A GREAT LOVE REBORN

As Emily Brontë's classic, Wuthering Heights, ended, Heathcliffe had just died, still grieving over the death of Catherine. Over the years countless readers have wondered if their two descendants, Hareton and young Cathy, would be haunted by their tormented passions. Would they marry and inherit the same tragic destiny of a love that was at once obsessive yet grand?
In this fascinating new sequel we learn that Hareton and Cathy do marry.
But their home is soon disturbed by the startling appearance of Heathcliffe's son, Jack . . . . a dark secret all these years. Jack has the same fierce attractiveness of his father and the will to use it. The inhabitants of Wuthering Heights and Thrushcross Grange seem fated to relive the primeval passions and hostilities of their forebears . . . .
Once again we feel the intensity of the windswept Yorkshire moors, the intricate interplay of familiar emotions, wild and poignant love, stormy violence, and rustic calm. Here is a captivating tapestry of romantic fiction that does not seek to imitate or recreate, but rather continues – with respect and affection – one of the world's greatest love stories.

Anna L'Estrange

Return to
Wuthering Heights

CORGI BOOKS
A DIVISION OF TRANSWORLD PUBLISHERS LTD

RETURN TO WUTHERING HEIGHTS
A CORGI BOOK 0 552 10608 9

First publication in Great Britain

PRINTING HISTORY
Corgi edition published 1978

Copyright © Anna L'Estrange

This book is set in 10 pt Times

Corgi Books are published by Transworld Publishers Ltd.
Century House, 61–63 Uxbridge Road,
Ealing, London, W.5.
Made and printed in Great Britain by
Hunt Barnard Printing Ltd., Aylesbury, Bucks.

Author's Preface

One does not lightly undertake a sequel to a classic one hundred and thirty years old. Since it was published in 1847, *Wuthering Heights* and its author have steadily gained such acclaim that by now it is one of the most famous books in the English language.

The extraordinary thing about it is that everyone has heard of it. Whether their acquaintance is through the book or the famous Olivier/Oberon film made in 1939, or merely by hearsay, everybody reacts to the words "Wuthering Heights." Along with the Bible, Shakespeare, and about half a dozen other works like *Gulliver's Travels, Robinson Crusoe,* or her sister's book *Jane Eyre*, Emily Brontë's one novel has achieved what is given to very few—immortality.

I knew, then, that when I was asked to undertake this task it would be a formidable one. I felt I could only come off badly because around the name of "Brontë" one encounters an invisible halo which is safely preserved by critics, some of them quite incomprehensible. In fact, along with the many very good books and essays I read about *Wuthering Heights*, I also felt I had never read such accumulated rubbish in my life. I felt so irritated by the verbiage, the ceaseless speculation that I wondered whether or not we were talking about a book and the human being who had written it, so abstract was the conjecture, so utterly phony the welter of psychological hypothesis.

But the very fact that *Wuthering Heights* is so many things to so many different people, that it has engaged the attention of scholars as well as romantics and readers of escapist fiction, seems to underline its importance in English literature. It is indeed a remarkable, a unique work; and its creator was remarkable and unique, too.

So, why attempt a sequel at all? Mainly, I think, because the novel cries out for it. It is a tribute to Emily's genius that after so many years it is still such a powerful force. Despite its faults, it lives in the hearts of all who have read it; it has an urgency and a dynamism that transcend time.

There is also the curious point I discovered in my reading that so many of the critics and writers on *Wuthering Heights* have speculated as to what might have happened next, as though they too were left unsatisfied. Did the ghosts of Catherine and Heathcliff haunt the Heights? Did the younger Cathy and Hareton live happily ever after? The author has created a web of such turbulent and conflicting emotions, that somehow a happy ending is not quite what one has expected; and one cannot really believe that she wanted it thus, but was rather bowing to the conventions of the time—probably under the influence of Charlotte. Although, to be fair, Charlotte was at pains to say later that Emily took not the slightest scrap of notice of what her sisters said. Indeed, says the elder sister rather crossly, "Having formed these beings she (Emily) didn't know what she had done."

Charlotte didn't know what Emily had done either. She had a poor regard for the book, was vaguely ashamed of her sister's monstrous creation, but thought she would have done better in time had she lived. ". . . her mind would of itself have grown like a strong young tree . . . and its matured fruits would have attained a mellower ripeness and sunnier bloom." In fact, Charlotte had said when her sister was still alive, Emily would do much better when she decided to be an essayist!

Dear Charlotte, in so many ways the most lovable of the three sisters; but I have no doubt that she was sure she was the genius, much as she loved the other two, and that their fledgling works would sink into oblivion with time. I have, however, gone into this in much greater detail elsewhere.*

So, how did it come about that I was the one to embark on this daunting and, many will think, impertinent task? What were my qualifications? Why me? Well, first and foremost, I was asked. Andrew Ettinger, the Editorial Director of Pinnacle Books, suggested the idea to me on one of his visits to London. He had read a previous novel of mine with a Yorkshire setting, and thought I might be the person he was looking for. Three other writers, he said, had attempted to do this, "all of whom failed to capture the special magic" he was looking for.

Before I agreed, and prey, naturally, to the greatest misgivings, I first re-read the book thoroughly and then I went up to Haworth in Yorkshire, home of the Brontës, like a pilgrim in search of enlightenment. Perhaps something would get through to me—I would have a sign as to what I should do. I should add that I am not personally in the least inclined to the psychic, but I was very hopeful.

For those who do not know it the town of Haworth lies on the slopes of the Pennine Chain—a range of mountains some two hundred miles along that stretch from Derbyshire in the south to the borders of Scotland. (In fact the Pennine Way, a track for walkers, passes the spot that I think Emily chose for *Wuthering Heights*, as I found when I was there.) The main street of Haworth is extremely steep and I suppose it is a realisation of what lies at the top, to the pilgrim, that makes the whole thing so remarkable. For first you

---

* Introduction to *Wuthering Heights* by Emily Brontë, Pinnacle Books, Los Angeles, 1977

come upon a church and then a churchyard consisting almost entirely of upright tombstones which completely surround the Parsonage on three sides. (Poor Charlotte, in one of her fits of melancholy, described the house as a tomb with windows.) On the fourth side are the moors and still, after a century and a quarter, the house is as it was, backing on to the moors and lovingly preserved since 1928 by the Brontë Society.

A wing has been built onto the Parsonage to house the Brontë Museum, and I suppose that even Haworth's main street must have changed in some respect. Late on a summer's day or out of season, however, with its cobbled streets and old houses one can still imagine what Haworth must have been like when the Brontë family lived there from 1820 to 1861.

Haworth may have changed, the Parsonage may have changed; but nothing can change the moors. They are as they were. No transport is available and there are no smooth roads to ease the journey of the twentieth-century pilgrim. The moors are bleak, as isolated and as majestic as they were in the days of the Brontës and as one tramps along the narrow tracks or through the coarse grass and heather it is not difficult to understand the influence of such rugged and wild beauty on a sensitive, introverted, motherless girl like Emily.

The most extraordinary phenomenon to the visitor from the south is the weather on these hills which can change from bright sunshine to a lashing storm in a matter of moments. I have been alternately soaked and bronzed by the wind and sun during a half hour's walk up a hill. When I went on my initial quest for enlightenment it was October and for most of the time a dark grey mist covered the moors and surrounding countryside. Cold and wet and squelching through mud, or with my ankles sinking deep in bog, I didn't exactly have the moment of profound revelation I had hoped for, but the conviction grew that I could do a sequel and that it would not be wrong to try.

After all, I grew up not very far from the Yorkshire/Lancashire border where Haworth is, and much of my adult life has been spent visiting Yorkshire, which I love best of all the counties of England. I had set a previous novel there; I knew a lot about that dour and peculiarly unfathomable Yorkshire temperament. Above all, like many before me, I had become fascinated by those remarkable Brontës the more I knew about them.

But the most important impediment, to my mind, was that Emily was a poet and a mystic and I am neither. According to Swinburne*: ". . . the younger sister's work (i.e. Emily's) is essentially and definitely a poem in the fullest and most positive sense of the term . . ." Or Mary Visick†: ". . . (Wuthering Heights) is the work of a poet who wants to write a novel." And that novel is really as much about the great metaphysical forces of creation, about Emily's poetic view of the universe as it is about the conflicting passions of the characters in it. The marvellous imagery, the facility of detail and expression is what has made Wuthering Heights a work of art and it would be quite impossible for me to emulate it and foolish for me to try.

And this realisation became my moment of truth. I wouldn't attempt to be like Emily. I would write a completely different kind of novel merely taking on her two main characters where she left off—Hareton and Cathy—and my interest would be solely in the interplay of human relationships, the development of character, and the influence of natural and unnatural forces on human destiny. I would extend, on more human terms, Emily's twin themes of storm and calm, light and dark: Heathcliff versus Earnshaw; the Heights on the windswept moorland.

But mystic or not, it has always struck me that Emily's psychological insight was well ahead of its time. Her

---

* The Athenaenum (1883)
† The Genesis of Wuthering Heights (1958)

pre-Freudian awareness of the effects of deprivation in childhood no doubt came from the loss of her mother; but papa was always on hand and that he loved his children and they returned his love there is no possible doubt. There was also the deep bond she shared with her sisters and brother. But Heathcliff had no one; he was a foundling, he was unloved and the absence of love in his early life precluded, as it does so many other deprived people, the giving of a normal kind of love to anyone else.

Thus I was profoundly interested, for my book, in the psychological ramifications of the Heathcliff/Earnshaw relationships. From a sociological point of view, too, I had the great expanding Victorian era as a background, a period that has always fascinated me. Emily never left the moors in her story; but I had to. I had to extend horizons, introduce new families, and even move away for a time from Yorkshire altogether. But I tried to keep very closely to the theme I had set myself and the book finishes where it begins—at Wuthering Heights.

As far as the topography is concerned, for those who are interested, I decided to set my Wuthering Heights where there is some agreement that Emily set hers—the farm known as Top Withens, which lies on the moorside some six miles from Haworth. Of course Emily could have set her farm—and Wuthering Heights is a farm—anywhere, and as a novelist I know how often one has a spot or place in mind but adapts it to suit one's own purposes.

Moreover, to anyone who has actually trodden the path from Stanbury to Ponden Hall and up to Top Withens, or stood half way and looked at the relative positions of Hall, farm, and village there dawns a positive conviction that this was what Emily had in mind and, seeing it as I did, I for one have no doubt that here we had the sites for Thrushcross Grange, Wuthering Heights, and the village of Gimmerton.

I deliberately saw the *sites* of the location because the ruin that is now Top Withens is nothing like the house described as Wuthering Heights. In my view, Emily took Ponden Hall, or a part of it, and put it on the exposed blustering spot where the wind "wuthers" continually, even, according to a local informant, on a calm day. It is a long, low farmhouse like the Heights, a substantial place, but not as palatial as Thrushcross Grange was, with its high white ceilings bordered with gold and candelabra "hanging in silver chains from the centre." (Ch. VI).

Significantly too, like the Heights, today Ponden Hall has a plaque above the door which says it was restored in 1801 and this is the date that Emily chose to start her novel, although above the door of the Heights is the year 1500 and the name Hareton Earnshaw to signify that the Earnshaws who lived there were farming stock going back three hundred years.

Speculation is always interesting—other people may have their view, but I visualise the Grange as a substantial Georgian mansion, perhaps in the Palladian style, with a colonnaded Doric porch and many outbuildings. Emily refers to the fact that steps lead up to the porch, and in the Parsonage museum there is a delightful pencil drawing by Anne of an oak tree under which is a house similar in style to the one I kept in mind as I wrote my book.

Many houses that may have influenced Emily have been mentioned such as High Sunderland Hall, Shibden Hall, and Walterclough Hall—the latter particularly interesting because of the similarity of its name to Wuthering Heights and also an actual link with the plot of the book.* Although when one thinks about it the names "Top Withens" and "Wuthering Heights" have a similar, interchangeable quality. There

---

* See also my introduction to the Pinnacle Books 1977 edition of *Wuthering Heights*.

was also the interesting fact that at one time the Heatons of Ponden Hall, who had lived there since 1541, and the Midgleys of Top Withens were related by marriage. The Heatons were a notable family in the district and Emily with her sisters would have visited the Hall a number of times, even allowing for her notorious reticence and dislike of company outside her own family.

So, with my territory firmly in mind, and the colors and the moods of the moors, I wondered how to begin the story, how to approach it. *Wuthering Heights* is told in retrospect by Mr. Lockwood, who has rented Thrushcross Grange, and Nelly Dean the housekeeper. I wanted to retain as few of Emily's characters as I could mainly because of the problems in presenting dialogue, etc. So I decided the story should be told in very much the same way but by Mr. Lockwood's son, Tom, and Nelly Dean's niece, Agnes.

I must say that although this device has been severely criticised for its artificiality, among other faults, from the writer's point of view it is extraordinarily effective, enabling one to maintain a kind of homogeneity that would be impossible in any other way.

The only other thing of any possible relevant interest I have to say is that from the moment of Andrew Ettinger's request to this very day I have, apart from the newspapers and historical reference books, read nothing that was not about Brontë or by Brontë, in order to keep in the mood and style of the period, 1801–1840, I was writing about. As an obsession this has its disadvantages, but as a labor leading to love for and a certain understanding of these three extraordinary sisters it has been infinitely rewarding.

I often wondered as I wrote what Emily would have thought of what I was doing. The unusual ease with which I was able to write, the way ideas flowed made

me think she would not have been critical of my under-
taking. Whether she would have approved of the result
I am quite unable to judge.

Anna L'Estrange
London, 1977

The Story of
Wuthering Heights

Although *Return to Wuthering Heights* is complete in itself there are, inevitably, references to Emily Brontë's book and for those who have not read it there follows a brief outline of the story.

The Earnshaw family have lived at Wuthering Heights since 1500; they are farmers and when the story proper begins Mr. Earnshaw has walked to Liverpool and back bringing with him a strange gypsy lad, a foundling to whom he has given the name Heathcliff after a son who had died in childhood. Mr. Earnshaw's children, Catherine and Hindley, are put out by the advent of the stranger—we are not told how old he is, maybe six or seven judging by the chronology of the rest of the book. Hindley, Mr. Earnshaw's son, is particularly jealous of Heathcliff whom he thinks has supplanted him in his father's affections. However Catherine and Heathcliff become soul mates and in time are inseparable. They grow up together.

In the valley below Wuthering Heights is Thrushcross Grange in which dwells the Linton family, landed and wealthy gentry: Mr. and Mrs. Linton and their children Edgar and Isabella.

Catherine and Heathcliff are spying on the Grange when Catherine is hurt by a dog and taken in by the family with whom she stays for some time until her leg is better. Edgar falls in love with Catherine and she eventually decides to marry him because she is attracted by the wealth and comfort of the Grange. In her heart she knows she loves Heathcliff; but since the death of Mr. Earnshaw he has been demeaned and reduced to servility by Hindley, who has married and had a son, Hareton.

Thinking she does not love him Heathcliff runs away and Catherine marries Edgar and enjoys some happiness until Heathcliff returns, despite the fact that she is a nervous, highly strung girl used to getting her own way. Heathcliff has been away three years and is transformed into a good-looking wealthy man, determined to upset the Lintons for marrying Catherine, and the Earnshaws for their treatment of him.

Worn out by various kinds of emotion and her hopeless passion for Heathcliff, Catherine eventually dies after giving birth to Edgar's daughter, another Catherine. Heathcliff spends the next eighteen years yearning for his lost love and steadily plotting the ruin of Edgar Linton. He brings about the death of Hindley Earnshaw—who is mourning *his* dead wife Frances—and debases Hindley's son Hareton by making him do the menial work that he, Heathcliff, was forced to do by Hindley. Hareton thus grows up unlettered and unkempt.

Meanwhile, at Thrushcross Grange, the young Catherine, Cathy, is also growing up into a beautiful girl, ignorant of what goes on at the Heights until Heathcliff plans to marry her to his feeble son Linton whom he has had as the result of a brief marriage to Isabella, Edgar's sister. Isabella has left Heathcliff, but on her death her husband claims his son and takes him to Wuthering Heights.

Heathcliff eventually forces Cathy into marriage with Linton and imprisons her; she escapes in time to be at her father's deathbed and after that Heathcliff owns both the Heights and the Grange. Soon after his marriage young Linton dies.

However Catherine's ghost continues to haunt Heathcliff and drives him to his death, whereupon Hareton and Cathy discover their mutual love and plan to marry.

The book is told in flashback by Mr. Lockwood who has become the tenant of Thrushcross Grange and Ellen Dean who is the housekeeper but who used to be nurse to both Catherines and thus knows the whole story. It ends in 1802 when we learn that Cathy and Hareton plan to marry in January 1803 and to live at Thrushcross Grange and begin a new life. Wuthering Heights will remain empty except for Joseph, the sinister old servant who lives there throughout the story, to look after it.

BOOK 1

Chapter 1

1840. Like my father before me I am a man of solitary disposition. Resembling him most of my brothers I, the youngest, could not help knowing that I was also the spoiled one, the darling, the one to whom he gave most favours in his declining years. And on his deathbed it was I who he called into his room, before all the others, and gave into my hands the manuscript in which he had written the strange story of the events that had befallen him in these parts so long ago—or rather events of which he was the recorder, because most of them had happened before he became tenant of Thrushcross Grange.

My father murmured to me that the story I should read had haunted him all his life, and that he had always wished to go back and find out what happened. He entrusted this task to me, knowing I should feel the same once I had read what he had to say.

It was a strange bequest and one which I had no time to heed until he was dead and buried and the formalities attending upon his demise had been seen to. As the one closest to him and still residing in Italy

3

where he died, I was given the major tasks of settling the estate.

And then one night, very late and rather tired, I idly flicked over the pages of the manuscript which my father had had bound in leather so that the state of preservation was perfect, each vellum page white and crisp, the lines of his fine italic handwriting flowing easily across the pages uninterrupted by marks or corrections. I realised than that my father judging what he had to say of sufficient interest to posterity, or his descendants, had made a fair copy of his narrative and the very idea of the labour he must have put into this awakened my sympathy and caused me to turn to the first page and read more carefully what he had so carefully committed to paper.

And so here I am in this desolate place bounded by moors and almost perpetually shrouded in fog or drenched in torrential rains or buffeted by gale force winds. Anything less like the sunny climate in which I was reared would be hard to imagine, and in carrying out my father's wishes I think that, like him forty years before, I may have paid the forfeit of my health, for no sooner had I arrived here than I caught a chill and have remained indoors cut off from my neighbours— the people it was the purpose of my visit to meet.

Yes, the manuscript did excite and intrigue me. My father knew me well, the imaginative, the dreamy one, the romancer—who would be captivated by the tale of the love between the foundling Heathcliff and the enchanting Catherine Earnshaw, the tempestuous, wayward Catherine Earnshaw, and its curious and bitter end. Who would wonder what had happened to Catherine's daughter, also a Catherine, and Hareton Earnshaw, Heathcliff's heir, who were due to be married in January 1803, when my father had given up the tenancy of Thrushcross Grange and returned to London.

So I grew impatient with my indisposition and the ministrations of good Mr. Duckworth the physician, and I longed to be away and see with my own eyes whether Wuthering Heights and Thrushcross Grange

4

still stood and, if so, who lived in them. Mr. Duckworth was new to the neighbourhood, having but recently graduated from St. Bartholomew's Hospital in London, and the servants we had engaged for my six months' tenancy of the Manor House, Gimmerton, were kept well away from me by my manservant, Nostro, who sometimes seems to see his role as something between a loving father and stern elder brother, protecting me almost from myself, cosseting or reprimanding me according to need. Nostro has looked after me since childhood and without him I should be lost.

Today, however, I persuaded him that I was indeed recovered sufficiently to take a short walk abroad with my mongrel dog Patch, who comes with me everywhere, and caped, capped, and gloved and with a suitably warm woolen muffler about my neck I was allowed out by my mentor. So I found myself with the aid of a local map of the area and, with excitement mounting, taking the track that leads across the moor towards Wuthering Heights and when, after much exertion and pauses for breath, I stood on the high moor and looked ever upwards towards the cleft in the hills I caught my breath once again because I knew that my goal was in sight.

Sometimes I think my father was lost to literature, such are his powers of narration, his gift for evoking moods and situations and portraying character. I knew Wuthering Heights so well from his description, how it lay on the bleak hillside isolated in its moorland setting. But nothing he said prepared me for the starkness of its beauty, the grandeur of its remoteness. By chance the weather was kind to me today, the air balmy and the sky blue so that one could almost see it as a harbinger of spring although it was yet early February and traces of snow lingered on the high ground.

I moved closer to the house, no longer tired or weary, uplifted by that buoyancy that is the reward of those who, travelling far or struggling long, find themselves within sight of their prize. I perceived how exposed the house was to the elements, standing as it did almost atop the rugged moor, and indeed how the firs

5

and gaunt thorns slanted away from the direction of the fierce north wind as it came swirling up the valley. Yet there was something tough and enduring about Wuthering Heights, something sure and solid that was to do with the land itself upon which it stood. The windows were tiny and latticed and, yes, there was the fir tree standing slightly apart from the rest down which Catherine had climbed on her escape from the house to be with her dying father.

Apart from the thin spiral of smoke from the chimney it was impossible to tell whether Wuthering Heights was inhabited or not. It was a house steadfast as a rock that would survive, whether a dwelling or no. At the end of my father's narrative old Joseph had been left in charge while Hareton and Catherine, newly wedded, went to live at the Grange. But Joseph, an old man then, must have been under the turf for many years now.

Yet there were fat cattle and sheep grazing on the moors nearby, and even from the distance I saw that the garden was neat and well kept, the soil turned over in preparation for the spring. Uncertain what to do I stood, hovering, and it was left to my dog Patch to decide the course of events. Where we live in Italy Patch very rarely wanders out of the grounds of our house as it is surrounded by a high wall, and thus the sight of the sheep must have seemed a welcoming one to such a friendly dog. I am sure it was his notion to offer them a greeting rather than worry them to death.

But such a charitable intention on the part of my pampered pet could not possibly have been divined by a moorland farmer and almost simultaneously with his bounding forth, leash and all, out of my hand, the door of the Heights opened and the huge fierce figure of a man appeared with a gun which he raised to his shoulder and aimed at Patch.

"Stop," I cried, holding up my arm in a futile gesture of command, "stop, stop!" I staggered through the coarse scrub, at a disadvantage with my cumbersome clothes and heavy boots; but the stranger had lowered his gun and was watching my approach, his expression

6

not one to guarantee a welcome either to master or dog.

I am tall but slight; he was even taller, but of such massive construction as to make me feel puny by comparison. Everything about him was on a large scale, yet in proportion to the rest of his body. He had a mane of thick curly hair, jet-black locks, and his complexion, though smooth, was swarthy like a gypsy's. The arms which held the gun were like young tree trunks covered with a mat of black hair. He wore only boots, trousers and a shirt the sleeves of which were rolled up over his forearms.

Out of the corner of my eye I could see that, however mild Patch's intentions, the sheep were not aware of the fact and had started to flee upwards over the brow of the moor. My reluctant host gave what I can only call a ferocious growl, raised his gun again and took aim.

"Stop, I beg you," I gasped and threw myself upon the man, knocking the gun from his hands. It was an absurd act of melodrama on my part and in so doing I fell heavily to the ground and must have presented a ridiculous sight as I lay there heaving from the exertion, as out of condition as my tormentor was positively fit. To my chagrin he leaned over and with a contemptuous gesture seized me by the scruff of my collar, raising me to my feet and giving me, for good measure, a thorough shaking.

"What . . ." he started to thunder when Patch, seeing his master manhandled, bravely rushed to my defense and jumped upon my attacker.

I thought my dog would be torn limb from limb. The man seized him by two legs, one front and one back, and flung him as far away from him as he could and Patch lay winded and whimpering while I shook myself free and rushed to his aid. All at once there was another intrusion and a small child hurled herself out of the house, past the man and on to my poor dog who lay groaning and rolling his eyes. She took his head in her arms and rocked it back and forth turning towards the man a look of malevolence.

7

"Father, I saw you! You were going to shoot him. How I hate you!"

Even in her fury I could see that the child was captivating. About five or six years old she had fair hair, deep blue eyes and chiselled aristocratic features; her nostrils flared as she stared at her father whom, I may say, she did not in the least resemble. In fact any two people less alike it would be hard to imagine.

"I have told you, Cathy," the man said, more mildly now, having apparently been subdued by the appearance of his daughter, "worrying sheep is punishable by death. There now, they've all gone . . ." He looked up at the horizon and, indeed, there was not an animal in sight. I recovered my composure and dusted my clothes, my mood also restored to one of benevolent forgiveness by the arrival of the pretty child.

"Lockwood, sir, Tom Lockwood," I said, "and I do apologise for the behaviour of my dog. But he is a friendly creature and would not harm the sheep."

"He harms them by chasing them," the man replied savagely. "Just the running sours the milk."

I felt abashed and, I hope, looked it. The child stared at me gravely, and smiled.

"He is a very sweet dog. I would like a pet of my own. All we have here are hounds who sleep in the barn."

"Perhaps your father will let me give you one," I said, "to make up for my behaviour."

I looked up at her father but he had turned brusquely back to the house, not reciprocating my introduction. I could see he was a churlish fellow, somewhat older than I, maybe about thirty, but not an uneducated one. Although his voice had the soft Yorkshire tones of these parts, he was by no means of the labouring class. A gentleman farmer, I presumed. He reminded me of the Earnshaw family who had farmed here when my father started his narrative in 1771. Maybe he was a relative of the Earnshaws, though seeing that I had so upset him I did not dare to venture an enquiry at that stage.

"Oh a puppy of my own!" Cathy clasped her hands

8

together and started dancing around, and then she ran towards the house to where a woman stood in the doorway, shielding her eyes against the morning sun. "Mother, I am to have a puppy of my own! That is if I may."

But her mother was watching the passage of the father who had rounded the corner of the house without a word. As I followed Cathy up the path I could see the woman's eyes had narrowed and her mouth was set in a grim line. She was a pretty woman, but her face bore the marks of early maturity as though life had been harsh rather than kind to her. Her daughter was not like her either, as she had brown hair and rounded features that must have once been ravishing, a dimpled sweetness of the kind that, I admit, appeals to me for I like women who are soft and feminine. I smiled at her and put out my hand, but she stared at me and I wondered if Wuthering Heights were afflicted with some kind of disease that renders it unfriendly to all who approach. This was very much the sort of reception my father had received nearly forty years ago; and dogs were involved then too. Thank God it was not snowing and I was in no danger of having to ask refuge for the night.

"Tom Lockwood, ma'am," I bowed and as the proffered hand had not been taken I instead turned it out and showed the palm. "Could I trouble you for water to wash my hands? Then I shall be on my way for I fear I have disturbed your household."

She had clasped the girl to her and they both stood to one side, Cathy now also reduced to silence. Before I passed through the threshold I could not help glancing upwards to ascertain that the grotesque carvings above the door described by my father were still there. They were, and also the date 1500 and the name Hareton Earnshaw. I saw the woman observe my action and look sharply at me, but she said nothing and motioned me to go inside.

With what quickening of the pulse did I step inside Wuthering Heights! I had journeyed all the way from Italy, endured inclement weather and much discomfort for this moment. And inside all was as I knew it would be. There was no corridor and I stepped straight into the parlour; and there was the huge fireplace and the fire brightly roaring, and the ranks of pewter dishes and silver jugs and tankards gleaming brightly on the tall oak dresser. The beams were still bare on the ceiling as my father had described them, yet there were no legs of beef or mutton or hams hanging there and the stone floor was covered with a rich though slightly threadbare carpet, and the furniture, also well worn, was substantial and comfortable. It looked a house of modest wealth, neither rich nor poor.

"The kitchen is through the door," the woman said pointing. "You will find water in the barrel by the door. Or do you know your way about this place already sir?"

I started and smiled.

"Why no, ma'am, I was never here before. Thank you for your direction," and I made my way through the door to the rear kitchen which again I felt I knew with its large fire and brightly shining utensils on the wall. Of course I felt I had been here before; it was uncanny. I took a pitcher and slopped water into the bowl, vigorously rubbing the dirt from my hands. As I did the woman approached me, proffering a clean white towel. Her attitude towards me was one of distrust and suspicion.

"I fear I am intruding," I said. "Your husband must be vexed both with me and my dog."

"He isn't used to strangers," she said, with a slight smile as though she excluded herself from the remark—as though she wanted to indicate that there was a barrier between her and this unfriendly fellow. I sensed an atmosphere of discord in the house and I was sorry for it, on account of the child. "Are you from London?" she continued as though wanting to atone for her spouse's behaviour.

"From Italy," I said. "I was born there and live there, though my father was a Londoner."

"Oh, how I would love to go to Italy! And you have come *here* from *there*?"

10

Her attitude was one of incredulity and I remarked to myself that she compared her homeland unfavourably with mine. I thought we were on the verge of establishing a *rapport*, for which I was grateful, when a shadow fell across our path and her brute of a husband stood framed in the doorway gazing at us. The woman moved to the table where I could see she had apparently been engaged in baking, for there was flour on her arms. Silently she commenced kneading the dough, and the chill of unwelcome was all-pervasive again.

"I am about to take my leave," I stammered awkwardly, "and again a thousand pardons for the dog." I looked around, but of the small girl there was no sign. The man stood aside to let me pass but I stopped by the table and smiled at my hostess.

"Thank you, ma'am. May we have the pleasure of meeting again? I am stopping in Gimmerton some months."

She didn't respond but went on with her work and sadly and silently I went towards the front door. Heaven knew when I would have the chance to come here again; to this place immortalised for me by my father.

Patch had been tethered to the post at the door and I untied him and put on my hat, staring squarely at my abrasive host.

"Might I know the name," I said, and then I stepped quickly back as he thrust his face within an inch of mine and bared his fine white teeth.

"Tell them," he said, "that you saw Anthony Heathcliff . . . Heathcliff, d'ye hear? And he's as mad as ever!"

And with that the amiable fellow slammed the door in my face.

Cathy . . . Heathcliff . . . the names revolved over and over in my head as I stumbled downhill across the black moorland scrub, my boots sinking in the gleaming sod still wet from yesterday's rain. Patch rushed ahead of me barking and yelping as though glad to be away from the place. I wondered if I was taking the fever again and had imagined the whole thing. *Heath-*

cliff? Heathcliff's issue was dead . . . and Cathy, why was the girl called Cathy? And lovely too, like the Catherines I had read about, one fair and one with brown ringlets; my father had remarked on the beauty of the hair of both of them.

I found that, by going directly downhill instead of following the track, I had come to some sort of road and I struck out in what I surmised to be the right direction, my mind full of my recent extraordinary encounter. The wind had risen and the thin whine through the valley, even protected as I was, made me realise what it would sound like higher up. True, the sun had gone in and those familiar black clouds were gathering in the direction I was hastening—towards Gimmerton. The trees swayed back and forth and then the gleam of grey slate and a cross leaning at a precarious angle caught my eye and I knew that this was the kirk—even more dilapidated than described by my father—where Catherine and Heathcliff, yes, and poor Edgar, Catherine's husband, were buried.

Half the roof of the chapel was missing and the naked beams beneath, exposed to the elements, seemed to me in my heightened imagination to resemble the bones of a skeleton, and the broken windows the sightless hollows of its eyes. I stood still and the blood seemed to chill in my body; there was a preternatural silence in which even the wind ceased its moaning and I glanced fearfully towards the moor expecting to see . . . what? The ghosts of Heathcliff and Catherine, lost souls still roaming in search of the peace denied them in life?

Half of me wished to hasten on; the other, and stronger, half undid the broken catch of the gate and made its way unerringly through the graveyard towards the corner that sloped towards the moor, knowing what it would find. And there, indeed, they stood; the three tombstones, apart from the rest as though accorded a solitary dignity by the passage of time. They were all three of them grey and encrusted with green lichen and the carving on them was scarcely discernible. Bending closer, I could just make out the names and . . . was it my overworked imagination again, or did the head-stones of Catherine and Heathcliff lean closer together, while that of Edgar looked isolated and apart?

I remembered how Heathcliff had ordered the side of Catherine's coffin to be removed so that in death he could be close to her, and how twice he had disturbed her coffin after she was dead. A terrible feeling of fear and dread, such as I have never experienced, overtook me and I knew I must run away from this accursed spot; but my feet were rooted in the wet earth as though pinioned there by unseen hands, and as I cried out the sky went completely black and the wind rose to a sepulchral scream and the trees began to thrash about like souls in torment, agonisingly bending this way and that, and with a groan the chapel door swung open and its dark, dank interior seemed not like a refuge but the pit of hell.

Then did the tombstones seem to bend towards me, swaying like the trees, in awful harmony with the discordance of nature round about me and the names stood out clearly in bold letters, dancing before my eyes:

HEATHCLIFF   CATHERINE   EDGAR
              LINTON   LINTON

and then a darkness engulfed me and I fell, insensate, to the ground.

Alerted by the stricken Patch running along the road, Nostro, who had already come in search of me, quickly found me, lying across the graves. At first he thought I was dead, and told me my pulse was but feeble. Swiftly I was borne home and the doctor sent for; but all I had taken was shock, and warmth and a good glass of brandy soon put this to rights and I was able to send a manservant to tell the doctor not to trouble himself.

Nostro was clearly beside himself with worry and fussed about like a mother hen with a brood of chicks; but I was in a curious state of excitement and after dinner I bade Nostro leave me and go to bed and I fetched my father's manuscript and sat by the fire with a good cigar and a glass of brandy by my side.

And through the night I sat there, alternately reading and dreaming until the book became the dream and the dream the book and I knew not which was which. Sometimes the awful forms of Catherine and Heathcliff would appear at the window, grimacing at me, arms outstretched, pleading "Let us in, let us in." And I would awake with a jolt and know they had no business in my home; the Manor House, Gimmerton, was not part of the story at all and here I was safe.

Occasionally Nostro hovered at my side urging me to bed, but I bade him make up the fire and let me be. At last towards dawn I fell into a heavy slumber and when I woke the household was up and about; there was a rug over my knees and a maid was rekindling the fire. The sun streamed through the window and I was filled with a firm sense of purpose, and knew what I must do.

Ellen Dean. Could she be still alive after forty years? She would be over eighty if she were. Only Ellen Dean or someone like her could bring the story up to date for me; someone must be able to fill in those missing forty years since my father went to Italy for his health, leaving Catherine Heathcliff and Hareton Earnshaw about to be married. I knew what had happened to my father. He had married a good woman and sired five children. Never in the best of health, he had nevertheless lived a leisurely comfortable life divided between his house in Rome and a villa in the Tuscan Hills, where I now lived. There had been trips to England after we boys were sent to school there. He had written a little, not much; painted a bit, not well; read a great deal and, by any standards, enjoyed a life well spent in the bosom of his family.

I jumped up and rang for Nostro who entered with that reproachful expression on his face that I knew so well. Sometimes I wonder why I tolerate it. But this morning I felt both tolerant and assured; I knew what to do.

"Banish that expression Nostro, my good fellow. I

have taken no harm for my fall in the graveyard. I am in capital form; the walk did me good. Nostro, after you have shaved and dressed me, pray bring our housekeeper to me. Her name is . . ."

"Mrs. Brown, sir."

"She will know what I want. Hurry Nostro, boil the water! And order a large breakfast while you are about it."

I dressed feverishly, completed my toilet and went down to the dining room where a dozen dishes were on the sideboard for my delectation. Sometimes I don't wonder we have riots among the poor when single fellows such as I live so well. However I piled a plate, and as I sat down there was a knock on the door and Mrs. Brown was brought in by the butler Timms. Mrs. Brown dropped an embarrassed curtsy and I got up and took her hand.

"Mrs. Brown. We have hardly met. I wanted to thank you for looking after me so kindly when I was ill. I wanted to thank you personally, you and Timms, and to ask you to thank the other servants for me."

Mrs. Brown blushed and tried to hide her confusion with her hands.

"Oh sir, we are glad you are recovered."

I sat down again while they remained standing and played with my cup.

"Mrs. Brown, I am come to Gimmerton on a voyage of nostalgia. I daresay you have wondered what brought me here."

Mrs. Brown assumed an expression which seemed to say that no well-bred servant would wonder any such thing.

"Well, it is a bleak place; not much to commend it; but my father stayed here a good many years before I was born."

"Indeed, sir?"

"He rented the Grange. You know Thrushcross Grange?"

"I was never inside sir. I hear it has been closed up since Mr. Earnshaw left. Some say it is for sale."

"For sale?" I cried. "What happened to Mr. Earnshaw?"

"I don't know the gossip, sir," Mrs. Brown replied primly. "Besides I am not native to these parts, having come from Bradford when I married the late Mr. Brown."

We Lockwoods are of northern origin and I know how closed the Yorkshire temperament can be. I could see that, unlike the good Ellen Dean of yore, my housekeeper had no inclination to gossip with the master of the house.

"Did you know one Ellen Dean, Mrs. Brown?"

Timms cleared his throat and stepped forward.

"As Mrs. Brown says, sir, she is not a native of these parts. I doubt she would have heard of Ellen Dean, as she was, because she married a man called John Roberts and moved to a farm some miles away. She is dead sir, quite recently and of a good age. I only know this because my Aunt Edna married a nephew of John Roberts, and was thus related by marriage in a very distant way to Ellen Dean. She knew her well. But Aunt Edna is dead, too, sir. She died last Easter."

The good Timms was about to embark, I could see, on the history of his Aunt Edna's demise and I interrupted him somewhat brusquely, I fear.

"Is there no one who would be closer than your late Aunt Edna to Ellen Dean?"

Timms drew himself up in injured dignity, but Mrs. Brown now intervened, anxious to be of help.

"I did know of Ellen Roberts, as we called her, sir, because her great-niece Agnes Sutcliffe lived but a few doors away when the late Mr. Brown and I lived in Gimmerton High Street."

"And is Agnes Sutcliffe still alive?"

"Oh yes sir, a widow, and she will tell you all about the Grange because she worked there. There is little she doesn't know about what goes on in these parts . . ."

Having discovered the whereabouts of Agnes Sutcliffe, I made haste to introduce myself to her. Her

16

neat cottage in the middle of Gimmerton was pointed out to me by Timms who, at my request, accompanied me no further. I wished the approach to be informal and as she answered the door herself I doffed my hat.

"Mrs. Sutcliffe? I am Tom Lockwood, ma'am, the son of David Lockwood who lived at the Grange about forty years ago and knew your great-aunt Ellen Dean very well."

This statement, though lengthy, was intended to put her at her ease and indeed the bewilderment on her face vanished as she heard the name of her relation and, her comely face wreathed in smiles, she stepped back and asked me indoors. The cosy parlour was aglow with polished brass and pewter; china cups and plates adorned the dresser and a good Yorkshire fire roared up the chimney. Would we had fires in Italy like they have here. I think the wood must not be so combustible; or maybe it is the easier access to coal now in these parts that provides the answer. However I saw only logs in the grate here. On the hearth rug an old dog lay sleeping, and scarcely raised its head to survey me.

Mrs. Sutcliffe bade me sit and patted the cushions of a comfortable chair.

"Pray be seated, Mr. Lockwood. I do recall mention of your father; because I was very close to my great-aunt and she used to talk about him and what a gentleman he was, unlike some in these parts that she knew. He was not here long on account of his health, and I do hear that you too have been ill since you came sir?"

Ah, village talk. Everyone knew everyone, of course, in a small place like Gimmerton; she probably knew more about me than I did myself.

"It is true I have been unwell due to the inclement weather no doubt. I am glad to say I am fully restored, and am come to enquire news that I believe only you can give me."

"I sir?" She looked at me with some surprise as well she might, and stirred the fire with the large brass poker.

17

I grasped the arms of the chair and settled back into it.

"Though dead, my father sent me on a quest. While he was here he heard from your aunt a very strange and long story which he wrote down and left me before he died. It concerns the Earnshaw family and one Mr. Heathcliff."

"Ah, now I mind why you are here. It was a very strange story, Mr. Lockwood, still is."

"Is?" I leaned forward with excitement.

"Oh, I knew all about it from my aunt, I mean the old part that you know before Mr. Heathcliff died; but nothing has ever gone right for the Earnshaws and I don't think it ever will. It is to do with the Heathcliffs, sir; they are an evil brood."

She got up and poured a glass of what I took for Madeira from a decanter on her dresser. This she placed by my side together with a box of biscuits.

"I always keep a little Madeira in the house. Mr. Sutcliffe was very partial to a drop after his dinner. He left me many years ago. But my aunt, now, she lived in a great age . . ."

She looked at me wistfully and clasped her hands.

"My condolences, Mrs. Sutcliffe. I feel I know your aunt as if we had been lifelong acquaintances. She must have been a great character."

"Aye, she was that."

"And forceful . . ."

"She needed to be."

I sipped my Madeira which was excellent and looked into the hot embers of the fire.

"Yesterday I went to Wuthering Heights. A very poor reception I had I must say . . ."

"Ah you'd have seen *him* no doubt."

"Heathcliff?"

"Aye, Anthony Heathcliff, as bad as the rest of them . . ."

"He said, 'Tell them you saw Anthony Heathcliff; and he's as mad as ever,' and he shut the door in my face."

"Aye, he would. I won't say he's mad, not that any of them were what you'd call in their right minds, like.

But he likes to pretend that he is, to keep people away, to keep her to himself."

"Her? His wife?"

Mrs. Sutcliffe snorted.

"Wife does he call her? She's a wife all right but not his. Jessica Earnshaw she is; wife to Mr. Earnshaw who has had to leave the Grange on account of the shame. Him a magistrate and all . . ."

"But," I gasped, floundering for words, "who is Anthony Heathcliff? How does he come to be there?"

Mrs. Sutcliffe looked at me thoughtfully.

"I think you had best remove your coat, sir. This will be a long story, being as how you want to hear everything from the beginning."

"From when Catherine Heathcliff, Linton's widow, married Hareton Earnshaw, which she did presumably?"

"Oh she did that all right, in January 1803. I mind it well because I was there, one of the bridesmaids to as lovely a young lass as ever you could hope to see."

She sighed deeply and gazed into the fire. I looked at her and a feeling of delicious anticipation seized me. My quest was to be realised at last. I was reminded of how Nelly had related the story to my father, as he recovered from his illness and I wondered how much Agnes resembled her aunt and how extraordinary it was that we should be in this situation nearly forty years after my father had encountered Nelly Dean.

I was amazed that she seemed so inclined to trust me and confide in me. Maybe it was because she was reminded of her aunt, or maybe she felt the need to unburden herself to a stranger of a story every bit as remarkable as that her aunt told my father, as I shall now relate.

Chapter 2

"Well I remember that happy day when Harcton brought Cathy back to the Grange as his bride," Agnes Sutcliffe said, settling back with her sewing into the deep armchair before the fire. "What a wedding it was; everyone in Gimmerton turned out for it because they were orphans without a relative in the world left between them.

"Squire Wolfer, who lived in the Manor House in those days, gave her away and six of us village girls served her as bridesmaids. She was such a beautiful bride; a tiny creature who looked as though she had been carved out of marble, with flaxen ringlets and deep blue eyes which in those days always seemed to be happy and laughing.

"My Aunt Nelly was overjoyed to see the change in her darling; she felt like a mother to her, having brought her up from birth, and she saw that the Grange was prepared as a fitting place to receive her. New papers were hung on the walls, the carpets were cleaned, fresh curtains were put on the windows and the woodwork on the outside of the house was done over with white paint.

"Hareton made such a handsome groom; all the girls were jealous. He was so splendid and strong, tall and robust with a healthy, ruddy complexion and thick brown curly hair. And he was so in love with Catherine that he never took his eyes from her all during the ceremony, or after for many a day. Squire Wolfer gave a great feast for the bridal pair and their first night together was spent at the Grange before Hareton took her to Italy for their honeymoon. They were away three months and when they returned in the spring it was to discover that a new romance had blossomed and my great-aunt Ellen was engaged to be married to a farmer, John Roberts, a widower with grown-up children.

"Miss Cathy was heartbroken and begged Aunt not to leave her, because the happy outcome of her union with Hareton was that a baby was on the way. But Aunt Ellen reckoned that much as she loved Catherine she deserved some life of her own and this was a good time to make a fresh start. She was no longer young, past childbearing age to be sure; but there was a lot that marriage could give her in contentment and stability and the love of a good man whom she had known as a girl. Some say he had wanted to marry her then but for her devotion to the Earnshaw family. Well, Aunt was determined and though Cathy broke her heart, off she went.

"Aunt turned to me to look after Miss Cathy. I loved babies and I felt flattered and privileged to be asked. It was something in those days to be asked to work for a grand family, and we considered the Earnshaws quite grand because they now owned two properties, the Grange and the Heights, and plenty of land.

"I mind still the day I went to work for Miss Cathy. It was a lovely spring day and my father took me in his cart as far as the gates of the Grange, then I had a walk of two miles or so carrying my things in a kerchief. I felt free and happy and quite grown up, and it seemed as though a new and beautiful life was beginning for me.

"And when I saw my young mistress she was yet abed, the sun streaming onto her golden hair loosed on the pillow and she jumped up like a young girl—which she was of course, but somehow one's 'mistress' was always considered more dignified—and clasped my hands.

" 'Oh Agnes,' she cried. 'I am so glad to see you! We are to be friends Agnes, aren't we? And you will look after me and my baby as Nelly looked after Mama and me?'

" 'Aye, miss, I will,' I said with genuine devotion, and she fell on me and kissed me."

Agnes fumbled for her handkerchief and blew her nose.

"Alas, such happiness was not to last. How unkind life is, Mr. Lockwood, how cruel fate, how uneven fortune. It seemed that the Earnshaws were cursed; that some evil blighted their family and drove out happiness."

"I thought my father's narrative had a happy ending," I observed sadly, thanking the good Mrs. Sutcliffe for the decanter of Madeira she proffered. "It seems, then, it was not so?"

"For a time, sir, they were like Adam and Eve in the Garden of Eden. Everyone and everything about them was happy. The servants went joyfully about their work, the place shone with care and Cathy and Hareton basked in the sunshine of mutual love. Although Miss Cathy had suffered a lot in her treatment at the hands of Mr. Heathcliff she seemed to have been able to put all that away from her. She never mentioned it to me and I don't think she ever talked about it to her husband. Of course, Hareton felt completely differently about Heathcliff. Despite the way he had been treated he seemed to worship him, and my aunt said he was the only person who wept for Heathcliff when he died. It was a mystery to everyone why this should be, because Hareton had been humiliated by Mr. Heathcliff.

"And another thing I marked was that Miss Cathy

23

took care always to avoid the Heights. She loved the moors and was out every day and in all weather, walking or riding in the pony cart when she got heavier; but go near Wuthering Heights she never would. When she was not out on the moors she would sit embroidering with me, making layettes for the baby and talking about the future with such joy and excitement. She and Hareton had decided to have a large family, she said, or as many as God would allow. Hareton had such plans for his children and one day we were talking about this when he entered silently behind his wife and planted a soft kiss on her cheek and rocked her in his arms. I was almost too embarrassed to look upon such love, and I found some excuse to leave the room but recovering herself, Cathy bade me stay.

" 'Darling Hareton, I was saying one of our sons is going to be an admiral.'

" 'Aye, and one a member of Parliament,' Hareton laughed, 'so that we shall have some good laws around here. Oh and Cathy, I am asked to be a magistrate. There, is that not respectability for us?'

" 'Oh Hareton! Now you are a pillar of the community.' She kissed him again, laughing.

"Hareton was very sociable that day and pulled a chair up to sit with us.

" 'I never thought I'd be so happy, Agnes,' he said, 'and I owe it all to my darling Cathy. Who would want anything else with her for a wife?' He looked at her adoringly and she took his hand.

" 'From what I hear you deserve your good fortune,' I said. And then I marked the expressions on their faces, both of them, and knew that I had blundered. I was never meant to refer to the past; but to me it didn't seem natural—to pretend that what had happened had not—and I should have taken it for a warning that happiness built on such poor foundations couldn't last.

"Well that lovely year ended, as all good things do, and almost a year to the day of her marriage Cathy was brought to bed of a lovely healthy boy, a joy to his parents and everyone who beheld him, Rainton Earnshaw. He was a sturdy lad like his father with the brown curly hair of the Earnshaws—her mother, Hareton's aunt, had the most beautiful auburn hair my Aunt Nelly used to say; whereas Cathy got her own fair locks from the Lintons. I loved Rainton the moment I took him from the midwife, washed him and laid him in his crib. Hareton and Catherine were overjoyed with their baby, and what a wonderful father Hareton was. Not remote, as some are, but delighting in the lad, spending time with him, playing with him and even helping me bathe him should he be home early from his duties.

"After the birth Hareton came into the nursery one day and drew me on one side.

" 'I want to thank you, Agnes, for looking after my wife so well. You have given her so much confidence, and I know that while you are with her she will always be well and safe. I want to give you this to remind you always of the gratitude of the Earnshaw family.' And he put round my neck a silver locket on a silver chain, and I have both to this day. Then he stayed with me for a while while I went about my duties, his eyes never for long leaving his son.

" 'This is the first of the new Earnshaw dynasty, Agnes. We are an old family, you know, good farming stock, not gentry. But now with our increased lands I will work hard to make us the finest family this side of Yorkshire, and it can be done, Agnes.'

" 'Aye, sir, it can,' I replied proudly. 'And you can do it, for you are a fine gentleman and deserving of your good fortune.' And his eyes shone and he shook me warmly, taking me by the shoulders almost as though he were about to embrace me.

" 'I thank you Agnes; you are a true successor to your great-Aunt Ellen who was always such a good friend to my wife and my aunt,' he paused for a moment as though mentioning her name had confused him, 'to my aunt, Cathy's mother. She was an Earnshaw too, you know, my father's only sister, and she married into the Linton family which, up to that time, was the grandest family in the district.'

25

" 'I suppose she married to better herself,' I said, feigning innocence because I was truly interested to hear Mr. Hareton's opinion of his aunt who caused such scandal in the area and still did—some say her ghost roamed the moors at night and she could not rest for her wickedness—but more about that later.

"Mr. Hareton was solemn and gazed away from his son, who was gurgling and laughing up at his father, out of the window, his eyes on the distant fells.

" 'Maybe she did,' he said, 'but she sorely grieved Mr. Heathcliff who had grown up with her and loved her all his life. She thought he wasn't worthy, that she was too grand for him and she married Edgar Linton instead with his big house and fine manners.'

"I thought Hareton spoke bitterly and it occurred to me that, close as he was to Mr. Heathcliff even though despised by him, he must have learnt a lot from him.

" 'That was why,' Hareton went on, 'Heathcliff worked so hard to become rich; to show Aunt Catherine he was as good as any Linton. Oh I know a lot of people hated him, Agnes, thought he was a fiend. But I understood him well; he loved the land and he used to talk to me and it made me close to him. He said my father, Hindley, treated him like a pig in a stye just because he had been taken off the streets; no one knew where he came from. And because I was Hindley's son he felt he had to do the same to me; but that when he wasn't hating me for being Hindley's son he loved me because I was so like my Aunt Catherine. He said he always saw her in me.'

" 'He was a very strange man, Agnes. A tormented man. That's why I couldn't hate him, and why I forgave him for treating me the way he did, and why I mourned him so much after he died.'

" 'You have a lovely nature, Mr. Hareton,' I said to him. 'My Aunt Ellen could never abide Mr. Heathcliff for all the things he did, for all the unhappiness he caused.'

" 'He was rough and cruel,' Hareton said taking his son from the crib and cradling him in his strong arms, so tenderly; it was lovely to see such a big man with

26

such a soft side to him. 'He was brutal towards many, including himself; but I understand it was because he was so unhappy and I forgave him, even for what he did to Cathy; even for that.'

"We looked at each other; the unspoken question between us. At last Hareton answered it.

" 'You must never mention this conversation to my wife, Agnes. It is something we never talk about—a mutual unspoken agreement, never to refer to the past.'

"And with that he kissed his son, replaced him tenderly in the crib, pressed my hand and left. I was very thoughtful for the rest of the day.

"It was a few months after the birth of Rainton that I first noticed any real change in my mistress. It was so slight at first I scarcely marked it, and maybe it had been going on for some time, and I was too busy with the baby to apprehend it. It was simply a restlessness about her; a desire to be even more out of doors than she had been before—so much so that she was never in the house. Her pleasure too in the child seemed diminished and she gradually withdrew from the nursery so that she scarcely appeared there at all and it was the father who spent more time with the child than the mother. And then one never saw them together, except at meal times. They now never appeared in the nursery to dandle the baby before his bath in the happy pleasurable way they had before.

"Oh, Mr. Hareton was busy with his estate, his books, his accounts. But it wasn't him, it was her. And then I felt she wasn't as close to me as she had been; she had withdrawn from me, and from her husband and son. For what?

"I don't think Hareton noticed anything then. His cup was still full with his new life, so very different from the old—a fine house, a beautiful wife, a healthy son, lands and servants, horses and cattle. Not long before he'd been like a servant himself, unable to read or write, a country bumpkin. No, Mr. Hareton was too blind with happiness to see that all was not so well with his wife.

"Or maybe he did see, and didn't let on because that

27

summer he took her abroad again, at very short notice, leaving Rainton in my care. I'd expected a long stay but they seemed hardly gone before they were back again and then I did notice a difference—very marked it was, and in both of them. The joy had gone and Mr. Hareton looked anxious and subdued, his wife indifferent to his care. Why the very hour her carriage returned she was ordering her old horse Minny to be saddled, and there she was flying off to the moors without even seeing her *son*! I was vexed, I can tell you; but Mr. Hareton shut himself in his study with his bailiff and his accounts and said nothing to me.

"I remember that day autumn seemed to have come early, and my heart felt heavy as I drew the curtains in the nursery and saw how the black clouds hurried very low over the moors and the wind whipped the leaves off the trees. And I imagined my mistress riding across the moors on her horse like some wild thing, not the fine lady of the Grange that she was. I recalled what my great-aunt had told me of her mother—how wild she was, how headstrong and fierce. There were parts of her mother in her, Aunt Ellen had said, but also the gentleness of her father Edgar Linton and this she hoped, my aunt, would be the calming, the strong influence. I had a deep sense of foreboding as I took Rainton out of his crib and held him in my arms.

"Well, that mood passed, as moods do; the household seemed to return to normal, though there was something lacking and it soon became apparent that the holiday, if not entirely successful, had been fruitful and the mistress was expecting again. But this time no happiness transformed her pregnancy, no eager anticipation, and I could see she was cross and angry about it.

" 'It makes me so tied, Agnes,' she cried one night as I prepared her for bed, 'tied, tied, tied to the home! Oh I hate it.'

" 'But Miss Cathy,' I answered mildly. 'You cannot spend all your time like a young bairn wandering on the moors. You are the mistress of a fine home, a mother, a wife. And Mr. Hareton becoming an important personage in the neighbourhood, a magistrate . . . you have your duties to perform, beside him.'

" 'Oh stuff!' cried my lady. 'You know I hate that sort of thing, and so does he.'

" 'I think not,' I said. 'Mr. Hareton told me not long since that he had ambitions for himself and his family. Why you yourself spoke of a *large* family, an admiral, I recall, and a member for Parliament. It is you who have changed, Miss Cathy, not Mr. Hareton.'

"She was examining her face in the glass and appeared not even to heed me; her hands touched her long neck and caressed her cheeks.

" 'Am I like my mother, I wonder? I never knew my mother, Agnes. She died when I was but two hours old. Isn't it sad for a girl never to have known her mother?'

" 'Aye, and a boy, too,' I said, unwisely perhaps because my mistress flew off her stool and rushed towards me.

" 'And what do you mean by that, Agnes? You must mean something. You never say anything by chance.'

"I moved away picking up the clothes she had strewn over the floor, and taking care to put as much distance between myself and her as I could. My aunt had cautioned me always to speak my mind to the Earnshaws, otherwise they took advantage.

" 'I mean your baby Rainton is growing up without a mother,' I said, 'and you know it, Miss Cathy, and your husband knows it now, too.'

"I thought Cathy was half mindful to throw the stool on which she had been sitting at me—and I recalled the rages of her mother that Aunt Ellen had described to me—but she thought better of it, if she thought of it at all, and came over to me quite gently.

" 'Rainton is a little baby, Agnes. Of course I love him; but I don't know what to do with him. Besides, he is your charge. Isn't he Agnes?'

"She was pleading with me to agree but I would not. 'It was not like that at the beginning,' I said. 'You were scarce ever out of the nursery, and, with your husband, so loving you could hardly bear for him to leave your

29

side. Now, you seem to see neither one or care for the other. You mind you do not take after your mother, Miss Cathy, and may I be forgiven for saying it; but she came to no good end. From what I hear she had awful rages too.'

"And thinking I had said enough I gave a little bob and quickly left the room, my duties completed.

"But I might have saved myself the trouble of risking instant dismissal, for all the good talk did. Cathy continued as strange as ever; Hareton withdrew more into himself and the house became an unhappy place in which to live. It affected the servants who started to leave; we had three housekeepers in as many months. They said it was a remote spot and there was not enough to do. And then, of course, it was winter-time and not the easiest part of the year for those of us who live here.

"But nothing kept Miss Cathy at home—storm, rain, sleet, snow; she was out and about in it all and then her horse would gallop into the yard at sunset, and she would appear almost exultant until she had quietened down and the excitement had abated, and then she would be very quiet and withdrawn and stay in her room. Sometimes when I went up to see if she wanted me I would find her sitting again in front of the glass, staring at her face, stroking her neck and cheeks as she had before. She would look at me but say nothing, and I knew she was thinking of her mother and the portrait of her that hung in the drawing room downstairs. Why she had this obsession about her mother I knew not at the time; all that was to come later.

"One night I recall it was near Christmas and the first winter snow had fallen. I begged my mistress not to go out but she would, pushing me impatiently away. As I watched her ride off I felt the stirrings of emotion I would not have had for the world about my mistress: dislike. Yet she had changed, not I; her obsession with her mother was turning her into a copy of her, and I no more liked the result, the temper and wantonness than my aunt had.

"But that day my mistress had not returned by sunset and when my master came in for his tea and found she was yet abroad he burst angrily into the nursery, not even a glance for the child.

" 'Agnes, where is my wife? Surely you would not let her out today, the snow fresh upon the ground?'

" 'Forgive me sir,' I said tartly, 'I am not the keeper of my mistress. I did plead with her but she brushed me away. I know not what goes on in her mind.'

"I turned away, close to tears because I liked Mr. Hareton and I felt I had fallen down in my duties. Hareton started to pace angrily up and down muttering to himself.

" 'I know not what ails my wife. She is not herself, Agnes. Do you think it is the baby? What is it? What does she do on the moors? Where does she go? Who does she see?'

" 'See?' I gasped. 'Whatever can you mean? You think she goes to see someone?'

"That such a thought had come unbidden to him shocked me; no such notion had ever occurred to me.

" 'You assume that all day she rides about on the moors?' Hareton snarled, his voice not at all the tone I was accustomed to. 'In this weather?'

" 'If you think your wife sees another then you should see to it, not I,' I said angrily, and started tapping the floor with my foot. Hareton put his head in his hands and sank on to a chair.

" 'Forgive me, Agnes. I am beside myself with worry about Cathy. She is not the girl I married, but more like the one who married Linton Heathcliff when she was sullen and surly, mulching about the house. I see in her that discontented look I saw then, and I wonder if people ever change; if they can change. I thought to make her happy, and she thought to teach me learning. Now I can read and write but she no longer smiles; I can do columns of figures and sit on the Bench but Cathy laughs no more. Who is to blame, Agnes? Is it I? Or is it she? Or is it . . .' he looked at me and paused. 'They say her mother was mad,' he went on. 'Deranged in her final days. You ask your Aunt Ellen.'

" 'Mrs. Linton had a fever,' I said. 'It was not

madness, but fever that took her. You cannot visit that on her daughter.' Hareton jumped up and I thought he was about to embrace me, his face transported with relief.

" 'Oh Agnes, thank you! You say she was not mad.'

" 'I never heard she was mad,' I said slowly. 'I heard many things about her—strange, wilful, stubborn, but not mad. In her condition maybe Miss Cathy takes after her mother a little more in—certain qualities, shall we say. But madness, no.'

"My poor master. I saw from the expression of gratitude on his face that his fear was that his wife was becoming deranged, and that had driven him to such agonies. That he loved her still I realised from his behaviour, and all I wanted in the world was for them to be as united as they had been the day they were wed.

"Quietened, Hareton went down to his study and the house was in silence until I heard the gallop of horses' hooves coming down the drive and Miss Cathy calling to the groom in the yard to take her horse. A feeling of apprehension seized me because of the lateness of the hour and the tone of her voice and, making sure the baby still slept, I hurried down to greet her in the hall.

"And what a scene confronted me. She was mud-splattered and windswept; her hair plastered wetly over her face; her expression was distraught as though she had seen a ghost and she shivered either with fear or apprehension, I knew not. When she saw me she rushed into my arms and as I held her I saw over her shoulder Mr. Hareton standing silently at the door of his room, his expression one of infinite anxiety and sadness. He seemed about to approach her, but I shook my head and led her slowly away from him up the stairs to the privacy of her own room.

" 'There, my bairn, there,' I said as though she were my daughter whereas in fact she was two years older than I. 'Get off your wet clothes and I will send for a hot drink.' I whispered to a servant who came to the door in answer to my bell and when my mistress was enveloped in her warm robe I put her gently by the fire and tucked a blanket around her. I could see she was numb with some kind of shock, the colour completely drained from her face. I didn't speak or ask her questions until the servant had brought a tray with a cup of thin hot gruel which I spooned gently between her lips. I noticed that her eyes stared strangely at the fire and I began to be afraid for her reason. I chafed her hands between mine and murmured to her like I murmured to her poor neglected baby.

" 'Joseph is dead,' she said at last, very quietly as though talking to herself. 'Dead.'

" 'Joseph!' I said sharply, thinking that her husband's suspicions were correct and she had been meeting a clandestine lover.

" 'Old Joseph, of Wuthering Heights.'

" 'You have been to the Heights!' I gasped. 'You never went near the place. You would go round and round it rather than approach near it.'

" 'Well, it all changed,' she said in that cold flat voice.

" 'One day I met old Joseph on the moors, wandering about with his stick, bent nearly double. I would have run from him for I hated the old man; but he looked so pathetic and forlorn that I stopped to ask how he did.'

" 'He said he was lonely at the Heights, having always been used to company and bade me visit him there. At first I said I could not, for the place had unhappy memories for me, and he said why was that? It was the place where my mother was born. Of course, Agnes, the very mention of my mother stirred me and I realised that of all people old Joseph would be able to tell me the things about my mother other people would not. Ellen would never talk about her, and you could not for you did not know her, and Hareton was but a boy when she died and Father was dead and Mr. Heathcliff was dead. I knew there were things about my mother that people would never tell me—strange things—and I knew she was supposed to haunt the moors. I have heard tales like this since I was a girl. You see, I went on to the moors looking for Mother. I was sure she would come to me if she could, for she

33

could, for she must have wanted to see me too.' Oh she looked so sad I could have wept; the poor orphan girl who had never known her mother. How she must have yearned for her, to estrange herself from her husband. I grieved that I had been so neglectful to find the reason for her wanderings.

" 'I know Mother was beautiful and sad and Father mourned her for the rest of his life; but father would never tell me about *her* as she was. But Joseph would know.'

" 'I told him I would come and visit him and it took some days to get up the courage, but then I did and oh, Agnes, I was so glad I had gone. The place was not the same; most of the furniture was gone; but it was clean and there was a good fire and Joseph made me tea and after I had got used to being back I went slowly upstairs and went into every room until I came to the one with the old-fashioned box bed that was Mother's room and where Mr. Heathcliff died. I felt something about the room, Agnes, I can't quite say what; a friendly warm presence that made me want to linger. Outside there was sunshine on the moors and little wisps of cloud in the blue sky, and I could see down towards the Grange, and a feeling of peace and security overtook me. I wanted to linger in Mother's room and take notice of things I had never even looked at before, and in her books I found scribblings she had made and little notes and then her name in her girlish handwriting, *Catherine Earnshaw*, and I realised I was Catherine Earnshaw too, having been Catherine Hinton just as Mother was.'

" 'I took the book down and showed it to Joseph who poked the fire and grunted; but his face remained friendly, not sour and gloomy as it always used to be.'

" 'Joseph,' I told him, 'you are the only person left who remembers my mother, from being a little girl.'

" 'Aye, I mind un,' Joseph said.

" 'Then tell me about her, Joseph,' I pleaded. 'All about her.'

"The colour had begun to steal back into her cheeks, and her eyes grew bright with remembrance and I tried to conjure up the picture of her in that gloomy old house with the ancient servant who was goodness knows how old, maybe eighty, maybe a hundred. And her with one bairn here and another in her belly, and a good husband fretting for her. All she wanted to know was about the mother who bore her and left her so many years before.

"And of course Joseph told her everything, about her mother and Mr. Heathcliff, how they grew up together and how she married Miss Cathy's father instead of Heathcliff whom she loved and who loved her. That's why her moods were so strange when she would return to us of an evening. It was so disturbing to know that maybe your mother had never loved your father, but someone else and that person a strange man who had imprisoned you and forced you to wed his sickly son. She tried to see in Mr. Heathcliff the good qualities which her mother had seen and Hareton had seen but precious few besides. She tried to understand Mr. Heathcliff's grief and resentment, and the bitterness he felt towards her father. It is funny that no one spoke to Miss Cathy about her mother and Mr. Heathcliff, seeing that she lived in the house. It seemed that people wanted to draw a veil over it because they thought it improper, which of course it was, by any standards. I tell you, sir, Yorkshire folk are right queer when it comes to some things; and not telling folks what they think they ought not to know is one of them. I suppose old Joseph had his motives, though I'll not judge him; knowing his reputation I daresay they'll not be good ones.

" 'And so I took to going to see old Joseph most days, Agnes, and wandering around the house, spending time in my mother's room. I still hoped she'd come to me and I used to linger in the graveyard and put flowers on her grave and Papa's, but not Mr. Heathcliff's. I don't know why I couldn't bring myself to do that; I suppose because I loved Papa so much and grieved that he had been so hurt.'

" 'But your mother hurt him too,' I said gently; but

no, she wouldn't have it, rushing to the defense of her mother.

" 'Mama couldn't help herself, even Joseph said that. He said it was love stronger than death. He said he couldn't abide either of them but that was a fact!' For the first time that evening Cathy smiled, but then her brow creased with pain again.

" 'And now he's dead, poor old man. I found him dead in his bed today; he must have died during the night for the house was cold and the fire unlit. I'd taken him a bottle of whiskey as I sometimes do and I couldn't understand where he'd got to. It was getting dark and I decided to take a candle and go up to his room where I'd never been. It leads directly up from the kitchen apart from the rest of the house. And I did and there he was; his eyes open, staring at the ceiling. It was horrible.

" 'I was so afraid, Agnes, I didn't know what to do. Of course I'd seen death before, Papa and Linton and Mr. Heathcliff; but there was something about Joseph that made me feel guilty and afraid. I wished I'd never come to the house and learned something that perhaps I would have been better not knowing. I was suddenly afraid of the Heights again, of the death and stillness it seems to bring and I thought of the warmth of the Grange and oh how I wished I was back. And then suddenly the wind rose as it does up there, with a shriek, it takes you unawares and I cried out too and ran down the ladder to the kitchen and when I got outside I saw Minny had got loose and was grazing on the moor, and she would not come to me when I called. Oh it was nearly dark, long past teatime and I wondered how I should find my way home, even with Minny because it was snowing again and the wind was howling round the house.

" 'I called and pleaded with Minny to come to me and I was nearly crying when up she trotted and bent her head to nuzzle me as though asking for forgiveness, and just as I was about to mount her I raised my head and looked back at the Heights and I saw a face, a woman's face, Agnes, at the window of Mama's room.

She was staring at me and as I looked at her she put out a hand and beckoned. I swear it Agnes, I swear it. It was Mama beckoning me to come back to Wuthering Heights.' "

Chapter 3

"I tell you, Mr. Lockwood, my blood fair froze in my body to hear those words, and to see the strange weird look on her face as she gazed into the fire and moved nearer as though she was chilled and wished to warm herself. Neither she nor I had heard the door open, or knew how long Mr. Hareton had stood there listening until a creak on the floor boards made us both look up to where he stood in the shadows. The life seemed to have gone out of him and, instead of the fine sturdy young man he was, he looked bent and old. Miss Cathy sighed deeply and rested her hands on her stomach, and I realised how near her time she was and how unfit to be galloping over the moors in all weathers. It was as though she wished to harm the baby inside her, to prevent it being born.

" 'I must go back to Wuthering Heights, Hareton,' she said, the words coming very gently on the end of the sigh as though they were all part of something deep and expressive inside her. 'Mama wants me to live there. It was so much part of Mama, she loved it,

39

Joseph said. She never was happy here and no more am I. I am so restless to be gone, Hareton.'

"Now Mr. Hareton gave a long low moan like an animal does, tugging helplessly at its foot which has been caught in a trap and is numb until it moves it. It was a cry of anguish and pain and loss, a plea for help. He didn't speak, but came up to her and tried to cradle her head in his arms as in the loving way he used to, and she so eager to let him then. But not now. The very touch of him seemed to anger her and she jerked sharply away. Then I knew she had rejected him and his love, and that was why she wanted to be rid of the baby inside her which was part of him.

"And I wondered about the stories that I had heard since I was a child of the woman on the moors, sometimes alone, sometimes with a man. There were many, I knew, who swore she was Catherine Linton, that they knew her and they'd seen her. But my Aunt Ellen never believed the stories; and to her dying day she denied that the late Mrs. Linton walked.

" 'Miss Cathy,' she used to say, 'was a wayward girl, wicked maybe; but no one who saw the peace she had in death as I did, the serene expression on her face, could believe she was anywhere but in the bosom of her Maker.' The sight of her mistress in death moved my aunt, who had lived through the turbulent years of her short life, so profoundly that she would never countenance the stories she heard or put any measure on them. Now Mr. Heathcliff, yes; she could believe that not even a merciful God would give repose to such an evil one as he. My aunt minded the awful fixed look of his open eyes in death, eyes that she tried to close but could not, and was sure that he had been taken straight to the devil who for aught anyone knew was his true father; for where he had come from no one knew and he never wreaked anything but misery to all about him except Catherine, and some say he caused her death.

"Of course, Mr. Lockwood, I, being strongly influenced by the sensible attitude of my aunt, was very reluctant to believe my Cathy's story and put it down to a temporary indisposition of her mind weakened by her experiences listening to the tale of wicked Joseph, and the coming event of giving birth. But Mr. Hareton, I could see, was of another mind altogether. He thought it was further evidence of the derangement of his wife's mind and after he had left, and I had got her into bed and sat by her until she slept, I found him waiting for me in the hall at the foot of the stair and he bade me enter the drawing room. Very stern and unbending he looked as he requested me to sit, standing all the time, himself, his back to the fire. 'I tell you Agnes,' he said, 'my wife is becoming deranged. She will be as mad as her mother was mad.'

"As I cried out in protest he held up a hand.

" 'Oh I know you said it was a fever; you wanted me to believe that and so did I. But after we spoke this evening I recalled that long ago Dr. Kenneth clearly gave me the impression that my dead mother-in-law was mad. Oh she was delirious at one time and she did have a fever, but she didn't die from *that*. She lived a few months longer, increasingly in another world, treating her husband as a stranger and neglecting the child in her belly as my wife does to hers now. He said she had always been a wild and strange girl subject to tantrums when she was young and when she was older they were almost like fits; the least little thing that disturbed her sent her into a paroxysm of rage. Now, after what has happened this evening, I know that your words do not comfort me, Agnes. My Aunt Catherine Linton was mad and so is her daughter, my wife. Kenneth was right. He knew.'

" 'He is an old man, sir,' I protested. 'Old men have bad memories. You are talking of events that happened twenty years ago.' Mr. Hareton looked me in the eye and I could see that, whatever I said, he had made up his mind. It is as though he wanted to believe it. It was the only way he could understand why the wife he adored no longer loved him. It was the only way he could explain her behaviour to satisfy himself. Before I had seen him *afeard* that she was becoming deranged; now he *wanted* to believe it. Just in that short space of time, those few hours, he wanted his wife to be mad.

" 'I am going to get rid of Wuthering Heights, Agnes. Let it or sell it, I care not which. But my wife must be prevented from going there ever again; she must be constrained to the house until her baby is born and if you cannot do this, Agnes, I must get someone else who will.'

"With that he nodded and turned his back to me in a gesture of dismissal.

"Oh with what foreboding in my heart did I go to my bed that night. I had never seen Mr. Hareton so stern and forbidding, so unmerciful and unjust. Of course I knew Cathy was not mad—wild, impulsive, but she was no more deranged than was I. Mr. Hareton was determined to make her a prisoner in the Grange and in this he would elicit the help of Dr. Kenneth; I could see that. My mistress, who so loved the moors and freedom, was to be forbidden them. Let someone else act as her gaoler; for I would not, I vowed as I went to sleep.

"But the following day my resolution was changed. For when I went into her room I could see that Mr. Hareton had already spoken to her, for she was gazing out of the window towards her beloved moors and her cheeks were wet with tears. She didn't even glance at me as I came in and I pottered about tidying her drawers. But eventually the silence wore me down, for she used always to greet me brightly in the morning as though she loved every new day and I turned to her and stood silently by the bed. At last she spoke, as though to someone else, not me, for her eyes never left the sight of the hills.

" 'Hareton is going to sell Wuthering Heights. He has forbidden me ever to go there again. Oh Mama . . .'

"And she wept afresh, and then I knew it was not to me she had spoken, and I wondered if she thought she saw her mother beckoning to her from the moors?

" 'Hush ma'am,' I whispered truly alarmed, 'do not disturb yourself. The spirit of your mother is all about you, not only in Wuthering Heights.'

"She then looked at me as though just aware that I was in the room. Now I was truly afeard for her mind, for I realised that indeed it *was* not to me she had been speaking. As she glanced at me she appeared different altogether, and I wondered if the conversation had been going on before I came into the room, or was it merely going on in her mind?

"My mistress gravely shook her head and I saw how pale her face was and how dark the shadows under her eyes.

" 'You know how I have searched the moors for Mama, Agnes, hearing the stories about her. They are not true. Mama is not on the moors. If she had been I should have seen her before. She was waiting for me to come to Wuthering Heights; she waited all that time before I came to her. She is there. In that room which was her room as a girl and where Mr. Heathcliff died. I rushed back into the house when I saw her last night. I didn't tell you that, Agnes, because Hareton interrupted us and I knew Hareton would not believe it. Although it was dark and the wind screamed I wasn't afraid any more because I knew that at the top of the stairs in that room was Mama, waiting to engulf me in her arms with her love. And, and . . .' my mistress gave a great sob and the tears once again gushed forth freely, 'she wasn't there, the room was empty, only the window was open where she had been leaning out to me. I was too late. Mama had gone; but oh, Agnes, I knew she had been there and I knew she would come back. I know she will come back I know . . .'

"Miss Cathy's voice rose and I could see that the pale face was covered with beads of sweat and to my touch her forehead was clammy and damp. She closed her eyes in exhaustion and I knew that Mr. Kenneth must be sent for, because whatever ailed her was beyond my power to heal.

"Indeed, like her mother before her, Miss Cathy fell into a fever and the doctor at times despaired for her life and that of the child she was carrying. He said he was reminded of those same winter months twenty years before when he nursed Miss Cathy's mother, my Aunt Ellen by her side, and also feared for the child in her

43

womb. Everyone in the house crept silently about and Mr. Hareton left all business to his bailiff so that he could be near my mistress.

"I know that my poor master reproached himself a hundred times for the harsh words he'd said to her when he'd forbade her ever again to visit Wuthering Heights. He told me he'd gone into her room before the house was astir that morning and found her already awake and gazing out of the window. But when she saw him she pulled the bedcovers over her head, and at this Mr. Hareton flew into a frenzy and tore back the sheets and shouted that she should hear him. She curled up on the bed like a baby and would not look at him, and he said this drove him to further fury and he shouted and stormed as he stalked up and down the room.

" 'You are my wife, and you will obey me!' he thundered. 'I will not have the mistress of Thrushcross Grange roaming like a gypsy girl upon the moor, and parleying with servants like a common slut.'

"At that she rose up from the bed and pointing a finger at him cried:

" 'You, Hareton Earnshaw, you who were brought up like a common servant, who are nothing better than a common servant, talking like that! You, whose place was always by the hearth with old Joseph or with the dogs in the barn, speaking like the fine gentleman you certainly are not! Fie on you, Hareton Earnshaw, for your snobbery and your pride, your wicked, wicked pride.'

" 'And she fell to the floor, Agnes, and wept, great sobs rending her thin frame, and I realised how wrong were my words and how the pride of my position, my new position, had gone to my head. I was a coarse, unkempt lad before Cathy took an interest in me and taught me nice manners and how to read and write and I had forgotten it.'

" 'Oh, Master' I cried, 'you must not talk like that for 'twas not your fault that your upbringing demeaned you so. Pardon, but you know I heard all from my aunt; for your father Mr. Hindley, Mrs. Linton's brother, was a gentleman and so my aunt said it was only out of spite that Mr. Heathcliff debased you.'

"Mr. Hareton bit his lip at that and turned away from me, and I knew that although he did not like talking about the past, indeed tried hard to blot it from his mind, it was always with him and he was very conscious of his new dignity.

" 'And then, Agnes,' Mr. Hareton continued, his back still to me, 'I knelt beside her and took her in my arms and begged her to forgive me and not distress herself for her sake and that of our child she was carrying, and then as we used to in the old days we clung together like lovers and she allowed me to lift her into the bed and to cover her and soothe her, but when she said to me "and may I not go to Wuthering Heights, Hareton?" I knew I must refuse because she was trying to take advantage of my loving weakness.'

" 'Nay Cathy,' I said. 'You never lived there as I did and loved the place as I did. I was born there and I grew up there; it is my home. But for you it is a fanciful place full of memories of the mother you never knew; you imagined you saw her ghost and you could not, Cathy. Your mother is at rest with your father in the churchyard of Gimmerton Kirk. Maybe when you are better and stronger and the baby is born we will take a year abroad, go to Italy again, Venice, Florence, and you will teach me about the great painters and sculptors as you did before—remember on our honeymoon, Cathy? About Giotto and Michelangelo and Leonardo, and we will forget the bad memories and start life again, as it was when we were wed.'

" 'But when I went towards her, Agnes, instead of the happy face of my bride I hoped to see, she had turned from me, her face to the wall and her body shaken by sobs.'

" 'Leave me Hareton, leave me.'

" 'And because my heart was so full of misery, bursting as it was with the love I had for her and the knowledge that I could not make her happy, and blinded by tears, I made for the door, Agnes, and saw

45

her not again until you sent for me. And now it is too late.'

" 'Nay master,' I said. 'It is not too late. The mistress is a young, strong woman. You have one healthy baby and will have another, and many more if it pleases God to send them. I think you are right to take the mistress away, go right away from here . . .'

" 'You mean *forever*?' He looked at me, a strange expression on his face.

" 'Why no, Mr. Hareton, I did not mean forever . . .' But he seemed excited and did not harken to me, talking as though to himself.

" 'Yes, that's it, Agnes. We will go away, to the South, to London maybe, start afresh. I will sell up and make a new life where we do not have the memories of the past always to haunt us. Cathy and I are without relatives, we have no ties. We are making the future in ourselves and our family. Cathy will be away from the talk of ghosts and spirits, away from the memories of her father and mother, and I . . . I am strong yeoman stock, Agnes. I can begin again.'

"I could see he was too elated by his words to listen, and deeming it not my business, I said no more, but in my heart there was a very strong conviction that the Earnshaws and their native soil were not soon to be parted.

"And so it was to be. As though sensing her husband's determination to uproot her, my mistress did not hasten to recover from her illness, but let it linger until the harsh snows of winter had melted from atop the hills and the glades and valleys were alive with the tokens of spring. She was not deranged. Her mind never wandered again nor did she talk to herself or to someone other, either in her mind or whom she thought she saw; but she would lie in her bed, her face turned for hours towards the window, her eyes seeming to see yet not to see. She would never talk to her husband when he came to see her and Dr. Kenneth remarked to me that this was exactly how her mother had behaved towards Edgar Linton, and that in the illness of the daughter he was seeing the counterpart of the mother years before.

"Mr. Hareton was desolate. He would sit for hours by his wife's silent bed trying to engage her in conversation, but she would not speak to him or allow him to take her hand and when she looked it was with an expression of such scorn as to freeze the heart of the most ardent wooer.

"Dr. Kenneth would urge that my mistress should be up for part of the day but, though she did as she was bade, she refused to venture downstairs or out of doors, but sat by the open window, her gaze forever towards the moors, in the direction where Wuthering Heights lay in the fold of the hills, out of sight of the Grange.

" 'Indeed ma'am,' I said to her one day while helping her to her chair, 'what is it that ails you, that prevents you greeting your husband or going back to your duties as the lady of the house? Doctor Kenneth can find nought wrong with you.'

"I know I spoke boldly, but I took my chance, hoping to anger her into some kind of activity. In the inert form that sat there I could scarce recognise in my mistress the youthful girl who had ridden wild across the moors, her face flushed with high good spirits. For it was not natural to see a young girl of but one and twenty years of age, in the full bloom of her youth, behaving like an elderly invalid.

"But my mistress was not even annoyed.

" 'You know what ails me, Agnes. I must go to Wuthering Heights where my mother awaits me. I will not be well until I am living there, where she was brought up; the place she loved. Mama was not happy here and neither am I. Hareton is too stubborn to see this; he has forgotten his roots but I have not.'

" 'But you were brought up at the Grange, Miss Cathy! You were born here in this very room; *this* is your home. Why, you told me you were never happy at the Heights. You longed to be away.'

" 'But all that changed, don't you see? It changed with Joseph, and seeing Mama there. She was there. I know it. I have always been seeking her and *that's* where she was.'

"And once again I grew afraid to hear her strange talk delivered slowly as she lingered over every word. That night I determined to talk to master and urge that he should at least let his wife visit the place she longed for so much. Women who are with child often get strange fancies, and I hoped that as Miss Cathy had only been so peculiar since she was in this condition, the fact that her husband humoured her would bring about some kind of change.

"As I knocked on the parlour door and was invited to enter I observed Dr. Kenneth sitting in the chair by the fire, a balloon glass of brandy in his hand. I was surprised to see him, for he was not expected and he had not been up to see my lady.

" 'Ah, Agnes,' my master beckoned me to enter and be seated. 'The good doctor and I are discussing my plan to move away.'

" 'An excellent idea,' Dr. Kenneth said. 'There is something very unwholesome about Mrs. Earnshaw's attachment to Wuthering Heights. I fear she may follow the affliction that deranged her poor mother, and well do I remember the misery *that* caused. I fear no good will come of her stopping in these parts.'

"I cleared my throat and spoke as boldly as I dared. But I must have betrayed my nervousness for I could not help twisting and untwisting my apron as I sat awkwardly on the edge of my chair.

" 'I fear my mistress will die, sir, if she is moved.'

" 'What are you saying, Agnes?' cried her husband, jumping up.

"Dr. Kenneth put the ash from his cigar into the tray by his side and smiled.

" 'I see she has the forthright manner of her great aunt whom I know well,' he said. 'And a lot of sense your Aunt Ellen spoke too when it came to the Earnshaws or the Lintons. What makes you say she will die, Agnes?' He looked at me kindly.

" 'Because I know it,' I said. 'I mind too well what my aunt told me about her mother, Mrs. Linton; about the stubbornness, the wilful streak. Miss Cathy is determined not to move from these parts. It is why she does not speak to her husband or heed him. She knows what is in his mind. She will never speak to him again if she is moved away, and then she will die.'

"Now Hareton let out such an explosion of wrath that I fairly jumped out of my skin and Mr. Kenneth dropped his cigar and had to remove the ash from his waistcoat, his face purpling the while from inhaling too great a quantity of brandy. I was reminded then that wild and unreasonable behaviour was not confined merely to the female members of the Earnshaw family.

" 'You are talking like a bigoted peasant!' Mr. Hareton thundered. 'You are back in the remote years of the seventeenth century when elves roamed the moors and fairies lodged in the glens. Have you no sense, Agnes Dean? Can you not realise we are now into the nineteenth century? That we know that a good and just God rules the world, and that it is governed by Him and those He ordains under Him, and not pixies and goblins and witches incarnate? We have modern medicine here in the person of Dr. Kenneth who has studied at the university and knows about potions and pills. My wife cannot die if she moves away from a *place*. *She cannot!*'

"The way Mr. Hareton walked about and ranted could not but draw from me the conclusion that he was about as stubborn as his wife and as unreasonable. But I kept my counsel to myself, knowing my place as I did.

"I could perceive however that Dr. Kenneth was looking no longer at Hareton but at me, and when my master had ceased his raving and paused for breath the doctor addressed himself both to Mr. Earnshaw and myself.

" 'I have known the family of good Agnes here for many years, Mr. Earnshaw, her aunt and all her relations. They are folk from this countryside going back as many generations as your own, and full of common practical good sense. Not learned, but knowing in the ways of the world. I have a good mind to listen to

49

Agnes when she says her mistress will die if she goes away, for she does not say it lightly.'

" 'That I do not,' I said, gratified by the attitude of the doctor, who was well loved by us, having dwelt among us for forty years or more ever since he came here as a young surgeon and apothecary to practise his skills.

" 'And I recall the strange illness of Catherine's mother,' Dr. Kenneth continued, 'and there was no rhyme or reason to her death either for she was a stout, hearty girl and I said so at the time to the aunt of this young woman here. Girls like her, I said, do not fall ill for trifles—it is hard work bringing them through fevers and the like. Oh I know there were strange goings on here and odd things were said and noised abroad, and rumours have continued to this day such that I do not know what to say about them or believe. I have seen people frozen with fright so that they had to be revived with *sal volatile* because they would swear they had seen ghosts on Gimmerton moor. I have seen them with my own eyes—the frightened people, that is—and not known what to believe. But I myself, in all my solitary journeys across the moor at all hours and in all manner of weather, have never so much as observed the flicker of anything pertaining to the supernatural, or anything which one could not give a rational explanation.'

" 'Some say it is only to the weak and ignorant that such manifestations appear; but Mr. Duff the curate was prepared to swear on the Bible that he had seen a young girl clad in white not once but several times. Squire Wolfers' bailiff—not an imaginative man—was almost driven to drink by the regular sighting of a couple wandering across the moors at dusk and seeming to vanish into the air. Once he followed them on his horse and he swore that they turned to observe him and then vanished laughing, while his horse frothed and foamed at the mouth and was almost put down by the vet who thought it had taken a fit.'

" 'No, we have grown used to the tales of apparitions on the moors and it is only since Mr. Heathcliff was put to rest but three years ago that I have heard
50

them. As far as I know your aunt slept quiet in her grave until Heathcliff joined her there—what but that Satan would not receive him into his home for ought I know.'

"He saw Hareton start and realised he had blundered.

" 'Pardon me, Mr. Earnshaw. I know that your feelings towards the late Mr. Heathcliff were that of a son to a stern father; but most other folk around these parts had no such feelings of kindness towards him at all.'

" 'Aye, I know he was hated,' Hareton muttered, 'but in his way he was good to me. He felt he had been badly treated and had a lot to bear. His early deprivation made him mean spirited.'

"Once again I marvelled that one who had been brought up as an urchin in his own house, denied his own birthright, could be such a simpleton as to kiss the hand that once had whipped him. In all the time I knew Mr. Hareton I could never explain this to my own satisfaction. It seemed that to Hareton and the late Mrs. Linton Mr. Heathcliff had shown an aspect of himself that was peculiar to them and no one else, for I seldom heard any other person say a good word about him. As I thought my quiet thoughts I also reflected that the room was strangely silent, as though both the doctor and my master were thinking about the disquieting facts which Mr. Kenneth had just narrated. I, too, knew many people who swore they saw the ghosts of 'Heathcliff and a woman' and sometimes in broad daylight too; but then all my life I had grown up with strange tales of fairies and hauntings in these parts, for we are canny folk ourselves. My grandmother had seen a witch burnt, and witches were quite common talk when my mother was a young girl, Pendle Hill being not many miles distance as the crow flies. Oh, the older folk amongst us are full of such stories at night as we sit round the fire and the wind howls in the chimney and buffets the doors. Still, I wonder.

"Well, Mr. Lockwood, I thought it was time I stirred

myself and I rose and bade good night to my master and the doctor.

" 'Stay Agnes,' said Dr. Kenneth, 'for I have a mind to ask you more about the illness of your mistress.'

"I looked at Mr. Hareton but I could see from the ease with which the doctor spoke that he knew about the disagreement between them. 'I understand she has a fixed idea that her mother is at Wuthering Heights waiting for her.'

" 'Aye,' I replied, 'and she has taken to her bed since Mr. Earnshaw told her she might go there no more. Now he wants to leave the district. I know my mistress. She has fixed notions and she is stubborn. She will let it kill her for she will have lost the will to live.'

" 'I believe we have sense spoken here, Hareton,' Dr. Kenneth said. He addressed him so familiarly because of course he had known him since he was a boy, delivered him if I recall, and no one knew more about the families than Dr. Kenneth unless it was my Aunt Nelly Dean. 'I would take heed of what Agnes has to say. I would put out of my head any notion of moving your wife until she is stronger and then maybe by that time either she will have come to your way of thinking, or she will have returned to normal and forgotten all about ghosts and spirits that lurk on the moors. Pray God that your love and affection for her and your joy in your new child will restore her to health, and the family at Thrushcross Grange will know happiness once more.'

"Had it ever? I wondered, thinking that Dr. Kenneth was but making an effort to cheer my master. As long as I'd known Thrushcross Grange it had been an unhappy place, with Mr. Linton sorrowing after the death of his wife and the house, lacking a wife and mother, seeming somehow deserted and cheerless. But my aunt told me that before that, the Linton family—my mistress's grandfather and grandmother—had been happy enough and that it was simply the advent of Heathcliff that had been the family's undoing. Yet I marked how quickly the young bride and groom had seen the shadow of sorrow and discord cross their

52

paths and how, but two years wed, Mr. Hareton was already talking of leaving forever.

"Mr. Hareton was about to reply, but then a scream rent the air and, knowing it came directly from the bedroom of my mistress overhead, I was the first through the door and flew upstairs as quickly as my feet could carry me. When I saw the way she moaned and twisted in her bed I thought she had taken the fever again, but Dr. Kenneth soon behind me going to her bedside and quickly drawing back the covers motioned me and told me urgently to fetch clean towels and have hot water sent up, for my mistress had begun her labour. The event that we had long awaited to restore her to normality was now due.

"But my mistress, although a strong young girl and one who had produced a lusty boy child so easily scarce a year before, laboured all night and far into the next day, rending the air with her screams and sending all the servants scurrying about in fear as they heard the pitiful sounds. Certainly it required all the skill of Dr. Kenneth, who never left her, and the midwife who was sent for, to save her life. For many times she seemed so near exhaustion that I thought she no longer breathed and her pale death-like face frightened Dr. Kenneth so much that he whispered to me he had seen the like on the countenance of her mother the night that she had given life to her daughter, who laboured now, and had thus forfeited her own.

"However when the long dark night and the wet stormy morning that followed it gave way in early afternoon to sunshine, and it broke as it does in such splendour on the moors that you cannot believe you are looking at a scene that was so grey and dismal a while before, my mistress ceased her moans and, looking out of the window, seemed to take courage from what she saw there. Her face was illuminated by a smile of such rapture that I feared she had seen the face of Our Lord, such as those who are about to die are supposed to do. She grasped my hand and that of Dr. Kenneth and, giving a tremendous push, brought

53

into the world the cause of so much anguish now and, although we could not know it, in the days to come, but of great joy too—the daughter who was to be given the name of Margaret Catherine Earnshaw."

Chapter 4

It was almost nightfall when I rose reluctantly from my chair, and bade goodbye to my kind hostess who seemed as much enraptured by the memory of the tale she was telling me as I was myself. I knew if I lingered any longer the protective Nostro would be wondering if I had taken any harm, and I was anxious not to embarrass the good Agnes Sutcliffe by being sought for like a recalcitrant schoolboy.

I promised her I would come on the morrow to hear more of her tale, if she had no objection; and indeed she had not, for I surmised she would be more comfortable in the familiar warmth of her own home than the somewhat spacious and impersonal atmosphere of the Manor House with its large rooms and the many interruptions as the servants went about their daily business.

But about one thing Mrs. Sutcliffe was right. That night my sleep was once more disturbed by strange dreams of ghosts on the desolate moors. I revisited Wuthering Heights again and again and, each time, I was received with a welcome even more hostile than the one I had had in reality, until Anthony Heathcliff seemed to have the huge jaws of a dog and his wife appeared like a ghostly Catherine Linton and her daughter an orphan waif in the storm. Several times I woke in a sweat and indeed I was up before Nostro had entered to draw my curtains and, such was my anxiety to hear the rest of the tale, I hurried through my breakfast and did not even complete my morning walk before delivering Patch back at the Manor House and hastening to the cottage of that good lady who would complete my father's tale. I think she was surprised to see me so early and I apologised for the hour.

"Maybe we could continue the story today, Mrs. Sutcliffe. I am anxious to be brought up to date and to know more about the present incumbents of Wuthering Heights."

Mrs. Sutcliffe motioned me to sit in the chair I had occupied the day before and once again took up her embroidery, pausing only a few times to furnish me with a glass of Madeira or a biscuit, take some light sustenance for herself, or stoke the fire.

"I wonder you are so interested in this tale Mr. Lockwood," she said pleasantly, as she seated herself comfortably and placed a pair of gold spectacles on her nose. "It must be a far cry from the smart fashionable world you are doubtless used to, this tale of folk in a far part of Yorkshire."

"I am very much my father's son, Mrs. Sutcliffe. He wished to be a writer or a painter but was too indolent. He also had the additional burden of ample means and a degree of ill health. He had me taught the art of composition as a boy, but alas, I too never fulfilled his expectations and to some extent have become a likeness of my father, being idle, not over-blessed with robustness and, as to me he apportioned the major part of his estate, I do not want.

"But we Lockwoods are a northern family descended from the ancient family of Lockwood who, in the reign of King Edward II were implicated in the feud with Sir John Elland, High Sheriff of Yorkshire. We have that vivid imagination, that almost Celtic relish for story-telling that is the portion of many of the northern race and my father, in penning this himself."

"But why did he never discuss it with you in life, Mr. Lockwood?"

"Ah, that I know not," I sighed and sat back. "Maybe he had forgotten it; although he told me it had haunted him, so that is scarcely the explanation. No, I think it dwelt in the recesses of his mind. There are some things, are there not? that we can write about more easily than discuss them and I think—for I have often wracked my mind to know the reason—that this was more likely why my father never spoke of it, but committed it to paper with such care. And then, as he was dying and reliving his past life, I imagine he was vividly reminded of the events of forty years before but, lacking the capacity to talk about it then, gave the manuscript into my hands instead.

"Perhaps he wished to console me for his death, for he would know that as soon as I had fulfilled my duties I would travel to these parts in order to discover more, to bring the tale up to date. Maybe we shall find a publisher in London, then all the world will know of Wuthering Heights and Thrushcross Grange."

"Oh, sir," said Mrs. Sutcliffe anxiously, "I would not wish to see my aunt or myself in such pages, for all to read."

"Ah never fear, ma'am. I would of course offer the tale suitably disguised, have no worry on that score. It is the custom with many of our fashionable novelists, I understand, to disguise the truth as fiction. Now pray continue. We have arrived at the birth of Margaret Earnshaw."

And Agnes Sutcliffe puckered her brow in the effort of recollection and proceeded:

"Whether it was on account of the anguish it took to produce her bairn or whether because she so resembled her, I know not; but from the day she was born Catherine Earnshaw could not abide her daughter. The joy as she gave birth was followed by a fretful sleep and then she lay there for days in the same inert fashion as before, except that she seemed spectral and drained of life. Dr. Kenneth came every day and stayed by her bedside until he was satisfied that his patient would not escape him as the last one had.

"The baby, born before term, was small but healthy and so perfectly formed that she seemed like a tiny doll delicately fashioned as are the porcelain figures on the mantle in the parlour. She had a crown of soft blond hair but, by contrast with this fairness, great dark eyes like her father and mother—the Earnshaw eyes. Her lips were formed like a bow and her cheeks were as soft as peach blossom. She was so different from her brother Rainton, now fifteen months old, that it was difficult to think they were sprung from the same parentage. Rainton was a lusty brown youngster with thick auburn curls and chubby limbs; he seemed forward in everything and walked well on his sturdy legs, laughed and played all day despite the neglect of his parents. Oh, the reverence with which he looked at his sister; the joy he had in her company. I remembered how his father had first held him and how moved I was to observe such strength and weakness together. Now, as the sturdy toddler gazed at his sister and tried to take her in his arms—I of course hovering close by—I could see so much of the kindness and gentleness of the father in the boy, and, oh, how I prayed that, despite her similarity of beauty, the girl would not resemble her mother in character. For, much as I loved my mistress, I could not abide her moods, and the damage she had done to her husband, home, and children by her waywardness and neglect. Even as she lay there I felt she was a pampered creature, and I reflected that money and property do not bring happiness. Our women, after they have give birth, are up and about the house seeing to the care of their menfolk scarce before the midwife has closed the door.

"A few days after the baby was born Hareton entered the room one day and stole up to his wife's bed, a tender look on his face. She watched him approach, unsmiling, and her mouth turned down in that spoiled childish expression as he took a chair and sat by her side. Then without a word he produced a leather case from his pocket and laid it on her lap.

"I could see now that by his action he had placed his wife in a predicament. She wanted nought to do with him, but she was intrigued. That it was a gift, a valuable one was evident by the soft leather of the box.

"She looked at him, then away, seeming to have the grace to blush, I am happy to say, and then one of her long delicate hands reached for the case and slowly she unfastened it. What she drew forth was one of the most beautiful necklaces of diamonds and emeralds I am ever likely to see. So fiercely did it sparkle that she gave a gasp and clasped it to her bosom.

" 'Oh Hareton!'

"Hareton sat and watched her, attempting neither to speak or touch her. He sat very erect and proud, like the gentleman he was, a landowner, a magistrate, a husband, the father of two children, a man of substance and of property. And so handsome—his face rugged and proud, his fine hair brushed straight back so that it fell onto the collar of his coat, his side-whiskers almost meeting on his chin so that they seemed to form a beard. His clothes were well cut by the best tailor in Leeds and his carriage was straight and firm. Any woman would be proud to have such a man for a husband, and here he was having to court her favour by giving her jewels! She pressed them now to her and then she smiled and touched his hand. I could see that he trembled and took her own small hand in his large one and then he bent his head and kissed her wrist, and then her fingers one by one.

"I turned with shame and embarrassment so that they should not think I observed them; but indeed I think they would not have known whether I stayed or went. He had bought back her love with gewgaws; but I doubted whether it would be half so permanent. When I turned, their heads were bent together and they were whispering as they used to when they were first wed, and even to go into the same room as them was to wish oneself away.

"Now I felt a desire to disturb happiness bought

59

with such artifice and dropped my respectful curtsy as I said.

" 'Shall I bring the baby ma'am?'

" 'Oh yes, Agnes!' Hareton cried, his eyes alive with joy. 'Do fetch our darling, for I feel now that my wife is on the way to recovery and she shall have her first proper look at her namesake.'

" *'Namesake?'* My mistress cried. 'She is to be *named* after me?'

" 'But of course my darling, Catherine Earnshaw.'

" 'I think we have had enough Catherines already,' Mrs. Earnshaw said with some asperity. 'I fancy a nice plain name like Grace or Charlotte.'

" 'You do not want her called after you?'

" 'No, I do not.'

"And I felt that, what my mistress was saying was that she neither wanted the baby called after her, nor wanted her at all. Twice every day since her birth we had dutifully carried the baby to its mother, and she, feeling it her duty no doubt, had inspected it casually and then sunk back on her pillow as though an unpleasant duty was completed. But to cuddle it or hold it or even touch it was not to be thought of, and because it was such a small baby Dr. Kenneth had a wet nurse sent from the village, a woman who had recently given birth and lost her child and derived some compensation for the loss in suckling and fondling our infant.

"While they were arguing about the name I slipped out to fetch the baby whom we had in fact called Catherine, knowing Mr. Earnshaw's wishes. She had just been laid down by the wet nurse from her feed and even tiny as she was I thought she smiled and raised her arms to me, though of course she could not do either; but it was a gesture of wanting and I drew her, all warm and smelling of milk, into my arms and wrapped her in the large shawl woven from soft Yorkshire wool and carried her along the corridor to her waiting parents.

"The contrast in the two was so noticeable I am not likely to forget it. Hareton reached out for his lamb while the mother shrank back into her large bed as though wishing to hide herself. Hareton took the baby from me and cradled it gently in his arms, then he offered her to his wife in a gesture almost of pleading as though to say 'take what we have produced with our love.' I would my mistress had reached for the baby as eagerly as she reached for her jewels. She looked at the baby and then at her husband and then she made a tiny gesture as though she would take her; and then she sank back again on her pillow and spoke.

" 'I can't. I am too weak, Hareton. Soon I will nurse the baby, but not today.'

" 'But my love, just hold her for a few seconds. Look, I will support you.'

"And he made as though to lay the baby in his wife's lap; but she pulled herself violently away and as she did the precious jewels slipped from the coverlet on to the floor.

" 'Oh my jewels, Oh Hareton, take care!' my mistress cried, and with all the vigour that she claimed she did not have she leaned over the side of the bed and groped about for them on the floor.

"I thought it was a terrible sight, my mistress grovelling for the pretty baubles and my master clinging desperately to the bundle of flesh and blood that was more precious to him than jewels. Then I saw not anger, not remorse, but resignation on his face and he slowly rose and, avoiding my eyes, handed the baby back to me.

"However whether the jewels had some secret talisman that made her well or whether it was some potion of Dr. Kenneth I do not know, but from that day my mistress began to recover. She started to eat all her food, took the glass of claret twice daily prescribed by Dr. Kenneth, and two weeks after the baby was born got out of bed. At first she was weak and had to be helped, but soon she dressed and came downstairs escorted by Hareton, who had kept her company for part of every day without ever again attempting the intimacy of the occasion when he gave her the jewels.

However at least they now talked to each other and smiled and occasionally he took her hand and, despite my reservations, I nurtured hopes that my master and mistress would be happy and contented again.

"Now it was May and it was as though nature conspired to adorn herself with raiment fitting for a Queen. The buds hung so heavy on the boughs it seemed they would burst into leaf before summer was nigh, the earth moved with new life and the birds gave forth a glorious melody of sound as they collected the grasses and twigs for their nests or the cattle spit and mud from the beck which they fastened to the eaves or lintels of the house.

"The day my mistress came down, the doors of the house were flung back and the windows open and everything seemed to gleam and sparkle in the beams of the sun. Miss Cathy ran across the hall to the door and then on the steps she flung her hands towards the sky and, as though offering her body to the sun, cried out.

" 'Oh Hareton look! It is alive, we are alive . . . oh, look at the sky, the sun . . .' and she flew down the steps onto the lawn and did a little dance, like a child who is beside itself with joy over a new dress or gift. I don't think that anyone looking at her could be but moved or deny her her happiness, even I, knowing what I did and full of foreboding as I was. And how beautiful she looked, Mr. Lockwood; all the fullness of motherhood with her yet, and her earthy golden hair which I had washed that morning in water brought from the beck—she never liked water from the well for her hair, but fresh running water carried from the stream—spun about her and she wore a pretty dress of green silk low at the neck as was the new fashion, and her face was clear and shining and bursting with youth and renewed health. She looked seventeen, nay younger, and with her sturdy young husband standing gazing at her with pride one would have thought that her cup was full to the brim. Then she stopped her dance and looked about her and seeing Hareton and the expression of love on his face, ran up to him and seized him by the hand.

" 'Oh, Hareton, fetch the horses. Let us ride over the moors. Hareton, let us go to Wuthering Heights. Please, please Hareton.'

"I saw my master falter and the expression on his face change from love to pain, and he seized her by both hands so that she was firmly held and looked into her eyes and said:

" 'No, Cathy. No. You are not yet fit to ride a horse. Why, you have been indoors for weeks. Tomorrow if the weather doesn't break I will have the pony and trap made ready for you, and George the groom will drive you round the grounds; but until Dr. Kenneth says so you may not wander beyond these walls.'

"But she still held him and then she tugged his arms and I thought that, but for the fact he gripped her fast, she would have gone onto her knees to him. She cried out, looking up into his eyes.

" 'Hareton I *beg* you, please, please let me go to Wuthering Heights. I have to see M . . .'

"And she stopped because of the terrible expression on his face as well, no doubt, as because of the enormity of what she had been about to say. I could scarce credit the fact that, although 'twas many months since my mistress had visited Wuthering Heights, and since then we had seen the winter pass and the spring come and the baby born, yet she still had not got this fixation out of her mind. Now that I thought about it, it was as though she had brooded on nothing else, lying in her bed gazing out of the window towards the moors, simply biding her time.

"Women take strange moods in childbearing and after; but I knew now that this was not something that was, as I had hoped, destined to fade. My master had tried to win her with his affection, bribe her with trinkets, make her aware of her responsibilities as a mother, but to no avail. I knew that Miss Cathy had never in her life owned such jewels—even those left by her mother were nothing to compare—and now I'd seen the way this wild moorland girl coveted them, nay loved them more than her own child.

"Hareton cast her roughly to the ground, leaving her

spread there and turned away, making an effort, I could see, to control his own violent emotions, such was the depth of his rage and misery to know that after all these weeks his wife was still of the same mind as before. Now I thought we would have trouble; now we would have more talk about going away and, just then, a cloud passed over the sun, the brilliance of the day was momentarily lost and as the weather has such sudden changes in these parts so did I see the fortunes of the Earnshaw family keep pace with equal caprice. I stole upstairs to my charges leaving the mistress lying where she was on the ground, the master turned angrily away biting his knuckles, not caring to remind them of my presence.

"The baby was to be called Margaret Catherine Earnshaw after his and his wife's mutual grandmother, the mother of Hindley and Catherine. Since my mistress had been recovered I had kept my place in the nursery where my charges were grateful for the care I lavished on them, and responsive, and I had known little about what went on in the house.

"It did seem to me however that Miss Cathy was more docile and resigned, as though she had had a good thrashing from Mr. Hareton—as might have been the case—and well would she have deserved it. As I have said the rages were not confined to the women of the Earnshaw family. Indeed Miss Cathy and her cousin, who was her husband, were too alike, although he had the gentleness that she lacked; yet I did not doubt that when occasion demanded a passion would be unleashed that he would find difficult to keep in rein.

"But now my mistress took her place at dinner every day and if the weather was fine—and it was a glorious spring such that those who dwell in these parts truly appreciate after the winters they have had to live through—she would sit out on the lawn reading or doing her embroidery. We continued to take the children to see her twice a day and on one occasion I ventured to suggest that a romp on the lawn would do young Rainton good and some air the same for the baby.

" 'Do you mean leave them here with me, Agnes?'

" 'Well, ma'am why not? I will be within call. I thought you would enjoy having your children around you.'

"She looked at me sharply, for my mistress knew I was not ignorant of her lack of maternal care, and I could see she was about to reprimand me for my sauce.

" 'You may bring them, Agnes,' she said, 'and stay with them; maybe the sight will soften the attitude of my husband towards me.'

"I ran upstairs and dressed young master Rainton warmly for, despite the sun, a chill lingered in the air. The wet nurse could scarce believe my news and she joyfully wrapped the baby in its shawl and placed a bonnet carefully on its head and followed me down, carrying her precious charge with her. Oh how it grieved me to see the care which that poor woman took of the young baby—having lost her own she lavished all her motherhood on our luckless bairn. She was a young woman and she surely would have children yet, and maybe Baby Margaret helped her to get over her grief instead of reminding her of her loss.

"She curtsyed before the mistress of the house and tenderly proffered the baby and, to my surprise, Miss Cathy reached up and took her in her arms while young Rainton danced around and laughed and would have me play tiggy with him and bouncing ball.

"It was on this happy scene that our master chanced upon us and the care on his face seemed to disappear, and the joy in his eyes was clear for all to see. The master had driven up the drive in the pony cart and I was surprised to see beside him a handsome woman of middle years but well preserved, dark haired but of comely complexion and dressed in what I, poor ignorant servant girl that I was, took to be the very height of fashion. Tall feathers nodded from a bonnet made of brown silk and she had a cloak of soft velvet adorned at the neck and the wristbands with lace. My mistress too seemed surprised by the sight, and diligently rocked the baby in her arms gently back and forth as she waited for her husband to escort his guest from the trap and lead her to where we were assembled on the lawn. The lady was tall for a woman and walked with a stately pace until she stood before Mrs. Earnshaw to whom she inclined her head.

" 'My dear, may I present Mrs. Ibbitson,' Mr. Earnshaw said. 'Mrs. Ibbitson, my wife.' My lady raised her hand and smiled at the newcomer, saying:

"You will forgive me if I do not get up, ma'am, I am but lately confined.'

" 'And so this,' exclaimed Mrs. Ibbitson with delight, 'is the daughter your husband was telling me about. To be called Margaret. May I?'

"The lady held out her hand and Mary, the wet nurse, took the baby from the mother's arms and placed her in that of the visitor who rocked her and murmured little noises and generally, to my eyes, behaved as though she was the baby's grandmother or at least some close relation. Mrs. Earnshaw did not know what to make of the visitor and eyed her husband who, however, avoided her glance and occupied himself in sending the ball over the lawn for his son to chase. The sun came out and dazzled us with its brilliance and to see the family dallying there surrounded by servants and in the presence of a guest you would have imagined them the happiest people on earth.

" 'And pray what brings Mrs. Ibbitson to these parts?' my mistress enquired at last, having managed to restrain herself, I could see, with commendable patience for one as impulsive by nature as she was.

" 'Why ma'am, I am interested in some property belonging to your husband,' Mrs. Ibbitson replied, taking the seat that one of the servants had brought out for her, casting him a grateful glance of acknowledgement as he did so. I could see she was a very gracious lady indeed.

" 'I am from Liverpool and have a mind to live away from the city now that trade has made it expand so. I saw an advertisement in a Liverpool paper about property to let on the moors and here I am!'

"She smiled at my mistress with an engaging frankness, having no idea of the boulder she had cast

66

in the pool of family tranquillity, as indeed I had, and I looked anxiously at my mistress who however appeared not to comprehend.

" 'Property? My husband has property to let?'

"I looked for Mr. Hareton but, whether by design or no, he was at the far side of the lawn playing with his son, apparently without a care in the world.

" 'Wuthering Heights it is called,' Mrs. Ibbitson said, glancing at a paper she had in her hand. 'I have just been to see it with Mr. Earnshaw.'

" 'Wuthering Heights!' cried my lady, rising to her feet, 'you have been to see Wuthering *Heights*?'

" 'I am hoping to come to an arrangement to rent it, Mrs. Earnshaw, from next month.'

"From the expression on my mistress's face our visitor was clearly under no doubt as to the commotion she had caused and she looked anxiously around for support from my master who was now walking in our direction carrying his son in his arms. My mistress had gone pale, that lovely glow but lately seen had been replaced by the deathly cast with which we were only too familiar and, as she stared at her husband, I could see the storm rising in her face.

" 'Wuthering Heights to let!' cried my mistress as soon as the master was in earshot. 'I never heard Wuthering Heights was to let!' and she clasped the arm of the chair and seemed to sway and steady herself.

" 'I told you, my love,' Mr. Hareton said easily, now joining our group and putting Rainton on the lawn. 'I told you I was going to let Wuthering Heights, now that Joseph is dead. We have no use for two homes.'

" 'But . . .' Mrs. Earnshaw gasped, appearing for the first time since I knew her at a loss for words. 'But it is a farmhouse, a simple country home. It . . .'

" 'It is just what I am seeking,' Mrs. Ibbitson said smoothly. 'I am a country girl by origin, not far from these parts, I'll not hide it from you; and I am attracted to the plain country life and the good air. I shall keep my town house in Liverpool but I dare say by and by I shall reside here much of the time and hope to persuade Mr. Earnshaw to sell it to me.'

"Mrs. Earnshaw had by now sat down and was looking at the ground as though to prevent herself from bursting into tears. Although she was headstrong and wilful she was too much of a lady to impair her husband's self-esteem in front of a stranger; her father had seen to that. As she kept back the tears I could see she was also biting her lips to check the hot words that would otherwise have flowed from her mouth.

" 'I am delighted,' Mr. Hareton said, taking care not to look at his wife, 'and hope we may draw up an agreement before the week is past. I explained to Mrs. Ibbitson that the Heights was *my* family home and I am pleased it is to be in good hands.'

"I marked how he dwelt on the *my* as though to emphasize to his wife that it was his home and not hers, but something she only had a fancy about. And he was right. Miss Cathy had been born and bred at the Grange, and had only gone to the Heights reluctantly as a bride.

"In the uneasy pause that followed Mrs. Ibbitson rose and said she must be about her business and Mr. Hareton said he would take her back to Gimmerton in the trap as he too had his duties to attend to. I guessed that he was pleased to leave his wife alone at this point to allow her anger to cool.

"Mrs. Ibbitson's face was thoughtful as she took my mistress's hand and bade her goodbye and I could see that she was aware of the turmoil that lay beneath the calm surface of Mrs. Earnshaw's forced smile.

"And indeed as soon as the trap was away up the drive Miss Cathy gave vent to such a tantrum that once again I feared for her reason and bade the wet nurse take the children and leave us while I attempted to quieten my mistress.

" 'How dare, how dare, how *dare* he!' She stamped her foot passionately on the ground so that the dust flew up and soiled the skirt of her pretty green dress and the green silk slippers she wore to match.

" 'But ma'am,' I ventured. 'Mr. Hareton is the master, is he not? Surely he does not have to consult you about what he does with his own property. In this land of ours the master's word is law.'

" 'Hold your tongue,' the mistress replied rudely, 'and remember *your* place. If I am servant to Hareton you are servant to me. But I am not his servant. All he has he owes to me. Without me he could not read or write; without me he would not have the money Papa left or this fine house or the servants or the horses in the stable, the carriage, or even the pony trap. Without me Hareton would have nothing, for Mr. Heathcliff left nothing; and even Wuthering Heights, according to the lawyer, would have been mine because I was the widow of Mr. Heathcliff's son Linton . . ."

" 'But Mr. Hareton was the son of the *legal* owner, the late Hindley Earnshaw, so I have heard told.' I murmured quietly, 'and I have also heard that Mr. Heathcliff did not lawfully own the Heights but acquired it by cunning.'

"Such information of course had come from my aunt; but this threw my mistress again into a frenzy and I thought she would hit me as she clenched her small fists and raised them in front of my face.

" 'You are on his side. Yet you are *my* servant!'

" 'I am merely saying he is the master, ma'am, and it is time you knew it and did as you were bid and become a good wife and mother, a companion by his side. You will forgive me speaking so direct, Mrs. Earnshaw, but such is the custom in my family and you would have heard the same good sense talked by my aunt. Why, Mrs. Earnshaw, you are but a girl, scarcely out of your teens and you have your whole life before you and I, who have seen you so happy and in love, mark with disquiet the storm you have brought upon the house by your stubborn, wilful ways. You were brought up here ma'am, the mistress beside your father, Mr. Linton. Why is it that you have taken on the common manners of a country girl, the air of a gypsy? Your mother has been dead these twenty years resting peacefully in her grave as my aunt always affirmed—such was her peace and tranquillity when she died. Your mother does *not* walk the moors, ma'am, or linger in Wuthering Heights. It is against belief and the teaching of our own Christian religion . . ."

" 'But people have seen her, Agnes. *I* saw her . . .'

"I shook my head firmly, believing that for once I had Miss Cathy's ear; she was listening to me without her customary inattentiveness. 'It is not possible ma'am. It is not Christian. You had these fancies only since you conceived baby Margaret; before I saw them not. It is not uncommon, according to my Aunt Ellen, for a woman with child to get strange fancies and in my opinion this is what happened to you. Some say it affects their appetite, or their liking for some people rather than others, and I fancy that with you it took the form of these strange romances, like this wild desire to be abroad all the time on the moors like a boy.'

" 'That happened before Margaret,' Mrs. Earnshaw replied quietly. 'I began to feel restless with all we had here; the change I saw in Hareton. Hareton has not the makings of a gentleman if you ask me. I always knew him as a rugged untutored farmboy and methinks I preferred him like that. Now he goes to Leeds to get his clothes and adopts all sorts of fine ways, but on occasions he holds his knife and fork in the wrong hands and slurps his soup directly out of the dish! I came to despise this change in Hareton and I sought the freedom of the moors where everything is wild about me and the lark flies high, the becks tumble in the ravines, and the heather is rough and springy underfoot. And then I remembered tales Nelly told me of how wild my mother was and how she loved the moors; she grew up on them because, of course, she was born and spent most of her life at the Heights and I felt I was like my mother and that this alone was true and everything Hareton wanted was false.'

" 'But you loved the jewels he gave you,' I said slyly and saw my mistress had the good grace to blush.

" 'Ah, they were so beautiful Agnes. I never saw anything so fine in my life. Yes I did love them and covet them and for a moment I thought I loved Hareton again because of what it must have cost him to buy

70

them for me. But I realised Hareton was only trying to *buy* me. With his new position he thinks everything has a price; but I am not to be bought, Agnes, and by his action over Wuthering Heights, Hareton has lost me forever.'

"Oh, I felt so sad in my heart, Mr. Lockwood, as I saw the proud stubborn expression on her face.

" 'Ma'am,' I pleaded, 'I am sure Mr. Hareton does love you for your sake. He wanted only to please you; to make you return to him. After all, if you have made him what he is, how can you reject your handiwork? For myself I think Mr. Hareton an admirable and a handsome man, a good, loving father, a husband any woman would be proud of. I see him taking pride in, yes, but not corrupted by worldly goods. He is living up to the station to which God has called him: his position as a man of property and a magistrate. He is good to the people he employs and kind to all and sundry. Mr. Hareton is well respected and thought of, ma'am, and it is you who are failing him. Not he you.'

"My mistress tossed her head and I thought a mocking smile played about her lips.

" 'And I? What do they say of *Mrs. Earnshaw*?'

" 'They say she is beautiful and an adornment to her husband and family,' I replied carefully. 'But they scarcely know you, ma'am. You do not go abroad as other wives do; you do not help in the church or visit the poor or sick bearing alms. You do not attend parties or entertain yourself. You have become too solitary here, Mrs. Earnshaw; you must go out into society. Forget about the moors and Wuthering Heights. Forget about them. Otherwise, ma'am, you will never know happiness.'

"I think this pleading tone in my voice moved her because she looked at me, and the heaving of her bosom ceased, and there seemed a recognition in her eyes that what I was saying was good and sensible and, oh, how I hoped she would heed me; how I prayed for her happiness.

"But even then, as you will see, Mr. Lockwood, I prayed in vain."

71

Chapter 5

"The baby Margaret was christened on a beautiful June day by the curate Mr. Duff at the new church in Gimmerton, the kirk having fallen by now into such a bad state of repair. I think none had been buried in its churchyard since Mr. Heathcliff and that by his own special request and provision made for it well beforehand.

"As though heedful of my words of a month past I had noticed a distinct improvement in the relationship of my master and mistress and, for ought I knew, she had never once returned to the subject of Wuthering Heights following the visit of Mrs. Ibbitson. She seemed intent on being an obedient and dutiful wife and as I never saw her sullen or heard her voice raised in anger, I thought that the particular aberration of childbearing with which we had thought her afflicted was past.

"I cannot say, however, that I noticed an improvement in her attitude to her children. Maybe she saw more of them, certainly in Mr. Hareton's company, but warmth, no. She would never pick them up or cuddle them or assist with their bath, and when I saw Mrs. Earnshaw at her most solemn it was when she was gazing at her children, her face unlit by a smile or the radiance of motherhood.

"Nor in that time did Mrs. Earnshaw leave the Grange unless she was accompanied by her husband to visit some neighbour or to go to Leeds or Bradford to shop; for they were making improvements to the house and ordering new fabrics and furnishings.

"But I did not feel close to my mistress at all. It was as though a curtain had descended between her and myself, and there were no more confidences as I brushed her hair or prepared her clothes for dressing or going to bed.

"In order to please her husband Mrs. Earnshaw had decided to give a large party for the christening; to throw open the doors of the Grange for the first time since she had come to it as a bride. All the staff seemed to enter into the spirit of this occasion and to welcome the opening of the house as a symbol of the Earnshaw's status and good fortune. For days before, the cook was in a state of agitation as she prepared for the feast and extra girls were hired from the village.

"The event was to be a tea party on the lawn following the christening and I remember it as an occasion of joy as I beheld the happy young couple and the baby whom I carried to the font. Just at the baptismal moment, when the curate poured water onto her forehead, a shaft of sunlight shone through the new stained glass windows straight onto the infant in the arms of its godmother, Mrs. Bradshaw, and the radiance illumined the faces of Mr. and Mrs. Earnshaw and Rainton, in his father's arms; and I took it to be an omen that the bad fortune that had afflicted the family was a thing of the past and only good times were in store. And I imagined them waxing ever more prosperous and the numbers growing until six or seven children stood about and the Earnshaws would become one of the best and most respected families in the neighbourhood. Surely God had sent that ray of sunlight as a blessing on my hopes?

"Although scarcely eight weeks old Margaret had grown strong and chubby with the careful nursing she had received and what an adorable baby she was, and so good as she smiled and gurgled in her godmother's arms, her cheeks pink and the golden hair curling under her bonnet. At the moment the curate named her Margaret Catherine her face broke into an open smile, which is strange and unusual in one so young, and I took this too as an omen that, lovely as she was, she would also have gifts and happiness showered on her in life. Indeed as I stood there at that sacred moment I had to reach for the kerchief in my pocket to hide the tears of happiness that were stealing down my own cheeks.

"The guests for the party—those who were not at the christening—had already started to arrive as we drove up to the Grange in fine style, three carriages and sundry gentlemen forming a fair crop of outriders. The guests gathered in the porch as the master and mistress alighted, I carrying the baby as I had travelled in the first coach with them, and many were the voices lifted in congratulation and admiration as they beheld the newly baptised. But my darling was yawning; it was time for her feed and sleep and I hastened upstairs with her to where the wet nurse, with aching breasts, was already waiting.

"While the baby was being fed I stood at the window which gave a fine view onto the front lawn and for the first time in my life I saw all the quality of Gimmerton and its neighbourhood as they circled and chatted on the lawn. To one side the white clothed tables groaned with an abundance of delicacies, cakes and jellies and cured hams and sides of beef, freshly baked bread and newly churned butter. All the servants were dressed in their best, wearing white gloves, and the men bore trays among the guests containing glasses of wine and cordial for the ladies.

"But it was my mistress who held my eye. I thought I had never seen her so beautiful or so happy. Her slim upright body a little more rounded now than when she was a maid, crowned by that head of lovely golden hair which she no longer wore in ringlets as when she was a girl but piled on her head in the fashionable style that they said was much favoured by the new Empress of France, Josephine. Despite our war with France, the fashion had spread across the Channel and, not stopping in fashionable London, had travelled as far north as the Yorkshire moors.

"Indeed to a humble person like myself the assembled throng could easily have been as *à la mode* as any seen in London, at the court of our own King George or that of the Emperor Napoleon in Paris. The women wore dresses of finest silks, satins and muslins, matching shoes and bonnets, some of which were adorned with feathers or flowers and the men strutted about like turkeys in their gorgeous coats, also cut in Leeds or Bradford like those of my master, with tight breeches, high cravats and tall hats with curled brims.

"It was while admiring the progress of my mistress that I observed, on the fringe of the crowd and accompanied by a man younger than herself, a lady whose name I had not heard mentioned since she had first set foot on the Grange property, Mrs. Ibbitson. Indeed the words 'Wuthering Heights' had not been mentioned from that day to this and I knew not what transpired there or aught about it. But the sight of Mrs. Ibbitson clad even more spectacularly than anyone else in yellow silk with an abundance of feathers about her brought the scene that day to my mind and I judged that she must have moved into residence in that bleak house on the moors.

"At that point, seeing Mrs. Ibbitson, my mistress made as though to move away from her and avoid her company, but Mr. Earnshaw was coming up behind her and, steering her by the arm, propelled her into the company of Mrs. Ibbitson and her companion, doubtless by design so as to be able to explain in company what he durst not do in private for fear of another scene.

"The man who was with Mrs. Ibbitson, a tall dark man whose features resembled hers although I was too far away to discern them properly, bowed to my lady and her husband and was soon chatting animatedly to my mistress until, at one moment, they seemed drawn apart and to be solely engrossed in each other which I must say, even at that time, I thought a rather curious event, to which however, I attributed no significance.

"But that night when I brushed her hair I thought my mistress unusually animated and considered that the success of the party, which had gone on against all expectations until late evening, had induced a rush of blood to the head for she smiled and talked in a manner I had not seen for months. I imagined that her success as a young matron at the side of her handsome husband with two beautiful children on show would have been to her great gratification, and indeed I think the party had pleased her; but, knowing how little she cared for society, I was foolish to think that a social gathering would be the occasion for such pleasure.

" 'Did you know that Mrs. Ibbitson has moved into the Heights, Agnes?'

"I paused in my stroke of the brush at the very mention of the dreaded words, but my mistress was smiling.

" 'She is a very charming lady and do you know she was accompanied by a most handsome man who is her son. I take it he cannot be any older than myself. His name is Jack and he is with the Foot Guards. He is anxious to fight against Napoleon! What is more, Agnes,' and in sheer exuberance of spirit my mistress seized the brush and began making the swift vigorous strokes she liked herself, 'I am invited to Wuthering Heights for tea! Surely my husband, who will accompany me, cannot object to *that*!'

"And then I realised that my mistress was elated not because of the party, or even on account of the attractions of a young soldier, which I had briefly dreaded, but because at last and after all these months, she was to return to Wuthering Heights.

"All Gimmerton was talking about the strange Mrs. Ibbitson who had elected to occupy the farmhouse of Wuthering Heights situated in such a desolate and unfriendly spot on the moors. So narrow was the path leading up to it that it could scarcely be approached by pony and cart, let alone horses and carriage, and yet all who saw it were amazed at the transformation wrought by Mrs. Ibbitson in the short time she had been there, and carried stories of it back to the village.

"You will know, sir, that Wuthering Heights is a fine, large house built of solid Yorkshire stone, but it is three hundred years old and many of the rooms are narrow and the floors uneven. I had never seen it myself before the day of our visit, about a month after the christening, and yet I was told that the garden, ablaze with shrubs and flowers, had been but scrub until the gardeners employed by Mrs. Ibbitson set to and transformed it overnight. Inside fine carpets and rare rugs adorned the floors, and the furniture was the very newest design from the workshops of the late Mr. Chippendale.

"The sun had blazed down all day and my mistress carried a parasol to protect her fine complexion as we drove up in the cool of the late afternoon, just Mr. and Mrs. Earnshaw and myself and the two bairns. It was a long drive up the moor from the Grange and I minded how my aunt used to run between the two as though 'twas no distance at all. Of course from the Heights to the Grange it was downhill all the way, but a hard walk for those going in the opposite direction.

"Mrs. Ibbitson must have heard the pony's hooves for she came to the gate and opened it herself, standing there smiling with a large straw hat on her head to protect her from the heat and a white muslin dress that made her look pretty and younger than I judged her years to be. Behind her, still in the shadow of the doorway, stood the tall dark man who was her son, and I remarked to myself how he did not go abroad with his mother but waited in the shadows, and I know not why I marked this, Mr. Lockwood, but I did. He was like some large bird of prey waiting to pounce, such as the owls or hawks do to the small animals on our moors, and, despite the warmth of the afternoon, I know that I shivered.

"When the trap stopped and Mr. Hareton got out to assist his wife, myself and the children, Mr. Ibbitson still did not move but waited in the doorway and I thought it was a rude and indolent gesture, not the sort one would have expected from an officer in the Guards. I could tell my lady was excited and looked quickly about her and then I saw that she gazed up at the window in front, but turned her head when she saw Mr. Hareton looking at her.

"A servant came out to help me with the children and another appeared to take the pony and trap to the back into the shade, and it became apparent that Mrs. Ibbitson maintained a fully equipped household, and once inside a maid took our things and yet another servant arrived with a silver tray on which were soft, cooling drinks. I was busy with my charges, but I perceived that Mr. Ibbitson had at last revealed himself and then I wondered if I had been lacking in charity as to his motives, for he carried a stick and it was obvious that he walked with difficulty and indeed sat down as soon as he decently could.

"There was such a hubbub with people and dogs and servants and little Margaret starting to cry, and Rainton rushing around and squealing with delight that my memory of the first moments of our visit are confused; but I do vividly recall the impact that Mr. Ibbitson made on the family for whom I worked, particularly my mistress. He was a tremendously tall fellow and muscular, with a dark, sallow face and eyes almost hidden beneath great black brows. The impression he gave was one not of refinement but of strength and vigour and, yes, an animal ferocity that I found frightening. He wore but shirt and trousers on that hot day, but one could imagine that in the uniform of a soldier he would topple the heart of any young girl. By the side of him, Mr. Hareton, who was also a finely built man, seemed almost dainty-like with his well-cut coat and breeches, his high cravat and his frilled waistcoat. Mr. Hareton on that day wore his hair tied at the back with a velvet bow, but Mr. Ibbitson's was cut short and a lock of it fell across his forehead giving him an appearance at once masterly and slightly sinister.

"My mistress had not worn a bonnet and, in her simple blue muslin dress caught under the bodice by a bunch of fresh cornflowers with a ribbon trailing down the front, she had never looked so lovely before. She had not wanted me to dress her hair, so that it hung loose, enhancing the effect of a young girl and the paleness of her complexion, contrasting with the dark brooding manliness of Mr. Ibbitson as they talked on a sofa in the corner, held my gaze and made me catch my breath.

"Mr. Hareton was kept fully occupied by Mrs. Ibbitson who had removed her hat indoors so that one could see what a thickly luxuriant head of dark hair she had and what a handsome bone structure and blue almost violet eyes. Yet her skin was of a ladylike whiteness and I was at a loss to account for the saturnine complexion of her son.

" 'Oh thank heaven, a breeze,' Mrs. Ibbitson cried. 'At last it blows through the door. It has been so stifling all day. Shall we sit outside? I will have Roger prepare the chairs; you see we have only a patch of lawn. How I envy you your fine grounds, but the view,' she went toward the door her hands outstretched, 'is it not breathtaking?'

"And indeed the view across the moors looking towards Gimmerton on that hot day was one of awe-inspiring beauty and splendour. For mile upon mile there was a carpet of heather, whose soft little buds were gradually breaking into the purple blossom that transforms our moors in August and September of the year, into a rich tapestry interspersed with patches of the coarse pale grass on which our mountain sheep graze. Crisscrossing the whole scene were the dark scars of the ravines which traverse the terrain, and through which our little becks flow swiftly towards the river from their sources high in the hills, each different valley a delight in itself. But from where I stood all that could be seen were the heads of the trees, unmoving in that still air, rising up from the ravines, and from their banks the dark green bracken which is as high as a man and in which we loved to play and hide as children, using the dead sticks for kindle in the wintertime.

"But that day a heat haze rose from the moors which obscured the sight of the dales and cultivated fields beyond; for from that height it seemed that one could see across half the county of Yorkshire, though I know it is not so. At a gesture from our hostess we strolled through the front door into the garden and our nostrils were assailed by the smell of stock, sweet william, and hollyhock; and the hum of bees busily flying from one flower centre to another, and the many-coloured butterflies winging in and out among the rich and varied foliage, induced in us all a sense of contentment and well-being, of laziness and sensual satisfaction that heightened our pleasure in the place where we were gathered.

"I don't think I ever saw my native countryside so clearly or appreciated it so well as I did on that hot July day some forty years ago and I still recall it vividly as I am describing it to you now. And then I knew why a fine lady like Mrs. Ibbitson would want to come and live here, or anyone for that matter who loved natural beauty, and why my mistress loved it so much that to be deprived of it nearly destroyed her mind. It was on that day that I realised for the first time why Wuthering Heights had formed such roots in the hearts of the Earnshaw family or in those who came in contact with that old stone house on the moors.

"The servants were bringing the tea onto the lawn, setting little tables and chairs in that small confined space and it was then that I noticed my mistress was absent and that Mr. Ibbitson, leaning on his stick, was listening carefully to my master who seemed to be pointing out landmarks of interest on the surrounding countryside because of course he knew it well. Mrs. Ibbitson was directing the servants and young Rainton was creating havoc among the flower beds, while the baby lay snugly in a carrying crib we had bought for her and which was placed in the shade by the wall of the house. I ran back inside, but Miss Cathy was not in the sitting room and then, not knowing my way, I paused and one of the servants who had served the tea things saw me and asked if he could help me. I told him I was looking for my mistress and he said he had seen her go up the stairs and pointed the way.

"I was undecided whether to go or not but then, on impulse, I ran up the stairs and found myself in a long corridor with many smaller passages and rooms leading off. I remembered what my mistress had said on her last visit to the house and I made my way to where I judged was the front and found one of the doors ajar. I pushed it gently open and saw that the room was empty except for a tall oak chest which stood near the window, and I was about to quit the room when I thought I heard a sound from the chest and I tiptoed up to it and peeped through one of the curious squares near the top which looked like little windows.

"I saw the chest resembled a tiny room in which there was a couch and there lay my mistress, her face downwards, her body heaving with great sobs. I couldn't find how the chest opened and looked in vain for a door, and then I observed a panel which at my touch slid sideways and I gained entrance to this odd structure that I must confess I had never seen before that day, but have since. They are like little rooms for those who would have solitude in a crowded house. My mistress heeded not the slight disturbance I made and even when I placed a hand on her shoulder she took no notice, but the sobs increased and the sound became a wail.

" 'There, Mrs. Earnshaw,' I whispered, not wishing the others to hear. 'It is I, Agnes, ma'am. What ails you? I thought how happy you seemed downstairs, and here . . .'

"My mistress turned over and took my hand in such an affectionate gesture that all the love I had had for her, and thought long since gone, came rushing back to me again. Her lovely face was stained with tears and her eyes so swollen that I could scarce credit the fact she had only been gone from our midst a few minutes, ten at the most.

" 'Oh Agnes, this was Mama's room; this was her

bed. On those shelves I found her books which I brought home. I was so *sure* Mama would be here waiting for me, and I came to the room with such a happy sense of expectation and I thought that I would bring up her grandchildren and that if she loved them I would too. But I came into this cold, silent room and I knew it was empty of anything save the chest, certainly any *presence*. It was from this window Mama looked out at me that night and I think she has waited for me too long and has now gone.'

" 'Hush, ma'am, hush,' I said, stroking the strands of hair from her forehead which had grown so moist and hot that I feared again for the fever. 'I thought that fanciful notion of yours was over and gone. Your Mama is in her grave, Miss Cathy, has been these twenty years and resting there happily with God. Try and see sense, Miss, I beg of you, for your own sake and that of your family. 'Tis idiotic to expect the ghost of your Mama to wait for you in this room; she lies in the old churchyard and always will.' And I pressed her hand and stroked her brow, for she burst into wild fretful sobbing again like a child, and would not be comforted.

"Soon Mr. Hareton came looking for her and found me tending her like a baby. As soon as he saw her his face clouded and I knew he repented of accepting Mrs. Ibbitson's invitation.

" 'I thought you would be here,' he said to her sternly. 'Catherine, get up!' and he pushed me rudely aside and caught her hand, but she struggled and twisted out of his grasp and she clung to the couch and looked up at him as I have seen a mouse when in the evil jaws of a stoat.

" 'Oh Hareton, don't be cruel. You love this place too. How could you *let* it? We could have lived here, been happy here. We can never be happy at the Grange, now, with what has gone before. Tell Mrs. Ibbitson to go. Let us come and live here, Hareton, where you were born, where Mama was born. I feel we *must* do it. I *beg* you . . .'

"He shook her again and I could see pain struggling

with the rage he felt at her betrayal and then unexpectedly he bent and kissed her fiercely full on the mouth
and I had to look away for embarrassment. But the act
pacified her, for she lay there and ceased her struggling; and he then kissed her gently all over her face
and took her in his arms and hugged her.

" 'Oh Cathy, remember the early days of our love,
here at Wuthering Heights? You teased me at first;
then you showed me you liked me and you helped me
to be educated like you. And we talked, Cathy, do you
remember, of the Grange and how happy we should be
to live there especially when the wind roared at night
here and we couldn't venture out of doors because of
the snow as high as a man's shoulder? And we said
how we would like to be rid of Mr. Heathcliff and old
Joseph and be by ourselves in a new world. And then
when Mr. Heathcliff died and it all became possible,
how happy you were to be going to your home with all
the space and freedom! What has happened to you
Cathy, my own sweet love? Have you forgotten it all?
Why have you changed?'

"The gentleness of his voice, the tenderness of his
gestures, brought tears to my eyes; but instead of the
mistress's face softening, as I had hoped and she returning his caresses, her aspect assumed a stormy expression and she tried to push him away from her.

" 'How *you* have changed, Hareton Earnshaw! And
not for the better. At Wuthering Heights you were
solid and sturdy, a force like the land, like the moors.
Now I recognise you not in those fine clothes and with
your fancy manners. I am trapped in the Grange with
you and the children. Trapped I say; and Agnes here
will tell you how I feel, like a lark imprisoned in a
cage. I care not for society or for bazaars or for entertaining. To me it is like being confined in a dungeon.
Even Linton Heathcliff was more *real* than you, for he
liked poetry and loved to lie on the moors and gaze at
the sky; but you do you ever think of anything but the
number of sheep you have, the acres of land, and the
quantity of cows? Do you? Do you, Hareton?'

"Mrs. Earnshaw's voice rose shrilly and I feared that

those below should hear it, but the window was closed and the fir tree had grown so close to it as almost to eliminate the light, and I hoped would serve also to muffle the sound. I could see my master was sorely hurt by her words and the mention of her first husband, Mr. Heathcliff's son, to whom she had been forcibly and briefly wed. Like Mr. Hareton, Mr. Linton was her cousin also, being the son of her Aunt Isabella, the sister of her father Edgar; but, according to my aunt although Miss Cathy was fond of her cousin, it had been no marriage in any way for the poor boy was dying when they were wed in order for Mr. Heathcliff to gain her inheritance. Thus I could understand how vexed my master must feel to be compared with one who, by what I have heard, was not much of a man by any standards!

"Mr. Hareton bit his lip and turned about and I thought would leave the room, but my mistress, not content at leaving well alone, cried after him:

" 'I *demand* an answer, Hareton. *Do* you think of anything else?' He slowly turned around and looked at her, and I could see he was tormented by the fact that his love clashed with wrath.

" 'I think of *you*, Cathy, and our children. All I do is for you and them. Is it so wrong for an orphan boy like me, unlettered and rough as I was brought up, to wish to be like the gentleman my father Hindley was, brother to your dear mother Catherine? We Earnshaws were not always thus, coarse as I was like a farmhand. I was only seeking my birthright; to be your equal, and that of your father who was so clever and fond of his books. I see no sin in this, Cathy, nor in wanting to sire a fine family and desire wealth. I work hard. I am never idle. I do what I can for the community in which we live. A wife other than you would be well contented with her lot. Why you are not, I know not; it saddens and bewilders me.'

"As it did me. I thought my master spoke nobly and I wished so much my mistress would match her mood to his. But no. She appeared not have harkened to anything he said, and I thought from all I'd heard she was

85

indeed her mother's daughter and that no compliment, for the late Mrs. Linton had also despised her husband, Edgar, Miss Cathy's father, and according to my Aunt Ellen made no bones about telling him either. Her daughter was saying the same thing to Hareton, and history was repeating itself.

"At that point the servant our hostess had addressed as Roger appeared at the door and said he came from his mistress to enquire if all was well. I glanced at him from the corner of my eye—I was still attending Mrs. Earnshaw—and saw that he was an upright, well-built young man with comely features and, although he spoke to Mr. Hareton, he too was looking boldly at me. I remember that, catching his eye, I blushed and dropped my gaze for although I was nineteen I had never had a follower or had aught to do with young men apart from my brothers' friends. My mistress by this time had dried her eyes and, feeling rather foolish in front of the servant, we all tripped out from the oak chest where we had been boxed and Mr. Hareton said he would descend directly and he begged Roger to precede him.

"I did what I could to straighten Mrs. Earnshaw's dress and combed her pretty hair, but for her swollen lids I could do nothing and I saw too that she was unwilling to leave the room, but I tugged at her arm.

" 'Please ma'am, for your own sake do not linger here or delay any more. It will sorely trouble my master and he is troubled enough already.'

" 'Hold your tongue, Agnes!' my mistress snapped sharply and with the reproof, the blood returned to her face and, whether with the tears or no, her eyes sparkled. Without a word she gathered up her skirt and ran from the room down the corridor and I could hear her light footsteps pattering on the stairs as I followed her.

"I know not what my master had been saying, or rather I guessed because, as my mistress came into the garden, Mrs. Ibbitson gazed at her with concern and took her hand.

" 'It is the heat, Mrs. Earnshaw. That surely is what

86

has caused your headache. Would you prefer to sit indoors awhile?'

" 'I am perfectly well, thank you,' Mrs. Earnshaw replied, not smiling or looking at her husband. It was plain for all the world to see that there had been some ado between my master and mistress because, whereas my mistress's usually pale countenance was flushed and angry, that of Mr. Hareton—normally ruddy—had an unnatural pallor. " 'I want to see the room my Mama had as a child and it upset me.'

" 'Ah, which room is that?' said Mrs. Ibbitson heedlessly, pouring the tea from a large silver pot.

" 'The one in the front,' Miss Cathy looked up. 'That by the fir.'

" 'Oh, that *is* a pretty room. I wanted it for my own but . . .' Mrs. Ibbitson stopped and seemed to be intent on her task.

" 'But?' my mistress enquired eagerly.

" 'Well, I don't know how to put this without seeming foolish, and as it was your dear mama . . .'

"Oh, the dread I felt, Mr. Lockwood, at her tone and the sudden unease that had fallen on the gathering. It seemed as though everyone was hanging on her words.

" 'Go on, Mama,' Mr. Ibbitson said testily, 'tell us. What?'

" 'Well the workmen tell such fanciful tales, I know, and one should not listen to them, but they told me it was haunted and that well known, too. It appears there is often seen at the window the face of a woman and she puts out her arms in a pleading gesture as though she were asking for something. And some say they have not only seen her; they have also heard her voice.' "

Chapter 6

"As Mrs. Ibbitson finished, my mistress gave a cry and swooned to the floor where she was hastily and anxiously attended by my master and myself. He held her in his arms while I fanned her face and the servant Roger, obviously a bright, observant lad, brought a bowl of cold water and a cloth from the kitchen. Mrs. Ibbitson stood rooted to the spot where she had made her inconsiderate announcement, her hands clasping her flushed and worried face. Mr. Ibbitson, I perceived, leaned on his stick and gazed thoughtfully at the face of Mrs. Earnshaw who by this time showed signs of reviving and, giving a low moan, passed her hand across her brow.

"Mrs. Ibbitson knelt by her side and took her hand.

"'Oh my dear, forgive me! It was the most tactless, tasteless thing I ever did or said! Of course it is not your mama, this spectre, if indeed a spectre exists . . .'

"'It *is* my Mama,' my mistress said in a weak voice. 'I have seen her myself, but none would believe me. Now will you believe me, Hareton?' And she glanced sharply up at my master whose face, as you would imagine, wore as careworn an expression as ever I saw. Oh what he would have given to have had these words of Mrs. Ibbitson's unsaid! How he must have wished he had never brought his wife to this place as indeed he had allowed not to. The events had proved his judgement right.

" 'Nay, I'll not believe it,' Mr. Hareton said, helping his wife to her feet and leading her indoors to a couch. 'I'll not believe you saw it, or that anyone else did. I was born in this house and know it well. It has no spectres, no ghosts; it is but a good Yorkshire farmhouse in which people have lived and bred and died and known sorrow and happiness; but there are no spirits. None. I'll not have it.'

" 'Mr. Earnshaw speaks well,' Mr. Ibbitson declared, joining us all in the sitting room. 'For I am a practical military man who will have naught to do wi' ghosts and fairies and the like. Mama, I am ashamed of you that you harken to such tales. I myself will move into that room and disprove your story.'

" 'Oh . . .' Miss Cathy gazed at him, but seemed at a loss for words. He looked at her kindly and from the expression in his eyes—as far as one could see an expression in eyes planted so deep in the forehead—I observed, as I had before, that he was a good deal taken with my mistress for his harsh countenance softened at the very sight of her.

" 'Fear not, ma'am. I know 'twas your mother's room and yours maybe; but my influence there will be gentle and good. Besides I am shortly to return to the Army as soon as this blasted leg is cured and then I shall be off to the campaign against France.'

" 'Pray what is amiss with your leg, sir?' Mr. Hareton enquired.

" 'Why, I fell while riding over the moors. I was galloping my horse, stretching her to the limit, and she stumbled in one of the ditches and, but for the fact I jumped clear, would have killed me as she fell and rolled over. Oh, but it was a splendid day with the wind almost a gale and the dark clouds tumbling over one another so that you felt you could race against

90

them. I like nothing better on days like that than riding or walking on the moors; my spirit seems to soar. I love this place as much as my mother. It seems familiar to me as though I was returning home after a long voyage.'

"I could see the practical Mrs. Ibbitson wished to put a stop to such talk and fussed about my mistress with the *sal volatile*; but my mistress harkened only to Mr. Ibbitson and, as he spoke, his eyes held hers and the colour flowed back into her face. I could see that in him she recognised a fellow spirit—one as wild and free as herself—and a terrible dread welled up inside me as I thought of the harm such recognition of like for like could do. The very gentleness of his voice seemed to quiet her as though she had met a master who could tame her own rebellious heart, which Mr. Hareton certainly could not.

"But whatever went on in his own mind he certainly felt uncomfortable because he began to walk about restlessly and finally said:

" 'I think I should get my family home ma'am, and thank you for your courtesy.'

" 'But for the unhappy incident it was a pleasure,' Mrs. Ibbitson replied graciously, 'and please do not let it spoil your promise to come again and again, as often as you like. There will be no more talk of ghosts and, indeed, I will have the room prepared for my son on the morrow.'

"Mrs. Earnshaw rose uneasily to her feet. I could see she was still under the spell of Mr. Ibbitson, or Captain Ibbitson as I learned he was called, and he eyed her bold as brass having no care for what her husband would think.

" 'Maybe when your leg is better you will go riding again?' my mistress said quietly, so that only I could hear apart from the man to whom it was addressed. Mr. Hareton was fussing about getting the children together.

" 'Ma'am, bad leg or no, I go riding every day. I am determined to punish that mare for making me fall.'

" 'Perhaps I shall see you, for I love the freedom of

91

the moors too,' my mistress whispered, and, with a frown, I tugged at her arm and indicated that her husband approached within earshot; but she, foolish girl, although a wife and mother of two children, stared at the Captain like a maid with her first beau. And I could see Mrs. Ibbitson's eyebrows rise a trifle and she looked with concern at the husband who, poor man, did not know he was being cuckolded.

"The journey home was an uncomfortable one, my mistress pale and silent, my master looking very stern and I knew not whether he was at war with himself for having taken her there in the first place or whether he had observed any commerce between her and the son of the new tenant of Wuthering Heights. None of us had eyes for the beauty of the evening scene as we rode down the hill; the haze had lifted now and the air was clear to the far hills many leagues distant. A gentle breeze came off the moor and the swallows and swifts flashed back and forth to the nests in the crevices of the rocks, and the thrushes and blackbirds deafened us with their evening call from their lodgements high in the branches of the trees which grew more plentiful as we descended towards Thrushcross Park. The grass and heather smelt sweetly and, apart from the birdsong and the ever-present hum of the worker bees, we heard naught save the crunch of the cart wheels on the uneven road and the clop of the pony's hooves. As soon as she got in, pleading fatigue, my mistress went directly to her room; my master shut himself in his study and I went swiftly to the nursery with my charges, for it was past time for the baby's feed and Master Rainton was in the churlish mood young children are when it is past their bedtime, those who have been used, as he was, to a steady and regular routine.

"I knew not whether Mrs. Earnshaw had made some secret assignation with the Captain or whether it was instinct that directed her out; but a few days after our visit she waited until Mr. Hareton had gone off to Keighley and then she bade the groom saddle Minny and when I made to remonstrate with her she sent me sharply about my business.

" 'I have a mind to ride in the park, Agnes! May I not do that in my own home? Even my husband says I may ride in Thrushcross Park.'

"But such was her elation that, remembering the glances exchanged between her and Captain Ibbitson, I doubted whether such colour was brought to her cheeks, such sparkle to her eyes by the thought of a canter round the walls of the park. I went slowly upstairs and climbed to the top of the house, unclasping an attic window to peer across the moors in the direction of Wuthering Heights.

"It was a day such as the one of our visit, except that the air was freshened by a light breeze and, if anything, the sky appeared even more blue and the heather a deeper purple. Even my blood, country girl that I am, quickened as I gazed upon the scene, but although my eyes searched every inch of the park I could not find my mistress. I decided then, rashly, to go after her, determined to warn her should my suspicions be correct. I bade the wet nurse supervise the nursery until I returned and then I slipped out past the stables towards the far gate that led directly on to the moors. Then I began that slow climb up the path towards the Heights which, as it lies just over the brow of the hill, is not visible from the Grange.

"Indeed I was happy enough walking, and reflected how little freedom I got; my mistress seldom gave thought to a day off, considering that my reward lay in the care of my charges and of herself when she needed me. It was many weeks since I had set eyes on my parents or my brothers and sisters. However, I decided on that beautiful day that my lot was in many respects a fortunate one. I was warm, well fed and clothed. My employers were not unkind, and the upbringing of my charges indeed a reward as in many ways I was to them mother and father as well as nurse.

"Mr. Hareton seemed unable to respond to the baby Margaret as he had to his infant son, as though taking the tone from his wife's behaviour, or perhaps he was anxious to avoid displeasing her by seeming to care too much for them. Certainly twice a day, morning and evening, the babies were brought to the parlour to be dandled and caressed by both parents, but never more than half an hour at a time and sometimes much shorter.

"As I walked occupied with my thoughts I heard the clip clop of a horse's hooves and thought to see my mistress descending the path towards me, and that I best prepare myself to receive the rough edge of her tongue for absenting myself from the house. Should I hide? I asked myself, thinking to lie on the ground among the scrub and gorse, but even as the thought crossed my mind the horse was before me and a soft male voice called in greeting.

" 'Why if it is not the very lass I was coming to see.'

"Startled, I looked up towards the rider, shielding my eyes from the sun, and I must confess my heart turned over a little with joy at beholding the comely face of Roger, the servant at the Heights. Indeed in my eyes he looked handsome with brown curly hair and a fresh young brown face scarcely past boyhood, really no more than nineteen or so, which was my age.

" 'Pray what brings thee from yonder?' he enquired, jumping down and gathering the horse's reins in his hands.

" 'I was seeking my mistress,' I said. 'She is not in the park where she said she would be.'

" 'Ah ah,' Roger laughed meaningfully. 'Did she then? In the park, eh?'

" 'My master does not like her to wander abroad for fear of some accident, such as happened to the Captain. He is anxious for her safety, so when I saw she was not there I decided to seek her.'

" 'I think thou had best not interfere,' Roger said. 'I can only assure thee that thy mistress hast come to no harm, at any rate by a fall from a horse!' And he laughed again and then the rogue had the sauce to place his arm about my waist and, pulling me close to him, kissed my cheek! 'Thou art a right gradely lass, Agnes Dean, as I have heard thou wert from thy

94

brother Arthur who worked at Daggert's farm where my father is head cowman.'

" 'But I have never seen thee before,' I said both angry and pleased and relapsing into the idiom which is the custom among the working people of these parts. 'Dost thou hail from Gimmerton?'

" 'Nay, lass; Daggert's farm is at Sharpthorpe on the Bradford to Bingley Road, but since I was fifteen I have been in Liverpool wi' Mrs. Ibbitson. I met thy brother last week when I returned home for the first time in three years to see my folks. I told him I was at the Heights and he said he had a right shapely sister who was nursemaid at the Grange. I tell thee thou canst do with female company there; it 'aint like Liverpool.' "

" 'How is Arthur?' I said, at a loss for words and not having seen my brother, next to me in age, for months. Distances make travel difficult in these parts if you are in service.

" 'I think he is working his notice and going to the city. He says he is interested in industry rather than the farm. Happen he'll go to Bradford to work at the mills that are springing up there.'

"I was still aware of his arm around my waist, but I didn't resist for I cannot deny it was pleasing, and I was flattered at the attention of this well-proportioned youth.

" 'And thou were coming to see *me*?' I went on. 'Hast thou so much freedom then?'

" 'Ah, I was coming to that, comely lass. I set off with my master to ride over the moors. He likes company because of his injury in case he should fall again, for his wound makes him unsteady on a horse though he denies it. We were rounding Penistone Cragg when your mistress comes galloping up on a big horse, and they both exclaim with surprise and delight at this chance encounter and rein in their horses. Then my master laughs and bids me be off; he is now not afraid of coming to harm it seems, and then he turns to your mistress and I see that, having eyes only for each other, they will not have a care to my whereabouts and

8   95

Mrs. Ibbitson thinks I am with him so . . . I set off towards Thrushcross Grange.'

"I had stopped and was staring at him, my eyes like saucers. 'Dost thou think they *intended* to meet?'

" 'With my master I think not; otherwise he would not have taken me. After all she is a married lady, the mistress of Thrushcross Grange. I dare say he would not like to have it noised abroad that they met secretly on the moors. But then if they had intended to meet the fact that I was there would make it look accidental and, if questioned, that is what I would say.'

"Young Roger smiled at me and I could see he was a man of brains as well as charm.

" 'Art thou loyal to the master?' I asked slyly.

" 'Aye, I am that; he is a fine man, Captain Jack we call him. I hope to go to the wars with him as his servant if I can enter the Army.'

" 'Oh.' The distress in my voice caused him to look at me with his laughing, roguish eyes and he drew me to him again and kissed me once more, this time longer.

" 'Dost thou care, pretty miss?'

" 'Of course I care not!' I said heatedly. 'What thou dost is of no concern of mine; I scarcely know thee.' And I drew away from him so that he would not think he had already captured my heart.

" 'Mrs. Ibbitson don't want me to go; but my heart is set on't if the master can buy me in. The Guards, imagine! I would be back often,' he said glancing at me and I thought how fine he would look in a soldier's uniform.

" 'If thou wert not killed,' I said and then I raced down the road ahead of him to tease him, and he followed after me, the horse trotting beside him. And so we came to the side door of Thrushcross Grange, and he caught me and, pressing me against the wall, kissed me hard until I pushed him away protesting that we should be seen.

" 'Thou *art* a bold young man,' I said, 'and the sooner thou dost get into the Army to check thy forward ways the better for all!'

"But he looked at me with his saucy smile.

" 'Thou dost not mean it, Agnes. I saw the other day how thou lookst at me at the Heights, and I knew that I would be welcome to call on thee. In the city the girls are a lot more forward; they think nothing of a kiss.'

" 'Indeed!'

" 'But thou art different. I have a mind to court you, Agnes Dean. Would'st like it?'

" 'I might,' I said, knowing already that my heart was his whenever he wanted it. 'I must go back to my charges. Wilt thou return to the Heights?'

" 'Aye, to wait my master. I'll not mention Mrs. Earnshaw to my mistress though she is indulgent toward her son whom she loves dearly. No doubt he will tell her himself; they are close for mother and son and appear to have few secrets.'

" 'And what happened to Mr. Ibbitson?' I enquired.

" 'He died before I went there. He was a very old man. I hear that she married late in life, and he had plenty of brass.'

" 'What did he do?'

" 'He was a considerable cloth merchant, and she has a fine house in Liverpool and a good income, and Captain Jack had the best education at Winchester School in the south and then a commission was bought for him in the Guards. It is a happy house. The mistress is kind without being soft and Captain Jack the very best.'

" 'He is a rogue,' I said, 'if he looks so boldly at a married lady and in front of her husband.'

" 'Oh aye, he's a rogue, and many a heart he's broken already that I know of. Women can't resist him; but that is only in matters of love. As a man and a soldier he is straight and true though he does have a wicked temper if crossed. He wanted his mother to go and live in the south as his barracks are in London, and he was really vexed when she came to these parts. But he bows to her in everything, although I have heard many hot words between them. Now he says he loves it as much as she does.'

" 'He has not seen it in winter,' I said.

" 'Nay, nor her; but then she will be back in Liverpool for the concerts and balls and card games. Happen she'll only be here in the summertime. I'd best be quick with my courtin', Agnes Dean.'

" 'Oh, I'll not be moving from the Grange,' I said, 'so long as my bairns have no parents.'

" 'What bairns?'

" 'My charges, my babies, Margaret and Rainton.'

" 'But they have parents!'

" 'Nay; they are ignored by both. She is a bad mother, a bad woman in many ways. I thought I could love her, as a good servant should love her mistress, but for the past year she has behaved so strangely. Oh she was a bonny, lovely bride; she and Mr. Hareton as happy as the day was long; but all changed after Rainton was born.'

" 'Aye they say love wanes,' Roger sighed.

" 'Nay, not like that; t'was almost vicious on her part, wilful. To reject husband and bairns; always off and away riding on the moors in all weathers. Her mother was a weird one—my Aunt Nelly Dean nursed her, and my mistress came to resemble her as she grew older. Oh 'tis a long story; I'll tell thee some day.'

" 'Aye, that sort appeals to Captain Jack,' Roger said. 'He likes the bold restless ones, as many faithless wives are!'

" 'Well they've no right to be,' I said tartly. 'Their place is at home by their husbands and children.'

" 'Wilt thou make a good wife, Agnes?'

" 'Aye happen,' I said, but as he came close to me again I pushed him away, for I did not want him to think I was 'easy' like the women who went after Captain Jack, or Roger himself for aught I knew. 'I must be back to my charges.'

" 'May I come and visit thee?'

" 'If thou canst get the time. Take the back entrance,' I said, 'for my mistress must not know of it.'

" 'She . . . !'

"But knowing what he was about to say, I shook my head.

" 'I care not what she does; or rather I care, but it

98

must not affect what I do. She would not approve of me having a follower and would be rid of me. I am too well placed to want that, Master Roger.'

"But I let him kiss me once more before we parted, and my head in a whirl I ran back to the Grange wondering when I should see him again.

"But, as you will hear, Mr. Lockwood, that was to be much sooner than I thought."

"I was in a spin that day because of the attentions of young Master Roger. Indeed I always enjoyed my work, but I went about it with a lighter step and a joyous heart so much so that it was apparent to the wet nurse Mary who upbraided me for my adventure. Indeed it was halfway through the afternoon that I bethought myself of my mistress and rang along the corridor to her room to find it empty. I then looked in the parlour, downstairs in the sitting room and had decided my mistress was still abroad, and my master expected back at any moment, when a movement on the lawn drew my gaze and I perceived that my mistress was sitting in the sun doing her embroidery!

"I felt abashed and went outside overcome with nervousness at my own misdeeds.

" 'Did you enjoy your ride, ma'am?' I enquired, stooping to pick up a ball of cotton.

" 'Indeed Agnes, and I stayed in the grounds as I promised.' I felt myself blushing at her lie, so that I could not help saying:

" 'Indeed ma'am? I looked for you and found you not.'

" 'And why, pray,' said Mrs. Earnshaw sharply, 'should you seek me?'

" 'To know that all was well, ma'am.'

" 'Then mind your business, you interfering girl! And be about it now, sharp mind!'

"I saw that I had needled my mistress and indeed I thought I should take care lest she send me home and deprive me of the chance of seeing young Roger again.

"But I need not have worried for a few days later one of the kitchen maids sought me in the nursery and

99

said I was wanted in the courtyard. She spoke softly and her eyes were bright with excitement, and my heart quickened for I knew something was afoot; but I assumed a grave expression, for she was a lot younger than I and very low in the ranks of the household servants, and I told her I should be out shortly and that whoever it was should wait.

"But as soon as she had left the room I hurried after her, through the kitchen and into the back porch and there giving water to his horse out of a bucket was Roger.

" 'Thou art bold!' I cried, 'coming when thou must know I am busy with my duties.'

" 'I told thee I should see thee soon,' Roger exclaimed and looked quickly about him before stretching out a hand to grasp me by the waist, but I neatly sidestepped him for I did not want to be observed by the other staff in this dalliance. 'And I am on business,' he said, and produced an envelope from his breeches pocket. 'There, this is for thy mistress.'

" 'From Captain Ibbitson!' I gasped.

" 'Aye. He said he wished to get a message to her but did not know how to do it. I told him the truth. That I had seen thee and liked thee well enough to pay thee court. He slapped his knee and laughed and was delighted, and said it was an ideal arrangement that, by my appearing to court thee, he should contrive to court thy mistress!'

" 'But my faith, I like it not!' I cried. 'It is a wicked thing you do and try to get me to do. I will not deceive my master whom I love and admire.' And I gave him back the envelope which he already had placed in my hand.

"Whereupon Roger tethered the horse to a post and taking me by the arm led me in the shadows of the stables away from the kitchen. Then he loosed my hand—not attempting to touch me as I thought he would, and gazed gravely into my eyes.

" 'Pretty lass, dost thou think thou canst order the ways of Providence? Or interfere with the intentions of our betters? Dost thou not know *thy* mistress is as ea-

100

ger for my master as he is for her, and that naught will part them now? He has told me he is besotted with her and that every minute that passes without her is agony for him. And he says, *she* feels the same, from the day they met on the lawn here. If thou dost try to interfere, thy mistress will send thee home and get another who will be more eager to oblige!'

"Then he seized me boldly and, pressing me to his young body, kissed me and murmured such sweet things that my head reeled with excitement and I knew that if I did not heed him he and I would soon be parted; for I knew my mistress and how great her wrath would be when she found I had sent Roger back with the letter.

" 'See,' Roger cried excitedly as he released me, having felt the returned passion of my own kisses, eagerly given, 'we can meet now and with our superiors' knowledge and blessing! Knowing that we know their secret they will do what they can to please us, because they need us!'

" 'Thou art a wicked one Roger,' I said, taking the letter, 'but thou dost speak sense. I have naught to gain by doing what I know is right before God and my master. No one will thank me when I pack my bags and trudge down the drive to the road; my bairns will not thank me for leaving them; my mistress might tell lies about me to a new employer and work is hard to find. But I am sad that my mistress should deceive her lawful husband so.'

" 'Oh fie!' that scamp said. 'My master will soon be gone to the wars, taking me too, I hope. Thee and thy mistress will be left all alone with plenty of time for virtue then. Until that time, why don't we make what sport we can?'

"I must admit his eagerness was catching, and I knew that every time I saw him I became more enamoured and I could not deny myself the pleasure of seeing him, whatever the consequences for my poor master.

" 'I must away now,' he said. 'My master is going shooting on the moors and he doth wait for me by the back gate. I think he makes an assignation for tomorrow and I am to come back for an answer later today. Show me thy room and I'll throw pebbles upon the window pane and so not disturb the kitchen staff who will be wagging their tongues.'

"One side of the nursery window looked onto the back court and I showed it to him and how near it was to the end of the house so that none need see him. With that he kissed me quickly and ran back to his horse while I, with many a qualm I assure you sir, sought out my mistress.

"She was in the parlour writing letters and looked up as I entered. She immediately saw the letter in my hand and, doubtless noting the expression on my face, jumped up.

" 'What is it, Agnes? Do you have something for me? Give it to me.'

"And she snatched the letter out of my hand and, turning her back to me, ripped the envelope and cast it on the floor and gave herself up to the missive within, of which I could tell there were several pages. I knew not whether to go or stay and was about to creep away when, with a cry, my mistress turned towards me, holding out the pages she was perusing.

" 'Ah! So you have a follower, you wicked Agnes Dean! You are using me to have secret meetings with this young scoundrel.'

"I was so wrathful at the injustice of her remark that I was about to retort when I observed that my mistress was smiling and, instead of being cross, had a tender expression on her face as she came towards me.

" 'Oh Agnes, I am so happy that you have found love too! For I am blissfully happy and I want everyone to share my joy but cannot. Now I can confide in you Agnes, and you in me. Here, sit down; tell me about him. Is he handsome?'

" 'Oh · ma'am.' I was so abashed that I knew not where to turn my face—that my mistress should take my arm and confess in me like a friend! Could the good days when I first came to serve her be returning? But could anything good come of wickedness? And what she was doing was very wicked; in my heart of that I had no doubt.

" 'I know! He is the tall one who brought the chairs, and he came up to fetch us! It can only be him, for he was the youngest and the best looking.'

"I marvelled that she had eyes for other than her paramour, but I said nothing, only lowered my head.

" 'It is he, isn't it Agnes! What is his name?'

" 'Roger.'

" 'Ah yes,' she glanced at her letter again, 'Roger. My trusty servant Roger, whom I hope to take with me to the wars. Oh Agnes, you and I will both suffer together when they go. We shall be able to give each other consolation.'

"I divined that my mistress was implicating me in her own misdeeds; whereas, as far as I could see, receiving a few chaste kisses from a man as single as I was myself did no harm to anyone on earth.

" 'Look at me, Agnes. Why do you avoid my eyes? Is it shyness? Or is it . . . yes you don't approve do you? You think I am wrong.'

" 'Oh I do, ma'am!' I cried, wringing my hands. 'You know I love and respect Mr. Hareton. I think him every bit as fine as Captain Jack, and he is your husband, ma'am, you owe him a duty.'

"My mistress did not give me the reprimand I expected, but instead rose to her feet and went to the window where for a long time she gazed out at the moors she loved so well.

" 'I know in your eyes and those of the world I do wrong, Agnes; but in my eyes and, I think, those of God I do Hareton no wrong. It is he who has changed, not I; he is not the sturdy Hareton I first loved, a creature of the moor and field, untamed, unlettered. Wuthering Heights meant more to me than I knew, Agnes. Mama and Hareton were both born there, and although I was not happy there at first, it was there I grew to love Hareton and, by custom, the place itself. Now, do you not see, it is not only Jack but the *place* that gives me freedom. Jack has the spirit of Wuthering Heights about him; the love of the moors. He is at

103

home there, he told me; and he is at home in my arms. Oh I know I shock you, Agnes; but the day I saw Jack here, the day the baby was baptised I knew we were destined for each other. He looked across at me and there was nothing I could do about it; in the deep pools of his eyes I saw my fate.'

" 'But ma'am, what will you do?'

" 'Do? I haven't thought what we should *do*. I think Jack will take me away one day to the south and then, when people have forgotten, we shall come back and live at Wuthering Heights one day when the War is over.'

" 'But people will never forget, ma'am.'

" 'Then they will have to live with it. I care not, and if Hareton cares let him move away.'

" 'But the *children*, ma'am!'

"My mistress paused and looked at me.

" 'You know that is one thing I am not proud of, Agnes. Oh there are many things, but that in particular. I have never loved my children. I do not seem to have it in me. I loved Rainton at first, I think, but that was bound up with my love for Hareton and then when I stopped loving Hareton I stopped loving Rainton. Maybe it is because I never had the love of my own mother that I am unable to be a good mother. I thought if I saw Mama, just once, she would help me to love the children. But they are beautiful, Agnes; you love them and Hareton loves them. Mary loves them; they will never want for love. They are better without me. I do them ill by staying with them; yet for a while I must. Pray God the War will soon be over and Jack can return forever.'

" 'Will he not stay in the Army, ma'am?'

" 'Oh I think he will stay. It is his profession; but I will go with him wherever he wants me and then, whenever we can, we shall always come back to Wuthering Heights.'

"I was but a young girl, Mr. Lockwood, nineteen, and had never been more than five miles from Gimmerton in my whole life. But, ignorant as I was, even I could visualise a live of extravagance and excitement, moving about from place to place, country to country. My mistress and Captain Jack and, who knew, myself and the Captain's servant, Roger. It was an absurd and wicked notion, but it had its attraction until I thought of the motherless children and the broken-hearted man who, as far as I knew, had never done harm to anyone and who would be left sorrowing. I wished then that I did not have this knowledge of Mrs. Earnshaw's infidelity; but I knew also that it was too late to change it.

"My mistress was at her desk writing furiously and after she had written her letter and sanded it, she kissed it and sealed it in an envelope giving it to me.

" 'He says Roger will come at three o'clock for an answer. I think he fears that I might say no; that I have repented of my folly the other days on the moors. But, oh Agnes, I have not. I love Jack Ibbitson; he is my life and without his constant presence, I can never be happy again.' "

Chapter 7

"For the rest of that summer I daily conspired to aid my mistress in her illicit relationship with Captain Ibbitson. Either she would send me to the Heights with a note, or young Roger would come on his horse and, throwing pebbles against the nursery window, deliver to me the latest missive from his master. Sometimes, even though the lovers had but recently met, a letter would come from the Heights, no doubt an outpouring of the sentiments felt by the Captain for Mrs. Earnshaw. And then I would take the letter to her and, while she scribbled a reply, would dally for a few pleasant moments with Roger exchanging kisses in the shade of the back porch.

"I must say it was exciting for a maid like me, the pattern of whose life had followed an even course from birth. And I was so enamoured myself that I could hardly reproach my mistress if she felt a joy similar to my own. And indeed I had never seen her happier or more pleasant and attentive to her husband who, poor man, never suspected a thing. His duties as a magistrate kept him from the house for long hours, and he had also developed business interests in the newly developing woollen industry in Bradford which was making great advances due to the inventions of Mr. Cartwright and Mr. Watt in the century that had just gone. It is quite common for us now, Mr. Lockwood, the factories and mills run on power and steam; but in the days of which I speak 'twas all very new and the factories were just beginning to be built, and replacing the cottage industries I had known as a girl.

"Anyway, Mr. Hareton was among the first in these parts to become interested in these new processes and if, eventually it made him a great deal of money, he deserved it because he took risks, and it also brought him great hardship and sorrow, as you will see, because money does not always bring happiness.

"So Mr. Hareton was away a lot, sometimes overnight and it was not uncommon, if that was the case, for my mistress not to come home which I was at pains to hide from the servants who, however, knew it all the time because the staff of a big house always do know everything, even though this did not come from my lips.

"In fact my mistress got bolder and bolder as one does with a reckless passion and seemed not to care whether Hareton heard about it or not.

"And then one awful day towards the end of September a double disaster befell that I am not likely to forget either now or until the day I die. Or rather the first was not so much a disaster as something we both knew was unavoidable and we must expect. Captain Ibbitson sent a letter early in the morning, indeed even before the Master had left, and I had to be careful to deliver it when he was not about. The news sent my mistress flying to the nursery.

" 'Oh Agnes, Jack is to return to the Army; his papers have come and he leaves next week. He begs me come today to the Heights as soon as I may. Oh Agnes,' and she fell on my shoulder and all that I could do did not relieve her weeping; for I too was sorely oppressed knowing that it would be the end of my own dalliance. But there was something about that day apart from the grim news we had at its commencement. Mr. Hareton appeared gruff and short with my mistress and then he announced that he was only going as far as Gimmerton and would be back for dinner, which we had at four in those days. I noticed that he did not kiss my mistress as was his custom on leaving the house, nor did he see the children to bestow on them his blessing for the day. It was as though he was preoccupied by news of some distressing nature; but my mistress was so distressed on her own account that she perceived it not and, scarce had the hooves of his horse receded into the distance, than she was away on Minny across the park and out by the back gate as was her custom.

"I, feeling ill at ease and unhappy for no reason I could recall, was left to brood. Just before dinnertime there was a pother of hooves in the court and, on looking out, I saw my master accompanied by a gentleman I recognised as Mr. Green, the lawyer from Gimmerton, whom I only know by sight because my sister Joan once worked for him. She found him of such an ill temper that she left and, for better or ill, now works in one of the new spinning mills in Keighley.

"The entire house was suddenly astir with noise and commotion like the evil sound of bats on the wing. My master, entering the hall downstairs, began to shout for my mistress and there was a scurry of servants up and down the stairs as they pretended to seek her, knowing full well she was not here. Then Mr. Hareton himself stormed into the nursery and enquired as to her whereabouts.

" 'I . . . I know not sir,' I stammered, whereupon Mr. Hareton seized me roughly by the shoulder.

" 'Don't lie to me, girl! You are her personal maid. It is your business to know where your mistress is!'

"I stared at him in fright when another clatter of hooves in the court told me my mistress was probably come home, hoping no doubt to arrive before my master. Quite forgetful of his position as head of the household, or that of his wife as mistress, Mr. Hareton went to the window, unhasped it and bawled:

" 'Catherine! Come up here this instant!' and he then strode down the corridor to the parlour which is on the first floor, the same level as the nursery. I hurried out to help divest my mistress of her cloak and found her red faced and disheveled, coming up the stairs, panting as though she had ridden hard. When she saw me she ran up the remaining stairs and clasped me saying, 'What is it, Agnes? What ails your master?'

" 'I know not, ma'am, except that he is sorely vexed and he has Mr. Green the lawyer with him!'

"My poor mistress started to tremble and clung to me piteously, but my master came out and, seeing her, shouted again.

" 'Catherine, we are awaiting you in the parlour.'

" 'May I not tidy myself, Hareton?' my mistress stammered, but he seized her roughly and, with her cloak half on and half off, dragged her into the parlour. I followed trying as best I could to relieve her of her garment, but no one paid any heed to me and it was thus that I am able to report what happened.

"Mr. Green was standing by the fireplace looking, I may say so, as green as his name. He is a man of ill countenance at the best of times being overweight through robbing people as all lawyers do; but his normally rubicund face was ashen and he seemed to shrink back towards the hearth as he saw mistress and the anger on my master's face. Mr. Hareton dragged his wife until she stood directly in front of the lawyer and then he gave her a little shove so that she almost fell on top of him. It was the most graceless thing I have ever seen Mr. Hareton do and it reminded me of the lack of breeding in his upbringing.

" 'Listen to this, ma'am! Listen to what Green here has to say and then tell me if you are not proud of yourself.'

"Mr. Green cleared his throat but no words came and he whispered if he might have a sip of water, but my master snarled at him.

" 'Get on with it man! Out with it, I say. Tell her what you know. All right, I'll help you. I'll tell her what you and all the village knows, and Agnes here and all the servants and everyone as far as York and beyond for all I ken. That I am cuckold! All the world knows, except me, that my wife is no longer my faithful spouse but lies in the arms of another man, and that man is my tenant at Wuthering Heights and not only that but this, I warrant, you do not know. Tell her, Green! Tell her!'

"My mistress was by now shaking so much that, still under the pretence of taking her cloak, I clasped my arm about her to give her courage, dreading what awful thing might come next. Green once more cleared his throat and then in a thin, reedy voice which did not tally at all with his robust frame stammered: 'Captain Ibbitson is the son of the late Mr. Heathcliff. He . . .'

"But at those words my mistress sank to the floor and I fell to my knees by her side. Her eyelids fluttered, however, and I thought she was feigning; but it was simply that she could bear to hear no more. However even in her extremity my master spared her not. He stood over her, legs astride her poor defenceless body, his mottled face glaring down at her.

" 'Did you know that Catherine? Did you know *that*?'

"My mistress moaned, but I knew that she apprehended what he said, for she tried to sit up, and her dazed eyes stared up at the frightening aspect of her husband.

" 'What are you saying Hareton? That Jack . . .'

" 'Aye, he's Heathcliff's bastard. Didn't you ever see the likeness? Of course you did. I did, except that we best remember his father as middle aged, and the son is a much younger version. But I noticed the likeness particularly that day of the tea party and then I started to make enquiries through this unprincipled rogue, Green here, who will do aught for anyone so long as his palm is sufficiently greased! He did all he could to deprive me of my inheritance, and you of yours when he dallied while your father was dying; and although he hated Heathcliff as much as anyone did he was well paid by him to cheat and steal and rob. So, I bethought me, who else but this blackguard to ferret out the origins of Mrs. Ibbitson and her fine son and the real reason for her taking a house in the district. I was already suspicious I can tell you when I saw him; but when I realised what a fine lady she was and how used to comfort, I knew she was as ill suited to the harsh life of the Heights as a sow in a gentleman's drawing room. So today . . .' Mr. Hareton strode over and seized Mr. Green by the ear which I thought as bold a gesture as I had ever seen, 'today this servile incompetent nincompoop summons me gleefully to see him, thinking I know what he knows and that is why I wanted to know more. He thought I *knew* you were seeing the fine Guards captain and that was why I wanted to ascertain his origins! So, at the same time as he informs me about his and his mother's background he lets slip that not a day passes but you and the Captain meet on the moor, or in a barn or up at the Heights where that evil woman can see nought wrong in the seduction of a married woman because she herself in the past has been no better than a whore.'

" 'Dorothy Ibbitson was Heathcliff's mistress on and off for three years when he left the Heights after hearing that your mother would not marry him, but preferred the nice manners of your father and the comfort of Thrushcross Grange. I was a baby at the time and you were not born, but I know it happened because after he came back he set about the ruin of my father and caused the death of your mother. And I loved him. Yes I say it! I had to love someone and I loved Heathcliff, for even in his rough way he did not treat me badly and he would talk to me even though he denied me my birthright and treated me like a servant. Poor orphan boy that I was I looked up to him as to a father, a master I suppose, and when he died I grieved for him. No more. Now I hope he not only rots in hell but suffers the torment and agony of the damned every minute of the livelong day, and writhes like a pig stuck on the end of a skewer . . .'

" 'Oh Hareton . . .' My mistress put out her hand,' but nothing would stem the tide of my master's wrath.

" 'Not only did he deprive *us* in life, but in death his

112

seed lives on to torment the Earnshaw family and deprive it of its deserts, all legally and honestly come by. You are my lawful wedded wife, I have given you all I have; yet as soon as you set eyes on Satan's Cub you are off like the strumpet your mother was before you! Is this why he came; to take the thing that I honoured and loved most in the world? The only thing, the only woman I ever loved and who at one time loved me?'

"My master choked and to my horror I saw his fine eyes fill and huge tears roll down his cheeks. It is an awesome sight, sir, to see a grown man crying. But he stifled his sobs and kneaded his fists in his eyes and his voice wanted nothing in strength and vigour as he cried out.

" 'I will rid Gimmerton of Satan's curse, and his mother, Satan's whore! I will sweep them before me.'

"Whether 'twas the break occasioned by Mr. Hareton's tears, or whether the weakling had found some unsuspected depths from which to draw strength I know not, but Mr. Green cleared his throat again and spoke this time more firmly.

" 'Nay sir, you cannot do that. I drew up Mrs. Ibbitson's tenancy agreement for you and I tell you it is watertight. You remember you were anxious she should not wiggle out of it so you would have a long let on the Heights. And on that account *you* may not either. She is the tenant for five years, whether you like it or not.'

"Green, like all cowards, was happy to cling to the safe log of the law while he floundered in these chilly and uncharted seas, and my master's brow clouded as he realised what he had done. It also interrupted his torrent of words and my poor mistress murmured.

" 'Hareton, may I not go to my room? My heart palpitates and I am unwell.'

" 'Get to your room!' Hareton cried savagely, 'and stay there until I decide what to do with you.'

"I noticed that my mistress's cloak was still half on and half off as I aided her along the corridor and into the room where she flung herself on her bed and com-

113

menced a torrent of weeping while I, as worried to death as I ever have been, tried to comfort her, feeling pity for the poor foolish woman who now saw her life in ruins before her; for, knowing Mr. Hareton's pride, I thought he would not forgive her now or ever.

"I was patting her shoulder and murmuring nothings when my mistress sat up, her tears still wet on her cheeks, but a brightness in her eyes that they had lacked before.

" 'Agnes! We must leave at once while Green is still with him; while they are deciding what to do. Look, it is almost nightfall; we must go at once.'

" 'Go, ma'am?' I said confused. 'Whither?'

" 'To Wuthering Heights, to Jack and safety. Hareton is a madman; he will never forgive me and, most like, will make me a prisoner and dismiss you because you are my friend. He may even have me put away in some sort of institution. I knew that if ever I crossed Hareton he would be unbending, because he is a peasant at heart and not a gentleman at all. You can see how violent and abusive he was both with me and Green. Quick; decend and get the boy to saddle Minny. You will ride behind me.'

" 'I, ma'am?' I cried aghast. 'But I must stay with your children.'

" 'Do you think he will allow you one night under this roof when you have connived at my escape? He will banish you into the dark and care not what happens to you or what goblins on the moors gobble you up during your long tramp home. No, you are with me, Agnes Dean. Quick; get your shawl and meet me in the court. We must be gone before it is too late.'

"I went into the corridor and, perceiving the parlour door still to be closed and voices engaged in conversation behind it, went swiftly to the nursery where breathlessly I told Mary that I had to go out on urgent business and she must mind the babes, and then I kissed them because I knew not when I would see them again and, tears stealing out of my eyes, crept down to the stables."

"Oh I will not forget that ride over the moors in the twilight, my arms tight around my mistress's back, clinging to her for dear life in fear of falling; for my mistress had decided after all not to alert the stable boy and we rode bareback. She being an excellent rider this was no hardship at all, but I being an indifferent one it was a nightmare. But I do recall how glorious the moors looked in the late evening with the rays of the setting sun illuminating here and there rich patches of purple heather, and gradually as we rode, Wuthering Heights—gaunt and forlorn—came in sight and behind it the sun threw its last beams and sank out of sight and darkness fell swiftly just as we clattered up to the gate.

"Then there was a commotion as a servant ran out to find out who approached and on seeing it was my Roger I almost fell off the horse into his arms, and then Mr. Ibbitson and his mother were there and everyone was talking and my mistress weeping and talking at the same time, until the Captain put his arm about her and drew her into the house.

"It must have been a comical sight to the idle onlooker—the mistress sobbing on the Captain's arm and I, the maid, sustained likewise by the servant while Mrs. Ibbitson, her face twisted with concern, walked up and down trying to press on my mistress a glass of brandy and on me some orange cordial. Finally my mistress's sobs grew less violent and the Captain sat her gently on the chair and bade her speak, but she shook her head and started her violent trembling again until he looked at me, and refreshed by the cordial, I said:

" 'Mrs. Earnshaw has run away from home, sir. Her husband has been told of her meetings with you.'

" 'Ah, I thought as much,' Mrs. Ibbitson said, stamping her foot. 'Who would have told him?'

" ' 'Tis common gossip, ma'am,' I said, speaking boldly. 'The only soul who knew it not was the lady's husband, and the lawyer told him.'

" 'Green?'

" 'Aye, ma'am.'

115

" 'But why should Green do such a thing? I liked him not, but what business was it of his, pray?'

" 'I think the master asked him to find out something ma'am,' I mumbled, not knowing how to proceed, and then my mistress gave a long moan and burst out:

" 'He has said you are the son of Mr. Heathcliff. my late father-in-law! Oh, say it is not true, Jack. That irks Hareton more than losing his wife to a stranger.'

"The Captain jumped up and looked at his mother, his dark eyes furious.

" 'Of course I am not the son of Mr. Heathcliff, whoever he may be. I am the son of the late Josiah Ibbitson, merchant of Liverpool. Why would he say that?'

"He looked wildly at his mother who, I noticed, was twisting and untwisting her kerchief in her hand, her face a veritable galaxy of warring emotions.

" 'Mother!' The Captain cried sharply. 'Why should he say that? Am I *not* Josiah's son?'

" 'Hareton says you are like Mr. Heathcliff and indeed you are. I perceived it not at first myself because I only knew Mr. Heathcliff when he was an old man, nearly forty, and he was grown corpulent and florid, though well preserved for his age by some standards. But now I do see it; you are very like him. It is the eyes above all, and the sallow complexion like a gypsy. And then I thought, oh Jack, listen to me and do not think me foolish. I thought that was maybe why I loved you at first sight because Mama loved your father and went to the grave for him, and Mama wanted me here at Wuthering Heights to be with you, to find in you the love and fulfilment she never knew with Heathcliff, for 'twas denied them.'

" 'But that is absurd . . .' the Captain began, his countenance as dark as any blackamoor's with fury. 'I am . . .'

"But Mrs. Ibbitson rose—making an effort at control, I could see—and walked over to her son, raising her head proudly.

" 'You *are* Heathcliff's son, Jack, I'll not deny it. Indeed I am proud of it for I too loved him as I never

116

loved Josiah Ibbitson, good man though he was, who married me when you were a baby, having courted me for many years. He was a good man, a widower much older than I was, and he treated you as his son and gave you as fine an education and as good a start in life as any gentleman's son would wish.'

"Captain Jack sank onto the couch beside Mrs. Earnshaw and put his head in his hands.

" 'But why did you never tell me, mother?'

" 'There was no need; you were happy and content. But I loved your father and I hated the Earnshaws who treated him like a servant, and had him eat and sleep in a different place. Yes he did love Catherine Earnshaw, your mother,' she said, looking at my mistress. 'They grew up together, but even she despised him because he was poor and ignorant, and rejected him for the master of Thrushcross Grange who she preferred because of his fine ways and his money.'

" 'So Heathcliff ran away to Liverpool from whence he had come—that was all he knew about himself— and he did hard work in the docks to earn money for his education to improve himself and that was how I met him. I was the daughter of his landlady and I kept a small school for young ladies, teaching them the elements of learning and deportment. I too had made my way up from humble beginnings, the daughter of a dockworker. It was almost impossible to rise above one's station in those days but, like Heathcliff, I worked hard and achieved it. But although I lived in a better district I did not neglect the mother who bore me, and I visited her weekly to see her and give her some money and there I met this fine young man, oh so dark and comely he was, struggling to better himself in the world and working all hours of the day and night to do it. Apart from the affection I instinctively had for him—no woman could resist him, he was so good looking; he had a magnetism for women which you have inherited, Jack—I admired his industry and wanted to help him, so I gave him lessons in deportment and manners as well as how to read and write and do arithmetic.'

117

" 'Oh, he was an apt pupil, eager to learn and with a gift for acquiring knowledge which made me think that his natural parentage must have been a good one. But he was ambitious and he wanted to make money in order to marry this girl, this Catherine Earnshaw, who he had loved and left. So he left Liverpool and every time he returned he looked more prosperous and as I had my own establishment then and my mother was dead he lodged with me and, in time, the inevitable happened and we became lovers. Oh I confess I hoped he would forget about Catherine and marry me; but he was always quite honest with me and told me that though I had a place in his heart it was she he wanted to wed. And he was generous with me and gave me money, and then he would go off again.'

" 'Well, finally he returned and said he had enough to live as a rich man and he would go and present his suit to Catherine and maybe purchase Wuthering Heights from her brother, who owned it, because she loved the place. I still loved him and gave myself to him, because he wanted me, and it was then you were conceived, Jack; but he knew it not, for by the time I discovered it myself, he had left and I never heard from him again until after his death the lawyer sent me a letter and some money that Heathcliff had intended for me. And in the letter he told me of his sad life and the fact that his beloved Catherine had married by the time he returned and was dead of childbirth ere twelve months had passed. And he'd vowed vengeance on her brother and the Earnshaw and Linton families for depriving him in his youth of an upbringing, and in his manhood of Catherine for a bride. He said he'd pursued this all his life and now that he had what he'd sought he no longer cared and wanted to die. But he remembered me with affection and had wondered what had become of me, and, if I was still alive and received his letter, to think kindly of him and buy some memento with the money he sent me.'

" 'After he had left I'd hoped he would return; but in time I thought all had gone for him as he'd wanted and he'd wed his Catherine and would not want to be

118

reminded of the past. You were born and after a while I decided to marry Josiah, who had courted me for a long time, to give me money and respectability: and I did and I never regretted it, but was happy with him until he died. But I never forgot Heathcliff, the love of my life he was, and after he died and the lawyer delivered me the letter and some money left in his will, and I learned about his years of grief and mourning I bethought me to come back and avenge his memory, and also take revenge for myself, for the fine man I had lost, and I have.' She smiled and looked at her son.

" 'Without any effort I have seen justice prevail. I have seen justice prevail. I have got his house and you have got his wife. Let the Earnshaws suffer for what they did to Heathcliff, a better man, a more straight and honest one I never knew.'

"My mistress's eyes were dry now and she listened as though spellbound to Mrs. Ibbitson, as did the son. Mrs. Ibbitson was a fine, tall woman with a resonant voice and she told the tale well. That she believed she was right and just no one could gainsay, though I myself knew that it was an evil ploy she had hatched, and mistaken at that, to wish to harm poor Mr. Hareton. She went over to her son and placed a hand on his shoulder.

" 'Have no fear, Jack; your father was an honest, upright man, whatever anyone may say, who was greatly wronged in his life. You are a credit to him and to me—vigorous, clever, and successful. He would have been proud of you and sometimes I wish he had known you because his own son, he said in his letter, was a sad disappointment to him. Maybe I made a mistake not telling him and maybe I didn't. But I regret nothing. What I have done is done.'

" 'And what are we to do now, Mother?' Jack said quietly, as though realising that not everything was as straightforward as his mother thought. 'If you came here hoping I would capture Hareton's wife you were right. I love her and she loves me. But what are we to do now? I am a Captain in the King's Brigade of

119

Guards. I am recalled to my regiment. How can I take her with me to the war in France? What would my commanding officer say? What are we to do now, Mother? It is for you to decide.'

"And she got up and began to pace about the room. 'I shall take Catherine to Liverpool,' Mrs. Ibbitson said firmly. 'For a while; then we shall be back. I don't want Hareton to think he can get off so lightly. Thrushcross Grange belonged to Heathcliff. He had it by right of inheritance; he told me in his letter. It is yours, Jack, as his son. Oh,' she shrugged, 'maybe not in the *letter* of the law as he and I were not wed and property cannot descend through bastards; but morally and in the eyes of God you own both Wuthering Heights and Thrushcross Grange and it is my intention to see that you get them, as well as Hareton's wife! Let him be harried from the district; let him be bankrupted; let him be ruined.'

" 'Oh, no,' Mrs. Earnshaw cried. 'Do not be harsh to Hareton. I wish him no harm, for I knew Hareton as a boy and he too was cruelly used by Mr. Heathcliff through no fault of his own, merely because he *was* an Earnshaw. Pray let this foolish feud lapse. I cannot return to Hareton, but I do not wish to harm him; let him keep the Grange. I want it not, nor money nor fine clothes; only Jack. Oh, Jack.'

"And she flew into his arms, and, big man that he was, he encompassed her in his protective embrace and softly kissed her lips.

" 'But, oh let me stay here. Let me stay in Wuthering Heights. I see now that Mother wanted me to be here with Jack and that was why she beckoned me that night. Please let me stay. Please.'

" 'My darling,' Captain Jack said. 'You cannot stay here. Once I am gone Hareton will come to get you back. He will send his servants and seize you; you are his property and he is a magistrate. Mother is right; you must go to Liverpool and then perhaps we shall try for a divorce, I know not at this moment. God, it is a bad time for it to happen.'

"And I could see the Captain was sorely troubled on

account of what had happened and had not bargained for this state of affairs. I imagine he had been content to trifle with a married woman, to take his pleasure while on leave and then desert her to take it elsewhere again, in London, maybe, or Flanders or France. I could see he was indeed the son of Mr. Heathcliff; like father, like son. And my poor mistress! What was to become of her now?

" 'Let me come with you, Jack. I beg of you. I will not be in your way. I will take lodgings near you. Oh, Jack. I love you so; do not let us be parted. I beg you.'

"She was still in his arms and he clasped her firmly again, but his grave face above hers was thoughtful. I could see she would be a burden to him, an appendage he neither desired or deserved, but which was all due to the wicked plotting of his mother.

"I'll not hide it from you, Mr. Lockwood. I thought my master had been made cuckold and my mistress deceived all for the spite of this woman interfering in something that was no business of hers. For why could the Earnshaw family not be left in peace? Why did Mrs. Ibbitson have to rake up the ghosts of the past? It seemed evil to me—an evil that reached out from the grave, and I thought of the ghosts that were supposed to walk and I wondered if it was they who took vengeance upon the living."

Chapter 8

"That night I put my mistress early to bed in the room she loved so well—that of her mother. The chest bed was still there and Roger transferred the few things Captain Ibbitson had—you could tell he was a military man by his sparse style of living—to another room. Mrs. Earnshaw was pale and fatigued after the events of the day; but there was in her face a kind of triumph born of deep happiness that I had not seen since she was first a bride and as in love with her husband as she was now with the Captain.

"For although I am not a clever or imaginative woman I realise that there are people who are nourished by love; whose whole beings are only fully realised in loving and being loved. And my mistress was one of these, as, alas her mother had been before her. I thought of my darling baby Margaret and sent a silent prayer to God to grant that she would not follow the family mold. The homage of a good man was not sufficient for my mistress and those like her; it has to be what, for want of a better word, I can only call passion renewed again and again and I doubted not that it would be her downfall as it had her mother's.

"Before she lay down my mistress spent a long time at the window. It was a starlit night with a full moon, and the moorland was bathed in golden light while the ravines and crevices appeared like dark and angry scars—a night of conflict such as must have had its echo in the soul of my mistress as she gazed at the well-loved scene. And indeed her eyes were bright and her face tranquil as she turned and bade me put her to bed.

" 'I have come home, Agnes, haven't I? Good servant, faithful friend that you are. For I know that though you do not approve of what I do, Agnes, you will be faithful to me always.'

" 'Aye, 'till death,' I said, moved by the emotion of the moment and the ethereal loveliness of my mistress in her shimmering white nightgown with her long fair hair combed over each shoulder.

" 'God grant there may be many years between then and now, Agnes; for I know I have not been a good wife to Hareton or mother to my children. I think it is something to do with the Grange. My mother wilted after she went to live there and was always ill and so was I. Spirits such as ours have a need of freedom and to us Wuthering Heights is that freedom. Jack and I were destined to meet, maybe hundreds of years ago. Do you believe in that sort of thing Agnes?'

" 'Fairy tales,' I scoffed.

" 'Oh, I think it is more than a fairy tale—or maybe it *is* a fairy tale if you believe in fairies and I think I do. For I believe in the spirit world and I know that my mother is with me and about me, here in this room. Do you ever think that she and Heathcliff meant for Jack and me to be united here, in this place where they loved each other?'

" 'You know what I think,' I said, helping her into bed. 'I think they are dead and buried and so shall we all be in time and no more heard about it.'

" 'Oh, no. 'Tis not so, Agnes. The meaning of my strange life has become clear to me since I met Jack.

How could I know that he was Heathcliff's son? It is an almost impossible coincidence is it not? I believe 'twas fate drew us together and now that we are happy, happen Mama and Mr. Heathcliff *will* rest peacefully in their graves.'

"She caught my hand in that gesture of affection that moved me so well and, drawing me down, made me kiss her cheek.

" 'God bless thee, Agnes, good friend. And thank you. I know what it cost you to come with me and I shall never forget it.'

"And as tears stole down her cheeks, tears of happiness, maybe mingled with the pain of separation. I quickly left the room after blowing out the candle for fear that I too should lose control of myself and break down.

"When I went downstairs I was directed to the back kitchen where my fellow servants were partaking of a late supper. I joined them and ate heartily for I had eaten nothing since breakfast. I could tell that Roger at the end of the table was keeping pace with me and as I finished he did too. When we got up we both met at the door and he caught my hand.

" 'Come outside. 'Tis a beautiful night.'

" 'Aye I know.' I was undecided because I was tired; but the sight of my own beloved did much to refresh me, and his kisses as we stood against the wall of the stables even more.

" 'Oh, I love thee, Agnes. I am bewitched by thee. How can I leave thee next week to go to the wars?'

" 'Dost have to?' I said.

" 'Aye. I am promised to go for the Army. Besides I confess I would like the challenge. When I come back, shall we be wed?'

" 'Oh, Roger,' I said, 'who knows when thou wilt come back and what will happen?' and my heart ached for the fact that the first man I had ever loved was about to leave me. I and my mistress would indeed be bereft.

" 'Aye we'll be wed,' Roger said, 'and maybe I'll leave the Army and we'll get a small farm of our own;

oh, nothing much, maybe a sheep or two, and we'll raise our own children and be as happy as two fleas in a pack of wool.'

"'Oh, thou art romantic!' I laughed and pressed my own kisses upon him in the bold way he had taught me and that I greatly enjoyed.

"Roger then took me into the stable and we climbed into the loft where the hay was stored for feeding the horses and we lay comfortably among the bales, and the warmth of our bodies kept the chill away for, despite the moon, 'twas a cold night.

"'What thinkest thou will happen to our master and mistress?' Roger said when he had taught me other delights that up to that time I had not known existed and, though I could tell it was not right, he justified on the grounds that we should soon be separated.

"'Maybe they will be wed in time. They say you can break a marriage.'

"'I think she will go back to her husband,' my beloved said. 'Mark my words.'

"'Nay Roger, she loves Captain Jack too well.'

"'Aye, but what when Captain Jack is no longer here? She will not be the mistress at Wuthering Heights, thou knowest that full well. Mrs. Ibbitson is very much the mistress, and Mrs. Earnshaw will not like being the daughter of the house after she has been used to being the owner.'

"'Oh, I think it will not bother her,' I said. 'She never took an interest in the affairs of the house, leaving it to the housekeeper and the servants entirely. She has no interest in domestic matters.'

"'Well, the Captain will want an orderly house,' Roger said, covering me with his jacket for I was trembling with cold. 'She will have to see to it then. I reckon the Captain will be less lenient with her than Mr. Earnshaw. The Captain has a fierce temper if crossed; thou shouldst have heard him tonight after thy mistress had gone up to bed.'

"'Oh?'

"'Aye, he fair let into his mother. It is a good thing the walls are so solid, or I thought he would tear apart the house. I was clearing up in the far corner but he did not even seem to be aware of my presence.'

" 'Mother,' he thundered, 'what do you mean by this revelation that you have concealed from me for twenty-one years? Didn't you think I was old enough to know who my real father was that I should be told finally by some sort of trick? Did you bring me here for a sport like some cock strutting after the first available hen?'

" 'I know you are partial to hens, Jack,' his mother said slyly and he crossed over to her and I thought he would strike her. But she is a proud woman and she stood up to him, her fine dark eyes blazing, a smile upon her face. 'But this is a particularly fine hen; she is a lovely girl. I'll not deny it has given me satisfaction to know you are avenged on your father who was spurned by her mother. If you had known about him do you think you would have run after her? I think not. No Jack, my regret,' and here she sat down wearily on the couch, '—if I regret anything it is that your father did not know of you, for you would make any man proud to have you for a son. You have nothing to be ashamed of and neither have I. I loved Heathcliff and, but for this mad obsession he had with the elder Catherine Earnshaw, he would have wed me. I feel bitter about it, I'll confess. I was every bit as good as her, *and* pretty too. I gave him all I had—I taught him, and gave him money and a home, aye, even my body though he treated it well and was welcome to it. And in return he respected me and I liked to think he never forgot me as indeed the letter showed. He left me and, not knowing I was well provided for, he sent money which I have put on one side for you. That was my generous-hearted Heathcliff.'

" 'But where did he come from, my father?'

" 'That he could never find out. He was brought here to the Heights by Mr. Earnshaw, your Catherine's grandfather who was a good man and loved by your father. Some thought he was a bastard of Mr. Earnshaw's because he loved and cosseted the boy to the exclusion of his lawful son Hindley, who thus came to hate your father and demeaned him after the old man was dead. But your father tried by every means after he came to Liverpool to find his origins and I helped him; but it was impossible and will be a mystery forever. There is no doubt he was of good birth, maybe even noble because he was regal in his manner and appearance and he dealt with people like a lord, and as I told you he was an able scholar. I was proud of you ever since, Jack.'

" 'But to tell me *now*. That, Mother, I find hard to forgive.' And the Captain raised his voice again and his face grew mottled with wrath. His mother got up and placed a hand on his arm.

" 'Forgive it, Jack. You are old enough and man enough to know it now. When you were younger, before you had known love yourself, it might have shocked you; any older and you would never have forgiven me. I think it was the right time though I am sorry it came about the way it did, through Earnshaw, and not in my own good time; that it was forced on us you do not like and neither do I. But now it is known, hold your head high and be proud you are Heathcliff's son.'

" 'And I *will* bear his name,' Jack cried. 'Aye, I'll call myself Heathcliff, so that all the world shall know who my father was. It can be arranged, can it not Mother?'

"His mother looked at him and I could see she was undecided whether it was a good thing or no.

" 'Jack,' she said. 'You are Heathcliff's son all right; you do not do things by half measures. You studied well and you are a good soldier and you wench well. Aye, maybe it is right you bear his name. But I hope you will not forget that good man Josiah Ibbitson who made it possible for you to follow your father and have the good things in life.'

" 'I'll not forget him, Mother. He was a good old man though I often thought he should be my grandfather and not my father. Aye, I loved him well. Cathy and I will call our first son after him. Josiah Heathcliff.'

" 'Well, you'd best fix up about a separation then,' his mother said, being a practical woman. 'There is such a thing as divorce. It is not easy but it can be done. When you are in London seeing to your name you can see to unfixing her marriage though I doubt it will be easy. Hareton Earnshaw won't be so happy to lose his wife.'

" 'She'll never return to him!' my master scoffed. 'She would give up anything she wished; she told me. She'll rest safe with you, Mother, until I come back.'

" 'Maybe you should see Earnshaw before you go?'

" 'Nay, he'll not see me. I'll let him cool and think about it and his position. Then when he sees my darling will have none of him maybe the simpering ninny will let her go, to preserve his good name.'

" 'He is no simpering ninny,' his mother said firmly. 'That I tell you. If you think so you have mistaken his nature. I am sure that he will employ subtle ways to try and regain his wife for he is a clever man and no fool. In fact were he not an Earnshaw I would rather like him. But as he is an Earnshaw we must try and squash him as flat as a fly and all his brood.'

" 'And how will you do that Mother?' my master asked, smiling for the first time since the conversation had begun. 'Roger, bring me a glass of wine. How will you squash the Earnshaw brood like flies?'

" 'I will hatch me a plan,' Mrs. Ibbitson said, motioning to me to fetch her some wine, too, 'and while you are away I will try and put it into effect.'

"And after I had given them the wine they indicated I should leave the room, but I know they are there still talking. Thinkest thou thy mistress will sleep well tonight?'

" 'Aye.'

" 'Maybe the master will keep her warm as I do thee?'

" 'Maybe.'

" 'Thinkest thou they will call us?'

" 'My mistress seldom stirs before dawn.'

" 'Then let us bide 'til dawn, and I will call thee when the cock croweth.' "

129

"All I can say about the week that remained, Mr. Lockwood, was that it was one of the happiest in my life and also, I think, that of my poor mistress. It was as though all nature conspired to do everything to make us happy. The late September offered glorious weather; my mistress and the Captain were out every day on the moors, and Roger and I would join them at some selected spot with a picnic and sometimes Mrs. Ibbitson would come too, though she stayed in the background, being the very model of tact and discretion. At night there were fine meals with plentiful wine and the mistress would sing after dinner accompanied at the pianoforte by Mrs. Ibbitson. Sometimes the Captain, who had a fine bass voice, would join her in a duet. And what they did at night I knew not, for after I had tucked her up and blown out the candle, I repaired more often than not to the loft where my cunning Roger had contrived to make a very handsome warm bed for both of us where, as he said, we were as happy as two fleas in a woolsack.

"But of Mr. Earnshaw there was no sign at all. It was as though we lived in a world of our own, cocooned from the outside in an atmosphere of tenderness and love. The servants plied to and from Gimmerton with provisions, but if they heard any tales they relayed them not and if they saw anyone they didn't tell us. But they were all natives of Liverpool and knew not the local folk, and I thought it unlikely that our people, who are very close and reserved by nature, would indulge in gossip or tittle tattle with strangers.

"And so the happy days of autumn fled by and then, one awful morn, Roger woke me before cockcrow because he had to prepare his and his master's baggage for the journey, and I stumbled with him through the dark of the yard, my eyes wet with tears at the thought of our separation.

"My mistress too was up betimes, and all the household was abroad before dawn and the fire roared in the kitchen and good smells came from the stove as the cook prepared food both for our breakfast and the journey. And after he had assisted his master to dress,

130

Roger went into the yard to groom the horses and I went into my mistress's room to find her already dressed and pacing up and down.

" 'Ma'am,' I said, 'are you all right?'

"She flew into my arms and laid her head on my shoulder.

" 'Oh, Agnes, I cannot bear to see him depart. He will not let me go with him. I begged him all night. I did everything I knew to make him let me, *us*, come with him. I said you loved Roger too and we were a healthy pair and could take the coach from Leeds while they rode beside us. The new stage only takes four and twenty hours to make the journey. In London I would be no trouble but would find lodgings for us; but he was adamant, all the time loving me and pleasing me as only he knows how.'

" 'My darling,' he said pressing me tenderly to him, 'I would not have you like a camp follower, for you are a lady and will be treated as such. If you come to London with me as my woman you will be looked down upon, because London is a small place and the fashionable world not a vast one. I am one of the King's officers and bad things will be rumoured about me, that I brought a married woman to London and then left her to fend for herself. Why, I might even be discharged from my commission and that is something that would dishonour my father's name. For now that I know, I am proud of being Heathcliff's son, and will strive to do all I can to be worthy of him.'

" 'At that I was silent, Agnes, for I knew Mr. Heathcliff and my dear Jack did not. I thought he had a fanciful picture of him, such as Hareton had, for Heathcliff was a mean and vengeful man; but I knew in time he would learn the truth and judged it was not best for our love that I should tell him then. And I thought what a strange man Mr. Heathcliff really was that he could make some, such as Mamma and Mrs. Ibbitson and Hareton love him so, while others, like Papa and Nelly and even his son Linton, detested him. But I was not certain now which way I felt since I had known for sure of the great love that Mama and Mr.

131

Heathcliff bore for each other that lasted beyond the grave.'

" 'But I was proud now to be the mistress of his son; and I thought Mama and Mr. Heathcliff would approve if they saw us lying together in the narrow bed in the chest in Mama's old room, the room where Mr. Heathcliff had died and where Jack and I plighted our love.'

" 'Jack lay beside me looking at the beam the moonlight cast on the ceiling and I asked him of what he was thinking.'

" 'Of when you are my wife and we can raise our heads for all to see; not that I am not proud, my darling, that you have given yourself to me, and your love for me to cherish and the memory of it to take with me to the wars . . .'

" 'Oh, Jack,' I took hold of his hand. 'I am so afraid of the wars; that you will be killed.'

" 'I know I shall not,' he said. 'I know I will come safe back to you, aye, and bring Roger wi' me for your Agnes'—oh Agnes is it not consoling to know he says that!—'and I'll get the name sorted out and the lawyers onto yon husband of yours.'

" 'I'll be Mrs. Heathcliff again,' I said. 'Won't that be strange? I'll have married both of your father's sons!'

" 'Aye, no wonder thou art a strumpet,' he said to me fondly, 'a thrice married woman.'

" 'But I was not married to poor Linton, in the proper sense,' I said quickly, 'for he was always puny and ill; and I have only really *given* myself to you with the sort of passion that is unlike anything I ever knew with . . .'

" 'Shh . . .' said my lover harshly, 'I do not want you to mention his name. I cannot abide it. Both for the fact of what his family did to my father and for the fact that he was wed to you, I will have my own vengeance upon him.''

" 'And then, Agnes, I was afeard and frightened for Hareton who is really innocent of any misdeed and I implored my lover for my sake to leave him alone, but

I could tell by the way he glowered that he would not, and then he bade me be quiet and took me in his arms and we lay bathed in the moonlight and drifted off to sleep full of happy tender thoughts and with no fear for the future. Oh now, Agnes, it is morning and my Jack is leaving me and all the fears he banished last night have come rushing upon me again. Oh Agnes, let us pack a bag and insist that we follow them!'

" 'Nay, ma'am,' I said. 'My heart is sorely grieving after Roger; but I know the Captain, and I would not risk his ire. He is doing things in the proper way, ma'am, as they should be and he is right.'

" 'But Agnes, I fear . . . oh,' My mistress clasped her hands before her, 'I know not *what* I fear. Yes, I fear that if Jack and I are parted nothing will ever be the same again.'

" 'Hush, ma'am. It is just foolishness. There is a long, hard path to tread and the way may not always be straight or even, and you may be buffeted by storms, but in his hands I would feel safe, if I were you. Leave it to the Captain and the goodness of Providence.'

"But, Mr. Lockwood, how could I *really* think that Providence smiled on the breaking of the commandments of the Lord as my mistress had so wantonly? How could I ever have hoped that such wickedness should have a happy ending? You see I was too blinded by my own youth and love. For a sturdy peasant woman I had too romantic a view of the world. But maybe it is best that we have our illusions while we are yet young for I assure you, sir, they evaporate pretty quick as we grow older.

"Oh, I can't dwell on that awful day as they mounted their horses and slung their bags behind them. The Captain had taken leave of my mistress in the privacy of her bedroom and all I got from my love was a rough, harsh kiss on the mouth as he bent down from the saddle. Then the Captain strode out, his face grim.

" 'Take good care of her, Agnes. Hasten up to her so as to console her when we ride down the hill.'

"And he kissed his mother who stood in the yard

133

and murmured something to her and from the brave smile she gave him I could see that she would miss him too. Then he hoisted himself into his saddle—flicked the flank of his horse with his whip and, together with my Roger, they turned out of the yard onto the road waving to the servants who had gathered in the yard to bid farewell. Then I hastened to my mistress who stood at the window in the room where they had spent their last night together and, her tears pouring down her cheeks, she nevertheless stood erect and, smiling bravely, waved him goodbye, and I doing the same beside her, until they were but pinpricks in the distance and then vanished out of sight.

"And by that time Mrs. Ibbitson stood beside us and when I left Mrs. Earnshaw's side to give vent to my own grief, she put her arms around the shoulders of the woman her son loved and whispered to her and murmured soothing noises, and methought that my mistress would find in Mrs. Ibbitson the mother she herself had lacked.

"And indeed for a few days we settled down and occupied ourselves with ordinary things, thinking all the time of the two brave men who were making their way on horseback to London. My mistress spent a lot of the time on her own in her room gazing out of the window, playing with her embroidery and often I would have given a mint of money, had I possessed it, to know what she was thinking, for many and mixed must have been the emotions warring in her breast. Did she think of her lover all the time, or sometimes also of her children and the husband she had once loved, that good man, who must be grieving and pining down the valley in Thrushcross Grange? Mrs. Ibbitson—that capable woman who would not even employ a housekeeper she was so particular about running the household—meanwhile made plans for the imminent move to Liverpool where she judged they would spend the winter. She had already deduced that her future daughter-in-law was not addicted to the art of good housekeeping and she bade me help her in the tasks of putting together my mistress's things, for few we had, having left

Thrushcross Grange without a stitch other than what we stood up in.

"I also assisted her in sorting the linen, and a few days after the Captain had gone we were in the sewing room at the back of the house when we heard the clipclop of the hooves of a solitary horse. I jumped up, thinking maybe it was news of the Captain and Roger and when I ran to the window and looked down into the yard I exclaimed and put my hand to my mouth.

" 'Madam, come quickly. For 'tis Mr. Hareton Earnshaw.'

" 'Ah, ah,' said that lady briskly removing the apron she had over her working dress. 'I wondered when we should see him. Is he alone?'

" 'He is, madam.'

" 'Then quick, descend, let him in.'

" 'Oh no, ma'am, I cannot.'

" 'Oh you're afeard, are you, he'll be vexed with you?'

" 'Aye I am, ma'am; he would say I had not looked after my mistress.'

" 'Then go to your mistress and say that her husband is here, but that I will see him in the sitting room and that if she does not care to she may stay in her room.'

"I hastened to my mistress's room, but she already knew, having watched him come up the hill on account of spending so much time at her window. She looked pale and aghast as I opened the door, and ran over to me.

" 'Oh Agnes, it is he, Hareton. He has come to fetch me.'

" 'Oh ma'am, I doubt that he has come to fetch you. Maybe talk to you, to know your mind. Mr. Hareton has behaved very well in this affair. I doubt that he would take you against your will.'

"But she was trembling and when Mrs. Ibbitson eventually came to the door she shook even more, so that the good lady exclaimed:

" 'Why girl, you are scared to death. I assure you he is most polite and well behaved; he does not rave or

135

rant. He says he wishes only to enquire after your health and to see you, if you are willing. I think you should do as he requests. He is behaving properly and I think you should too.'

" 'Oh, but I am terrified, Mrs. Ibbitson. Will he scold?'

" 'I assure you he will not. I have the situation well under control. He has given me his word not to make a scene, and begs you not to either. Come, my dear, he is your husband; you must brace yourself for this task and then it will be over. Would you like to see him alone . . .?'

" 'Oh no, no, with you . . . and Agnes. I want her with me.'

"Well, I was petrified, too, but to give my mistress the courage she sorely lacked, I straightened my dress and squared my shoulders and resolved to encounter my late master with as much bravado as I could manage.

"He was standing by the window looking on to the moors when we entered, and when he turned the expression on his face was pleasant, though I could tell from the lines beneath his eyes and the pallor of his complexion the strain that he was under and undoubtedly had been ever since our departure.

"He went to his wife, bowed, and took her hand which he kissed very correctly and then he nodded to me—I perceived a flicker in his eyes which was not so friendly and I hoped he would forgive me one day when he knew the truth—and stepped back.

" 'I have come to see how you are, Catherine, and whether I can do anything to assist you. I understand Captain Ibbitson has departed for London and I wish to know whether it is your desire to remain here or if you wish to return home or what.'

" 'Home? To Thrushcross Grange?' my mistress said, startled.

" 'Why certainly. It is your home, Catherine, and you have two children waiting for you in it. I make no demands on you and no conditions. If you wish to return you may and no questions asked. You can take up your old life as it was.'

" 'You would have me *back*?' my mistress gasped. 'Why, Hareton. I know not what to say.' And she collapsed into a chair, her face a merry picture of bewilderment.

"Oh, then I admired my master and the skill he showed in handling my mistress. Had he shouted or wept the result would have been the reverse of what he wished. As it was he had her confused, and I noted that she did not immediately send him about his business.

"And then I thought of what I had learned about the character of Mrs. Earnshaw and how she needed a man about her to give her the love and admiration she craved. Oh she loved Captain Jack with passion, I was sure of that; but he was not here, nor likely to be for many a long month. She must have thought about this and brooded upon it all the days since he had left and, although she got on well enough with Mrs. Ibbitson, it was not at all the same thing as having her son.

"In short I had quickly perceived that my mistress was growing bored and knowing her and her passion for the moors, I reckoned that she viewed the projected sojurn in the commercial city of Liverpool with some dismay.

"But the expression on Mr. Hareton's face remained impassive and when a servant entered with some wine he took a glass and raised it to his wife.

" 'Your health, Catherine. Health, and happiness. Pray think about what I have said and if you wish to come home send Agnes with a note and I will come myself to fetch you. It is your place, Cathy, and I want you.'

"Then to my astonishment, he quaffed his wine, replaced the glass on the tray, took up his hat, doffed it to Mrs. Ibbitson and Mrs. Earnshaw and made his way to the door. It was as dignified and as commendable a performance as I ever saw in my life and it left confusion in the house behind him, as well he might have calculated it would.

" 'Well, the impertinence!' cried Mrs. Ibbitson, rushing to the door and then closing it with a hearty slam so that it should echo in my master's ears. "I have never *seen* such nerve!"

"But Miss Cathy was lying back in the chair, her face flushed and a smile playing on her lips.

" 'Oh, I know not, ma'am. I think he behaved with dignity. Did you not, Agnes?'

" 'Aye I did,' I said sincerely.

" 'Forsooth!' cried Mrs. Ibbitson. 'Are you for going back to the bed of your husband when that in which you lay with my son is scarce cold?'

"My mistress gave Mrs. Ibbitson a glance of scorn as though to reprimand her for the coarseness of her words.

" 'Did I suggest such a thing? I merely said Hareton behaved with dignity. You should see him when he loses his temper, ma'am! Of course I do not plan to go back; but, then, to be frank, I do not fancy going to Liverpool either with you. I have no taste for the city, ma'am, I am a country girl born and bred. My very existence depends on the moors. That is why I wished to go with Jack. Either his spirit or the country here makes me free. Not Liverpool, certainly.'

"Mrs. Ibbitson flushed. I could see she was angry.

" 'I thought you had never been there, Catherine, so I do not see how you can judge. Yet if you do not propose to return to Thrushcross Grange—and it would be the end of the affair with my son if you did, even if he didn't return to kill your husband which I can't promise he won't—and you do not wish to go to Liverpool, what is it you would like to do?'

" 'Stay here.'

" 'In Wuthering Heights? Alone?'

" 'With Agnes.'

" 'It is impossible. You would be the scandal of the neighbourhood and, on account of your recent behaviour which everyone knows about, the prey for any man of coarse disposition. I know these are enlightened times, Catherine,' and I detected a dangerous note creep into Mrs. Ibbitson's voice, 'but they are not so

138

enlightened that everyone condones the behaviour of a married woman who leaves her husband and children and runs off with another man. Besides, I promised Jack I would stay with you. I have a sacred duty to him, even if not to you.'

"And I could tell that the affection between the two women or what there had been of it, was at an end, for my mistress rose from her chair and stalked over to Mrs. Ibbitson, raising her head, her expression proud.

" 'Is that so? A wanton am I? And anyone may fall upon me because I went off with your son! Cannot you comprehend the meaning of passion, you silly woman? Did you ever feel it yourself? The love Jack and I have for each other is greater than the sordid affair your words imply.'

"Mrs. Ibbitson flung back her head and laughed, bright red spots of anger on each cheek.

" 'Cannot *I* comprehend passion! Huh! Did not I compromise *myself*, incur the censure of society for *my* liaison with Jack's father? And *you* talk of passion.'

" 'Ah, but he never loved *you*. He loved my mother. You he merely used.'

"My mistress stopped abruptly as, advancing towards her, Mrs. Ibbitson administered a resounding blow on her cheek. She was about to deliver another when I took it upon myself to catch her arm and begged her to desist. Miss Cathy nursed her cheek, but the tears in her eyes at the pain were held back by the anger at being so abused.

" 'There, slut!' cried Mrs. Ibbitson, not content with the furor she had already caused. 'Take that and more. If I am to have you in my charge I can see a daily whipping will be in order. Wait till my son gets back and hears ...'

" 'Wait. Yes, wait!' my mistress spat out. 'He will send you to an institution for the insane and lock you up and cast away the key ...'

"But Mrs. Ibbitson's hands were blocking both her ears and she cried:

" 'I will hear no more! Away to your room! You shall be treated like the intemperate child you are and locked up. And tomorrow we shall leave for Liverpool first thing so that I can have you better under my control. Agnes, take your mistress to her room and try and talk some sense into her. Then lock her in and bring me the key.'

"I was aghast at the nature of my duties and indeed at the turn events had taken so suddenly. My mistress to become a prisoner! We stole together upstairs and shut ourselves in her room and she lay on her bed and ran her hand over her brow.

" 'So now we know my future mother-in-law for her true worth. The dockworker's daughter, indeed, who has reverted to her origins. And how do you think will my Jack turn out, with a mother a shrew and a father like Heathcliff?'

" 'But what will you do, ma'am?'

" 'I must think. Do as she bids you now and return with my dinner and I will tell you what I have decided. Meanwhile do not defy her, good Agnes. She is a termagant.'

"But when I got downstairs and dutifully gave Mrs. Ibbitson the key I found her in a very changed mood. She was sitting on the sofa and quietly sobbing into her kerchief.

" 'Oh dear, Agnes, that I should have forgotten myself thus! She will never forgive me, nor Jack neither. I am not like this at all, you know, not given to abuse really. You ask my servants.'

" 'Indeed Roger always spoke well of you, ma'am.' I murmured politely, and truly he had never had anything but praise for the kindness and care of his mistress.

"Mrs. Ibbitson dried her eyes and smiled.

" 'There, and he was with me nigh four years. Oh I have a temper, but I keep it under control; but there is something about that headstrong young woman that provokes me.'

" 'Maybe it is jealousy, ma'am, on account of her affection for your son?'

"Mrs. Ibbitson looked at me sharply.

" 'Nonsense, girl. I am his mother, not his mistress!

Jack has brought many girls to see me; but none with quite the verve and sauce of that young madam. Of course she is an Earnshaw, I forget all the time. They are an impossible breed. Well, doubtless when we get to Liverpool things will settle down and I shall try and forget what has happened here.'

" 'I doubt if Mrs. Earnshaw will forget, ma'am. She has always been used to being her own mistress except for the brief time she was locked up in this very house by Mr. Heathcliff. She was the apple of her father's eye and the darling of Mr. Hareton. She is used to her own way.'

" 'Well, she better be unused to it!' Mrs. Ibbitson snapped, her temper returning, 'while she is in my care. What an impossible task my son has left me.'

"But as I reflected that Mrs. Ibbitson had brought this dilemma on herself I felt for her no trace of pity and indeed I began to dislike her as heartily as did my mistress.

"The rest of the day I was occupied with household tasks and saw little of Mrs. Ibbitson who was with her own maid in her room, and nothing of my mistress who remained locked up like a small child. Dinner was late and Mrs. Ibbitson ate alone, bidding me to take up a tray to Mrs. Earnshaw and inform her that we should be leaving for Liverpool by first light and she had best compose herself to a better frame of mind.

"I went up with the tray and found my mistress still lying on the bed, her eyes closed as though she were asleep. There was no light in the room except for the dusk and she whispered as I closed the door.

" 'Agnes, is it you?'

" 'Aye mistress, with your supper. You are to eat it up and be ready for an early departure.'

" 'We shall depart even earlier, Agnes. Quick, sit beside me,' and my mistress drew herself up and seized my hand.

" 'I have decided to return to Thrushcross Grange,' and as I gasped she quickly went on. 'Oh, do not be surprised. What else can I do? Hareton loves me; it is my home; I am mistress there. Mrs. Ibbitson clearly hates me and, if she has me a prisoner here, what will she do to me far away from my own kin in her own place? Poison me, doubtless, and tell Jack my death was an accident. No, Agnes, take out my tray and lock my door and prepare to go to bed. Make sure to give Mrs. Ibbitson the key so that she is not suspicious. Then when the household is asleep steal downstairs and, if you can, get Minny from the stable and bring her under the window. See, I will escape from the window here as I did before!' My mistress laughed bitterly. 'Oh I am practiced at it, I tell you, Agnes. The fir tree is my good friend and Mama's room my refuge.'

" 'But what will Mr. Hareton say, ma'am?'

" 'You think Hareton will throw me out? Then I shall be a wanderer. Will you wander with me, Agnes? Who shall take us in? No, Hareton will not throw me out. He is a good man and in his face today I saw love still and forgiveness, and he will have much to forgive.' Her clasp on my hand tightened as though to give herself strength for what she was about to tell me. 'You see, Agnes, if I mistake not, Jack has left me with child.' "

Chapter 9

"I had scarce time to take in the terrible import of what my mistress had said when there was a banging on the door and Mrs. Ibbitson cried:

" 'Well, has madam dined? Fetch the tray, Agnes, and bring me the key, and be quick about it and be sure your mistress is ready and packed for her journey.'

"My mistress pressed my hand in the dark and murmured in my ear.

" 'Under the tree. When I see you there I shall descend. If Minny demurs do not force her. We can walk, though I fancy not that long journey on foot.' And she kissed me lightly on the cheek. And, oh, my heart flooded with love and pity for this foolish young woman, scarce a maid, who had been led to such folly through passion. I prayed that my Roger's love had spared me a similar fate to her!

" 'Aye, I'll be there,' I whispered, and, taking the tray, eased out of the door, locked it loudly and descended the stairs where Miss Cathy's gaoler was waiting, her face grim and unsmiling.

" 'Well, is it done?'

" 'Aye ma'am, she is abed.'

" 'Good. Wake her at dawn for I want to be abroad before Mr. Earnshaw gets wind of what is happening.'

"Oh, I bethought me, Mr. Earnshaw will get wind of that long before *thee*!

"The servants were not late in going to bed because of the early start. I was lucky because I had the small attic room all to myself, or I don't know how I should have left as I did, guessing the time, after the house was quiet. I stole down the stairs, pausing on the landing to make sure there was no light under Mrs. Ibbitson's door and then I tapped very lightly on my mistress's door to indicate that I was ready and I went on down the dark stairs, through the house and out through the kitchen door, the key of which had been left in the keyhole, and into the yard.

"But this is where the first part of our plan went wrong. I could not get Minny to budge. I identified her and she knew it was me all right because she appeared to look at me in a knowing way, the whites of her eyes gleaming. But when I tried to put her bridle on she whinnied and tossed her head and when I tried again she reared her head, nearly knocking me over. I then put down the bridle and attempted to lead her by the mane but this was useless too; she backed against the stable wall and I thought that if there was any more commotion our plans would be discovered.

"Still the mistress had oft made the journey between the Grange and Wuthering Heights on foot and I was a young woman and, with her to guide me, surely we should not come to harm? Still I was apprehensive and I tucked my cloak more securely about me because it was a grim, gusty night and, even as I walked round to the front of the house, the rain started to fall.

I stood directly below my mistress's room and I could perceive the window was open and saw the dark outline of her head. However, expecting the buck of a horse, I fear she did not see me and I stood there for some time vainly signalling with my hands until at last I was forced to give a low call and say that I waited beneath. Then the fir tree shuddered and down it, lightly as a cat, came my mistress dropping softly to earth as she reached the bottom and clasping me in her arms.

" 'Agnes, what is it? Where is Minny?'

" 'She would not come with me ma'am. She whinnied and shied and I thought she would wake up the house.'

" 'Then I must go get her.'

"I grasped Mrs. Earnshaw's arm.

" 'Oh ma'am, let us go. I am sore afeard while we stop here. The least little sound and we shall have Mrs. Ibbitson and the servants swarming around us.'

" 'But it's so cold and wet, Agnes.'

" 'Aye, ma'am, I know. But we are both strong young women and you well know the way.'

"Oh, Mr. Lockwood, when I think back on my words now I do repent me that I urged her forth on that cold wet night; but if we had the vision to see into the future we should not be mortals, should we? Anyway, Miss Cathy and I, clasping hands like girls, crept towards the gate and then when we were on the road we walked very quickly to put as much distance between the house and ourselves as we could; every now and then we glanced back but, in that intense dark without moon or stars, we could only see the Heights as a grim shadow in the cleft of the hills. All was still within. Knowing the condition she was in I begged my mistress to slow her pace and she clung to me, poor thing, her teeth chattering against the cold, while the rain soon had us both drenched.

" 'Agnes, I know a way we can take if we leave the road and go direct over the moors. It will save us an hour or two in this terrible weather,' and her teeth chattered the more and I realised that, because of the fine autumn we had been having, the only clothes my mistress had were light and unfit for such a night as this. Thus, although it was against my instinct to leave the path for the soggy moorland—and well I would have done to have harkened to my instinct, but I did not—my one wish was to have my mistress fast in the

145

safety of her home, and I agreed to turn off the path when we did to take the steep descent directly to Thrushcross Grange.

"Oh, Mr. Lockwood, words cannot describe what a journey it was. For my mistress, thinking she knew every inch of those moors, had never before attempted them in inky blackness and in such cruel weather conditions. Soon we were crashing through heather ankle deep, falling into ditches and being up to our knees in the bogs. Meanwhile the rain had us soaked to our very skins, the clothes clinging to us and our hair plastered over our heads. The wind buffeted us from the north so as to impede our progress and then I realised we were utterly lost with no familiar landmarks to guide our way. However, my mistress resolutely forged forward and I think that it was not want of bravery nor motive that prevented us from reaching our destination as we should have.

" 'Ma'am,' I cried as we stopped to get our breath, 'we are lost. We are going in circles.'

" 'Nonsense, Agnes; we are going downwards. This must ultimately take us to the valley, even if we pass the Grange, and we shall be in shelter away from this weather.' And my mistress tugging me plunged ahead and suddenly she gave a cry and, letting go of my hand or I should have followed her, fell forward into the darkness. For a dreadful moment I thought she had gone over Penistone Cragg, knowing not where we were, but then I heard her moan and, oh thank God, could feel the shape of her wet bedraggled, but still alive, body as I knelt beside her cradling her head in my arms.

" 'I think I have broken my ankle, Agnes. Oh, oh the pain . . . oh when I lift it. Oh, Agnes, we are done for. We shall perish in this bleak spot 'ere help can get to us. Oh Jack, Jack, why did you leave me? Oh Jack.'

"Her words struck terror into my heart and I feared she was delirious and, in truth, I did not know what to do, whether to leave my mistress and seek help or try and warm her with my own frozen body when, suddenly as I looked about me in the dark in desperation,

146

I saw, far off, the light of a candle which seemed to gleam and then fade as the wind wailed and shrieked about us.

" 'Oh ma'am. I see a candle! Look ma'am. It *must* be the Grange.' My poor mistress feebly raised her head.

" 'Where, Agnes? Where? Oh go to it, Agnes, or we shall perish. Leave me and go quickly.'

" 'Oh ma'am.' I chafed her hands and kissed her cheeks. 'Oh do not faint or sleep, or you will die with the cold. Do everything you can to keep yourself awake, ma'am, and I will be back as soon as I can.'

"With that I rose to my feet and stumbled in the direction of the light, across ditches, over hillocks through the marshes. Sometimes my foot would be held by a root and, fearing to have the same fate as my mistress and be marooned on the moor, I went more slowly, my eyes never leaving that uncertain flickering light which several times appeared extinguished altogether and then would shine forth with renewed intensity like a beacon to guide me.

"Oh, I knew not how long the awful journey took me. It seemed I would see dawn 'ere I arrived; but at last the outline of the wall of Thrushcross Park grew nearer and, not even wasting time to look for the gate, I found purchase for my feet in the crumbling stones of the plaster and, not caring how much I lacerated my hands or bruised my knees, propelled myself over the top of the wall to fall gratefully at the other side. Then, drived on by a renewed frenzy and glad to be out of the merciless command of the wind, I ran helter skelter across the park until I all but collapsed on the main steps of the Grange pounding against the door with my fists.

"Yet on that night with the wind screaming through the eaves no one heard me and then I saw that the light which had guided me came from my master's study and, half walking, half crawling along the ground, I came to the window, and peering in, perceived him sitting by the fire half asleep over a book. I then commenced a banging of the windows until my

147

master, his face white with alarm, jumped up and peering out almost fainted with shock when he saw who it was pummelling on the pane. He quickly disappeared and before I knew it—I was half dazed by this time—I had been seized by the waist and guided into the house where, sobbing now that I was safe, I collapsed in a heap in the hall.

" 'Oh sir, my mistress has fallen on the moor. Hurry, lest she die of exposure.'

" 'Your mistress!' My master cried in alarm. 'You have left her on the moors?'

" 'We were escaping from Wuthering Heights. We decided to leave the path so as to get here more quickly, my mistress being certain that she knew the way. Then she fell and lies with a broken leg halfway between here and Wuthering Heights.'

" 'But how shall we ever find her in this storm? Oh, Agnes, what have you done?' And my master strode to a gong that is kept in the hall for summoning folk to dinner and banged it for all he was worth.

"In a moment the whole house was in an uproar as servants, some still clad in nightshirts, poured down the staircase, rubbing the sleep out of their eyes and demanding to be told where the fire was.

"My master bade them dress as soon as maybe and said my mistress was hurt on the moors. He then sent another servant to fetch Dr. Kenneth, bade the women prepare fires in my mistress's chamber and warm the bed and put hot fuel on the stove and then, with all the available men gathered, he prepared to lead them to the search. Then the noise and hubbub subsided and I realised that everyone was looking at me as, my teeth still chattering, I remained where I had been in the hall.

" 'Agnes,' my master said, having apparently forgotten me.

" 'You are the only one who can guide us. Have you the strength to come with us?'

" 'Aye, master,' I said, my courage returning as I rose to my feet. Then the housekeeper, Mrs. Kemp, hurried me into the kitchen where she had a maid fetch

148

me warm, dry clothes and in a jiffy I was changed and ready and all the better for some hot milk being poured down my throat and my aching limbs rubbed with linament."

"The horses were saddled and waiting us in the yard and, with the dogs alongside of us we set off at a brisk pace, I riding on the saddle behind my master who wanted to be in command of the operation. We were aided by the fact that the rain had ceased and I think the wind had dropped, at least on the low ground and, if I was not mistaken, in the east the sky was breaking up with the imminence of dawn.

"In fact it was the light that saved us for, although I had fancied I had come straight to the Grange and that if we went in an imaginary straight line between the Grange and the Heights we should find my mistress, of course I was wrong because in the dark distances are deceiving. And so it was not until the moors were revealed in the pale light of dawn and the blackbirds had started to carol their throaty song that we saw on the horizon an arm raised and then flop back to earth again—my master saw it first—and crying 'She is there! She is alive!' urged his horse into a gallop.

"It was now about three hours since I had left my mistress, maybe more on account of the light, and she was in a sorry state though alive and indeed conscious. She told us afterwards that she had despaired of us finding her before Mrs. Ibbitson sent servants from the Heights and then when she had seen our horses she had not been sure; but feeling close to fainting or expiring, she knew not which, she had raised her arm and waved not once but again and again and it was only after a long time and her arm was becoming too weary to move that she saw us respond.

"I dismounted to assist my mistress whose leg had now become numb and, indeed, it dragged unnaturally as my master gathered her to him and lifted her onto the horse. Then turning quickly and leaving me to make my way as best I could—luckily one of the servants spotted I was without a mount as they were about to charge off in the same direction—he rode ahead of us at full gallop to the Grange where a warm and loving welcome, as well as medical aid in the person of Dr. Kenneth was awaiting one, who by any just reckoning scarce deserved it; but then there is little real justice in this world is there, Mr. Lockwood?

"For the best part of the next month, that is between the end of September when we made our escape and the end of October, my mistress hovered twixt life and death. She had indeed broken her leg and Dr. Kenneth had sent for an expert bone-setter from Bradford, as the break was of a complicated nature and he feared my mistress might walk with a permanent limp. But even before the bone-setter was called the havoc wrought by the weather on my mistress's slight frame had done its work and she took pneumonia.

"I might say I too caught a chill and was confined to my room for a few days, but my illness was nothing compared to that of my mistress and passed unnoticed, certainly by my master who sat constantly at her side and indeed had to be led away to sleep. I marvelled that such fickleness of her part was met with such fidelity and devotion on his, and I bethought me that maybe it was the best way, after all, to treat a man as she did.

"I, of course, was worried about the child that my mistress carried and then I thought that if she lost it maybe it would be a good thing and she could really start life afresh. But no, it was not to be and though she suffered so grievously and so long, being unable to take water or any nourishment unaided, she did not part with her baby.

"And talking of babies, oh, the thrill to see again my own bairns after such an absence. Little Rainton refused to acknowledge me for days as though to punish me for going away; but the baby Margaret, oh! she had grown into a beauty—a fine round bonny baby, a credit to the mother who bore her and all who nursed her. I think that, at first, Mary who had taken charge after my defection was jealous to see me back; but soon my own illness, causing more absence from the nursery and the much graver illness of my mistress, made that kind of thing seem unimportant. Indeed I was uncertain of my place in the house and of my station when one day the master called me to his study, said he had learnt of my own ill health and hoped I was better. I bobbed, and stammered that I was not sure how Mr. Hareton would treat me after helping my mistress to flee the Grange.

" 'You know, Agnes Dean, that you have a lot to answer for,' he said sitting, but keeping me standing before him.

" 'Aye, I do, sir . . .' "

" 'But for your help your mistress would not have flown from hence in the first place . . .'

" 'Oh but she would, sir!' I cried, wanting to speak in my defense. 'She was determined on't whether I aided her or no, and I did not wish to for I loved and revered you, Mr. Hareton, and always have done. In fact I urged my mistress not to go, but she said she would and that if I did not go with her you would make me walk home on my own.'

" 'Ah, maybe she was right, Agnes,' my master said, pursing his mouth ruefully, 'and it ill becomes me to blame you, for I know how determined she can be. But then again you showed lack of judgement in coming back here on such a stormy night; whatever pursuaded you to do that?'

" 'Ah, my mistress had fallen out wi' Mrs. Ibbitson who had locked her in her room and was taking her to Liverpool early the next day, where my mistress thought she would be killed.'

" 'I see,' my master said, and paused for a long while. 'Thus you had no choice?'

" 'No sir, and Minny would not be moved otherwise we should have gone all the way by road and have been saved. 'Twas fate, sir.'

" 'I can see that,' my master said. ' 'Twas fate indeed. Dr. Kenneth says that my wife is with child. Did you know that, Agnes?'

" 'Yes, Mr. Earnshaw.' I hung my head as though it

were something of my own doing though, God knows, whatever else I did wrong I could not be blamed for that.

" 'My wife told you?'

" 'Yes sir, the day we fled.'

" 'But the child cannot be mine, did you know that, Agnes?'

"Again I mumbled something because I was embarrassed with talk of this nature apart from anything else.

" 'Because I have not lain with her in the time; it is impossible. It therefore must be Mr. Jack's. Did Mrs. Ibbitson know?'

" 'Oh no, sir.'

" 'Nor the Captain?'

" 'I think not sir, for my mistress had just discovered it.'

" 'Good. Now, Agnes. I want you to listen to what I am about to tell you and then I want you to go away and never open your mouth upon the subject again, or your ears, or say to another living soul what I have told you. Do you understand?'

" 'Oh yes, sir,' and trembled at the awful responsibility that he was thrusting upon me.

" 'I will never tell anybody else this child is not mine. Dr. Kenneth does not know nor will he ever need to. I will bring it up as my own, and it will rank after my own children when my estate is shared out after my death. I will love the child as my own for I love Catherine and what is hers is mine. I have not spoken to her for she can scarce talk sense yet, but if she is willing I will take her away until the child is born and once again I will give a thought to leaving here altogether, for I think that some fate besets us here and we can never be happy in this place.'

" 'Now in exchange for your secrecy, Agnes, I shall reinstate you in your position as nursemaid and maid to my wife, but if ever you do wrong again and do not come to me with any plans your mistress may have *before* she can carry them out I shall not only dismiss you, I shall also have you disgraced and sent away from the district, is that clear, Agnes?'

152

"Now I was trembling violently because I have never seen Mr. Hareton so stern and solemn.

" 'Yes sir.'

" 'Good, then you may go. Oh and remember Agnes, 'twas not you who saved your mistress that night but the goodness of God. For I could not sleep and, in sending me down to my study to find a book, He enabled the light from my candles to guide you here. Otherwise you would have perished on the moors along with your mistress. Never forget that it is God who ordains all things, not we, Agnes.'

"And without replying I fled up to my room where I lay down on my bed and had a right good weep."

"Even at last when my mistress was out of danger and her leg on the mend and the fever gone she seemed to me permanently weakened and wondered at the life that clung so tenaciously inside her. She spoke but little; indeed, for a time, she recognised no one and seemed perpetually in a world divided between Wuthering Heights and Thrushcross Grange only peopled by spirits of the past as, although she often mentioned her mother and cried the name Heathcliff! she never called the names Hareton or Jack.

"And indeed, apart from hearing that Mrs. Ibbitson had left for Liverpool as planned on the day after our escape without a word to anyone, we heard nothing from either her or her son and I was grateful that my mistress was restored once more to the bosom of her rightful home.

"As a result of her pneumonia my mistress was left with a tiresome cough and, to my consternation, I often noticed that her face was flushed and her eyes bright. Dr. Kenneth sounded her lungs and said they were in good condition, but I could tell that he too was puzzled by what ailed her and once again was reminded of her mother.

" 'There is bad blood in this family,' Dr. Kenneth once confided in me after a long spell at my mistress's side. 'It seems to affect the female line. Temper, wilfulness, a tendency to fever and a slight derangement if you ask me, though this one is not so deranged as her mother. But see how she lies inert all the time? Does she ever speak to you?'

"I shook my head sorrowfully.

" 'She will ask me for water, or to draw the curtain so that she can see the moor; but direct conversation, no.'

" 'They're a bad lot, these Earnshaw women,' Dr. Kenneth muttered in his gruff manner, for he knows our folk and our ways like no one else. 'Went off with the son of Heathcliff, I hear, just as the mother went off with the father.'

" 'I understood Mrs. Linton never actually "went off," sir.'

" 'Oh, 'twas the same thing. Unbridled passion. It is just that in twenty years we are become more advanced and demoralised by the example of the Prince of Wales and high society corrupting our morals and standards. They say that the Prince keeps his mistress in a house in the very same part of Brighton as he has his pavilion; and the doings of the royal princes, none of whom are lawfully married, is more than scandalous. In her mother's time things had not come to quite such a pass. 'Tis the age. Unbridled passion, that's what it is. Lust gone mad. Anyway, Earnshaw seems happy enough that the child is his—and *he* should know.' And Dr. Kenneth packed his bag with pills and instruments and, pulling on his coat, departed for the day.

"My mistress, who had been lying there, we supposed asleep, opened her eyes as he went out and, oh my heart filled with joy as she, looking at me directly, smiled for the first time in weeks.

" 'Unbridled passion!' she said weakly. 'Tut tut.'

"I rushed to her side and clasped her hand.

" 'Oh ma'am, you are better.'

" 'How long have I been ill, Agnes?'

" 'A month, ma'am. It is the Eve of All Saints. You had a fever and your chest is weak.'

" 'And I am mad, too, if Mr. Kenneth is right.'

" 'Oh no, Mrs. Earnshaw, that you are not. Do not say that.'

154

"The smile left my mistress's face—oh how lovely she looked lying there, her golden curls spread on the pillow, her face wraithlike even against the whiteness of the sheets—and she coughed.

" 'I am not mad, but I am done for, Agnes. I feel it. I shall not ride on the moors again until they take me to the kirk to lie beside my mother. And, Agnes, I want you to be sure I am placed beside her, or rather next to my father, for I do not want the graves disturbed . . .'

" 'Oh, ma'am. I beg you do not speak like that. You have everything to live for. Two children and another on the way and Mr. Hareton every bit as loving and as fond as when you first wed.'

"My mistress sighed and this set off the coughing again as indeed every movement she made seemed to do to her.

" 'I know it, Agnes. Mama came to me one night and told me I should be with her soon. I am done for, Agnes; I do not want to live. Jack is gone and will never have me back now and Hareton . . . what is life with Hareton? It is nothing after the passion I have known. No, I want to die; and maybe Jack too will die in the wars and we shall be together as Mama and Mr. Heathcliff are.'

"I confess that the tears stole down my face at the sight of this wretched, unhappy woman. And I thought what a waste her life had been and what a misery she had proved to others. Was it worth it; this brief flicker of a candle that we call life?

"I knew now that why she did not speak was because I had the strange feeling that she had already advanced in time and was ahead of us.

"By Christmas time my mistress was allowed up, but she never went downstairs because of the pain which still ailed her leg and caused her to drag it. It was so sad to see such a beautiful woman walking with a limp, and Mr. Hareton used to give her his arm and go with her so gently because he did not want her to feel maimed.

"But maimed she was, in body and in soul. In her

155

mind I'll not say she was maimed at all. She was fully in her senses and aware of what went on and what she was doing; but with Mr. Hareton she was like a puppet, smiling when he wanted her to smile and answering when he spoke to her; but there was no commerce or intercourse between them at all of any kind. She was lifeless and he was sorely perplexed.

" 'It is the damage to her lungs,' he said to me one day after he had tried in vain to make her walk the length of the corridor. 'After the baby is born we shall be off to a hot climate. God grant it could be sooner!'

"But God granted nothing of the kind, and a terrible winter we had of it an'all. Oh, I well recall that winter. We were confined to the house for weeks while the snow stood higher than a man's shoulder on the moor, and even the tall posts that were meant to guide travellers disappeared from sight. We even ran short of provisions at one time and Dr. Kenneth could not visit, while Mr. Hareton chafed at being kept from his business which I heard was expanding, though he had given up being a magistrate on account of the scandal caused by his wife.

"My mistress was so thin and her cough so much worse that sometimes I thought she would die before the baby had come to term. It was a miracle to me that the baby survived and, indeed, maybe it *should* have died in its mother's womb and we should have been spared all the trouble that it has caused up to today.

"For in due course the snows cleared and once again the first crocuses appeared and the birds shook themselves from the long winter, those who had stayed and survived, and went about nest building in that timeless ritual we call spring. And at that time of the year when the earth opens and brings forth my mistress we delivered, before term, of a tiny dark-haired baby boy, and he was called Anthony Earnshaw . . . who you know today as Anthony Heathcliff, Mr. Lockwood, though how that came about we'll come to by and by.

"Well my mistress had as little interest in this new creation as she had in any other and, by the shallow way that she breathed and the deathless cast of her

156

countenance, I thought she was not long for this world. She now had someone to sleep with her all night to assist her when her relentless coughing threatened to choke her. She recovered from the baby, but she was dying of consumption and at last Dr. Kenneth told Mr. Hareton it was useless to hope.

"Oh, I minded Mr. Hareton in those awful days. His eyes were ringed with dark circles and he looked like one who too had not long to go before the earth closed over him. He would spend hours by her bedside, always entering the room with a posy of spring flowers that he had gathered himself, placing them on her breast if she was awake or on her pillow if she slept. And, although she could only talk with difficulty, my mistress was kind to him and would occasionally lift her hand and stroke his suffering face.

" 'Oh Hareton,' she whispered one day. 'I have been useless to you. I want you to marry again and get a good mother for the children; for I have been neither good mother nor wife. Forget me Hareton, for I did not deserve you or one as good as you . . .'

" 'Oh, Cathy . . .' he sobbed, clasping her thin, emaciated hand. 'You are going to get better; we shall go abroad. You are weak after the winter, after childbirth. You are only a young girl, Cathy. Do not leave me.'

" 'I must, Hareton. I do not want to stay here any longer. I realise I was only meant for a short life and that a hectic one. I have loved and been loved . . . oh, Hareton, can I ask you one last favour.'

" 'Oh, anything, my darling, anything,' and then buried his face in the bedclothes.

" 'Let me die in Wuthering Heights. Do it for me, Hareton. Let me die in Mother's room.'

"And with that my master's sobs became louder—and no wonder because it meant that in her last days she was not even thinking of him at all—and when he could control himself once more he rushed out of the room without answering, leaving me to bathe my mistress's fevered brow.

" 'Agnes,' she pleaded, 'let me die at the Heights.'

157

" 'Oh, ma'am, do not distress your sorrowing husband more. Think of him for once in your life!' And although it was a harsh thing to say to the dying I turned away for I could not abide her selfishness any longer, though I dare say she knew not what she did, because I do not like to be uncharitable about the departed.

"But here was a woman I'd at times loved and hated, admired and despised and who was the cause in me of as many mixed emotions as I drew live breaths.

"But that very night of which I speak something occurred which no one in their wildest dreams had anticipated and which determined the subsequent, all too brief, course of events.

"At sunset there was a commotion in the yard and on looking out I perceived the young handsome face of my lover Roger and, behind him dismounting from his horse, his master Captain Ibbitson. I remained transfixed to the spot—rooted they call it—and then, my senses reeling, I flew down to the hall just at the same time as Roger and Captain Ibbitson stepped inside. They both wore travelling cloaks and looked strained and spattered from a long journey.

" 'Ah, Agnes!' the Captain cried, on seeing me, his voice none the less vigorous for fatigue. 'Lead me to your master. Say Captain Heathcliff calls—and mind the Heathcliff, Agnes, for I have changed my name to that my father bore. Now hasten, Agnes, and you can dally with young Roger anon.'

" 'Oh Captain,' I cried running up to him, 'the mistress is near death, and the master . . .'

" 'Aye that's what I heard,' the Captain roared, 'and I've come to take her away, to her proper home. Hasten, find your master.'

" 'My master is not at home,' I said. 'He was but recently at her sickbed, but has gone to Gimmerton on a call. Indeed I think he had gone to make preparations for her funeral which we were sure would not be long delayed.'

" 'All the better then,' cried the Captain and he ran up the stairs two at a time. I could only glance anxiously at Roger before I followed him. But when the Captain came to her room, as though sensing the delicacy of the invalid, he slowed his pace and looked back to me.

" 'Here, Agnes, precede me into her room. Oh my God, is she very ill?'

"It was late afternoon and the rays of the sun streamed into my mistress's room casting a golden glow about her bed. Indeed I thought her already dead and summoned by the angels, for she lay there so pale and still. But as I entered she opened her eyes and fixed them not on me but a spot behind me and her countenance was illumined by such bliss that I thought she had seen the Blessed Lord come to take her.

" 'Oh Jack,' she sighed.

"And with a sob the Captain went swiftly to her bed and knelt beside her.

" 'Oh Cathy, Cathy . . .' and he took her tiny hands between his large ones and, pressing them, covered her face with gentle kisses while large tears ran down the cheeks of both of them.

" 'Jack, I am dying. Take me to Wuthering Heights.'

" 'Of course my love, but you will *not* die. Not now that I am here. You will get better up on the Heights with the wind blowing and the clouds rolling over our heads. And we shall get out, on our horses, eh Cathy, as we used to? And Roger and Agnes will bring us a picnic and then we'll set out and look for the cowslips, forget-me-nots and marsh marigolds; the dog daisies, hairbells and campions and I shall make you a garland and put it on your head, for you are my Queen, Cathy, and there is none to compare with thee.'

"But by the way he held her hands and wept I knew he believed it no more than she did and, such was the confusion of grief and joy, that I saw my Roger had tears in his eyes and mine were wet too.

" 'Just take me, Jack, take me there for I feel I have not long. Mama is waiting for me there and she will guide me to where the blessed souls have eternal rest. Hurry, Jack, hurry.'

"The Captain looked to me and I was beset with anxiety and uncertainty.

" 'Oh sir, she is too ill to travel. Besides, Mr. Hareton . . .'

" 'Oh Agnes, good Agnes, help us,' cried my mistress. 'I have not long and you have always been a true friend to me. Help me now in my extremity.'

"Captain Jack had drawn back her bedclothes and he scooped her into his great arms, she who was now like a wraith and not the plump, handsome woman he had fondled not so long before.

"The effort of talking had brought on her cough again and I held a bowl for her and mopped her brow.

" 'Hurry, Agnes, a blanket. Wrap your mistress well. Once she is at the Heights she will make such a recovery as you never saw.'

"I put a shawl over Mrs. Earnshaw's head and wrapped blankets round her and the Captain strode out carrying her as though she were thistledown.

" 'Quick, fetch her things and come too!' Roger whispered, 'or Mr. Hareton will kill thee.'

" 'I fear not the master,' I said sorrowfully. 'He knows I serve my mistress well. But I'll not fetch her things for I think that, 'ere dawn breaks tomorrow, she will be at rest.'

"In the hall the servants stood in a bunch to see the departure of their mistress, alerted by curiosity at the strange situation as well as by sympathy. But the Captain heeded them not and strode out to the yard where Roger helped him mount his horse and then settle the mistress in front of him so that he could hold her. Then I mounted up behind Roger and it was a sad little procession that, without a backward glance towards the Grange, set out once more for Wuthering Heights.

"Slowly we climbed up towards the house; the earth was very dry now as there had been no rain—a contrast to the last time we had come this way and, oh, I bethought me if I were to blame for the sorry state my mistress was now in, and then I thought God does take these things out of our mortal hands and bends us to

160

His will. I saw that my mistress was upright, not slumped against the Captain, as though savouring every moment of this last ride to the place she loved so well; her last view of the moors over which she had ridden and romped all her life, and the sight of the hairbells and the buttercups and the cowslips that lurked in the ditches. Her last smell of the new grass and the burgeoning heather. But, above all, her last view of that glorious sunset that transformed everything with colour as it set behind Wuthering Heights casting its lingering beams towards Catherine Earnshaw as though in a welcome on her last journey.

"And then we were at the house and the Captain alighted and bade Roger and me run quick to make the beds and light a good fire in my mistress's room and I ran up and preceded him, there, and then, Mr. Lockwood, the most extraordinary thing happened which I shall recall to my dying day as vividly as it happened then. When I opened the door of the chamber which, by rights should have been cold, not having been occupied for nine months, we were greeted by a draft of warm air and the room was fresh and pleasant smelling and about us there was an air of repose and joy, yes, joy. And as the Captain placed my mistress tenderly on the bed which again by rights should have been both cold and damp it also seemed dry, even warm, and as I hastened to make it up I bethought me that I was in a place that had been ready and waiting for my mistress for some time. I never had an explanation for it from that day to this.

" 'There love,' said the Captain tenderly, tucking her up after I was finished. 'I'll go and take off my coat and Agnes will prepare thee some supper and by tomorrow you'll be feeling on the road to recovery again, you'll see!'

" 'Oh Jack, don't leave me. Give Roger your coat. I have come home, don't you see? Mama is here in this room. We have not long together, Jack, and I want to tell you how I loved you and thought of you and prayed that I should see you before I died. And we have a little son, Jack, Anthony, who I want you to

161

protect and love as you would me. He looks just like you. I have been a bad woman in many ways, a bad wife and mother, but you . . .'

"And here my mistress was troubled by another fit of coughing and again I knelt and wiped her damp brow and her breathing was so quick 'twas a wonder she spoke at all.

"'You have given me nothing but joy,' the Captain murmured brokenly. ' 'Twas I who should never have left you. You wanted to come and I should have taken you, for well you knew what would happen if I did not.'

"My mistress smiled at him tenderly.

"'Aye I knew. I wanted to go with you so badly; and then maybe you and I and Agnes and Roger would all be happy and well now and together.'

"'Oh do not say that, my soul! Do not leave me with that reproach, that memory for the rest of my life. That but for me thou wouldst have lived! Oh do not say it. I beg you. But what am I saying! I am *here* my love; I am come in time and by bringing you here, why, in no time at all you will be well. Is it not so, Agnes?'

"And he stepped back, looking at me, his tone pleading.

"'No 'tis not so Jack,' my mistress went on, her voice growing fainter so that I could tell some crisis was approaching, 'and do not weep, for I am resigned to it. I could never have had you for my own while Hareton was alive; your career doesn't leave you free and he would not let me go. I grew weary with the struggle.'

"'Hush, my love,' the Captain said once again getting on his knees and warming her hand with his kisses. 'Try not thyself. Rest.' And he took her in his arms and kissed her face again and again as though trying to give it life, and she with difficulty returned his kiss and, weakly, with her hand trembling, stroked his face in a last loving gesture.

"'I shall not rest,' she said softly, 'because I am shortly going to that long rest, and I want to look at you and take your memory with me. Why Jack, don't cry; see I have no tears. I am happy. And Agnes. why do you weep? Is it so sad to see me go? Have I not been a burden to you?'

" 'Oh no, ma'am, no,' and I wept afresh and knelt to kiss her hand.

" 'Ah thank you for that kiss, dear Agnes. Think not too harshly of me for a lot of what I did was in my nature, not by design.'

"And as the two of us knelt by her bedside my mistress suddenly sat up and her eyes opened wide and, unglazed as they had been, stared out of the window into the dusk. The Captain hurriedly made a cradle for her with his arms and lent her support as she reached out with her hands and a beatific smile lit up her face.

" 'Oh Jack, see, towards the sky and the top of the moors. How beautiful it is; the larks are hovering and the first swallows have arrived to build their nests. And look Jack, do you see, oh *look* there is Mama, I can see her clearly . . . oh Jack, can't you . . .'

"And then my mistress gave a shudder and her limp body fell back against that of the Captain, her eyes still open, the expression on her face serene. And, I am prepared to wager any money that Catherine did see her mother then and, as she did, her spirit went out to greet her.

"At first I could not believe she was dead, but the Captain gently laid her on the bed and as he closed each eye he kissed it and then he broke down in such a spasm of grief and sobbing that Roger and I withdrew to the room below, where we stayed all night without supper or fire or candles, locked as much in our own particular grief as the Captain was in his.

"And then at dawn as the new sun rose up fresh from the valley in the east we went upstairs and found him as we had left him, stretched over her bed and she lying there still with peace on her brow and a beautiful smile fixed on her lips.

"Roger tried to rouse the Captain and told him it

163

was dawn and he should rest or he himself would be ill.

" 'Oh I would go with her to wherever she is gone. How can I stay here without her, Roger?' his master cried and then allowed himself to be helped up and gently led away. And I, feeling too a peace I had not felt before, washed my mistress and laid her out, putting into this last act I could do for her all the love I had felt over the years for this strange tormented woman, Catherine Earnshaw."

I was stiff as Mrs. Sutcliffe ended her tale. It was past dusk and I wondered that Nostro was already not abroad seeking me. I got myself up and dusted my coat.

"I remember your Aunt Nelly said of her that her beginning was as friendless as her end was likely to be; but she did not die without friends."

"Nay, with love all about her, and her mother coming for her as though to make up for the fact she had died at her birth. Later that day Mr. Hareton came, stunned with grief, and the Captain allowed him to be alone in the room with his wife, but what happened I know not for I waited outside.

"It seemed that grief temporarily reconciled the two men, and also the desire to do the proper thing and not cause more scandal, for the Captain allowed Mrs. Earnshaw's body to be removed to the Grange and did not trouble her husband again, until the funeral which he attended as a guest, not pressing himself forward.

"But as they laid my mistress's body beside her father in the old churchyard I minded how the two men who had loved her, more than she deserved, wept alone of all the mourners and how, after the others had gone, they remained for a long time by the side of the grave. Then as the gravediggers started to toss in the soil, together and without exchanging a word, they left, one going up the hill towards the Heights, the other turning downhill to the Grange."

BOOK 2

Chapter 10

After I had dined that night I sat up until the small hours making notes of the story told to me by Agnes Sutcliffe. Was Roger called Sutcliffe, I wondered as my pen tore across the pages; had at least one thing ended happily? Had Agnes Dean married him? For her story, told to me shyly though with engaging frankness, was almost as poignant as that of the main *dramatis personae*.

Yes, I would turn it all into a book one day and my father's wish for me to be what he was not, an author, would be accomplished. Maybe he knew that, in leaving me his manuscript, I would be fired by his own endeavours to add to it the story of my later discoveries.

I knew poor Nostro could not understand what had overtaken me—out all day, morose and preoccupied by my thoughts the rest of the time. He hovered over me anxiously all evening and would not go to bed until I threatened to have him shipped back to Italy, confound him, if he would not leave me alone. So, sullenly and silently, he left the decanter of brandy by my elbow and without even bidding me goodnight withdrew from the room.

So that was Anthony Heathcliff, grandson of the first Heathcliff and like his grandfather too in looks as well as nature if I was not mistaken. Then who was the pretty careworn woman with him? And the child? *Also* a Cathy? Dear me, where would this story end? And the events we had been talking about happened thirty-four years ago. Catherine had died in 1806! How vivid Agnes made it all seem. By slightly embellishing her plain country style I could make a good narrative of it, fit for a London publisher.

The following morning I did not rise so early, and the day was fairly well advanced before Nostro woke me with a smug smile on his face as though pleased that I would be late for my rendezvous with Mrs. Sutcliffe. But I felt also that I wanted to complete my own narrative before I saw her again, so I sent round a note begging permission to come the following morning, and sat all day at my desk recording the story she had told me.

At four I broke off and, before it was dark, took Patch for a long walk on the moors until again I was within sight of Wuthering Heights and noticed how the smoke spiralling from the chimney seemed to emphasize its remoteness from the rest of the world. Then I cut across and took the road to Thrushcross Grange which already I could see nestling in the valley, a good two or three miles distant. Unlike the Heights it looked unoccupied; no smoke came from the chimneys and there were no signs of activity in the large grounds or among the outbuildings. And indeed when I got to the gates they were barred and padlocked and, peering up the drive, I could see that already the place looked desolate and forsaken and the lawns in need of scything.

So Wuthering Heights remained while the Grange was deserted? What strange turns in fortune's wheel had Mrs. Sutcliffe yet to reveal to me?

When I got home there was a letter waiting for me on the silver tray on the hall stand. It had been delivered by hand and I strode into the warm of the drawing room while I read it.

It was from my brother Dalby and contained the news that he was going to pay me a visit before the week was out. Not even so much as "may I?" or "by your leave?." No, not from Dalby. Dalby Lockwood is one of those men who are convinced from birth that nature has singled them out for particular approbation. He is older than I by two years, but my earliest memories are of Dalby already ruling the house from his high chair and of everyone rushing about at his beck and call.

Dalby and I are not in the least alike; we do not even look alike; in fact there is not a single feature that we have in common except our height and we are tall after our father. Dalby is a big man; a forceful man; a handsome man—very attractive to women, with whom he is continually in trouble. He has broken every marriageable heart in London where he is much sought after for, as well as his looks and charm, he has a fine voice and a great gift for repartee.

And not only has he these natural gifts. He is also clever and although only twenty-seven has already entered Parliament. And it is said that Sir Robert Peel has his eye set on Dalby for advancement, should he again think government, though that maybe is just Dalby talking.

Oh dear, Dalby coming here. I sank into my chair and summoned Nostro who I think had already steamed open the letter because he surely knew, from the smirk on his face, what it contained.

"My brother Dalby is to visit us, Nostro."

"Indeed sir? It will be very agreeable to see Mr. Lockwood again."

I shrugged with annoyance.

"Nostro, when *will* I teach you the rules of etiquette? My borther John, the eldest, is Mr. Lockwood. My brothers Horace, Dalby and I are known by our Christian names, Mr. Dalby, Mr. Horace and so on. My sister Frances as the only girl was always *Miss*

169

Lockwood until she married the Marchese di Serrafini, that is, and became the Marchesa."

My poor sister, God help her, had married an Italian nobleman and was already, though but thirty, the mother of six children and showing no signs of stopping. However Giuseppe di Serrafini had ample means to support them all and more if necessary and, as they seemed to enjoy no end of connubial bliss in their villa in the Tuscan hills, I was happy to let them get on with it.

"Pardon, sir," Nostro bowed with just that slight lift of the left brow that was on the verge of insolence, "Mr. *Dalby*. It will be nice to see Mr. *Dalby* again, sir."

"I am not sure. I am intent on composition. I do not know that I care to be disturbed. However, he is up in the north to do a survey of the factories on behalf of his Party, I understand. He is anxious to raise the age of child labour. Always doing good, my brother Dalby, with his eye on the chance of preferment of course. He never does anything without being sure first of all that it will be recognised in the right quarters, but then that is politics is it not, Nostro? I will dine early tonight, and will hope that Mrs. Sutcliffe will be through with her tale and I have it all written down before Dalby comes to distract me."

Mrs. Sutcliffe greeted me warmly the following morning, saying she had missed me the previous day, and I told her about the visit of my brother, and she was very impressed at hearing that a Member of Parliament would soon be staying in the village. I seemed continually to bask in Dalby's reflected glory—which is why I was glad that I lived in Italy to be out of Dalby's tiresome orbit, shining brightly all the time—and her respect for me and kindness towards me, though always very marked, seemed exaggerated on that day, if I recall. But because the story did not end that day or indeed the day after but went on until the eve of Dalby's visit I shall set it down as she told it to me, without pausing because otherwise I shall never get to the end.

170

"Well, we got to the funeral of Mrs. Earnshaw," Mrs. Sutcliffe began, her embroidery growing vastly by this time, "and the silent parting of Captain Heathcliff and Mrs. Earnshaw.

"I could scarcely bear to leave my mistress there in the cold ground; she was but two and twenty and indeed seemed to have lived life enough for one three times her age. Twice married, the mistress of another, and the mother of three with but a year between each of them. And Mr. Hareton, six years her elder, seemed like an old man bent by the cares life had bestowed on him, so undeserved in my opinion. I even detected grey hairs at his temples and his back was beginning to be arched with the worry of it all.

"And indeed as one strode up the hill, and one down, on that grey day in late May with the clouds whirling across the sky giving the promise of rain, I wondered which one I should follow, for did not Roger go up the hill with his master and now what would Mr. Hareton have to say to me? Since the death of his wife he had scarcely spoken a word to anyone and none to me except to enquire if the children were well. He neither came to see them or had them brought to him.

"But the example of my mistress, in seeming to do what was best for herself and using people to her own ends, was not lost on me and I knew that Roger and the Captain would be off to the wars whereas, with a little pleading on my part, Mr. Hareton would continue to give me a warm home and enough to eat. I hastened after with him, with only a backward glance at Roger, taking care not to catch up with him before he had entered the house. And once there he shut himself up in his room and was seen by no one but his valet, for over a week.

"Thus I assumed my position was secure and resumed my care of the nursery. But, oh, how I longed for the sound of a horse's hoof on the yard and the scatter of pebbles upon the window pane that would tell me my Roger had come 'a-courtin.'

"Anthony was not a pretty baby. He was puny and dark and disagreeable and in some ways he was to con-

171

tinue like that through life, though many found him striking to look at both as a boy and as a man, particularly women, as you shall hear. But to me he was the cause of his mother's disgrace and death, albeit an unwitting one, and I could find little love in my heart for him. Rainton and Margaret were too young to know their mother or, of course, to miss her, and the joy and sunshine they brought to the house did much to gladden our hearts in the sad days and, indeed, years that followed.

"But before I talk of bringing up Master Rainton and Miss Margaret I must tell you of what happened about a week after their mother's funeral as I was nursing young Anthony and trying to get him to sleep after his feed.

"Mr. Hareton had finally emerged from his mourning and paid his first visit to the nursery where he neither smiled nor spoke but gazed at the children, shaking his head. It was then I observed how aged and changed his appearance was which I mentioned to you. He just opened the door without a word and walked in, and Rainton, indeed, seemed to regard his father as some kind of stranger and made haste to get out of his way while the baby smiled up at him from her cot, bless the darling, and held out her little hands for him to take her. But he just stood and stared and then came over to me where I was winding Anthony after his feed. Mary's milk had long given out and we fed Anthony from a bottle, there being no other wet nurse available. I often wonder too, Mr. Lockwood, if it was the lack of the breast that made Anthony such an ungrateful and difficult boy. They say it is an old wives' tale, but I have sometimes observed that children who are weaned too early before the mother has been able to feed them are often petulant and difficult and lack the warmth and lovingness of breast-fed children.

"Well, I sat there rubbing Anthony's back and gazing half fearfully at the master.

" 'It's the wind, sir,' I said by way of explanation.

" 'Does he always cry like that?' asked my master.

" 'Aye, he is not a contented baby, like his brother
172

and sister.' I looked at Mr. Hareton to see if he would object to the terms "brother" and "sister," for I wondered if the death of his wife and the sad turn of events taken had changed his mind towards the child whom he knew was not his. But not only did Mr. Earnshaw not seem to object; he smiled for the very first time since coming into the room and, bending down, took the child in his arms. Immediately Anthony stopped crying and his little eyes, scarcely focusing, seemed to gaze at Mr. Hareton as though in approval of what he saw. At that moment, I believe was born an affection which was marked for life between Anthony and the man who was not his father but whom he thought for much of the time was. In fact, Mr. Lockwood, from now on until a much later stage in my tale I shall refer to Mr. Hareton as Anthony's father for such did Anthony grow up to think of him, and for his entire years he enjoyed the enviable status of favourite child.

"However on that particular day of which I speak Mr. Hareton took Anthony in his arms for the first time since his birth and was fondling him when there was a commotion from downstairs and once again in a short space I heard the familiar tones of Captain Heathcliff shouting 'Where's Earnshaw?' I really did not know what gave that man the right to storm unbidden into someone's house and begin shouting for the owner. The very idea of it incensed me as it did my master who, giving the baby to me, moved to the door of the nursery, squaring his shoulders as he did so.

"I hastened after my master and we were both standing at the door when the Captain bounded up the stairs and strode down the corridor towards us, my Roger coming somewhat fearfully behind him.

" 'Ah, Earnshaw. There you are! I want words with you.'

"So loud was his voice that all the servants could hear it and, no doubt fearing what he would say next, Mr. Earnshaw drew him into the nursery and shut the door. Little Rainton backed against the wall in the presence of this fearful monster, and I bade him get on with building his bricks while I put young Anthony back in his crib. I was comforted by the presence of Roger, for I knew he would not let violence occur in the front of myself and the children.

" 'Now Earnshaw,' the Captain said, not giving my master the chance to utter a word. 'Where is my son? I have come for him!' My master took a deep breath and, his face as grim and forbidding as the Captain's was angry, he said:'

" *'Your* son, Captain Ibbitson? You have no son here that I know of.'

" 'Curse you, man,' cried the Captain, advancing nearer. " 'Of course I have a son. Anthony. He is my son. You know it. Look . . . this is him! My God, he is the image of me.'

"And he advanced towards the crib and bent over it, looking eagerly at the little face which did indeed resemble his in every particular, I am sorry to say. But Mr. Earnshaw stood beside him and he seemed more relaxed as he too gazed at this infant countenance.

" 'He is the son of my late wife Catherine, sir. He is her son and my son. I know of no reason why legally or morally he should be *yours*.'

"The calm words of my master and the manner of his delivery impressed themselves on the Captain who turned slowly and faced Mr. Hareton; his face, I may say, a picture of incredulity.

" 'But you know quite well he is not your son.'

" 'No I don't; why should I?'

" 'But you know that Catherine was my mistress . . .'

" *'And* my wife. I believe there is nothing you can prove as to the paternity of the child.'

"And, as though appearing to realise it for the first time, the Captain resembled one on whom a thunderbolt has unexpectedly fallen.

"He was a man not used to being thwarted.

" 'But he *looks* like me,' spluttered the Captain.

" 'He also looks like *me*,' said Mr. Hareton, unperturbed. 'I'm sure any resemblance to yourself is a mere coincidence. See, he has a broad nose, as I have . . .'

" 'And I have,' said the Captain feeling his snout, somewhat comically in my opinion.

174

" 'And my *wife* had,' Mr. Hareton replied. 'We were first cousins and shared many similar features. We have also all dark eyes, as you will observe and, as for the hair, I grant you that what there is of it *is* black, but my mother Frances Earnshaw, although I never saw her for she died shortly after I was born, had, I was told, jet black hair. So you see, Captain Ibbitson, this child has a very fair inheritance of my wife's characteristics and my own.'

"The Captain gave what I can only call an animal-like growl and seemed to perceive for the first time that his brutal strategy against my master had failed and he had underrated him. I recalled how at the Heights he had called Mr. Earnshaw a ninny and failed to learn from his mother's admonition that indeed my master was no weakling. It seemed to me that, because he had captured my mistress so easily, the Captain had nothing but contempt for the husband who had let her go, and indeed this was one of the strangest aspects about Mr. Earnshaw that I myself was at a loss to account for. All I could think of, then and afterwards, was that he knew his wife and her stubborn will too well and had let himself be conquered by it, and this had diminished him in the sight of her paramour who stood glowering before us now.

" 'You know that what you are saying is arrant nonsense,' the Captain said bitterly, but in a much more respectful tone of voice.

" 'Then what will you do about it?' Mr. Hareton said. I could see his confidence mounting with every word. 'Will you go to the law, or tell the world that you have designs on a child who is my wife's progeny and bears my name?'

" 'But you know she was not with you; she was with me!'

" 'But I believe not long enough for there to be sufficient doubt that the child *was* mine,' Mr. Earnshaw replied smoothly. 'Certainly, it never occurred to Dr. Kenneth to raise the matter. No, Anthony is my son and he bears my name and you will ruin yourself, Ibbitson, if you pursue the matter. You will be laughed to scorn.'

" 'Aye, so I hear," Mr. Hareton replied, 'and I knew your father, if indeed he was your father—for we can never be quite *certain* in these matters can we?'

"I could see that the Captain was about to take hold of Mr. Hareton's throat at this taunt, but Roger advanced and gently placed a hand on his arm restraining him, and Mr. Hareton also cautiously took a step or two back.

" 'I loved him, sir, even though in many ways he was a cruel man and debased me; but in his way I think he loved me too, although it was against his nature to do anything for me because he hated my father so much he was trying to wreck our family. I perceive that you resemble Mr. Heathcliff in this particular too, except that, to me at any rate, you do not appear to have his kindness or charm. You walk into my house as though you own it; you abuse me in front of my servants and try and run off with my newly-born son. You seem to be doing everything you can to debase me and my family too, and to this end you bewitched my wife. I see you are motivated by evil designs against my family, sir, and I ask you to be gone and never trouble us again.'

"I could see that the Captain was battling with himself, for his face worked with emotion; but, for the moment at any rate, he had lost, and turning on his heel he strode to the door. Then turning and motioning to Roger he addressed his last words to my master.

" 'We are joined in battle, Earnshaw, you and I; and don't forget I am a fighting man and you have not heard the last of me. For you have my son and I'll not forget it. I loved Catherine with the kind of love you cannot comprehend, and she returned my love and she gave me a child to remember her by. On her deathbed she told me Anthony was my son, and I know it; I can see it with my own eyes. If I hadn't been a cross fool I would have taken her with me when she begged me; but I wouldn't. I was too sure of myself, and of her. I did not reckon that her enormous strength was also her weakness and that her love for me was so powerful that without me she couldn't live. She told me I gave her life, and I did. You watched her die, Earnshaw, and I'll never forget that either. You *allowed* her to die and, in as much as you did that, you killed her as though you had plunged a knife into her breast.'

" 'Aye, I am my father's son and Catherine was her mother's daughter and mortals like you have no place in the spheres of folk such as we.'

" 'But never rest in your bed easily for one moment, Earnshaw. Never think that I have forgotten or that too much time has gone past. For I will remember, Earnshaw, and I will be back!'

"And with that he strode from the room and Roger after him, with never a backward glance at me.

"Now that he had left I could see the effect on my master who had grown pale and stared fixedly at the shut door. I went up to him and looked into his eyes.

" 'Sir? Mr. Hareton? Are you all right?' He didn't see me for a while. He was still looking at the door, no doubt still seeing that huge evil man standing there, or maybe he was following him out of the house and up to Wuthering Heights in his mind's eye. Then he shook his head as though blotting out the awful picture and looked at me.

" 'Ah, Agnes. Yes, I'm all right. I'm not afraid of Ibbitson, or Heathcliff, as he now calls himself. *If* God is good he will be killed in the wars. If he is spared he cannot live with a grudge for the rest of his life . . . even *if* he *is* his father's son.'

"And with that he left the room and me to my charges. But you see, don't you, Mr. Lockwood, that Mr. Hareton had learned nothing from all those years that Heathcliff mourned Catherine and steadily set about the ruin of the Earnshaws and the Lintons. We of all people should have known the passion that lurked in the Heathcliff heart, the evil that possessed its mind; and he of all men should have realised that when the Captain said he would take his revenge he meant it.

"You can imagine how sad I was for the rest of that

177

day and how worried about my responsibilities; but above all my heart grieved for my love, Roger, with whom I had not exchanged a word since the funeral. And now that my master and his were locked in mortal enmity what hope was there of the wedding he had so gaily talked about the winter before?

"I was still sorrowing late that night and sitting up in the nursery with the candles lit because Margaret was teething and was restless when suddenly there was a scatter of stones on the window pane and, my heart lurching with joy, I ran to it and unhasping it saw my Roger in the court below beckoning to me to come down.

" 'I cannot,' I whispered as loud as I dared. 'Come up, through the kitchen. I will meet thee on the stairs.'

"I need not tell you my emotion as I strode out into the corridor, the candle lit, and saw my eager young love appear at the top of the staircase and run lightly towards me, clasping me in his arms so tight he would have stifled the life out of me.

"I then drew him into the room, but he continued kissing me so that the candle almost fell from my hands.

" 'Oh Roger,' I gasped when he would let me, 'oh, what is to become of thee and me?'

" 'We can be wed,' Roger said slyly, 'and I can leave thee a reminder of me as my master left thy late mistress!'

" 'Oh, do not talk so!' I said crossly and pushed him off. 'Thou thinkest I would want *that*—with three motherless bairns here needing me, and thou in France and no one to look after me or care.'

" 'But I want thee, Agnes, for my wife, and one day . . .'

" 'Oh how can it be?' I said sadly. 'Thy master and mine will never tolerate sight of the other again.'

" 'Then I will leave the Army in due course like I said and thou wilt leave the Grange. Nay, Agnes; thou dost owe them nothing. We will do our duty by our masters. Dost want to be like thy aunt and lose the chance of bearing children because of thy service to a family who forget it as soon as thou dost turn thy back?'

" 'Aye,' I said, remembering that love my Aunt Nelly had for children and how she was too old to have her own when she finally wed. 'Happen when you come back we will do that and the children will be older then and I can leave them. But oh thy master today . . .'

"Roger laughed.

" 'I'm used to him. They call him "the devil" in the army. 'Tis his nickname. They say he rides rougher, swears harder and wenches longer than anyone else; and that he is a clever shot too and a neat swordsman. He is a cruel man, a harsh man. He gets obedience out of those under him because they know he will show no mercy. But he is fair too and won't ask anyone to do anything he won't do. I have seen him ride until the rest of the troops drop. And because I am loyal to him he is good to me and will see I come to no harm; this is what thou dost want in a commander, Agnes. Survival depends on't.'

" 'You see, the Captain has grown up at public school and in the Army. He and Mr. Earnshaw have nought in common, except love for the same pretty woman! And the Captain was bound to win. He means to, and he always does.'

" 'But will he keep up this idea of revenge?'

" 'Oh, aye. He'll find a time during campaigns and come up here and plague Mr. Earnshaw like he promised and, Agnes, you see he is right. We *know* Anthony is his son, don't we? And so does Mr. Earnshaw. That's it; the Captain is always right and I have never known him act unfairly if he is wrong.'

" 'Mr. Earnshaw is getting his own back,' I said unhappily. " 'He knows the Captain can't prove it.'

" 'Yes, but he is *wrong;* it is not his son.'

" 'But what would the Captain do with his son?'

"My love caught me in his arms and tried to undo my bodice which I would not allow with the children in the room—much as I yearned for him and his impa-

179

tient wooing—so I pushed him away, reluctantly I'll admit.

" 'That's not the point,' Roger said. 'What he would do with him is not the point, as he explained to me. It is *his* son. As a matter of fact I think he would have left him with his mother and then they would both have let Mr. Hareton alone. He has his own bairns and he could have wed again. But now he's landed himself a heap of trouble and the Captain will never let go. I know him. Now let us lie on the bed and have a kiss.'

" 'Nay I cannot,' I protested. 'Not with the children. 'T'ain't decent.'

" 'They'll not see.'

" 'No Roger, I cannot.'

" 'But tomorrow we're going.'

" 'I can't,' I said. 'The children will worry us and I will feel ashamed.'

"Oh, I wanted to give myself so much to that young warrior, so straight and handsome he looked in the candlelight; but when passion conflicted with duty I knew what to do and *this* is more than I can say of my late lamented mistress, which is happen why she is in her grave these thirty years and I am still alive. I have always done my duty, Mr. Lockwood, and I'm proud to say it."

"Well my lover went and Captain Heathcliff went and neither of them were heard of again for years until everyone had forgotten about them and the feud that the Captain had pledged himself to keep alive.

"But someone who had not quitted the district was the Captain's mother, Mrs. Ibbitson; but all I knew was that she came regularly in May and left in September. I never had sight nor sound of her and neither had Mr. Earnshaw who, deciding to leave well alone, did nothing to injure or aggravate her as long as she paid her rent regularly through Mr. Green which she did. He even consented to renew her tenancy which, in view of what was to happen, was perhaps the most foolish thing he ever did. I think that he reckoned, as he grew older, that the past was forgotten and the least said soonest mended. Indeed Mrs. Ibbitson troubled us not, at least until Margaret was older and we have not reached that point yet.

"What can I say about those years, following the death of their mother, except that the children, well cared for and nourished, grew from young saplings into fine trees. Margaret was a winsome beauty from very tender years, loving, eager and anxious to please and be pleased. Rainton did not have quite her charm; but he was a handsome lad, tall for his age and taking after his father both in looks and manners. And what can I say about the cuckoo in the nest, young Anthony? Except that he grew up as unlike the other two to look at as chalk is from cheese and that he seemed, in my eyes at any rate, to have neither charm nor a happy disposition. He was sulky if thwarted, demanding if gratified so that you could never satisfy him, and utterly ungrateful for anything that was done. I never heard the words 'thank you' pass his lips and he was as cordially disliked by all the servants, who at one time or another managed to offend him, as Margaret and Rainton were loved.

"It was an unfortunate situation. Yet I can honestly say that although Anthony's behaviour was vexatious in all those years that I was their nursemaid it never disrupted what was a well-run household; Mr. Hareton, that conscientious father, that good man, saw to that. And the second extraordinary thing was the tender love which Mr. Hareton bore for Anthony and which, as far as Anthony could demonstrate any tender emotion, was honestly reciprocated. Margaret also loved her younger brother to the obvious detriment of Rainton who, though he was the legitimate heir, grew up with the feelings of inferiority that should, in justice, have been accorded to Anthony. Rainton had a lovely nature, perhaps just because he had to work so hard for any love from his closest relations. Any pleasant word they said to him gratified him so much that it was pathetic to see his joy, and he was forever doing little acts that would find favour with them, any of them, including the ungrateful Anthony who wielded the power of an elder, not a younger, sibling.

"Mr. Hareton was away a good deal and the care of the children was left entirely in my hands and I was given the help of a junior nursemaid. As I was not a learned woman the children, as they grew older, received lessons from Mrs. Tinkler, a widowed gentlewoman who was fetched every morning by the pony cart from Gimmerton. Thus it was that at an exceptionally early age Margaret and Rainton were able both to read and write, which is more than I can say of myself to this day, Mr. Lockwood, except in a most rudimentary fashion, letters and the like. Margaret proved herself a veritable bookworm, as I believe her mother was and her grandmother before her; but Rainton was a slow scholar, preferring the outdoors and taking a particular interest in the glories of nature and the wonders of animal life, so that soon he could name every shrub or flower that grew in the park, every tree and every bird that flew.

"Anthony was none of these things; nothing seemed of particular interest to Anthony unless it was the satisfaction of his own needs and the doing of his own will. Of course he was younger than the other two and, consequently, his sister seemed to feel, in need of her special care and protection. But what he lacked in scholarship he made up for in cleverness and cunning and I think that if his life had not been so sadly thwarted he would have made a good lawyer or politician, being naturally devious and unscrupulous by nature—present company always excepted of course, Mr. Lockwood, by which I mean your distinguished brother Mr. Dalby.

"So the years passed and we were snug and quite unaware for the most part of the events that were taking place abroad in the struggle against France and Emperor Napoleon. I say for the most part because, of course, we were not *altogether* ignorant, for Mr. Hareton's business interests now frequently took him to London—where some said he had a lady friend though I never knew the truth of it, and indeed I wished with all my heart he would find someone nice and suitable and marry again but he never did.

"The Earnshaw women seemed to exercise a truly fatal attraction on their men when you think of Mr. Heathcliff pining for his Catherine for all those years, and Mr. Edgar the same. And now in the next generation Mr. Hareton could not rid himself of the memory of his wife and, when he was at home, he never missed his weekly visit to the grave or the chance to talk about her with me when he would come and play with the children.

"And in many ways Mr. Hareton was a *contented* man. That haunted, elderly look had long since left him. He was adding to his lands and now owned a good part of Gimmerton and beyond and, I believe, his business interests were very extensive indeed and included coal, iron, wool, canals and the new railways which were just being talked about then. He took an active part in civic and philanthropic affairs, and above all he was devoted to his children. And how they loved him in return; how eagerly they ran to greet him when his carriage drew up outside the front porch after one of his journeys! And he would hug them and swing them up, kissing them, and then his servant would divulge a bagful of goodies.

"One day, a good many years after the death of Mrs. Earnshaw, when Margaret was about ten and it was a fine spring morning with the park ablaze with daffodils and the trees bending under the masses of tight new buds, Mr. Hareton came into the nursery, or playroom as we later called it, the children being busy in the schoolroom with Mrs. Tinkler. Mr. Hareton strode to the window and looked out.

" 'A fine day Agnes, but I never see a day like this without being sad. Do you remember your mistress?'

" 'Aye, well I do sir.'

" 'It was on a day like this in May that she died if you remember.'

"I didn't say anything but bustled about with my tasks.

" 'Tell me Agnes did you ever hear again of that man, Roger, the servant of Ibbitson who courted you?'

183

"Now whether this was an indirect way of finding out whether I knew ought about the Captain I know not, for I would not have the temerity to question my master, so I said what was the truth.

" 'Nay, sir. I never heard a word from that day to this.'

" 'It's nearly ten years, Agnes.'

" 'Aye it is.' I swallowed hard and just the mention of his name made my eyes swell with tears. 'And long since married I've no doubt, or killed in the wars.'

" 'Goodness, how the time flies,' Mr. Hareton continued. 'And will you never have a mind to wed Agnes?'

" 'No,' I said not wishing to discuss the matter. 'I will not. I have my duties here, and well content with them. And you're one who can talk, Mr. Earnshaw, if I may say so; a fine man like you must have every marriageable woman's eye upon you!'

" 'Oh, I've enough to do.' Mr. Hareton turned to me and smiled. 'I am not without lady companions from time to time you know, when I go to London, to mix a little pleasure with business; but a replacement to Mrs. Earnshaw, never. No, I feel I have a full life and what man could wish for three more handsome children?'

"Indeed, sometimes I wondered if Mr. Earnshaw forgot that Anthony was not his real son, so readily did he include him with the other two. Just then they rushed into the playroom, their morning's lessons finished, and Margaret and Rainton gave cries of joy at seeing their father while Anthony stood pouting on the threshold causing himself, as always, to be the object of attention for being different. I could see Mr. Hareton's eyes raised above the heads of the others looking for the youngest.

" 'Ah, Anthony, why don't you come and greet your Papa. Are you not well?'

"And, careless of the kisses of Margaret and Rainton, Mr. Hareton walked quickly to the door and bent down solicitously.

" 'Tell Papa, darling boy, what ails thee?'

184

" 'I have a headache,' said Anthony petulantly and drew his hand across his forehead in the artificial gesture I was well accustomed to, but which always deceived his father.

" 'Oh, my darling, you're working too hard. I must talk to Mrs. Tinkler and see that she is not forcing you to keep up with the others. Come into the garden with Papa. Maybe the fresh breeze will do you good.' And putting his arm round his darling and without a backward glance at the other two he strolled with his youngest son down the stairs and out into the park.

"It was not the first time or the last that something like that happened and what I always found remarkable was the fact that the other two took it in such good part; but that day I remember thinking that, for once, Rainton did look rather angrily after his father and why I recall that day so well and can pass the events in detail on to you is because it was the day that, inspired by my master's queries, I made a decision that was to have consequences that a poor serving woman like me could never have foreseen."

Chapter 11

"You can imagine with what trepidation, with what memories I climbed the hill towards the house I had not set eyes on for nigh ten years. Neither the Heights nor its inhabitants were ever mentioned at the Grange and indeed the older children were unaware of its existence. Unlike her mother and grandmother Margaret had no yearnings for the moors, but preferred playing with her dolls or reading books or looking after her little brother Anthony whom she idolised quite as much as her father. She was, indeed, a very *motherly* kind of girl—warm, loving, and compassionate.

"No, if anyone liked the out of doors it was Rainton, who was quite the little naturalist and it was he who had to be restrained from wandering too far afield and he was forbidden to leave the confines of the Park under any circumstances unaccompanied. Sometimes their father would take the children onto the moors when they went to visit their mother's grave; but he took care never to let them climb up too far so that their curiosity was aroused by the house in the cleft of the hill.

"So I can say that those ten years passed with very little thought either of the house or its past being allowed to creep into my memory.

"And here I was on a fine May morning about to see the woman who, indirectly, had caused my mistress's death so many years before. As I walked I noticed the small wild primroses and violets nestling in the ditches, and the swifts darting about over the high moors telling us that winter was indeed past and summer about to come.

"I knew that Mrs. Ibbitson had arrived, for otherwise I should have thought the house empty—there was no bustle in the forecourt or smoke issuing from the chimney. But as soon as I lifted the clasp on the gate the front door opened and Jeannie her maid stood there eyeing me suspiciously. Then my heart began to pound in the presence of her hostile stare and I wished I could turn and run back the way I had come.

" 'What dost want?' said Jeannie without greeting.

" 'I wish to see thy mistress,' I replied. 'Is she within?'

"Without further words Jeannie, who no doubt had been watching my approach from a window, shut the door and left me standing wondering what I should do; but after a few minutes the door opened again and in her far from friendly fashion, she indicated that I should go inside.

"Her mistress sat in the front sitting room doing her crochet work. I marked she was as fine as ever though her hair was practically white. Her figure was good and she sat erectly in a high-backed chair by the window, the fire unlit in the grate. I thought maybe after all it was she who had watched my approach. As I went in she neither looked up nor ceased her sewing and, feeling awkward and ill at ease, I stood first on one leg then on another while Jeannie stood watching me with an expression of malevolent satisfaction on her face.

" 'Well, Agnes Dean,' her mistress said at last, still without looking at me. 'What brings you here after all these years? Are you seeking a position, maybe, as confidential lady's maid?' I noted the scorn in her

voice, for my face burned, and I decided that she had
forgotten nothing about my mistress's escape or liked
me any better than she had.

" 'No, ma'am. I wondered if . . . if you had word of
Roger, ma'am.'

" 'Roger?'

" 'Your son . . . Captain Heathcliff's servant.'

" 'Oh, *Roger*,' said the lady in a very different tone,
settling back and looking directly at me for the first
time. 'Yes I have news of Roger. Why do you ask?'

" 'Oh, ma'am,' my words came tumbling out with relief. Then he was not dead! 'He took a fancy to me,
you know, and I did hope in all these years I might
have heard a word; but I know that he can neither
read nor write and . . .'

"Mrs. Ibbitson's face softened and she smiled
sweetly.

" 'All these years and you wondered about your
sweetheart. Poor girl.'

"She stood up and came over to me, indicating to
Jeannie that she should leave us alone by a toss of the
head in the direction of the door. But knowing how
sneaky Jeannie was I had no doubt she would be listening at the keyhole. Mrs. Ibbitson looked into my
face, standing close, and I noticed how her face was
powdered and rouged, and the fine lines on either side
of her eye and the deep furrows by her mouth and I
decided that she had aged and had suffered a good deal
in these intervening years. But her eyes, which were of
a curious violet colour, were clear and sparkled, and in
them there was a strange expression as she said:

" 'And all these years I wondered about my grandson, Anthony, Agnes Dean; so I know well how you
feel. Tell me about him.'

"I was so abashed that I nearly sank to the floor. I
had of course forgotten that she was Anthony's grandmother, so used was I to regarding him as a member of
the family, Mr. Hareton's own son. Maybe if I had
thought of Mrs. Ibbitson as Anthony's grandmother I
would not have made the journey.

189

" 'Why ma'am, he is a fine lad . . . tall, dark like the Ca . . . like you, ma'am,' I faltered not knowing how to choose my words. 'Bright, strong willed . . .'

" 'I would like to see him, Agnes.'

"She looked at me and held my gaze until I was forced to lower my eyes in confusion.

" 'Will you bring him to me? And then I will tell you all you want to know about Roger.'

"So that was it! I had been tricked and deceived! Oh, how like someone connected with the name of Heathcliff to behave dishonourably.

" 'Oh, I don't mean for *good*, girl!' Perceiving my apprehension, Mrs. Ibbitson laughed. 'Just for a visit. I promise you no one will know of it, if you can contrive it from your end. I can send a gig for you, if that's what's bothering you; pick you up outside the wall. Will you do it, Agnes? Let me have a sight of my grandson?'

"Her voice was so sweet and plaintive and urgent that I felt myself compelled to grant her request; besides that, I did want to know about Roger and how his feelings were towards me. I had waited so long, never looking at another.

"I often feel, Mr. Lockwood, that where my Aunt Nelly was of a very clear, quick-thinking turn of mind I am muddled and weak; prey first to the command of one then of another. I knew I would give in to her request even though something inside me told me I should have to deceive Mr. Hareton to do it and this I did not want. My aunt would have gone straight to him with the problem; but not I.

" 'If I can manage it, ma'am.'

" 'Oh, I'm sure you can, Agnes. I hear Mr. Earnshaw is grown very prosperous and is often away. Maybe then; send me a message and I'll send the gig. Bring the other two. I'd like to see all Catherine's children.'

" 'About Roger, ma'am, could you not . . .' but already she was steering me to the door.

" 'When we meet again, Agnes. Let it be soon.' "

190

"Well, you can imagine how I felt, knowing that I had done something I should not have done and wondering where it would lead me. Every time I looked at Mr. Earnshaw I felt guilty and the blood rushed to my face; but I knew that I was too curious about the man I'd loved—the only man I'd loved—and that I would comply.

"And so a few days later when Mr. Earnshaw went to London I sent her a note by one of the younger men-servants who I trusted to keep quiet and, later on in the day, I took the children to the back gate of the Park and there I waited for the cart I had asked her to send to pick us up. The children were agog with excitement and I told them that they should not tell anyone about this expedition or it would never happen again.

"They left the Grange but rarely. I thought it was a pity for children to grow up so remote from their own kind; but their mother had before them, being taught by Mr. Edgar. Sometimes I wished their father would remove them all to London, or to some city where they could lead more of a normal life, having a town house and lots of friends. I knew he could well afford it; but whenever I spoke to him of their isolation he told me that they were fortunate to have such a nice house in such a fine park with a governess and nursemaid, which is more than what he had as a boy, and we would leave it at that.

" 'And who is Mrs. Ibbitson, Agnes?' Margaret enquired as the trap set off up the hill.

" 'An old friend of your father's and your mama, too.'

" 'And has she just come to the district?'

" 'Ask no questions and I'll tell ye no lies,' I said, 'look yonder, see how fine the view is.' And I diverted her attention while Rainton gazed eagerly about him noting the wild flowers and the birds who soared overhead.

" 'Agnes, look!' He pointed excitedly upwards to where a large bird circled over the crest of the moors. 'See the curlew! I have but rarely seen one in the park; they like high open spaces; oh I wonder if there is a nest there. I must ask Papa to take me more often on the moors.'

"And my heart sank, I can tell you, as I wondered what I had let us all in for.

"But soon we were in calling distance of the house and Margaret and Rainton exclaimed and marvelled at the sight of such a splendid place all alone on the top of the moors, and I knew that this would never be kept from their father who would hold me responsible for the disruption of their domestic harmony. And then I saw Mrs. Ibbitson at the gate waving and as we drew nearer she hurried forward, her eyes scanning each young face; but of course it was not necessary, for the identity of her grandchild was obvious. To me he was the one who had taken least notice of anything about him; least interest in the expedition; and who was looking around for something to complain about which would give him the chance to sulk for the rest of the day.

" 'Welcome, welcome,' called Mrs. Ibbitson and, as the trap stopped, she held out her arms towards Anthony. 'Come darling, let me help you down. I can see you are the baby. Oh dear, have I said something? Shall I help your sister first as she is a girl?'

"And she turned to Margaret perceiving that she had said something to upset her darling and, indeed, I knew that she had given him the cause for complaint that he had been looking for and that he would now go into one of his moods.

"But I was mistaken. I had reckoned without the charm of his grandmother, or maybe it was the blood bond, I know not. I think Anthony was merely abashed at being called the baby for he jumped down after his sister and then when Mrs. Ibbitson turned to him he allowed her to kiss his cheek and solemnly shake him by the hand.

" 'And your name is?'

" 'Anthony, ma'am, Anthony Earnshaw. I am nine years old.'

" 'Oh Anthony, what a pet you are. And this big boy is Rainton. And Margaret, you are a beauty! I knew your dear Mama and you are so like her, is she not Agnes? And Rainton, you are just like your Papa. Do you know that you were here years ago but you have forgotten it. You were tiny babies.'

" 'In this house?' asked Rainton wide-eyed, and I well recalled the circumstances of that visit for it not only cemented the bond between my mistress and the Captain, but also it was the beginning of the attraction between Roger and me.

" 'Yes, darling, with your Mama and Papa, and little Anthony was not yet born. Not yet *thought* of, was he Agnes?'

" 'No, ma'am,' I replied feeling uneasy; but she led us into the sitting room where a table was set with goodies enough to delight the heart of any small child and Jeannie came forward with, for once, a pleasant expression on her face and was told to start feeding them while Mrs. Ibbitson had words with me. So, after a while and some more talk and questions to the children, she drew me aside and took me into the garden where the lupins and marigold and rhododendrons were in bloom and the red-currant bushes giving off their heady lingering perfume which is always summer to me.

" 'Well, Agnes, you kept your bargain, and I'll keep mine. But tell me first, how is Mr. Earnshaw with Anthony?' and her eyes eagerly searched mine.

" 'Why, ma'am, he loves him as his own. He always has done. Indeed he prefers Anthony to the other two. I know not why, but 'tis the truth, ma'am.'

" 'He's a lovely boy,' Mrs. Ibbitson exclaimed proudly. 'I can see why he is the apple of Mr. Earnshaw's eye; he is so quick and intelligent compared to that Rainton who looks dull-witted to me.'

" 'Nay, ma'am,' I protested, 'that is not true! Rainton has a lovely nature; he is kind and cheerful and loving . . .'

" 'No doubt Anthony is those things as well,' said his grandmother fondly and I realised how the ties of blood do blind people so that they can see only those things they wish to behold. She instinctively preferred

193

Anthony because he was her grandson. To compare the two, Mr. Lockwood, anyone else would go for Rainton because he *looked* cheerful and happy and healthy and his outgoing nature was such a contrast to that of the surly Anthony.

" 'Anyway, ma'am,' I said, 'now that I have done as you bid can you not tell me about Roger?'

" 'Yes, Agnes,' Mrs. Ibbitson drew me to a bench in the shade, 'but I want you to promise me something else!'

"Oh, how my heart quailed because I knew that indeed I had set my foot in a trap from which she would not lightly free me.

" 'And that is, ma'am?'

" 'I want to see Anthony more often. I want you to bring him to me whenever you can. Will you Agnes? I have small consolation in my old age. Will you do this for an old woman?'

"Really I was not deceived because by my reckoning she had a good few years of life in her yet, but I nodded my head thinking that maybe when Mr. Hareton heard about this adventure he would dismiss me and the matter would be out of my hands.

" 'Good girl,' Mrs. Ibbitson clasped my hand. 'Now Agnes you have not heard from Roger since 1806?'

" 'No ma'am.'

" 'Well he is alive and well and, like my son, has covered himself in glory in the wars. I too have not heard from my son for a long time, months not years, nor have I seen him since he embarked for Portugal in 1808 with his regiment.'

" 'Although he was a man of great capabilities my son was extraordinarily fortunate for, in his very first engagement in Portugal in 1809, his commander was Sir Arthur Wellesley who is now the great Duke of Wellington. It was at the Battle of Oporto, and my son fought with such distinction that he came to the attention of one of the officers close to Sir Arthur who brought him to the notice of the great man.'

" 'Although in many things Jack is reckless, in war he is disciplined though fearless and these qualities

194

commended themselves to Sir Arthur who admired good soldierly qualities when he saw them and saw that he fought near him in all his major campaigns.'

" 'And so Jack has gone from glory to glory through Portugal and Spain fighting at Burgos and Badajoz— names that will mean nothing to you, girl—Salamanca and finally at the decisive battle at Vitoria in June 1813. Jack pressed on into France with Wellington's Army until the victory and then he was due to come home last year, but he went back to Spain as part of the Duke's diplomatic mission and now he is with the Army in Flanders; but I expect him home later in the year and what then I know not, whether he will continue in the Army or stay here. I think he will find it difficult to accommodate to civilian life.'

" 'And all the time Roger has served him faithfully as his servant, many times fighting in the thick of battle and Jack says never had a man more faithful a servant or more loyal.'

"My eyes had long since filled with tears at the thought of all the hardship in the hot Spanish sun my Roger had had to endure, but my heart too was proud that he had covered himself with glory and perhaps in all this had remained steadfast and had not forgotten me.

"Before I could ask Mrs. Ibbitson more, the children, having eaten their fill under the watchful eye of Jeannie, ran into the garden where my lady set about making friends of them all which was not difficult as, with the exception of Anthony, they responded to love and kindness; but even Anthony seemed to be drawn, albeit unknowingly, to his grandmother and I had seldom seen him so companionable, friendly and, well, at home.

"Soon the time came for departure and after I had give my promise to return as often as I could we were waved off fondly from the gate."

"And how, you might ask, did Mr. Earnshaw react to the news of the meeting? Well a most extraordinary thing occurred which meant that the report I gave him coincided not only with his arrival home after an absence of many weeks, but also with the news of the glorious battle at Waterloo in June where the Duke had trounced the Emperor Napoleon and sent him packing for good. He told us all London was hopping with the news and the balls and parties had delayed his return home.

"So that when, not wishing him to hear it from any lips other than my own, I told him of the visit to Anthony's grandmother, he cried.

" 'Why Agnes, that was a capital idea! So many years have passed that I'm sure the two families no longer bear rancour towards each other—I know I don't. Indeed London is buzzing with the fame of Colonel Heathcliff, as he has become. He is rumoured to be in one of the close circles around the saviour of our nation, the Duke himself. I'm sure the Colonel, covered in medals and glory, will have no mind to an idle threat made over ten years ago. I'm not one to brood on past misdeeds and seek revenge, and what he did to me would still make me reluctant to welcome him to my house; but I daresay if he put in an appearance I would be magnanimous.'

"I might say that in all these years Mr. Earnshaw had never again referred to Anthony as being the son of anyone but himself, and I, knowing my place, would of course never refer to it either. So it lay unspoken between us, and I only hoped for all our sakes that the Colonel would be as magnanimous towards my kind master as Mr. Earnshaw was prepared to be towards him.

" 'We can thank God, Agnes,' my master continued, 'that Boney has been despatched once and for all—this time they are putting many leagues between him and his native France. There will be no escape a second time. It has been a bad time for business, a bad time for the country. These long years of war with France and recently with America have drained this country of its wealth and resources. We had no outlet for our goods, no opportunities for trade; that and an impotent government at home since Pitt died has reduced this

196

country to a sad state. Now we shall see a resurgence of British vigour unparalleled in history for it is we, and we alone, who have brought Bonaparte to his knees and that is mainly thanks to the Duke of Wellington and the icy snows of Russia. God be praised for them both.'

"But although we were indeed thankful for the Peace, and I doubt that you were born at the time, Mr. Lockwood, or maybe only just, we also had a lot of suffering at home. The factories were expanding and people were being forced off the land to work in them and the conditions were awful, I can tell you. They're not much better now but then they were terrible. There were riots worse here in the North than anywhere else and the machinery was broken and men not only flogged and deported but hanged an' all. I recall a young lad not sixteen being hanged in these parts and calling for his ma to save him he was that tiny, being underdeveloped from lack of food. It was a terrible time because the old order was broken up and people no longer knew their place or where they belonged, and those in authority were awful mean and cruel, or so it seemed to us folk. But thank God, nothing much changed at Thrushcross Grange where we all knew our stations in life and were content with them. And no one could have wished for a better or kinder master than Mr. Earnshaw and a further example of how good he was I will give you in an instant.

"A few weeks after Waterloo there was a commotion one morning in the yard and, because we lived a peaceful life with not many visitors, my heart beat quicker for hearing the horses' hooves, for I wondered if, released from the wars, my Roger had come home to me. I looked out of the window and saw to my consternation that it was my younger brother Will who is a farrier in the village and works near my mother's home. Will had borrowed one of his master's horses and as I looked out of the window I could see him talking to one of the servants.

" 'Will,' I called, opening the window, 'what is't with thee? Is Mother all right?'

"Will looked up at me and I could see his face was grave.

" 'Thou art to come quickly, lass. Thy lover is returned and is gravely ill.'

"Oh, I can't tell you the dread in my heart as he uttered those terrible words. I rushed into Mr. Earnshaw who, happily, was working in his study and asked permission to return with my brother which of course he gave me and then, before minutes were passed, I was in the saddle behind Will and we were galloping for dear life across the park towards Gimmerton, me without even asking Will what had occurred. I hung on to him and prayed with all my might that Roger would not die before I could get to him.

"Such was the speed of Will's horse that within half an hour we were outside Roger's cottage, which lies in the next village to Gimmerton and, trying to keep my face smiling and stifling the dread in my heart, I rushed into the main room where a bed had been made for Roger, and where he lay, his eyes closed, his face deathly pale. His mother ran to me and clasped my arm, telling me that since he returned with a fever Roger had done nothing but call my name, but she feared he would not know me. I smiled at her to try and cheer her and took my place by the bedside. Indeed, judging by the colour of his countenance, I believed it to be his deathbed.

"He was so thin and haggard you would have thought he had marched for weeks and then, to my grief, I saw that his left arm had been severed just below the shoulder and the stub was covered with bloody bandages. He looked like a man who would never see youth again and there were flecks of grey in his brown curly hair, and him not yet thirty! Oh, I cursed the war which had reduced him to this state and Colonel Heathcliff for ever letting him get this way. My heart was full of hate and resentment as I sat by the bedside of my beloved, not only that day but many more, as he wavered between life and death bathing his face and, when necessary, dressing his awful wound.

"But I think I knew he would recover when at last

198

he recognised me, after calling my name continually and being told I was by his side, and he gave me a smile of such joy and relief that for the first time in many days I allowed myself to cry and buried my head on his chest. And, as though comforted by my presence, he fell into the first natural sleep he had had. Dr. Kenneth who had looked after him well, God bless that good old man although his bill, I know, was being paid by Mr. Earnshaw, told me one day the crisis was past and Roger would get well. Gradually Roger took a little solid food and some wine that Mr. Earnshaw had sent for him, and Mrs. Ibbitson sent food too for she had been told of the poor condition in which her son's trusted servant had arrived home.

"One day Roger opened his eyes and they were so clear and free from suffering and the shadow of death that had hovered round him constantly that I clasped him in my arms again and wept.

" 'Eh, lass,' he said speaking in strong, clear tones for the first time, 'art thou here yet? Hast no work to do?'

" 'Oh, Roger,' I cried, 'dost thou not know we nearly lost thee? Not once but a hundred times? How could I leave thee? Mr. Earnshaw has seen that the children are well taken care of and has told me to remain with thee as long as I am needed. All thy sisters are away and thy mother was sorely pressed.'

" 'Nay, lass,' Roger said smiling, 'I was but teasing thee. Well have I minded thou wert by my side, and grateful I am to thee for it,' and he gave me the first kiss I had received from him in nearly ten years and, weak and feeble as he yet was, it was good. After a while he was able to talk more and remember what had happened and this is the story he told.

" 'Thou hast heard how well Colonel Heathcliff did in the war; a right brave soldier but not a foolhardy one. It was this that brought him to the attention of the Duke who said that gallant men were fools. He liked men who were brave but also careful. He was a very strict disciplinarian, was the Duke, or Sir Arthur, as we called him in the old days "Wor Arthur" we used to say among ourselves because, although he was not a man you could love, being too keen on hanging and flogging among the lower ranks for any lapse of discipline however slight, he was a man you could respect. For he cared for his troops and lived like them, sharing their hardship. He saw that they were all well fed and provisioned as he could and when you saw the state of the Spanish troops or the Frenchies you realised what a lot we had to be grateful to "Wor Arthur" for.'

" 'I was there when he first came to the Peninsula as commanding officer and the sad state of the men, officers as well as ranks, was unworthy of the British Army. We'd fought with Sir John Moore until we had our backs to the sea at Corunna, and we knew what war was about, I can tell thee. But Sir Arthur changed the Army completely, making it into a first-rate fighting force. Of course the Colonel was a very junior officer in those times and although he had money his class made it difficult to get much higher, for most of the officers in the Guards were of nobility or gentry. But Sir Arthur was not impressed solely by birth and he early on saw the merit of Heathcliff especially in the battles we fought in Portugal and Spain, Vimeiro, Badajoz, Albiera, Salamanca and the great final battle at Vitoria.'

" 'Colonel Heathcliff was always in the thick of the fight, where he was most needed and thou never saw anything so cool and capable in thy life. He always saw that his men were safe and had the least casualties—and I tell thee I have seen Wellington weep when the list of casualties was brought to him—and he always praised my master for his coolness and care when many an officer threw his men into the fray regardless.'

" 'And I was always there along with him, of course, seeing to his care and fighting by his side. Many was the time he saved my life and I like to think that once or twice I saved his, or helped to prevent him coming to harm. Like Wellington, who also was always in the front line, my master seemed to have a sort of divine guidance, for he was never hurt or injured in any way while those about him fell like ninepins. At Waterloo

200

almost all Wellington's suite were injured in some way except him, and he was right up in the front line along with his men.'

" 'Well, after Boney was sent to Elba the Duke left the Army and became something of a diplomat I understand and that was the first time he and my master had been parted, for my master stayed to command his troops. I well recall how moved the Duke was to bid my master farewell and he embraced him which I have seldom seen him do, for the Duke abhors any display of emotion or affection and couldn't abide the Frenchies who were always hugging and kissing. After a time my master was sent for to join the Duke's entourage in Spain. Well, before very long as you know, Boney escaped and the Army encamped first at Quatre Bras outside Brussels then at the village of Waterloo. This the Duke chose because it had a hill there, Mont St. Jean, and gave a view of the surrounding plain, which the next day included the French Army taking up its position with much pomp and playing of marches. I was with my master who was alongside the Duke at the time and I recall the Duke chuckling and saying that we could clearly see the position of all the best units like the Imperial Guard and the Polish Lancers, first rate corps used by Napoleon in his campaign. Indeed for the first and last time in my life I saw the Emperor himself, a little fellow riding on his famous white horse, Marengo. One of the gunners asked the Duke permission to pick off Boney, he was so near, but the Duke ticked him off right and good and proper, saying that it was not the business of opposing commanders to assassinate one another. The Duke was a real gentleman and that was more than you could say of Napoleon.'

" 'Oh, it was a tense business waiting for the start of the battle. It had rained all the previous night and was a grey and cheerless day and the gun teams had their guns into position—the ground was that sodden. We were not afraid because we had Wellington with us, even though we knew that our Army was much smaller than Napoleon's and we had no notion where the Prus-

201

sian Army, who were to come to our help but had been dispersed by the French at Ligny, were.'

" 'For five hours we lay facing each other, Wellington testy and anxious for news of Blücher and the Prussians, so much so that he snapped at Lord Uxbridge which was a thing I had seldom seen him do before a battle where he was always cool and calm—though he afterwards apologised to His Lordship, who later lost his leg in the fight. Well, I won't tell thee the details of the battle for they'll only bore thee. Indeed I can hardly recall them myself, it was such a fracas. The Guards were defending the outlying farm of Hougoumont and my master left the Duke in the height of the battle to bring relief to the battalion there because the Frenchies were pressing them and the casualties among our men were terrible. The whole farm was ablaze and it was hard to tell who was fighting whom, red uniforms and blue were covered in blood and mud. Marshal Ney had, for some reason, decided he must take Hougomount and he threw in division after division when his troops would have been better used against the main army and Wellington; but our lads held out even though we heard the other farm of Le Maye Sainte had fallen to Ney who had all but pierced the line. It was a close run thing, closer than many people know, but late in the afternoon Blücher arrived and with that the day was saved. But long before that I had ceased to have any part in the battle. I remember I was separated from my master, who was fighting on foot right in the thick of it, and I too had my bayonet out and was thrusting and parrying and then I felt a terrible blow on the arm and it fell useless to my side and the next thing I knew I woke up in the field hospital tent and my arm was off and lying by my side, and the room was full of fellows like me with limbs scattered all over the place. And the smell of blood and dirt and brandy fumes was stifling, and the agonised cries of the wounded was overwhelming and they gave me a glass of brandy to dull the pain but before it took effect I passed out again.'

" 'In the confusion of the battle and the victory my master lost track of me and it was the next day before he found me, for they had taken me to Brussels along with the other wounded men. My master wept when he saw my arm and knew that I could serve him no longer for we had grown to know each other well. He was needed with the Duke in Brussels and charged me to get home safely and said I would be well provided for. But I warrant my master didn't know, or the Duke either, how badly we fighting men were treated by the country we'd fought so hard to preserve for so many years. When we got ashore in England we were discharged before our wounds were fully healed and it was thus I found my way to London where I was set upon by foot-pads and robbed and, having nowhere to turn I started to walk home, still weak from my wound which opened again and the sight of the blood running out disgusted all who saw it and they would not help me. I can tell thee it were a miracle I survived that awful walk: occasionally a good man would give me a ride in his cart or a country woman give me a bed for the night and sommat to eat. I can't tell thee how many days or weeks I walked thinking all the time of the glory I had shared with my master on the battlefields and away from them, for to be the servant of a soldier so well thought of by his men as well as by the commanding officer was an honour for one such as I. And now I was reduced to this pitiful state without money, my clothes rags on my back, my feet tired and bleeding for my shoe leather had long since worn through.'

" 'And then at last I saw my mother's house and as I came over the hill my strength gave way, because I have often found after a weary battle that a man is so weak as to wonder how he ever fought it in the first place; and as I saw my mother's cottage and the smoke rising I wondered how I ever made the journey from London or managed to survive. My brother found me collapsed in the field and the rest you know.'

"And he clasped my hand as the effort of telling the tale had weakened him, and he laid his head on my
203

breast and I was filled with such love and emotion as to let some tears steal silently down my face while my Roger slept in my arms.

"Well, Mr. Lockwood, I know you are more interested in the affairs of the Heathcliff and Earnshaw families than mine, but as you are a kindly man—for I could see how concerned you were when you heard of Roger's misfortune—I must tell you that God was very good to us. For Roger recovered and we were wed in the new church at Gimmerton and Mr. Earnshaw gave us a cottage in the grounds of the Park and took Roger on as a handyman, while I became the housekeeper because the children were too old for a nursemaid but they still lacked a mother. I saw to the running of the house and the welfare of Mr. Earnshaw and the children whom I loved dearly even after I had my own. For Roger was a good father and nursed our bairns, two girls and a boy, and all doing well now, thanks to Mr. Earnshaw, when I had my duties up at the house.

"And the Earnshaw children treated our cottage as an extension of their own house and were always in and out the doors playing with our young ones, Margaret in particular who looked after and played with them as though they were her dolls.

"Oh what happy times we had; they seem like golden years to me now alone in this cottage, my children away and my Roger under the turf in the churchyard, for I would say he never recovered his strength after Waterloo; he was always a thin, ailing man and had lost the robustness of youth. But oh, he was a lovely man, a good man and a wonderful husband and father and, yes, *friend* to me and mine in all the years of our marriage. And a good servant too; he never shirked his duties despite his disability or expected of others what he would not do himself. He always used to say that he had this example from the Duke of Wellington in all the years of campaigning under him. And the Duke still lives, Mr. Lockwood, and my Roger dead; some say he is so hale and hearty he will live forever.

204

"But you will be asking yourself, with impatience by now; and what of Colonel Heathcliff? And it is to his return sir, and the awful consequences of it that I must now reluctantly address myself."

Chapter 12

"I well remember when Colonel Heathcliff came home to Wuthering Heights because Margaret had just turned seventeen, and her father had given a ball for her—the first to be had at Thrushcross Grange within living memory. Anthony and Rainton had come home from school—they had both gone at thirteen to Dr. Arnold's school at Rugby—and all the quality of the area was present, and many of Mr. Earnshaw's business acquaintances came from as far as York and Hull just for the occasion.

"Margaret had developed into a lovely girl, by nature as well as looks. She had none of her mother's wilfulness or petulance but much of her father's inner strength and a serenity, unusual in one so young. Unlike her mother too she was tall and, though very blonde and with the flashing dark Earnshaw eyes, altogether seemed to have little in common with her, for which I thanked God, I might add.

"Yet she had always been told about her mother, and her father talked of her and how much he had loved her—though of course nothing about the affair with Colonel Heathcliff had ever passed anyone's lips from that day to this, and the servants in these intervening years had almost completely changed with the exception of Roger and myself. Roger had become Mr Earnshaw's bailiff when the old one died and, as I was the housekeeper, we felt we had bettered ourselves in the world and had done well for our children.

"It was Roger indeed who first heard of the Colonel's arrival. All the village was talking about how he had swept through it in a fine carriage and then had to return and leave it there and proceed on horseback because the carriage was too broad for the narrow track up to the Heights.

"Roger ran in looking as excited as I have seldom seen him crying; 'Agnes, the Colonel is back. My master is back at the Heights!'

"I remember that day. I was in the linen room mending some sheets and looking out of the window when I could, marking what a fine June day it was and how the leaves tossed in the breeze and the tiny clouds, like wisps of cotton, drifted lazily across the sky. My eyes were not what they had been and the fine stitching meant that I had often to pause and gaze out on this tranquil scene. I minded how I had known it since I came here as a girl nineteen years before—we are talking now of the year 1822—and how I had grown to be and to feel part of the place as though it was my real and only home; and how Roger and I had at last found happiness after all these years. My cup seemed very full until he burst into the linen room and, at his words, I felt a shiver go down my back as though someone had thrown icy water over me.

" 'Oh Roger!' I said, and the expression on my face caused his smile to vanish.

" 'What is it, Agnes? Art not pleased?'

" 'Pleased?' I cried. 'Do you remember the last time the Colonel was here the trouble he caused?'

" 'But Agnes, that was *sixteen* years ago. It is long over and forgotten, all that happened then. Colonel Heathcliff has become a famous soldier and Mr. Earnshaw a prosperous business man. Naught can go wrong now.'

" 'I wonder you're so pleased,' I said bitterly, 'after the way he treated you. Left you to find your way home alone and nearly dying, and not a penny in back pay have you had that the Army owed you.'

" 'Oh, 'twas not the *Colonel's* fault, Agnes; be reasonable, lass. You can be sure the Colonel will see about getting my arrears in pay now. I am going to see him as soon as I can.'

" 'Then I shall come with thee,' I said biting through my cotton thread, 'for I want to see fair play.'

"And so it was that Roger got out the pony cart two or three days later and, as I put on my bonnet, Margaret came dancing into the cottage as she often did whenever the fancy took her.

" 'Aggie, are you going out? Oh *do* take me. Papa has been in London nearly two weeks and I am dying of boredom. Where are you going?'

"I had a strange feeling, as I went on tying my bonnet strings and saying nothing, that somehow I had known this would happen. At the same time I experienced a sensation of alarm and apprehension such as I had not had for years. Yet for why I could not tell. Margaret was used to the Heights; had been there two or three times a year for many years when, keeping my promise, I took Anthony to see his grandmother during the school holidays. And Mrs. Ibbitson behaved beautifully and correctly and the children felt only fond admiration for her.

" 'To the Heights,' I said.

" 'To see Aunt Dorothy?' for such did the children call her.

" 'Nay, to see Colonel Heathcliff who has come home from the wars. Roger has some back pay to come and he hopes the Colonel will be of help to him. Besides, he wants to pay his respects.'

"Margaret clasped her hands and her face lit up.

" 'Oh let me come with you! I hear he is such a hero! I would love to see him. Oh do.'

" 'I don't know what your father would say,' I said gravely. 'I have my doubts he'd approve.'

" 'But he does not object to our seeing Aunt Dorothy?' said my little mistress winsomely.

" 'No, *but* in the past—I'll not go into it now for there's no cause—there was some bad feeling between your father and Colonel Heathcliff.'

" 'Oh what, Agnes? I can't imagine anyone having bad feelings about Papa.'

" 'Well, as I said I can't tell you. It isn't my place; but . . . Oh, I daresay no harm will come of it. Certainly you are bored; you have not enough to do, with your papa and the boys away and no young company near enough for you to visit regularly. Get your bonnet and meet us in the porch.'

"And with such casual words did I determine the strange and unhappy events that were to follow. Would that we could see into the future, Mr Lockwood; but, as we know, we cannot and maybe it is better that we don't."

"At first I thought the place was empty. The house was very quiet as wc trotted up to it, though the windows were open and there was smoke from the chimney. Roger had put on his best suit and sat looking very pale, and I thought that he was apprehensive about his meeting with the man he so admired. Because we had Margaret with us we did not drive round to the back, but stopped in front of the gate and Roger got down and helped Margaret out, then me, and we stood there not quite knowing what to do when the door opened and Mrs. Ibbitson herself came out.

" 'Oh, Margaret, what a lovely surprise! Did you come to see *me*, darling? Are the boys not with you?" And she kissed her cheek and took her arm and was about to lead her into the house when she glanced at Roger, and said abruptly:

" 'You can take the horse round the back, my man, and get a cup of tea in the back yard.'

"I felt my face flame at her words and then I realised she did not recognise my husband as the sturdy bonny lad who had served her years before. Indeed his hair was quite grey and although his face was still youthful—he was but thirty-seven after all at the time—he looked older than his years, for he had a stoop and the lack of balance in his arms had given him a curious crooked walk.

" ' 'Tis Roger, ma'am,' I said abruptly. 'Your late servant and that of the Colonel, and my husband these past seven years.'

" 'Oh Roger, I did not recognise you. Oh please forgive me, and your poor arm, Roger, was that . . .'

"She had forgotten so soon, I thought; that is if she had ever known what was wrong with him. Just another soldier wounded in the war.

" 'Aye, ma'am. At Waterloo.'

" 'Oh, you poor fellow.'

" 'I was lucky, ma'am; most who had limbs cut off died. 'Twas only my youth and vigour saved me.'

" 'That's what he has come to see the Colonel about ma'am,' I said firmly seeing Roger redden and knowing that he would best like to drive home without doing what he had come for. 'He has back pay owing from the Army. He thought the Colonel could help him.'

" 'Oh . . .' Mrs. Ibbitson seemed lost for words and her arm tightened about Margaret's shoulder. 'The Colonel has left the Army. I don't think there is much he can do now. However he has gone riding and will be back shortly. Agnes, will you take Roger to the kitchen and get some tea. I want to talk to my darling Margaret.'

"It was the first time I had been sent round to the servants' entrance and I was fair vexed about it, I can tell you. Every other time I was always welcomed into the sitting room because I had the children with me and had tea with them. I was indignant and so, I could see, was my lamb because she gave Mrs. Ibbitson a dark look and then pursed her lips and shrugged at me as though to say 'what can I do?' Roger was a very humble man, used to serving, and seemed not to be angry at what had occurred; but I, through my close position to the children—indeed I often felt I was their

211

mother and had six children, not three—did not like being considered a mere servant, so I said: 'We will wait in the trap in that case, ma'am,' and, with that, I climbed back into the trap and summoned Roger to do likewise.

" 'But I'd *like* a cup of tea, love,' that simpleton said to me, his face puzzled.

" 'Get into the trap!' I said sharply. 'You're no menial servant and don't you forget it. You're Mr. Earnshaw's bailiff. I am the housekeeper of Thrushcross Grange and no scullery maid either.'

"But by that time Mrs. Ibbitson and Margaret had disappeared inside the house and, soon after, a servant appeared with a tray and served us our tea in the pony trap while I berated Roger for being such a bumpkin and having no pride.

"I must say it was pleasant sitting there in the sun with a soft breeze sighing off the moors and mingling with the scent of grass and flowers from the garden. It was warm not hot, but already the flies were buzzing round the horse's ears and tail and he flicked them lazily while Roger nodded in the front seat and I almost closed my eyes too.

"Then there was the clopping of a horse's hooves and, looking up, I saw that familiar figure on a chestnut and my heart filled with a sort of dread that I was at a loss to account for. I hadn't such a short memory as everyone else; I'd been too close to the events of sixteen years ago to be likely to forget them lightly. What's more I had a good memory for history too and the very name 'Heathcliff' seemed to ring doom in my ears.

"As he drew nearer I observed that his figure was ramrod straight in the saddle, his years as a soldier had seen to that, and that unlike my poor Roger, he had the air and manner of a man a good deal younger than the thirty-eight years I knew him to carry because he was the same age as my late mistress. I thought he was going to go around the back straight to the stables, but his eye was caught by the trap and he came over to us appearing at first not to know who we were. But the sight of Roger nodding in the front seat caused him to reign in his horse.

" 'By God, I know that face! Roger Sutcliffe!'

" 'Sir!' Whether he had been asleep or no I know not but, at the words delivered in a tone used to command, Roger jerked himself up and nearly fell off the driving seat when he saw who it was addressing him. He jumped down and stood as straight as he could which wasn't saying much because the lack of an arm made him permanently lopsided. The Colonel sprang off his horse with the agility of a youth and ran over to my husband clasping his good shoulder: 'Roger, my good man, my old servant. Often have I wondered what became of you after we were separated. Why my good fellow, don't take on like that. I never saw tears all during the Spanish wars, Roger, nor at Waterloo either. What would the Duke say!'

"And indeed my husband was crying like a baby and his poor thin frame shook with sobs while the Colonel looked to me for help.

" 'And you are? His wife? Why 'tis Agnes! So it all ended happily. Thank God for that.'

"I got down rather stiffly because I had my dignity to consider as housekeeper at the Grange and I wanted him to know it, however we were treated by his mother.

" 'Nearly *not* happily, Colonel Heathcliff,' I said carefully. 'Roger all but died on the way home from neglect and his wounds . . .'

" 'Oh Agnes!' Roger exclaimed, his voice still trembling. 'Do not bring that up, I pray thee. Leave it be.'

" 'Aye, I will bring it up,' I said advancing, my hands on my hips like any washerwoman, for I am a peasant girl at heart and always will be. 'I'm not likely to forget it neither, having nursed you back to life.'

" 'But don't bring it up with the Colonel when he has not seen me for seven years. It weren't his fault.'

" 'Not *his* fault?' I said, beginning to feel angry at my man being so spineless. 'Not his fault to see that the servant who served him faithfully for nearly ten years, who risked life and limb for him, got home safely—'aye—and with his pay into the bargain. What kind of thanks for being half killed for your country is that?'

"I was fair snorting with rage now and I looked up to see the Colonel smiling down at me—my goodness he seemed to have grown taller an' all, or I'd shrunk as they say you do when you get older. And he looked fit. His face was bronzed as though he spent much of his time in the sunshine, and his eyes sparkled with the clarity of one who had a good liver and did not over-indulge himself as some do. His hair had grey flecks in it but that added to his handsome appearance and his riding clothes were well cut and sat easily on his tall angular frame.

" 'A woman of spirit still, Agnes! I see *you* have not changed. Do you have children to bless your union?'

" 'Aye three, sir, two girls and a boy.'

" 'And right glad I am to hear it. I will give you a sovereign for each of them.'

"And he thumped Roger cheerfully on the shoulder as though that were the end of it and made as if to go into the house. I was fair incensed, I can tell you, to think how emotional my poor man got at seeing the Colonel and how little the meeting seemed to matter to him! So do the upper classes look upon the lower orders, I'm sorry to say, not always, but often.

" 'Colonel Heathcliff,' I said. 'Pray do not go indoors before you hear what *I* have to say. Roger has come up here about his money; he never got his back pay owing from the Army.'

"The Colonel was about to lead his horse away and he turned and looked at me sharply.

" 'I am not in charge of back pay, my good woman. What do you expect me to do about it?'

" 'But you were his master; he followed you faithfully for ten years . . .'

" 'Aye 'aye 'aye 'aye . . .'' interrupted Colonel Heathcliff sharply. 'He was doing his duty like the rest of us. He was a soldier and that's what was required of him. Eh Roger?' The Colonel strode up to my husband and glared at him. 'You remember what the Duke

214

said? A soldier's duty is what is required of him, no praise or thanks for it either. He gets hanged if he doesn't do his duty, and he don't get praised if he does. That was the Duke's axiom and it's mine too. Roger knew what he was doing when he joined the Army, as I did. No one asked him to or forced him into it. He begged me to get him in and I did. He was well fed and looked after, as were all the Duke's men. If he didn't get his pay, blame the government, not the Duke. The Duke did all that was required of him. He looked after his men and turned them into a body of troops fit to fight Napoleon or any army in the world. Do you think Roger would have survived that wound if he hadn't been so fit? You can thank the Duke of Wellington for that!'

"And the Colonel was about to stride away as though saying all that was to be said, but I wasn't haven't any, not if I could help it.

" 'Then why doesn't the Duke of Wellington see he gets his money?' I said. '*He's* done well enough for himself hasn't he? A Duke, plenty of land I hear and fine houses, the thanks of the nation. Why doesn't the Duke of Wellington see his men get what's owing to them; no more and no less. That's all Roger asks—what is his due.'

" 'And what about *my* due, Mrs. Sutcliffe? Didn't I fight for year side by side with the Duke, having his most intimate confidences and his trust? What did I get. Nothing. I went in a Captain I came out a mere Colonel and I *bought* my commission, no one gave it to me. And why? Because for all his words the Duke wouldn't promote men who were not from the nobility. He was a noble himself—his father was a Lord—and a noble he remained. I've seen him prefer the sons of lords and earls before the finest infantry commander in the battalion and why? Because he knew their mothers or their fathers. Men who came in younger than me and without my experience are now generals with honours heaped on them the way they were heaped on Wellington, from his campaign in India way back in the 80s and 90s to Waterloo! Much as I admired the

Duke as a commander I had no love for him as a man. He was hard and he was on the side of birth and privilege. He also found out the circumstance of my birth because I had changed my name and that was enough for him. No promotion for Heathcliff because he was born on the wrong side of the blanket to the wrong sort of people. Commerce. No matter how much money he has he is not one of us. Blood, blood, blood, that's all that counts and I tell you *I'm* bitter too! If you think I made money out of the war I didn't. I'm not one bit better off now than I was before. All I have is the reputation of a good soldier, which I can be proud of, and the thanks of King George when I resigned my commission writ on a bit of paper.'

" 'Why do you think I came up here? Because I was rejected by London society once the war was over and there were no more daring feats of arms to perform. Merely an ageing Colonel in the Guards which were stiff with the sons of nobility. All I could hope for was a post in India out of the way. There was more to the war than back pay, I'll tell you. Don't think I'm not bitter too. And . . .'

"The Colonel was giving full throat to his resentment and spleen when he looked up and the words died in his throat. Margaret stood at the door and though, as I've said, she was taller than and different in every way to her mother, there was a likeness especially at a distance, and I could tell that the Colonel had seen it immediately and it made the word die in his throat. Even beneath his tan I could see his face grow pale and his hands tightened on the bridle of his horse which he had held during all his tirade.

" ' 'Tis her daughter,' I said softly, so she should not hear. 'Margaret.'

" 'Margaret Earnshaw,' he whispered as though all the breath had been knocked out of him. 'It's incredible.'

"Margaret was as much struck by the Colonel as he with her and as she walked slowly towards him my mind flew back seventeen years to the meeting of him and her mother on the lawn at Thrushcross Grange.

The slow way that they seemed to see each other and then be drawn together as though attracted by a magnet. Oh my heart turned over with the shock and I looked to Roger to see if he had seen it too; but he was locked in his own misery and his head hung on his chest like some village idiot. Then I recalled that the Colonel was old enough to be her father and I dismissed as fanciful the notions that had flown to my head.

"Mrs. Ibbitson was hurrying after Margaret and caught up with her just as she reached the Colonel.

" 'You don't recognise the baby, Jack, do you? This is little Margaret who must have been about one year old when you saw her last.'

" 'Aye and grown up,' the Colonel managed to find his speech at last.

" 'And lovely too, if I may say.'

" 'This is my son Jack, Margaret dear. He has become a very famous soldier in the war as I told you. Preferred by the Great Duke of Wellington himself.'

" 'So you did Aunt,' Margaret said still looking at the Colonel, her eyes shining with admiration, and I realised how attractive he must seem to her with all his years of experience, in other things besides war I might say. Add to this fact that she had no opportunity to mix with young men who would be suitable for her, and so had nothing with which to compare Colonel Heathcliff. All the young men at her birthday ball scarce had whiskers on them and had been drafted in from outlying areas and thus a normal bairn with the desires and emotions that young girls have, as I know from my own experience, was denied an outlet. I then perceived how womanly Margaret had grown, a thing which due to being in constant touch with her I had not noticed, for to me she was still a young girl, my own darling.

" 'You're not going, are you, Margaret?' the Colonel said, handing the reins of the horse to Roger as though he was still his servant which I greatly resented even if Roger didn't, the oaf, meekly taking the bridle. 'I knew your mother well. You are very like her, and yet as I see you closer you are not so like her. Taller I

217

think, and the features more defined. Is it not so, Agnes?'

" 'Aye,' I said grumpily. 'And very like her *father* too.'

" 'Nay, she's not like her father,' said the Colonel. 'Not at all. Come inside, my dear, and tell me about yourself.' And, seeing that they only had eyes for each other, his mother stood back to let them pass giving me a very curious look while my face, I knew, was black as thunder.

" 'He is old enough to be her father!' I hissed.

" 'Sshh, Agnes. It will pass. He is momentarily taken with the snippet. It was the resemblance to her mother whom he told me only last night he has never forgotten. Why the first thing he did when we came here was to lay flowers on her grave.'

"Seeing that everyone had forgotten I was a servant, I followed Mrs. Ibbitson indoors and I motioned to Roger to follow, that clodhopper digging his heels in the earth like some shy pony. But he shook his head and said he would take the master's horse to the stables and rub it down, and I thought some fools never changed or grew up and Roger was one of them.

" 'Master' indeed! So I tossed my head and went inside.

"There on the sofa the Colonel and Margaret were engaged in deep conversation as though they had known each other all their lives as, of course, they had when you came to think about it. He was laughing at something she had said and, by the set of her head and the look in her eyes, I knew she was captivated already, just as her mother had been all those years before. At that moment for me she seemed to grow up and I saw her as a young woman who was ripe and ready for marriage, and not the darling child I had loved any more. Mrs. Ibbitson too seemed aware of the danger and strutted about in front of them, backwards and forwards, like an anxious mother hen with two wayward chicks, trying to intervene by saying something or passing a glass of cordial which she poured from the jug on the table.

218

" 'I see you are at home here already?' the Colonel was saying.

" 'Oh yes, I've been often with my brothers to see Aunt Dorothy. She is not our real aunt as you know; but she is as good and sweet as any. You see neither our father or mother had brothers or sisters so we have no aunts or uncles of our own. She has often told us of you and your famous exploits abroad.'

" 'I am very proud of my son.' His mother came and stood behind him and kissed his cheek. 'He has brought glory to the name of his family.'

" 'But why are you called Heathcliff?' Margaret said innocently. 'I knew you were Jack but I did not know your other name was different from your mother's.'

" 'Because my father was called Heathcliff, my pretty,' the Colonel said. 'And I am named after him and proud of it. Did you never hear the name Heathcliff before?'

" 'Yes. It is on the grave next to my grandmother's. Just the name "Heathcliff;" but when I ask my father or Agnes who he was they pretend not to know. Was he *your* father then?' And her eyes grew wide as she looked at him while I experienced a distressing fluttering in the breast.

" 'Aye, he was my father, and right proud I am of that.'

" 'And is *that* why you and Father had a disagreement?' continued Margaret, to my renewed consternation. 'Is that why you don't talk?'

" 'Did your father say aught to you?' the Captain was smiling, though I thought the expression in his eyes agitated.

" 'Never. Agnes told me that years ago you and he had a disagreement."

" 'Well, it was not about my father; and I can't tell you yet what it was about. But I'm sure it is over and forgotten, for it was many years ago. What say you, Agnes? Has Mr. Earnshaw forgotten, do you think?'

" 'Forgiven, 'aye, for he is a good God-fearing forgiving man,' I said, 'but forgotten, never, if you ask me, Colonel Heathcliff. Come missy, put on your bon-

219

net or you will be late for dinner.' I was anxious to get my charge away from here and angry with myself that I had ever allowed her to come, and I lamented the designs of Him who leads us on such devious paths and through ways the directions of which we know not until it is too late to mend.

"Well, I needn't tell you that Margaret was full of the handsome Colonel all the way back and ceased not to talk of him for many days afterwards, so that when her father returned, the first thing she did was throw herself in his arms and exclaim:

" 'Papa, I have met Colonel Heathcliff, the famous soldier.'

" 'What, is he here?' said my master in some agitation, looking over his daughter's head at me.

" 'Aye,' I said grimly, 'and just as *charming* as ever he was.' And I motioned with my head in the direction of missy and gave him a knowing look with my eyes.

" 'Oh Papa, he is *very* handsome though Agnes says he is almost as old as you, and *older* than Roger, Papa! Imagine, Roger looks twice the age of Colonel Heathcliff!'

"Oh, I felt such anguish at hearing how cruelly the darling girl I had brought up as my own spoke; with what levity and lightness of heart! Had she so swiftly forgotten the lessons of her careful upbringing instilled into her by me? Never to mock the aged; never to prefer the superficial to the real. Yet I knew she spoke carelessly and without malice and I said sadly, for I always spoke frankly to her: 'It grieves me, Miss Margaret, to hear you speak thus of my husband who is but thirty and seven yet looks and walks like an old man due to the severity of his life in the Army and the terrible wound he sustained which was enough to kill a weaker man. Your father will mind, as I do, what a fine young man he was and is in my eyes, and what a *good* man—which is more important than looks, is it not Mr. Earnshaw?'

" 'Aye, it is indeed, Agnes,' nodded my master in agreement and I could tell he was sorely perplexed at the turn events had taken.

220

" 'How did Margaret come to meet Colonel Heath-cliff?' he enquired, mildly enough, but his eyes searching my own keenly. And I explained the circumstances of the visit and told him about the Colonel's tirade against the Duke for good measure.

" 'Ah, he has not lost his harshness, then,' my master lamented.

" 'Indeed not, sir. If you ask me he is full of bitterness and hate and expected to come out of the Army grander and better rewarded than he is.'

" 'That is our old Heathcliff,' my master said. 'It sounds familiar. Ah well, maybe we shall not see him again; for I doubt that he will be contented with life in these parts after the excitement of London and the Continent.'

"And he seemed to put the affair out of his mind, as I suppose he wished to, refusing to answer any of the questions Margaret nagged him with not only then but for many a long day afterwards. And I knew it would not be long before she would have to learn the truth one way or the other."

"But not a week had passed since our visit to the Heights when a servant came with a note for my master from the Colonel asking for an interview. I was in the room at the time because as housekeeper it was my duty to report on the running of the Grange to my master and discuss sundry items with him.

"My master read the note for a good while and then told the servant to give Mr. Heathcliff's messenger some refreshment while he pondered an answer.

"He sat thoughtfully for a long time in his chair, the letter in one hand, his head resting on the other.

" 'Well, Agnes, what shall I do?' he said. 'Shall I see him?' He had already read the contents of the note to me.

" 'Oh sir, that is a question I cannot answer,' I said, my heart already quailing at the prospect. 'But I fear nothing good can come of a visit of the Colonel here. I feel it in my bones.'

" 'And I feel it too, good Agnes,' my master said

sighing. 'But I know not how I can refuse him. I mean he asks me politely; he does not stride in as he did years ago. It would be a discourtesy of me to refuse.'

" 'You are a gentleman, sir,' I said, 'and he is not.'

" 'Maybe he has become one under the influence of the Duke,' my master said, laughing. 'They say he has perfect manners, even on the field of battle.'

"Accordingly my master replied, setting a date and time, and on the specified day I hovered anxiously in the hallway wanting to receive Colonel Heathcliff myself so that I should be party if possible to the interview, but hoping it would seem casual.

"As it was he rode directly up to the front steps and not to the porch at the back, and as a groom hurried forward to take his horse I stood at the top of the steps awaiting his approach. I remember how well he looked that day in a green riding coat and brown breeches, his tall hat in his hand and the sun gleaming on his luxurious black locks flecked with grey. Suddenly he stopped and raised his hand towards an upper window and waved; then, still smiling, he came towards me.

" 'I think she is waiting for me, Agnes.'

" 'Who?' I said, a cold hand already gripping my heart, knowing full well who he had seen.

" 'Margaret. She was waving to me from the window. Ah, here she is,' and to my dismay and consternation Margaret was flying down the staircase into the hall, her face alight with happiness. How lovely she looked that day, in cornflower blue muslin and a blue ribbon round her hair which set off her golden locks.

" 'Colonel Heathcliff!' she cried. 'What a surprise! Does Papa know you are coming?'

" 'I am expected, Miss Earnshaw,' and he took her hand bending low to kiss it and at the same time contriving artfully to gaze full into her eyes, the wretch. I saw her blush and her dark eyes gleamed and I knew with an awful certainty that she was halfway to being in love. For what did it take for a handsome, accomplished stranger to capture the heart of an impressionable young maiden with too much time on her hands? Not much, to be sure.

" 'I will take you to Mr. Earnshaw, sir,' I said, wishing to part him and Margaret as quickly as I might. 'He is expecting you.'

"The Colonel nodded and bowed and did not neglect to smile into Margaret's eyes and whisper something to her that I could not catch, but I saw the blood rush to her face so that I could well guess what it might be about. As we entered her father's study I glanced down the corridor and saw that she was gazing after him, and that he stopped just for a moment and looked at her again.

"Mr. Earnshaw stood awaiting his guest and as he gave me a very clear signal to leave the room I shut the door, full of foreboding, and went back to the hall to join young Margaret.

" 'Oh what does he want with Papa, Agnes?'

" 'Business, I expect,' I said sourly.

" 'I think he is the most handsome man I ever saw,' she exclaimed, joining her hands in rapture. 'Don't you?'

" 'No, I do not,' I said. 'My Roger was a very good-looking man before being destroyed by the war. Your father is a fine-looking man . . .'

" 'Oh yes, I know, but Colonel Heathcliff . . . he is as I imagine Lord Byron to be, or some romantic knight from the novels of Sir Walter Scott.'

" 'You read too many novels. That's your trouble, my girl! Come now into the garden and find something to do.'

" 'But *what* must I do Agnes?' And, surprised at the tone of her voice, I perceived two fierce red spots on her cheeks and I saw that she was full of suppressed rage of some sort. 'I ask, what must I do? What *is* there for me to do? I have read all my books, sewn all my dresses, finished my embroidery. I have no one to write letters to, so pray Agnes, *what* must I do?'

" 'You have never spoken like that before,' I said testily, leading her onto the front porch. 'You have always been very pleased with what life had to give you. And it has given you much. A nice home and a father to be proud of, an easy way of life and a full belly which many do not have in this land of ours. What makes you so discontented now?'

"She looked at me without answering, but the intensity of her young gaze made me quail. Her teeth were clenched and her eyes blazed with a passion I had never seen there before.

" 'It is him, isn't it?' I said. 'Colonel Heathcliff. He has made you restless. I don't think a day has passed since you met him that you haven't mentioned his name. I rue the day I brought you there.'

" 'Oh, we should have met,' Margaret replied calmly, and the words had an ominous ring in my ears. 'I know we should have met some day.'

" 'That's a silly way to talk,' I said. 'I don't know I ever heard a sillier, like some novel or the other. The Colonel has more to do than look at a girl young enough to be his daughter.'

" '*As* you've said before, Agnes,' she said turning away and running down the steps. 'But he didn't ever marry did he?'

" 'I know nothing about the Colonel's private affairs,' I said, following her slowly. 'I . . .'

"And I forget what I was going to say, for at that moment our ears were assailed by a commotion coming from Mr. Earnshaw's study and loud voices raised in anger. Margaret looked at me aghast and I tried to draw her further into the park so that she should be away from the unpleasant sound.

" 'What is it, Agnes? Why are they shouting at each other?'

" 'I know not, miss,' I said with some agitation. 'Come, let us go down to the bottom field and pick some willow herb and meadow sweet for the downstairs parlour. We can . . .'

" 'Oh, Agnes, don't treat me like a child! You tell me *nothing!*' and my young mistress wrenched her arm from my hand and, bursting into tears, ran away from me towards a thicket at the far end of the park. I followed clumsily after her; but then I decided to leave her alone and made my way slowly back to the house just as Colonel Heathcliff strode on to the steps bellowing for his horse, his face mottled with anger. Oh I would that Margaret could have seen him thus, his fine looks blotched and choleric, his tall frame quivering with wrath. Before I had time to reach him the groom had his horse, and he was on it and galloping away up the drive as though he had the devil on his tail, and so I hurried into the house and to my master. I found him sitting slumped in his chair, his face as pale as Heathcliff's had been purple, breathing so fast I thought he was sobbing.

" 'Did he strike you, sir?' I said with consternation, bending over him. He shook his head, but could not speak, so that I was surely troubled to see him so disturbed and asked if I should fetch Robert, his valet.

" 'No, no Agnes. Pour me a glass of sherry from the decanter. That will revive me. My God, *nothing* has changed Jack Heathcliff, he is as rough and as brutal as ever he was. That polish of the soldier is only a veneer to cover the rotting cracks beneath.'

" 'Tell me, sir, what happened?'

" 'Well,' my master thanked me and sipped from the glass I proffered him.

" 'It began civilly enough. We talked about the war, and I offered him sherry and then he said:

" 'To reach the point, Earnshaw, I am here to enquire after my son.'

" 'I do not know to whom you are referring, sir,' I said. 'No son of yours is here.' Because of course I have always maintained that Anthony is not his son . . .'

" 'But sir, he knows . . .'

" 'Oh, I know,' my master said, 'and I know you have known these many years, although we agreed not to speak of it, but I do not admit it for fear it should come to court. Anyway, this angered him.'

" 'You know full well Anthony is my son,' he said, 'and you as good as acknowledged it publicly by letting him come to visit my mother.'

" 'But all my children visit your mother,' I said smoothly. He then thumped the table so that the flower vase on it upset.

" 'By God, Earnshaw, he *is* my son and Cathy's son and I want all the world to know it. And they will know it. I've nothing to lose, Earnshaw. If I had ambitions in the Army sixteen years ago they are gone now, with a puff of smoke. I should be a general and a baronet, but all I am is a colonel bought and paid for, and tossed aside by Wellington as though I had never existed. I tell you in many of his battles and skirmishes *I* saved the day, and well he knew it.'

" 'Tossed you aside as you tossed Roger aside,' I said sarcastically. 'Luckily I was here to provide a home for him.'

" 'Roger was one of the *men*, damn you," Heathcliff said springing up. 'Cannon fodder we called them, the scum of the earth. I was an *officer*, a man used to command. I tell you . . .'

" 'You sicken me, Heathcliff,' I said. 'Roger is the salt of the earth and so are all good soldiers like him who helped to save this country. And badly treated they have been. I hear not only in these parts but also in London of starvation and death and the countless wounded who walk the streets without home, work or money . . .'

" 'I have no patience with this talk, Earnshaw,' Heathcliff said, his voice already beginning to rise. 'I came civilly to ask after my son and to tell you I wish him to go into the Army.'

" 'You have no son,' I said and as I looked at him I thought he made a move to strike me and I stepped aside; but he controlled himself.

" 'I want Anthony to go into the Army. I will pay for him, and I want him eventually to be acknowledged as my son, and be damned to you, Earnshaw!'

" 'He is not your son and never has been,' I said losing my own control now. 'He knows nothing of you and cares less, and I would trouble you to leave me and my family in the peace we have enjoyed these many years in your absence.'

" 'And then I went to the door and opened it; but he seized me by the collar and I thought would throttle me and I couldn't even call out for Robert, but I man-

226

aged to get a punch to his stomach and he released me and staggered against the wall and we stood glowering at each other like prizefighters.'

" 'I'm a bitter man, Earnshaw,' he said. 'I haven't got out of life what I wanted. I'm nearly forty and I've plenty of money; it was wisely invested for me while I was abroad. I'm going to put some of it into the railways which I hear are going to transform civilisation and I'm going to take part in business affairs locally. I'm going to hound you, Earnshaw, and make your life hell, and one day I shall tell Anthony that I am his father and you can do what the devil you like. We are at war, Earnshaw; we always were . . . for I hate you and I have not forgiven you, not by a long chalk!'

" 'And do you think I have forgiven *you*?' I muttered, beside myself in wrath at his impudence, scarcely able to speak for the pounding in my chest. 'You seduced my wife and it led to her death; do you think I forgive *that*?'

" 'Oh, she came willingly, Earnshaw. I don't think you used her well. She was eager for my embrace, I can tell you. As for killing her that is nonsense. I wasn't even here. Had I been she wouldn't have come back to you, that's for sure. That was my mistake in ever letting us part; then there would have been no doubt as to whose son Anthony was! I haven't got even with you Earnshaw, and by God I won't rest until I have.'

" 'And with that he strode out shouting for his horse. Did Margaret see him?'

" 'Oh no, sir. She heard the noise and was already upset. She had fled into the copse. I think she has an eye for the handsome Colonel.'

" 'I must take her away,' my master said. 'Away from him, curse the day he was born. We shall go to London. The season is nearly over, but if we go quickly I can get in some balls and parties, then maybe on to the continent.'

" 'Oh sir, that is a wonderful plan!' I exclaimed. 'You should have done it before. She is too enclosed

227

here; too isolated from young folk or people of her own kind.'

"Her father nodded.

" 'I should have seen it sooner; but she seemed so happy; so contented. She has been an ideal daughter, has she not, Agnes? Never any trouble, no tantrums. And I have been too busy to see that maybe all the time she was lonely.'

" 'She is a young *woman*, sir,' I urged meaningfully. 'She needs to be married.'

" 'Married!' cried my master in horror. 'She is but a child.'

" 'She is older than her mother when *she* was first married, I grant you by force, but still,' I said. 'And when her mother fell in love with you and married you she was but nineteen, two years older than Margaret is now. Women develop very early, sir; it is the natural thing.'

" 'But Margaret married! Oh no. She would leave me, leave here. How could I live without her?'

" 'Oh sir,' I said appalled by this display of fatherly possessiveness. 'You must accept the course of nature. Margaret is a beauty; haven't you noticed *that*? How the young men at her ball jostled to dance with her? She will not stay unmarried long or she will be married to the wrong type, I can tell you. But she is old for her years and men of her own age are mere boys in her eyes—like her brothers; too young to attract her. The mature charms of Colonel Heathcliff appeal, I can tell that.'

" 'You can't mean it!' my master cried anxiously. 'He is much too old for her.'

"But I could tell he was worried enough without me mentioning what she had said about the Colonel only half an hour before.

" 'Oh I'll take her away,' he said. 'Yes, and the boys can join us from school. I shall take a house. I'll leave you and Roger to look after the Grange; but of course I will be back from time to time for business.'

" 'Oh, you are not going forever are you?' I said in

alarm, for I felt that to lose my family—and I thought of them as my family—would be the death of me.

" 'Not forever, Agnes! We shall be back by and by; but I want to show Margaret something of life. She is a beauty, you are right, and she shall marry well; but not yet. You see, when she is in London she will soon forget all about Gimmerton and Thrushcross Grange . . . aye, and Wuthering Heights.'

"But, as you will see, Mr. Lockwood, my master was quite wrong. For Margaret was not leaving trouble behind her; she was going straight into it with her eyes wide open and, unknowingly, all of us helping to push her there."

Chapter 13

"Well as you know, Mr. Lockwood, I am no reader, but the year she was away from us my young mistress did not neglect to write to me, sometimes just a note, but more often a long letter telling me of her doings, of the excitement of being in London or going to Bath or Brighton for outings with her Papa. I thought how unlike her mother she was, or her grandmother, come to that, to whom absence from the moors would be the equivalent of death. Margaret seemed to thrive on the bustle and excitement of the city. I would take the letters to Mrs. Tinkler who had by now retired from her teaching and was living in the village and see, I have them here, Mr. Lockwood. You may look through them for yourself and the last one, the most important one, I will keep for you until you have finished.

June 19 1822

Dearest Aggie,

Oh, it is so exciting to be in London! I feel as though I am in another world. Papa's lady friend (she is *very* nice and respectable), Mrs.

Wright, has secured the lease for a house for us in George Street, Marylebone, and we moved into it straightaway after stopping a night in a hotel. It is quite a small house, but with room enough for us all and oh Aggie it is *right* in the centre of the city. Around the corner is the grand house belonging to the Marquis of Hartford in Manchester Square and not far away is Hyde Park. To the other side is the wonderful new road that Mr. Nash has constructed for the King all the way from Carlton House to Marylebone Park that is renamed Regent's Park, and the broad new street—such a handsome way with colonnades—is named Regent Street.

London is vast and the streets filled with horses and coaches all day long and half the night. Mrs. Wright lives but a short journey away in Devonshire Street and she accompanies me everywhere while Papa is about his business. She has taken me shopping and, oh Aggie, I never saw anything *like* the variety of goods offered: silk stockings, ribbons, laces, and trimmings of all kinds, French gloves, muslins of every description, and from every country, satins and brocades, furs, plumes, and feathers of all colours in the rainbow. And the food shops full of such delicacies you cannot imagine! I never saw anything like them in my life.

Papa does not allow me to the theatre but he has been with Mrs. Wright twice since we have been here, and the other evening she gave a dinner party to introduce me to the immediate circle of her friends.

Mrs. Wright is quite young, much younger than Papa, and very pretty. She was married to an officer who died at Waterloo and when I told her about Roger she cried a good deal and said that there were some worse off than you. I think she has ample means and is obviously very attached to Papa; but he has told me that he has given her no hope in that direction and I think it a pity, for Mama has been dead sixteen years and Papa and Mrs. Wright look well together.

I think Mrs. Wright has been charged to introduce me to some *young men,* for wherever I go there are an assortment of earnest gentlemen who kindly pay me a lot of attention and try and engage me in conversation. But, truth to tell Agnes, I feel like a country bumpkin as I have no knowledge of the world and its way and I sit there silently for the most part and see they soon lose interest . . .

September 22 1822

Dearest Aggie,

We have just come back from a visit to the Continent! Papa had business there and first we stayed at a hotel in Paris but I was accompanied everywhere by another friend of Papa's, Madame Jules Rébart, a bit older than Mrs. Wright and smart rather than pretty. I think Madame Rébart *has* a husband but he was never mentioned, and she is obviously very fond of Papa. It seems that he is quite a lady's man when he is away from Gimmerton. Paris is so gay now after those terrible years of war. Madame Rébart says it is as though Napoleon never existed and everyone breathed a sigh of relief when he died at St. Helena last year.

We were only in Paris a week and then we journeyed south to the Mediterranean and stayed at Nice, just Papa and I and the boys who joined us in Paris from school. Anthony has grown enormously tall and outstrips Rainton. There is a lot of bad feeling between the two which distresses Papa and which I cannot understand. They quarrel incessantly. Rainton has now finished at school and is going to Oxford in October which Papa says will be a good thing.

There was a large English colony in Nice and Papa gave a dinner at our hotel for some

233

friends and we were out every evening at parties and dances. I found the Frenchmen easier to talk to than the English; they are flirtatious and only want to ogle and make advances. Papa never left me alone for an instant!

Then we journeyed into Italy where Papa used to love to take Mama and stayed at Genoa which is an ugly commercial city though beautifully placed. Oh Aggie, I can't *tell* you all our adventures abroad; it will have to wait until I see you! But we travelled up through Switzerland and Germany to Brussels and back to England again arriving last week...

November 8 1822

Dearest Aggie,

Thank Mrs. Tinkler for writing such a nice letter on your behalf. It was good to have news of home and to hear that Roger and the children are well. I miss them all. But London is so exciting and full of things to do that I can hardly imagine how I survived at Gimmerton with nothing to do all day and no one to see. Mrs. Wright was immediately in attendance on our return and she says I am advanced out of all recognition. I think she *did* think I was a dimwitted country cousin but was too polite to say so!

Of course I have a lot more to talk about now and I find the young men more entertaining and interesting. There is a very nice friend of Rainton's called Henry Livingstone who is always about the place and who Papa says comes to see me, not Rainton. Like Rainton he too likes botany which he is going to study at Oxford. After that he says he wants to go into the Navy...

January 4 1823

Dearest Aggie,

We saw the new year in at such a fine party and I danced most of the night with John Fair-

234

fax who is quite *old*, nearly twenty-two, and a friend of Hettie Wright (I now call her Hettie. It seems she is but ten years older than I! I wish Papa would marry her; she is quite besotted by him and talks of him all the time).

John Fairfax is very handsome with beautiful manners and he says he has fallen madly in love with me! *Imagine*, Aggie! I can hardly believe it. It is so different from Gimmerton. Hettie says he is a very good match having inherited a small fortune from his grandmother. He is a gentleman of prospects with estates in Hampshire. He wants to take me to visit his Mother, but Papa says he won't hear of it yet . . .

January 25 1823

Dearest Aggie,

I wanted to tell you that I consider I am in love with John Fairfax, for I cannot get him out of my mind and wait all day for his visit. Do not you think that is being in love, Agnes? Through influential friends of his he secured tickets for Almacks, the Assembly Rooms in King Street, which are very grand, and I was so excited at the prospect but Papa said he would not hear of my going. I think Papa is afraid that I will get too serious about John and he thinks he is too young and an idler! Papa likes men to be gainfully employed either by the Army or business and John is in neither . . .

February 26 1823

Dearest Aggie,

There has been the most awful tragedy and sorrow of my life. John asked for my hand but was swiftly despatched by Papa who gave no adequate reason other than that I was too young. We had time for the briefest parting and now he has gone back to Hampshire broken-hearted, but says he will wait for me and write to me through

235

Hettie Wright. Though saddened I am not *quite* as broken-hearted about John as I thought I would be. I have now met a very nice lieutenant in the tenth Hussars (which used to be called the King's Regiment) called Charles Talbot who is really much more *fun* than John (who was forever given to mooning and sighing over me and really a girl wants a *little* more entertainment)!

Papa talks of returning home for Easter. I do a great deal of sketching and embroidery, but mainly visiting or being visited or walking down Regent Street or in the Park. We have also seen the amazing waxwork museum of Madame Tussaud in the Strand—the figures are quite lifelike. She came from France as an emigré—early in this century. Charles's family live in London and he has a vast army of brothers and sisters and one of his sisters in particular, Laetitia Talbot, and I are very well disposed towards each other. She says Charles is in love with me, but that he has *no* money, having several elder brothers, and that I must not hope. I have asked Hettie to return all poor John Fairfax's letters unopened . . .

"Ah, I see, Mr. Lockwood, that you are coming to the end. Well the others were more or less the same— parties, dances, young men and then after these regular missives there was a long interval during which we neither received letters from Margaret or heard anything from the master. I was worried I can tell you as the spring gave way to summer, but I thought that no news is maybe good news. I did not expect anything as *bad* as I eventually heard when late in July of the same year I received a letter addressed to me in Margaret's hand with a foreign postmark and here it is, Mr. Lockwood, and I need say no more for it will explain itself."

Brussels July 29 1823

My dearest, dearest Aggie,
    I know not how to write to you after such a long interval or how to tell you what has hap-

pened since I last wrote or maybe Papa has by now returned home and you know everything. Do not condemn me, Aggie, until you have heard what I have to say.

Shortly after I last wrote to you I was escorted to a dance by Charles Talbot with whom I imagined myself falling in love. I could spare no dance for anyone but him and I could see Papa, who had escorted Hettie, approved, for he stood on the floor gazing at me and smiling at Charles, which was a good sign.

We were dancing the *waltz*, Aggie, which is the very daring new dance in which the partners actually hold each other round the waist! At first, few couples dared dance it, but it has become quite acceptable now and I have even seen Papa and Hettie engaging in it! However that particular evening my heart was full of nothing but happiness in Charles's company. Everything was so well with us and Papa was contented too when, from the staircase which led into the ballroom, I perceived a man looking at me intently and, oh Aggie, my heart turned over and I felt faint. It was *Colonel Heathcliff*, who looked ever more distinguished and splendid than before in a blue coat and white breeches with a very high cravat. He saw that I had seen him for I waved my hand and when the music stopped he came over to me and bowed.

"Miss Earnshaw, I am delighted to see you. I could scarcely believe the evidence of my own eyes, seeing you dance the daring waltz, when I imagined you safe home in Gimmerton. And now you are here, may I have the honour of the next dance?"

And he looked into my eyes, Aggie, and held them so that I was aware of nothing in the room but him. Charles cut in coldly. "Miss Earnshaw is engaged to me for the evening, sir. Be good enough . . ."

237

But I cried:

"Oh Charles, this is an old friend from home, pray be good enough to spare me." And rather gracelessly he withdrew while Colonel Heathcliff drew me onto the floor, and again it was a waltz and I could feel his arm about me and, oh Agnes, it seemed like heaven, nothing I had ever known before, just to be touched by him. And then everything else was swept away—Papa and John Fairfax and poor Charlie Talbot—in the flood of the great passion I felt for the Colonel and as I looked into his eyes and he into mine, I knew I was absolutely and irrevocably in love with him and had been since the first day I saw him. I felt then, Aggie, that there were only the two of us alone in the world despite the crush of dancers around us and the noise of the orchestra, and even when the dancing had stopped I couldn't take my eyes away from his and I was still in a trance as he led me off the floor and began to talk to me urgently and quickly.

"We have met again, Margaret. It is fate, is it not? May I see you? May I call? Where are you staying? How long are you here? Margaret, I must tell you that since I last saw you I have not been able to rid my mind of you, and, as I could not call at the Grange, I have thought desperately of ways to approach you. Knowing, however, how your father felt I could see no way out of this dilemma so I travelled abroad to seek distraction and now I have found you again . . ."

And as we had been unaware of the dancers so we didn't see Papa approach until we heard his icy voice saying:

"Margaret, I believe you are engaged for the next dance!" And there was Papa looking very angry and Charlie Talbot quite flushed and even the Colonel, normally so poised, at that moment looked as though he didn't know what to do when Hettie cried:

"Why, it is Colonel Heathcliff! He was James's commanding officer in the Foot Guards. Colonel, do you recall James Wright, a lieutenant . . ."

"By God, I do, ma'am," Colonel Heathcliff cried, thankful for the diversion, "he was one of my men, a fine young officer. And you his widow, ma'am? Pray accept my deep sympathy . . ."

Of course Papa looked outraged, but what could he do? Hettie was obviously entranced by the Colonel, who quickly saved the situation by asking her for the next dance and whisked her out of the way before Papa could explode. He wanted to leave the floor immediately and as Charles was looking sorely perplexed I can't tell you what a commotion it all was, observed by not a few people close by. At length I prevailed on Papa not to cause a scene, for all our sakes, or to involve Hettie, who clearly venerated the Colonel, in some countryman's quarrel that she would neither know about or comprehend.

At that Colonel Heathcliff delivered Hettie back to Papa, bowed to her and to me, nodded to Papa and was gone with a polite murmur of farewell. I believe he was with a party of people for I did not observe him again or see him go.

Papa was very silent for the rest of the evening, but no more was said on the subject, though there was a constraint among us that made me glad when the dance was over.

But, Aggie, you can *imagine* my consternation at the discovery I had made on the dance floor. I wanted to write and tell you but I thought you might not approve, and so I had to keep it to myself and try and imagine it a young girl's fancy; but when I saw Charles Talbot again I wondered with what eyes I had gazed at him previously for to me he seemed insipid and stupid and dull.

239

For days I was in a torment, Aggie, knowing not what to do or where I would see Colonel Heathcliff again, if ever, and then one day Hettie Wright came to call and she said she had a surprise for me and looked at me very mysteriously and asked me to walk over to her place. Papa was out and I was alone in the house but for the servants.

Well, I put on my bonnet and hurried off with her and begged her to tell me what it was, and, just as we were at the door, a thought occurred to me and I turned to her and said in dismay:

"Oh Hettie, it is *not* John Fairfax . . ."

And just then the door opened and Colonel Heathcliff stood awaiting us, and I could not restrain myself from crying out with joy at seeing him and, Aggie, yes, I *ran* into his arms and, right in front of Hettie and the butler who stood in the hallway, but I cared not, he hugged me and his lips brushed my forehead. Then, both of us very much moved, he let me go and escorted us into the drawing room where we sat for a while gazing speechlessly at each other while Hettie bustled about ordering tea and pretending that the whole thing was not unduly untoward.

We chatted over tea in the most ordinary way, she telling me how much her husband admired the Colonel and how honoured she was to have him in her house, and he just sat there looking a bit fierce as though the whole intrigue irritated him as I knew it did.

Then she made an excuse and left us alone together and he said he had been in a torment since he saw me because, although he wanted to see me as he had some inkling as to how I felt about him because of the way I looked at him and behaved, he was indeed old enough to be my father and out of sorts with Papa into the bargain. I was so abashed, of course, and

240

amazed to know that such a distinguished man, a man of the world, could feel *this* about me, that I told him I felt I was not worthy of him and he got up and paced agitatedly about the room and said he must have time to think what to do and would I continue to meet him at Hettie's?

I said that, of course, nothing in the world would please me more even though it meant deceiving Papa, and then Hettie came in and he begged of her to render again the favour and she said of course she would and she would talk with my father to try and mend the rift with the Colonel, but he cried out:

"Oh no, I beg you, ma'am, discuss it not with Mr. Earnshaw who on this matter is as intractable as a mule and would take his daughter to India or China, far enough I know, if he thought he would thus get her away from me."

At this we all fell silent and the Colonel said he had to go, but we made another rendezvous and he kissed my hand and my cheek and was gone. And after he left I found the matter was too much for me and I wept on that good lady's bosom and she, very agitated herself, did what she could to comfort me. And we discussed the matter until nightfall and she told me about the Colonel approaching her and begging of her this service just for once, and that she knew not to what she was committing us, but that she could not refuse her late husband's commanding officer a favour.

"Besides, Margaret," she said sadly, "when your father gets to know of it, it will be the end of things for us. I didn't know *half* how serious it was between you and Colonel Heathcliff . . ."

And she looked so grave and upset I was sorry to distress her and I replied that, in truth, neither had I for we scarce knew each other; but that I felt committed to him and he to me and I knew not what would become of us because

241

Papa disliked the Colonel so and of course I was Papa's loving and respectful daughter. And then she said that, oh, it was terribly romantic and her eyes filled with tears and we both wept until it was time for me to go home.

And after that the Colonel and I contrived to meet every day either at Hettie's or in the Park, and each time it was more painful for us to part and I knew that the situation could not continue thus much longer. Then, one day late in the afternoon, as we walked under an avenue of trees in Regent's Park through which the sun glinted down, and the birds around us sang as though we had been in the heart of the country, the Colonel stopped and looked into my eyes.

"My heart, we cannot continue this," he said, "deceiving your father, compromising our good friend, Mrs. Wright. You know I am a man of action and I propose to have it out with him."

"Oh no, no, I beg you," I cried. "Papa will take me away; you know he will not allow us to meet."

"I want to *marry* you," the Colonel said, "I'm not talking of meeting but a wedding. Is it not what you want too, my Margaret?" And there and then he crushed me in his arms, and we cared not what the other strollers thought about it, nay, nor the birds or the squirrels either, or all the world.

"Oh, Jack," I breathed at last. "I am under age. Father will never let us meet or be wed. We are doomed . . ."

"We are *not* doomed!" my bold lover cried. "By God, not while I have life in my body, and I am used to my own way, Margaret. Well, if you will not let me see your father, and I think you are right—as a minor you are still his property and he can dispose of you as he likes—then we must go away. I have friends in Paris and Brussels, or Rome or Geneva, if it comes to that. We will find a parson to tie the knot and then there is naught your father can do. We shall elope, my love!"

"But Jack, Papa will never forgive me. I am all he has."

"Stuff. He has *two* fine sons, has he not? A pretty lady friend, whose heart incidentally he has already broken, and I know not how many more besides. He will never forgive *me* but he will forgive thee, Margaret my love. Say yes, and I will arrange it instantly."

"And if I say no?" I said, greatly daring, to test my love. Then his face grew black as thunder and he pushed me away from him.

"Then I will be gone and trouble you no more. I am not a young man, Margaret, to have his affections trifled with. I have never asked a woman to be my wife; for the one I loved I could not have, and the others were merely amusement to me. But you, Margaret, you have captured my heart and my head and if you will have me, old as I am, I am yours; but if you dally and play with me I shall leave you and never see you again. For I am no boy."

"Oh, Jack," I cried, moved by his words. "You know I am yours; and I know that if I harken to Papa and tell you to go I shall regret it all my life. Though I *am* afraid, Jack, of what I am about to do. I fear to hurt Papa and sometimes I feel frail and alone in the world; but if you give me strength I will do your bidding all the days of my life."

And so Agnes we plighted our troth on that sweet day in June only a month past, and I have never regretted it for a moment nor ever shall. Jack fetched me the following day for, thank God, Papa was still away or I feel I should never had been brave enough to go through with it once I had seen his kindly face again. Hettie lent me her maid so that I should not be unchaperoned and, after stopping at Dover, we arrived in Brussels where some kind friends of

243

Jack's accommodated us. And last week we were married in the English Church and as we are about to embark on a journey to Italy I thought I should write to you my dearest Aggie, and tell you what has passed.

I want you to know that I am *very* happy; the *happiest* woman in the world and Jack is as wonderful and considerate a husband as he was a passionate wooer. Oh, and Aggie, he has such style and such a manner: People do everything he bids them, and gladly—you can see they worship him, as I do. I feel I am so fortunate to have for a husband a man such as he, experienced in the ways of the world and not as gauche and awkward as were the young men I knew.

I have written to Papa and I hope he will forgive me. Do what you can for me with him. I love you and leave you, my dearest Aggie, who was always for me the only mother I ever knew.

Margaret Heathcliff.

"Margaret Heathcliff, sir! Can you imagine, Mr. Lockwood, my thoughts when I had the letter read me and saw the signature with my own eyes.

"Mrs. Tinkler and I fell onto each other weeping for I knew that Colonel Heathcliff had not told her the truth and she knew not that she was wedded to her mother's lover, the father of her own half-brother Anthony. Oh my God, if such wickedness cannot be punished in this world, what hope have we for the next?

"And what of my poor master, the kindest man ever made? Did he deserve to be treated thus by his only daughter, to whom he only ever gave love and happiness; whose welfare was his only thought; whose protection his main consideration? I scarce dared breathe for thinking what my master would do as I hurried home to break the news to Roger, only to find that that very day my master had arrived back and that Roger was already in his study with him.

"I never saw a man so changed; even the elopement and death of his wife had not moved him as this had. He had lost so much weight that his clothes hung on his body and the hair had left his head so that he was almost bald, that fine thatch of curly hair had vanished! It was a terrible sight. And the eyes were so sunken in the cheeks as to make one wonder if he had ever slept and his hands trembled as though he had the palsy. Why my Roger, who was far from strong, looked robust by comparison, and I doubted not that while Margaret's husband waxed fat and healthy her poor father had taken several steps nearer the grave.

"I even held her letter in my hand as I approached my poor master and curtsyed low to show the extent of my respect for him.

" 'Ah, you've heard, Agnes.'

" 'I just got the letter yesterday, sir. I took it this morning to Mrs. Tinkler to read to me. Oh sir, what can I say?'

" 'Say that I am finished, Agnes, done for. My own daughter, my little Margaret, to whom I tried to be not only father but friend, to do this to me.'

" 'You must not blame *her*, sir. 'Tis he!' I cried. 'He is the monster who should be stoned and whipped and transported to the colonies for life.'

" 'Aye, and hanged, too,' growled Roger which was the first time I ever heard him speak thus of his old master, even though he had failed him on his return from the Army and Roger never received a penny that was due.

" 'Is there naught you can do sir?'

" '*Do*?' said Mr. Earnshaw, leaping up so violently that it brought on a fit of trembling again. 'He has married her. They are wed; united in flesh as well as by the spirit; tied up all legally, I doubt not, knowing the blackguard the Colonel is. What can I do when I do not even know where they are?'

" 'Brussels,' I said, showing the letter. 'Oh, but she said they were leaving.'

" 'Then it will be Switzerland and Prussia and Egypt

245

. . . no, my daughter is gone, Agnes. Heathcliff has revenged himself on me most brutally and finally.'

" 'You think he did it for revenge, sir?'

" 'Of course! You think he *loves* her? She is but a child. Eighteen years old and he nigh forty, if my calculations are correct, he was the same age as my wife. He is *more* than twice my daughter's age. How can a man like that love a mere maid? No, he toys with her . . .'

" 'Sir,' I spoke respectfully, quietly. 'I do not want to anger you or add to your grief; but you know I have differed with you before on this subject. Margaret is a *woman*, sir; she is not a little girl and it is through a father's eyes that you see her. Eighteen she may be, but fully mature and capable of experiencing and inspiring passion. I have heard of many men who when in love have married women half their age, and no doubt you too sir; but because Margaret is your child you see her not in this light. I have no doubt the Colonel *could* love her as a woman, for that is what she is. I do know that after his own fashion he loved my late mistress sir, and again I hate to cause you pain' for at this, Mr. Lockwood, my master actually groaned aloud. 'He stole her from you and he was wrong to do it; but he *did* love her, that I doubt not, and wanted her and pined for her all these years. Then he sees her daughter, who is fully grown up and like her mother in looks and spirit. I think it is natural that the Colonel should find her pleasing . . .'

" 'No he did it for *spite,* Agnes! The whole thing is for spite, I tell you! He is getting his own back on the Earnshaws for what they are supposed to have done to his father, that scoundrel Heathcliff. My God, how I rue the day he came into the world, wherever it was, a man I once thought I loved. Jack Heathcliff wants to pay me back, don't you understand? And now he's taken my daughter as formerly he took my wife. I've got *his* son, but he's got *my* daughter. It is to get even with me because I denied him Anthony. My God how we *are* at war. If ever he shows his face in these parts again I'll whip him to death.'

"Oh, how my heart was filled with pain and trepidation as I looked at my master, enfeebled by sorrow. The thought of *him* putting a whip to the strapping Colonel, as I'd last seen him, would have made a cat laugh. Oh, I was full of woe and misery as Roger and I returned to our cottage and our own happy family, leaving my solitary master to his frenzy of remorse and grief."

Chapter 14

"From that time onward—it was the summer of 1823 that Margaret eloped with Colonel Heathcliff—the master seemed to banish all thoughts of his daughter from his mind and she was never mentioned, by him at any rate, by name again. And although he was but in his forties he seemed more like a man of seventy as he sat alone in his study wrapped up in his thoughts. He no longer bounded abroad every day to see to his business affairs or rode round his estates to be sure that all was well. A lot fell on the shoulders of Roger who was thus weakened by riding out in all kinds of weather and, as we had a series of bad winters, though all winters are bad in these parts, he grew thinner and kept me awake at night with his harsh and persistent coughing. The next day I would beg him to stop at home but off he would go.

"They were quiet years and there was an air of sadness about the Grange that we had not known in all the happy days of Margaret's childhood. Rainton was at Oxford and the cheerlessness of his home made him want to stay away during the vacations and I can't say

I ever blamed him. No, Rainton's place was taken by Anthony who, after he left school at eighteen, became his father's main support and gave him any small pleasure he was still able to get out of life.

"By the time Anthony came home, the year after Margaret had eloped, Roger was feebler than ever, and Anthony began to take an interest in his father's affairs and accompany Roger on his trips round the estates. Anthony was a big fierce-looking boy, very much as you see him now. He did not have the striking good looks of his natural father, or his charm, and he offended a good many people by the brusqueness of his manner and the sharpness of his ways.

"But I will say this about Anthony, though I could never like him because to me he was always cold and unsmiling—maybe he resented the fact I had never been able to mother him as I had the others, mainly because he did not seem to want it as much as they did and spurned what loving advances I had made until in time I ceased to make them—I will say this; he was a model of respect and affection towards his father, as he thought of Mr. Hareton, and gave up the chance to go to university or into the Army or Navy to be with him.

"Mr. Earnshaw and Anthony thus grew closer together in the years of which I speak, and Rainton when he came home was received like a stranger and soon made haste to depart, and Margaret was not spoken of at all.

"Meanwhile Roger worried more and more about Mr. Hareton's neglect of his estates and his business and told me we should all be ruined and cast out on the moors if something was not done soon. Business acquaintances were forever coming to the house to see Mr. Earnshaw and being turned away dissatisfied by Anthony who said his father was unwell. And times were very bad for industry in the North, Mr. Lockwood, as you may have heard tell. When the Combination Acts were repealed the workers immediately went on strike for better pay and conditions which caused misery and distress in many a home, for their demands went unsatisfied and because of their action some mill-

250

owners went out of business. In Bradford the wool-combers and weavers went on strike for *twenty-three weeks* to no avail and much suffering and even death resulted.

"And then in 1826 two terrible events occurred almost at the same time, one of them deeply affecting me, the other us all.

"My Roger fell ill in the February, Mr. Lockwood. That great good man could not rise from his bed one morning and never left the house again on his two feet. The consumption which had got hold of his chest in the bad winter took him off in a few weeks, and nothing I or anyone could do to help him was of avail. Dr. Kenneth had retired by that time and gone to live in the South, and the new doctor used all the powers of modern medicine, the mercury cure, cod liver oil, bleeding, all the best known remedies without any success. My eldest daughter was ten and a great little help in the home and about the house, the other girl nine, and the little boy eight.

"In those days children had already grown up at eight and many of them worked in the mills a twelve-hour day and my children were pampered compared to those poor mites; but they were expected to help in the big house and run errands and generally make themselves useful and earn their keep.

"And, oh what a comfort they were to me during those sad days after we buried my man. Ten years of great happiness we had, such as are given to few, and but for the war and the savagery of our winters I daresay he would be alive now and sitting with me on the other side of the fire.

"Then we had scarce got over that terrible blow when the big firm of Butterworths collapsed and there was such chaos and confusion that hundreds of firms and banks, large and small, followed suit. You might have heard it, called The Butterworth Panic, Mr. Lockwood, and it brought awful distress and hardship to masters and men alike all over the north of England. Mr. Earnshaw was affected like everyone and I have heard tell that in a space of a few hours the fortune he

251

had worked so hard to build up was reduced almost to nothing.

"I often feel that had Mr. Earnshaw been his old self and not so diminished by grief he would have seen this coming and have been able to do something to prevent it. They say a lot of these mill owners had their businesses based on shaky foundations. As it was, it came as much of a surprise to him as anyone else, but even then he didn't rise from his stupor, and he let the whole untidy mess flow over him while lawyers and businessmen came and went and someone tried to create harmony where discord had reigned.

"And that person was Anthony Earnshaw, as he was then. He was but twenty at the time of his father's business collapse, but he worked day and night burning the candle at both ends to save him from complete ruin. He sat in on the business discussions, had talks with the lawyers and bankers, and was to his father a pillar of strength and brought a measure of salvation to us all.

"But what a price he had to pay! He had to put almost all of Mr. Earnshaw's property hereabouts on the market and I have told you how at one time he owned most of Gimmerton and beyond. That way Anthony hoped to preserve the Grange and some measure of comfort for his father.

"And Wuthering Heights was put up for sale too. We had not seen or heard of Mrs. Ibbitson since her son had gone off with the daughter of Thrushcross Grange—at least she had the decency to keep out of the district and, as her tenancy had ceased in 1825, the house was free to be sold.

"And what did I do in this time of upheaval you may well ask, Mr. Lockwood? I went about my daily business as best I could, trying to make economies and getting my children to work in the house for nought so that we could manage with fewer servants. I owed Mr. Earnshaw too much to grudge him any little service I could render. He was not ungrateful, I know that, though he said little. We hadn't talked for years as we used to talk in the old days and he was content to let

252

me run the house and Anthony his business, or what was left of it, while he sat in front of the fire or in the sunlight, according to what season it was, his head sunk on his chest like a man in whom life was but a token, a little flickering light.

"And it was thus that in the autumn of that year, 1826—I'm not likely to forget it—Margaret came home to us, yes home, knocking on the door as her mother had done many years before, damp and distressed, with her cloak clinging about her and her hair damp on her forehead.

"I was the one to whom she came. It was late afternoon in October. The winter had set in early and I thought that it was like to be as harsh as it had the previous year, and I was sitting by the fire in my cottage, thinking about Roger and those happy days of courting in our youth, when a sharp knock at the door of my cottage raised me from my lethargy and I told my son George to be quick about seeing who was there.

"Oh, Mr. Lockwood, my eyes still fill with tears at the memory of the sight before me, my young mistress thin and bedraggled, her eyes half staring from her sockets. At first I hardly recognised her and thought some stranger had mistaken the way, but she stood on the threshold and stretched her arms towards me.

" 'Oh Aggie, dear Aggie, thank God,' she cried, and she fell on my bosom and gave vent to great silent heavings of her shoulders that were worse than any tears and, indeed, when she looked at me I saw her face was dry and that all the tears were from within, great choking sobs in her chest. Oh, it was a terrible thing to hear and see!

" 'Ah Margaret, my darling,' I said, taking her by the hand. 'Sit a while, my baby. Your Agnes will see to you. George, get up quickly to the Grange and fetch some brandy from the dining room, and not a word to anyone, mind. Sharp now.'

"And without another word, looking fearful, my youngest scampered out of the house to do as he was bid. I helped my mistress—for I still thought of her as such—out of her wet garments and, oh, Mr. Lockwood, I saw that her belly was swollen and that she was great with child! Her thin frame and her swollen belly were such a contrast as to make me fear she might be ill and I wondered if she had come home to die before her time, just like her mother and grandmother. Oh, the unlucky fate of the Earnshaw women, I thought, as I made up the fire and chafed her cold hands and, when George returned with the brandy, I forced it gently between her lips, wondering if I should call the doctor.

"But the heat and the good strong liquor revived her and the colour came back to her face and soon she smiled at me—still that serene, beautiful smile which then was in such a pathetic contrast to the rest of her state.

" 'Oh Aggie, thank God you were here. You are my mother, Aggie, always here when I want you and oh, I want you now, Aggie. I need you as much as ever I did when I was a little girl.'

" 'Tell me, my darling,' I said, 'tell your Agnes what has happened. Where is Colonel Heathcliff? Has something happened to him?'

"At the mention of his name my mistress shuddered and clasped her hands to her ears as though she would cut out an unpleasant sound.

" 'Oh, do not say his name! I cannot bear it. Oh how I hate him; what a fiend . . . he is not a man, Aggie, he is an animal.'

" 'But your letters,' I stammered. 'You were so happy.'

"She sat back and gazed into the fire as though recalling happier days.

" 'How long ago was it, Aggie? Only three years? Is it possible that I was once happy? Yes, I suppose it is and I was, rapturously happy for the first months of our marriage. I was so honoured and thrilled at being selected by him as his bride. I think I was blind to the fact that he was indeed so much older than I and twenty times more experienced. Had he not fought in the Peninsula and at Waterloo? Had he not had any number of women companions, and was he not well versed in the ways of the world? Oh he was, Aggie, in every way. But at first I think he did love me for they were happy days and he did all he could to please me and took me all over the continent, to Spain and Italy and then quite suddenly he seemed to tire of me. Just like that,' my lady snapped her fingers. 'He started to neglect me, and to sneer at things I said and find fault with things I did and to belittle me in many ways.'

" 'He said I was not a fit companion for him, for I was not sufficiently well educated and had nought to talk about, and I was boring and trivial and, oh Aggie, . . . it was terrible, for in a way I felt it was all true. I had been too cut off here and, even in a year in London and abroad, I could not acquire the polish that a man like Jack required, was used to.'

" 'So he would leave me wherever we happened to be living and stay out all night and soon I would hear that he was frequently to be seen in the company of this smart hostess or that and, on the rare occasions he did take me anywhere, he would immediately leave me and make off in the direction of the ladies, many of them of the *demimonde* and not at all respectable.

" 'But did you never speak with the Colonel or plead with him or seek some explanation?' I enquired, horrified at my mistress's tale.

" 'He would give me the same answer. I was too young for him; I bored him; I had not enough to offer him; he had made a mistake in marrying me. He did nothing to spare me humiliation and remorse; but last year when we returned to London, this time to settle, Jack said, I renewed my friendship with Hettie Wright who in fact was married again, to a banker, and was comfortably set up in Mayfair. Unfortunately Jack made the acquaintance of her husband which immediately interested him because he said he was of a mind to settle down and invest his money in industry. Despite all his profligacy and spending, all-out travelling, he still seemed to have plenty of it left.

" 'Now that I was so unhappy I was of a mind to crave father's forgiveness and asked to be allowed to visit Gimmerton, but Jack would not hear of it even though he now threw himself into his business interests and took to spending a great deal of time in the north of England, where the new industry was developing so fast. How I longed to go with him; how I begged him to let me, but he would not.

" 'And so I remained in our rented house in Wimpole Street alone and unhappy save for a few visits from Hettie or her friends.

" 'Then at the beginning of this year, Aggie, when I thought I could not be more miserable or unhappy, or more unkindly treated by fate, I discovered that I was with child. Colonel Heathcliff, although considering me unworthy of his time or conversation, did not leave me alone altogether when the fancy took him. I was quite far advanced before I told Jack of my condition and, instead of it making him feel tender towards me, he was glad merely that he would have an heir, because of course he is sure it will be a boy, to carry on his accursed name.'

" 'But Aggie, the worst is not yet told,' and she clasped my arm and leant earnestly over towards me. 'While he was in the North my husband came across information through the husband of Hettie about my father's affairs and investments. It seemed they were in a poor way and likely to collapse because he had speculated unwisely and was allied with merchant banks that were overloaded and trading beyond their means. And, instead of helping my father or informing him as to the danger he was in, Jack deliberately stood back and when the crash came manipulated things so that my father's position was even worse than it had been before. And now, Aggie, the awful part is that Jack has bid to buy all of father's property, which is going for a song to pay his debts, and that includes Wuthering Heights and all the surrounding land. In fact he said he would have the very coat off his back if he could get it.'

" 'And so, dear Agnes, when Jack was away I made my way to the stage unaided and have travelled on the top because I lacked the means to pay for a seat inside, and I have been jostled about in all weathers until a kind man gave me his seat below and insisted that he took mine. And then I was put off at Leeds and have made the rest of the way on foot and many a time the pain tore at my belly and I thought I should deliver on the wayside and Aggie, here I am and that is my story.'

"And here my poor mistress clasped her stomach and gave a loud groan and, judging by the size of her, I thought her time had come, but it was only fatigue and emotion after the harrowing tale she had told me and, after a rest and some more brandy fortified by a thin hot gruel I had on the stove, she rested quietly, holding my hand, saying nothing but looking into the fire.

" 'And Papa, Aggie?' she said timidly, at last. 'I hear he is not well. I have so much to answer for, have I not, dear Agnes?'

"And what could I say, for indeed she only spoke the truth. Bewitched or no, Margaret had only herself to blame for what had come to pass; she had not thought of her father when she had made off with the Colonel or, if she had, it was not enough to deflect her from her path of wrongdoing.

" 'Your father is a changed man,' I said sorrowfully. 'He is bald and his face is sunken . . .'

" 'And it's my fault . . .' Margaret whispered, 'oh how can he ever forgive me?'

" 'I think since you came to him in your distress,' I said gently, 'that will do something to atone, for the rest . . . I cannot say. Your brother Anthony has been a tower of strength; but Rainton we don't see at all. Your father could no longer afford to keep him at Oxford and last year he went abroad, I think something to do with his botany; but we have not heard from him since. Pray God he is not dead, killed by the heathens or lost at sea. I know worry about him is an additional burden for your poor father.'

"At this Margaret again pressed her head in her hands, still not weeping but with her shoulders shaking in this curious and frightening way she had of expressing emotion.

" 'To what have we come?' she said at last. 'Can there be a curse on the Earnshaw family, that everything we do ends in ruin?'

" 'Nay,' I said trying to cheer her up. 'There's no such thing as *ruin*, lass. There are bad times and good times and things always pick up; your brother Anthony is a capable lad, and your father is not dead yet—and Rainton, there's a fine strong pair of shoulders and a good head set on them, *if* we ever see him again. Your father still has the Grange, he told me he'll not put that on the market before his dying day, and if need be we can dismiss all the servants and I'll do the cooking and my three bairns are eager and able to work . . . they know full well that children of their age are working in the mills and down the mines and without a decent bed to sleep in or sufficient food to fill their bellies. We'll survive, lass. Now let us go up to the house and see your father.'

" 'Oh Agnes, can't you tell him? Can't you go for me?' she pleaded, but I knew the master still loved her so well that the sight of her pitiful condition would do more to appease him than any words of mine."

"And so it was, Mr. Lockwood. It was dark and the candles were lit by the time we went up to the house and I knocked on the door of Mr. Earnshaw's study, and then I stepped back to let Mrs. Heathcliff in and she stood on the threshold while her poor father, looking so much older than his years, screwed up his eyes to see who it was. And it was Anthony standing by his side who cried: 'Margaret!' and running up to her embraced her and drew her over to her father who took her hands and, gazing into her eyes, slowly rose and then held her in his arms and, for the first time that day, Margaret gave vent to the tears that had for so long been stifled in her bosom.

"What a picture it was—it has remained firm in my memory all these years—that sad family reunion grouped together by the fire whose rich blaze was so much at variance with the circumstances of those whom it warmed. All around the pewter and the silver glit-

258

tered, and the polished furniture shone and one would have thought the family as protected by affluence as indeed they had always been, for we servants had worked as hard for them as we had ever done, as much to keep our own spirits up as anything else. The whole house gleamed and sparkled with polish and good care, and the linen was fresh and clean and sweet-smelling on the beds, and in the larder lay good solid sides of beef and lamb and quarters of sheep and pigs.

"But for how long? How long could it last? And its destruction was all brought on by the viciousness of this good lady's husband who had sought deliberately to destroy her father as he had promised he would.

"Mr. Earnshaw had tears in his eyes as they appraised Margaret's figure and he perceived that he was about to become a grandfather.

" 'Sit down my dear,' he said tenderly. 'You are welcome home once more.' And no Biblical father could have given a more loving welcome than Mr. Harcton did that night to his prodigal daughter. And while she began her tale I slipped out so as they could be alone together and I enjoined the servants to lay on a fine feast and open some good wine because, I bethought me prayerfully in the words of the Bible, she who was dead had come to life again, she who was lost had been found.

"When I returned to announce dinner Anthony was sitting on the arm of his sister's chair, his hand on her shoulder and such a loving expression on his face that I wondered if, as sometimes happens, bad fortune would restore Anthony to a happier disposition. As for Mr. Earnshaw, the poor man wept uncontrollably and the hand which held his handkerchief trembled; but Margaret's eyes were dry and on her face was still a trace of that serenity that had been so much a feature of her as a girl.

" 'He will come and get you back,' Mr. Hareton was saying. 'Once he finds where you are. He will not leave you here.'

" 'But father, he does not know I am here until he returns to London; then let him look. In the meantime we shall have a few days together. Oh I know Jack; he will want me back all right; in his house; under his eyes to make sure that his progeny is born on his property. What can I do, father? Can I flee somewhere else? Is there someone who can shelter me so that Jack will never find me again?'

" 'I'll kill him,' Anthony said very slowly and quietly, 'before he takes you from us. I will. I mean it.'

" 'Oh Anthony, darling, do not say that, I beg thee,' his sister cried. 'You will be hanged if you kill him and then what shall we do?'

" 'Hanged or not, 'twill be worth it to be rid of him!'

"And I observed that Mr. Earnshaw, for all his grief, was looking at me as though to say if only Anthony knew about whom he was talking.

"Thinking about the situation as I did then and later, it occurred to me that I could scarce comprehend anything *worse* than the fact that, not only was the Colonel Margaret's husband and the father of her unborn child, *and* the enemy of her father, but he was also the lover of her mother and the father of Anthony and all this unbeknownst to the children. No wonder the knowledge of it made Mr. Earnshaw ill.

"Be that as it may my efforts at cheer did not go unrewarded, and that night the family contrived to make merry over the dinner table and I had the happiness that night of tucking my mistress into her bed and stroking her forehead while she fell asleep.

"And indeed all the week I saw her gain colour and improve under my very eyes. We made her rest as much as she could; she never moved but there was someone to help her or pick up a fallen object for her, and under our loving care and the watchful tenderness of her brother and father she was transformed from a sickly waif into a vibrant beautiful young woman again, on the verge of motherhood, despised and ignored by her own husband, but who would be the envy of many another man.

"And then, of course, inevitably one day there was the sound of a carriage being driven furiously up the drive, horses neighing and pawing on the gravel outside the porch and, once again, the house rang to the strident harsh voice of Colonel Jack Heathcliff raised in anger, as only he could be angry, fiend that he was.

" 'Where's Earnshaw?' he bawled out in those by now familiar and hateful tones. 'Earnshaw, I want my wife!' and I heard him bang on the sideboard in the hall with his riding crop as I ran downstairs and found that I was the first to greet him.

" 'Ah, Agnes Dean,' he said threateningly, perceiving my whitened countenance, for I will not hide from you the fact that I was afraid. 'Mischief-maker if ever there was one. Where are you hiding her, eh?'

" 'Sir, Colonel Heathcliff,' I said, recovering my composure and with it my voice, for the sight of him in full health and vigour, while I thought of the master and of my poor Roger now under the ground, made me angry. 'The poor soul came to us for refuge. Why don't you show some compassion and leave her be? Don't you think you have caused enough grief in this house?'

" 'Grief? Compassion?' he thundered. 'I know not the meaning of such words, at any rate when it comes to the Earnshaw family, for they have shown none towards mine. My wife is about to bear my child and I want it under my own roof although one day I expect this property will be mine too.' And he looked about him with an expression of proprietorial greed and satisfaction on his face. 'Aye, a fine house to bring up my family in; for now the cow's in calf and we know she's capable we'll keep her that way; that will take the restless spirit out of her for a few years more, bearing sons for me. Aye, I'll keep her at it.'

"Oh, the cruelty of him; it was hard to think he was talking of a fine lady and not some animal in his barn with his coarse words and inflamed complexion. In his face I saw unbridled lust and avarice and, though still a fine figure of a man, he had put on weight and was beginning to show the signs that come to those who debauch themselves or drink a lot.

"And then, aware of a movement behind me, I beheld Mr. Earnshaw standing erect and proud, as much

261

as his poor bent shoulders would let him, and saw the Colonel was staring at him, as if unable to believe the evidence of his own eyes.

" 'What! Is it *Earnshaw* I see before me? Ho, ho, ho,—thou hast gone to seed man, or, truth to tell, you could do with a *sowing* on that bald pate of yours. Ho, ho, ho, if Cathy were to see thee now; the fine fellow of a man you were! Is it the soft life that has reduced thee thus?'

"I went up to the Colonel as though I would hit him and indeed I feel I would have if the master had not spoken quite firmly and calmly.

" 'I fear it is not the soft life, Colonel, but a life of bereavement and shame that has ravaged me and, indeed, had Cathy been spared to me and had we been denied your presence in our lives, I think I should not be in the state you find me. Pray step into my study and tell me your business.'

"The Colonel continued in his overbearing way, flicking his cane on his thighs.

" 'My business is my *wife*, Earnshaw, whom you are holding from me. It is against the law I believe, a criminal act.'

" 'She is here of her own free will,' my master replied proudly. 'indeed she came to us as a refuge.'

" 'Nevertheless, my wife is my property. The law states it thus.'

" 'And my wife was my property when you took her from me,' Mr. Earnshaw replied in a whisper so that none should hear but he. 'Or is there one law for you and another for the Earnshaws?'

" 'Yes, there is,' bawled the Colonel. 'I always said you were a puny ninny, Earnshaw, and indeed you are.'

" 'How dare you talk like that about my father?'

"We turned round and saw Margaret slowly descending the staircase, looking proud and beautiful and dignified despite the burden she carried. Her head was flung back and her curls, brushed by me until they shone like beaten gold, hung over either shoulder. Even the Colonel seemed temporarily overawed by her

262

magnificence and she stood back as she came up to him.

" 'I said how dare you talk like that about my father? A finer man never breathed, Jack Heathcliff, and I should know—aye, having been married to you for three years—I tell you I well know the difference between a fine man and a rogue.'

"Oh, I was so proud of her; her fine bearing, her slow and measured speech and indeed I thought the Colonel saw, maybe for the first time—for women are fools in love are they not, Mr. Lockwood?—what manner of woman he had married. He had never seen her tested before; she had always been, until he started to neglect her, a pampered darling and this does not breed moral fibre; but sorrow and suffering, such as my mistress had known, had turned her from a girl into a woman and a fine one, to be proud of.

" 'Margaret, get your things and come with me,' the Colonel said sullenly, his voice much quieter than before. 'I want no scenes. I have my rights and I know them, but if you force me I shall carry you from here kicking and screaming, see if I don't.'

" 'I'll not give you that pleasure, Jack, to take me by force,' my mistress said scornfully. 'No, you shall have me as I am, knowing how much I hate and despise you, and how contemptible I find you and will to the end of my days.'

" 'I care not for your contempt,' the Colonel muttered, but I could see, even in the gloom of the hall, that his complexion had darkened, 'or aught about you except you are my lawful wife about to bear my lawful child. I have the Heights prepared for you and there we shall live for the meantime. Ah, did you know, Earnshaw, that I have acquired most of your property to save you from debt? Wuthering Heights is now my own.'

" 'My daughter told me,' Mr. Hareton replied quietly. 'Had I known you were the buyer I would not have sold.'

" 'That's just what I thought, Earnshaw, which is why I used an intermediary and, as you were anxious

263

to complete the sale, I got it for a good price. You're a fool, man, you don't deserve to succeed. I was prepared to pay more. Now I have my eye on . . .' and he looked around him, but dared not or chose not to utter what he had said before, that he would one day have the Grange. Oh I longed for Anthony to be there, to have his fine strong body to protect his sister, but maybe God was merciful; for I doubt not that Anthony would have gone for his real father with a pistol and who knows what might have happened to my mistress in the delicate state she was in? Nay, Anthony was out on his duties somewhere and in many ways—though vengeance was only delayed as you shall see—God be praised that he was.

" 'I want to take Agnes with me,' my mistress said, 'that is if she will come. Papa, may Agnes come, just until the birth is over? For I feel it will be very soon now.'

" 'Of course my love, my darling,' her father said, his voice cracking. 'That is if she will.'

" 'Need you ask, sir!' I cried. 'I am honoured to be so needed by my mistress.'

" 'But can you leave the children, Agnes?' enquired my kind master, his concern always for others.

"And I did indeed pause, for my eldest child, Jennie, was but ten years old and since their father had left us they clung to me the more. But I knew where my duty lay.

" 'Dora in the kitchen will look after them, sir; she is devoted to them and they to her. Maybe you would let her move into the cottage with them until I return?'

" 'That I will,' my master said, 'and a noble sacrifice you have made, Agnes. But you must come often to see them and they will come to see you . . .'

" 'It is only until the baby is born after all,' Mrs. Heathcliff said, but by the pleading look in her eyes I knew that she would need me by her side long after that.

" 'Of course, ma'am!' I cried to still her distress. 'My children can well fend for themselves for a while with Dora to keep an eye on them. I'll accompany you right away and I'll tell Jennie what is happening and that she is to be the mother to the family. 'Twill make her feel important. She can fetch up my things later and see for herself how near I am. There, sit thee, Mrs. Heathcliff, and I'll prepare your baggage.'

" 'Aye be quick about it,' the Colonel replied recovering his harshness. 'I want to be there by nightfall.'

"My mistress sat in the large chair in the hall and her father stood by her taking her hand in his and kissing it. It was a sad leavetaking and I compared it with the joyful reunion only a week before; but how I admired the dignity showed by the Earnshaw family that day, that contrasted so well with the brutal manners of Colonel Heathcliff—would that the Duke of Wellington could have seen him thus! By not resisting her husband my mistress was not only doing the dignified thing, as became her, but sparing my master more pain. She showed herself, on that day, to have the makings of a truly great lady.

"I had packed in a trice and one of the few servants we had left brought down Miss Margaret's bags, and a sorry sight they were, so few possessions did she have. Then she got up and, kissing her father murmured something in his ear, and looking at me to follow, walked proudly out of the place she loved to the hated home of her husband. The Colonel followed her silently, saying nought to Mr. Earnshaw and, driving the small carriage himself, whipped the horse into a trot up to the gates.

"It seemed to me during that short drive that much of my life had been spent passing between Wuthering Heights and Thrushcross Grange and always at some watershed in the family's history. But I never ceased to admire the fine view of the moors particularly on a day like that day, late October, when the sun had sunk low on the horizon and the patches of bracken were beginning to brown and wither and the storm clouds hovered in the west and the wind rose, suddenly as it does, from over the hill.

"How proud and fearless my mistress looked as she sat gazing out of the window, her eyes full of memories

265

of I knew not what, conscious of her destiny. I reached over and touched her hand and she smiled at me and pressed my own.

" 'Dear Aggie, my friend. I thought, looking out just now, how little I know of the moors which my mother loved; really I have hardly ever observed nature the way Papa told me she did. I think Rainton takes after her, not I. Oh Aggie, I have made so many silly mistakes, have I not? I was a foolish girl, empty-headed, trapped by the excitement of London life and the false charm of an older man.'

" ' 'Tis not unnatural,' I said. 'Your father should have seen to it that you did not spend so much of your childhood without young company. That way the Colonel might have not swept you off your feet so easily. You were a normal high-spirited girl—were, indeed,' I laughed, 'are, for thou art but one and twenty!'

" 'I have to keep on reminding myself of my age too, Aggie,' my mistress smiled wanly, 'for I seem sometimes to have lived a thousand years, I feel so old and bitter; but I must not let bitterness and unhappiness cloud my mind must I, Aggie? For I do not want it to affect my baby. I felt the child stirring strongly within me today. I feel my time will be very soon now and I want to be as tranquil as I can—as Jack will allow me—for that ordeal. Thank God I have you with me, dearest Agnes.' And she sat back in her seat and, once more, turned her face towards the moors and the sight of Wuthering Heights which loomed nearer with every step of the horses.

"And indeed the Colonel had made some sort of attempt to furnish a welcome for his wife. The place was clean and warm—the larder was well stocked with provisions, fires roared in all the grates, and he had a complement of servants to see to our needs. Indeed, as my mistress walked into the sitting room I saw her eyes light up with pleasure at the warmth and cosiness which the housekeeper had contrived to provide for her, and she bent down by the fire to warm her chilled hands.

266

"The housekeeper was a village woman I didn't know, Mrs. Baines, and she seemed not at all put out by the strangeness of the situation and courteously bade my mistress welcome.

" 'I have prepared Mrs. Heathcliff's chamber in the front of the house,' she said to me. 'The master thought she would like to have her mother's old room.'

'I thought it tactless to say the least, her mother having died in the room; but Margaret did not know that and she was not the kind of girl, as her mother had been, to imagine spirits. It was just the sort of ill-considered gesture I would have expected from the Colonel, trying in his bluff soldierly way to do the right thing. Indeed he seemed nonplussed, not that he had attained his object so easily, and he paced up and down the room rubbing his hands, for my mistress did not address a solitary word to him.

" 'Dinner will shortly be ready, sir,' Mrs. Baines said. 'Maybe madam would like to go upstairs and see her room?'

" 'I'm happy here thank you, Mrs. Baines,' my mistress replied. 'Agnes will take my things up for me.' And she smiled graciously and sat down in the arm-chair where I left her while I went upstairs.

"Oh what memories that room had for me, and I minded how we had brought Miss Cathy there the day she died, and how it had seemed warm and welcoming. This night as I entered I thought I detected a breeze and I knew not from whence it came for the windows were shut and the curtains drawn and there was a good fire in the hearth. I remembered the stories I'd heard as a girl of her grandmother haunting the moors, and indeed I had continued to hear them through the years, idle village gossip which had become part of the folk-lore of our area, but I doubted that Margaret had ever heard the stories, for which I was thankful.

"The old oak chest had been removed and there was a decent-sized bed in its place and a wardrobe and a chest of drawers and over by the window a little dressing table with a mirror mounted upon it. At the windows were pretty drapes. I judged that this had been the work of Mrs. Ibbitson and I wondered what had happened to that lady, almost as fierce as her son, whom I had not seen now for some ten years or more. Whatever had become of her, she had done her vengeful work well. Her evil plan had more than succeeded.

"While I worked upstairs the master—for such I had now to think of him—and mistress had dinner served to them downstairs and, from what I heard in the kitchen afterwards where I ate with the other servants, not a word had been exchanged between them and sorely perplexed everyone was, but I enlightened them not, thinking it was not my place to tell or their business to know.

"My mistress went upstairs as soon as she had finished dinner. She was tired and I got her into bed and sat with her until she fell asleep, and I marvelled at the courage and serenity she showed and the smile that played on her lips as though she had naught to worry about in the world and all the tomorrows to live for."

Chapter 15

"The rest of the week passed quietly—too quietly in many ways—as my mistress still refused to converse with her husband and the unease was felt by all in the house. She was polite enough and civil in that she sat with him at table; but not one word did I hear her say to him except 'please' and 'thank you,' with an agreeable, courteous nod of her head. It was as though he did not exist for her, not that she hated him, but that he was not *there;* and for a man of his temperament I think this was the worst burden he could be made to bear. Reviled or scorned, yes; hated or shouted at, yes; but silently ignored, no.

"However, anxious for her condition, for she now moved about with difficulty and lost her breath at the slightest exertion, he was careful not to provoke her, though that did not stop him being rude to me or shouting at the other servants when they did anything to displease him. Indeed I was worried about my mistress and the size she had attained in case it should damage her health, and the doctor who came every day was worried too and feared she might have a stillbirth if labour did not occur soon. But my mistress passed the days tranquilly and quietly, sewing, reading and looking now increasingly often towards the moors as though, for the first time in her life, she was beginning to appreciate their natural beauty.

"Every day her father sent for word of her, usually by one of my children, together with a little note, and thus we kept in touch with the Grange, for I knew Mr. Earnshaw feared to provoke his son-in-law and hazard his daughter's health. I also felt a closeness to my children who, despite missing me, were well looked after and lacked nothing. Seeing one or another of them daily kept my spirits up.

"To the relief of us all the Colonel went out most days to see about his business, or to ride on the moors which he loved, and often he brought back a fine bird or a rabbit for the pot and then I saw him at his best for he was content with what he had done and prepared to be agreeable, or to *try* to be—for it seemed he had long since lost the habit of amiability due to his years of acquisitive greed and debauchery when he neglected his wife and coveted his father's possessions.

"It was impossible to feel truly sorry for Colonel Heathcliff; but an emotion akin to sorrow possessed my breast on his behalf, although I cannot name it, for I am not a learned person. I think the word I want is that there was something pathetic in this proud, strong man who had served his country with honour, who had revered his father's name and loved his mother, and yet who could not keep the love of a woman who had once worshipped him and now regarded him only with the most blatant contempt. I often saw him looking at her as though he would fathom the mystery she had become. Sometimes he would try and gain her approval by a smile or a cautious gesture, or his bringing her a posy of wild flowers plucked from the moors, sparse as they were at that time of year, or a much grander bunch he had purchased at a florist's in Leeds or Bradford. She would accept everything he brought with a gracious inclination of her head to accompany her gentle words of thanks, and that would be all she would allow him. He would then sweep out of the room in rage and be heard striding about upstairs or pounding on his horse along the path to the moors or towards Gimmerton.

"And then the day came when my lady was taken with a sudden cramp, and her face creased with pain and, knowing her time was near, I sent one of the servants post haste for the doctor, thanking God for my own experience in giving birth to three children. I waited with her as the pains came quicker and her agony grew worse and still neither the doctor or the midwife came. And there she lay in the room in which her mother had died and sometimes her suffering was so great that I feared she would follow her, but she was a strong girl and I was glad that I had had the care of her in the last weeks of her confinement so that she was rested and well prepared.

"Then, after what seemed hours, when the pains were harsher and stronger, so that she knew no moments of ease at all, I heard the thud of hooves and a gig came up the hill with the doctor and the midwife and Colonel Heathcliff ahead of them on horseback, galloping for all he was worth while the servant followed behind.

"But the worst was over. The doctor scarce had time to roll up his sleeves before he delivered my mistress a fine boy and what a joy he was to behold as the midwife held him up, sound in every limb and huge to boot. But, that was not all! My mistress continued in labour, the doctor quickly examined her beneath the sheet and said that another baby was expected and, before half an hour had passed, a girl had joined the boy and her first lusty scream as well as her fine proportions proclaimed to all that Colonel and Mrs. Heathcliff were the parents of beautiful, full-term twins. They were yelling heartily, one at each end of the single crib I had prepared, and the midwife was almost weeping with joy, and I too, as I washed my mistress's face and saw the peace and gladness in her eyes before, after

271

she had briefly held the babies, she fell into an exhausted sleep.

"To say the Colonel was beside himself with happiness is to minimise the matter. He was almost berserk and ran about the house shouting 'It is twins, it is twins—no wonder she had such a girth. Thank God for a boy and a girl: Master and Miss Heathcliff!' And he gave the doctor a glass brimful of whiskey and thumped him on the back as though he himself had brought off this miracle, which indeed I can say was not so, and the midwife was kissed on the cheek also and given whisky every now and again, and they all agreed that the twins were the finest, healthiest, best-looking pair of babies born in Gimmerton or anywhere else for as long as anybody could remember.

"Oh it was a happy day. We had not many I can recall at that time, but that day was one of them. I was so overjoyed to see my Margaret safely delivered, and the size and health of the children meant they would not struggle in their infancy as some twins do—they are often puny things and in many cases one or both soon die. And yes, I'll admit it, I was overjoyed to think that again I would have babies to nurse for I am a very domestic woman, Mr. Lockwood, child-loving and always have been; all my own grandchildren are now a source of much joy to me. Five I have in all, and two more on the way—my daughter and my daughter-in-law are both expecting.

"My mistress slept all that day and when she woke it was to see my master bending over the crib. Indeed he had scarcely left it since the departure of the doctor and the midwife, and she stared at him for along time before he realised she was awake then. When he turned and saw her eyes upon him, he bent his head as though he were ashamed of himself, as well he might be, and he stood by her bed and said simply:

" 'Thank you, Margaret; they are fine children,' and he bent and kissed her forehead and his face stayed near hers as though seeking an answering response from her, but she gave none; so he straightened up again and I could see a shadow of anger pass over his

272

face, for maybe he then realised that the event of the twins had changed nothing and she would still not talk to him. So he went to the window and with his hands behind his back said:

" 'I would like us to be friends again, Margaret. I may have behaved badly, and I'm sorry for it. Now we have something besides ourselves to live for; may we not be friends on't?'

" 'I'll want to see more proof than words,' my mistress said softly. 'I'll want to see you give my father back his lands and make full amends to our family. I'll want to know that when you go to town it is not to the bed of a lady of easy virtue, and I'll want you never again to bring bad women or men into my home as you have not once or twice, Jack, but time and time again to my shame and mortification.'

"The Colonel stood where he was staring angrily over the moor, his hands twitching behind him.

" 'I can't give your father back what I bought honestly and legally; they were on the market, Margaret. I did him a good turn by keeping them in the family. Why his grandchildren will inherit this some day, instead of which they would have gone to strangers. I'll have young Green up and alter my will at once.'

" 'Alter?' said Mrs. Heathcliff. 'Alter?'

"The Master looked confused and I could see he had blundered, for of course, strange as it was to believe, his wife still did not know about his relationship to her brother and I daresay there was a provision for him in the will. Indeed the Colonel's interest in his natural son seemed to have diminished altogether, for I had never heard him mention his name. I daresay now his concern would be only for his legitimate issue.

" 'Why, my love, my estate is willed entirely to you. I want our children to share in it now.'

" 'Leave it all to them,' she said, 'but give Father back what is his.'

" 'Oh, you're unreasonable,' stormed the Colonel. " 'All right I'll put it down to childbirth when women have strange moods! I am not going to make a present to your father of something I purchased with my own good money. He and I do not like each other well enough for that! Now put it out of your mind. As for the women . . . why, if I reform I shall expect my rights too as far as you are concerned, and willingly and freely given. So think on that ma'am!' And with that he strode out of the room.

"For a long time my mistress gazed out of the window, her face curiously impassive, then she turned to me and smiled:

" 'Give me the babes to suckle, Agnes. You must teach me how.'

"Oh, a beautiful mother she was with a babe at each breast and, as she nursed them, her face became transformed with the joy and satisfaction that the suckling of one's own give, though among women of fashion it is often not considered the thing, I understand. And how I wished that she had joy in her husband as well as her children, but even then I feared that it could never be. They were too different. And as she nursed them I marked for the first time that the golden hair of the Earnshaw women had now ceased; for both the babies had hair as black as their father's and by black I do not just mean dark, but jet black and shiny such as we see in gypsies or in people from sunny lands like Italy or Spain.

"And I thought how curious it was that that very dark complexion and hair was so strong that it proceeded to the third generation, for these two were the grandchildren of the original Mr. Heathcliff and, from what I could see, as every bit like him as their father and half-brother were. Oh how I prayed that they would not turn out like them; deep in my heart I prayed for the twins that day.

"In fact, as though reading my mind in uncanny fashion, my mistress said, scarce had the thought left my mind:

" 'Agnes, see how the babies are like Anthony. There must be a dark streak in the Earnshaw family . . .' and her voice trailed off and I gazed at her, fearful that her mind was running along the same lines as my own, but although she was frowning I did not see

274

how she *could* arrive at the right conclusion. For she had no idea of the connection between her mother and her husband, and thank God she hadn't. I prayed that she never would, for every time I thought about the *unnaturalness* of it—and we have some unnatural things in country districts, I can tell you, Mr. Lockwood—it made me shudder, for this was one of the murkiest of all I had heard, as though the very Devil himself had had some hand in it.

"Very soon after the birth Margaret was up and busy about her maternal duties like the country woman she was. Unlike her mother, she loved nothing better than to take care of the babies herself, to nurse and bathe them and dress and undress them and all those fond little tasks that babies need and that we mothers dote on. And often I perceived how Colonel Heathcliff would come into the room and stand there watching his wife—indeed his eyes more on her than them, as though he coveted *her*—but he too would take them and fondle them and I think he did this because he wanted to try and find favour in his wife's eyes; he was wooing her all over again.

"There was another thing about my mistress, too, and that was that she had not inherited her mother's and grandmother's love of Wuthering Heights; the smallness of the rooms oppressed her and the view of the moors seemed to tire her, for she was used to the trees and shrubs and flowers of Thrushcross Grange and the gently undulating landscape of the valley in which it lay.

" 'Oh Agnes, why does he stay here?' she said to me one day as we were folding baby linen, and enough there was of it I can tell you. 'There is not enough room in this house.'

" 'Why, ma'am,' I said, 'it is a big house by any standards except that of the Grange; but it is an old house and was built solidly to withstand the north wind.'

" 'But I cannot understand his attachment to it. He says he has all the money in the world; why do we have to live here?'

275

"And then I saw my master had come in—for he could move as stealthily as a cat, and he said:

" 'I have a deep-rooted love of the Heights, Margaret; 'twas where my father was brought up. I feel I have roots here, bedded in the soil. That is why I wanted my children to be born here, so they have their roots here too. But, my love, if it irks you, and you have done your duty by having the babies here, I'll buy Thrushcross Grange for you, for I hear your father is sorely oppressed by debts.'

"My mistress gasped and her hands flew to her inflamed cheeks.

" 'What! Are you making more mischief for my father?'

" 'I, my love?' protested the Colonel, whited-sepulchre that he was. 'I have never made mischief for you father, on the exchange anyway. All I have is bought by lawful means. But I hear he is in a very bad way and that the new stock he has bought with the proceeds of the sale is now worthless. He cannot hope to be successful. He does not attend to his affairs himself, but leaves them to young Anthony who is still wet behind the ears. For though this is a time when great fortunes can be made—and I know for I have made one myself—they can be lost just as easily. I have asked your father to call on us today. I sent him a note a few days back telling him of the birth of my children and informing him that I would let him know when it was convenient for him to call. Well, I sent that note yesterday and asked him to come today.'

" 'You just order my father about as though he were some kind of lackey,' my mistress shouted at him. 'Well, he's not. He is my father and he . . .'

"The master cocked his ears and then went to the window.

" 'He is here, Margaret. I perceive him in the gig with young Anthony. My, what a fine strapping-looking boy he is—he'll break a few hearts, I'll warrant. Like his father . . .'

" 'I know not what you mean,' my mistress said. 'His father was never a man for flirting or breaking hearts.

276

As far as I know his one and only love was my mother . . .'

" 'Oh, I heard a few things in London,' the Colonel said craftily and of course I could see how deceitful he was being because Mr. Hareton had, in fact, trifled with the affections of a few wordly ladies, but not half so much as the Colonel, as we all knew.

"But Margaret cried out and, passing the boy to me, she ran down the stairs to greet her family before the gig had stopped at the door.

" 'Why Margaret, up already!' cried her father. ' 'Tis not a week since the birth . . . oh, my darling, you look so well,' and he put his arms around her and kissed her, his eyes wet with joy.

" 'Oh Papa, I am perfectly well. See, I am a fit country girl, as Agnes is always telling me, and the babies—wait until you see them, Papa.'

" 'Is your husband at home?' Mr. Hareton replied cautiously—no, I must use another word if I am to be honest, Mr. Lockwood. He spoke *nervously*. For a tremor in his voice betrayed his anxiety at meeting with the Colonel and how my heart grieved at the depths to which this worthy and good man had been reduced.

" 'Aye, he awaits you,' Margaret replied briefly and, after kissing her brother, she drew her arm through her father's and led him into the house where the Colonel stood with his back to the fire and his hands under the tails of his coat.

" 'Welcome, Mr. Earnshaw,' he cried coming towards Mr. Hareton with every appearance of affability. 'Fine babies I have given your daughter, as you will see. You have something at any rate to be thankful to me for. Fetch them will you, Agnes, so that their grandfather may see how like they are to me. There is not one Earnshaw characteristic that I can perceive, sir. Not one.'

"Oh how hateful I thought him then, to so taunt a man already tasting the bitter dregs of humiliation. He was crowing over his rival and he was about to administer another blow as I knew from the conversation I had overheard upstairs. Margaret remained by her father's side staring at her husband with the contempt to which he must surely by now have grown accustomed. That cool serene brow of hers rose loftily, the proud chin jutted out and her dark eyes sparkled with an anger that should have warned a man less sensitive than her husband.

"Mr. Earnshaw's joy at seeing the fine pair of babies which I shortly brought down was so great that once again he was reduced to tears, and I marked how his hand trembled as he wiped them with his handkerchief. Comparing the proud father and grandfather standing side by side, and remembering that there was but five years or so between them, you would have thought you were looking at men separated not by one generation but two or three, and the way that his hands shook, and his general frailty and debility made me wonder if Mr. Earnshaw was afflicted by some mortal disease that had diminished his once sturdy frame. But Margaret's arms were tenderly around her father; and I knew that she neither touched or permitted the embrace of her husband, much as he yearned for them.

"The twins had opened their eyes for their grandfather and though they were unfocused, of course, they still seemed to gaze directly at him and you could see how proud he was and how the sight of his progeny restored to him some feelings of dignity and self-respect, for his chest swelled and he seemed to have grown in stature.

" 'They are fine children, aye, fine indeed. I congratulate you both. And their names?'

" 'Josiah and Elizabeth Heathcliff,' the Colonel boomed, and not only did I look at him in surprise, but the Mistress too, for the last I knew of it the names had not been decided, and I knew that Mrs. Heathcliff was pressing for the use of her father's name, Hareton, which was perhaps a trifle overoptimistic of her.

" ' 'Tis the first I heard of it,' my mistress said quietly.

" 'Is there aught wrong with two good English names like that?' queried the Colonel. 'Josiah, after my stepfather, that good man who provided the wherewithal for me to make my fortune, and Elizabeth which is my mother's second name—I care not for Dorothy as such; it has not enough command to it. My daughter will be a person of importance in the community. Aye, Elizabeth it is.'

" 'I think you should have consulted me,' my mistress protested.

" 'And when should a wife be consulted?' the Colonel replied brusquely. 'When she carries out her husband's command and does as she is bid! When she is loving and dutiful and sweet and pleasant. *Then* she might be consulted, but there is no law on't that I know of. It is for the head of the house to make the decisions. Is it not, Mr. Earnshaw? Pray be seated, sir, and I will have tea brought in for I have something to discuss with you. Be good enough to take the babes upstairs, Agnes—have you noted by the way, Mr. Earnshaw, how like *your* son Anthony they are?"

" 'I thought you said they did not have one feature of the Earnshaws?' my mistress said gently and I saw again that frown of bewilderment trouble her clear brow, as though she were trying desperately to understand something. I gazed anxiously at the Colonel but obviously it did not suit him yet to make mischief, for he said:

" 'It must be some remarkable coincidence, my dear. Now, sir, I have heard in business circles in Leeds that you are sorely pressed for money yet again. Once more you have invested unwisely, this time in continental iron which was foolish when we have plenty of our own. I learn that the company importing it has gone bankrupt. Did you know, sir, that there is iron ore in Middlesbrough enough to provide for the whole of this country, or so they think? So that to invest in *continental* ore is a folly, sir, a folly. I myself had the foresight to purchase stock in the Middlesbrough fields a few years ago and my investment has already trebled.'

"At that, tea was brought in and I took the opportunity to take the babies up and put them in their cribs, and hurry down again because I was curious to know how this conversation would develop, and I dismissed the maid and served tea myself so that I should not seem to be conspicuous or prying.

"'Now sir,' the Colonel said, stirring the sugar in his cup. 'I want to make a proposition to you, for I am not a man of mean disposition and I know that your daughter is greatly attached to you. I wish to take Anthony here into my employ; he shall receive a good wage and be grounded in the elements of business of which, as I have heard, he has at the moment no knowledge at all. Untried, sir, untried; 'tis not your fault, boy,' and the Colonel gave Anthony what was no doubt intended to be a kind smile but which looked more like a grimace to me. 'Secondly, Mr. Earnshaw, my wife finds the Heights not to her liking. It is too cramped for her, she says, too bleak. True enough. If you do not have a love for the place as I do it *is* cold, remote and, if you are used to the space of Thrushcross Grange, cramped.'

"'I will buy Thrushcross Grange from you, and the park and all outbuildings for a fair sum as a dwelling for my wife and Anthony here . . .'

"'And my father?' cried Margaret, breathing quickly. The Colonel shrugged, putting his tea cup to his lips.

"'I cannot provide a home for your father, my dear. He must make his own arrangements. If he ceases his unwise speculation and husbands the money he receives for the Grange he should be well enough set up to buy some small house in Scarborough or such place as he chooses. What say, Earnshaw, is it a fair offer?'

"Mr. Hareton was sitting upright—that is as far as his poor back allowed—and his eyes were staring fixedly at the Colonel as though he heard but yet he did not hear and, for a time after the Colonel had finished speaking, he said nothing.

"'Did you hear me, sir? I need an answer.'

"'I am not going to accept your offer, sir.' Mr. Earnshaw said at last, speaking slowly and with dignity as though considering each word. 'You have taken everything. The Grange you shall not have and if I do have to sell it, it will not be to you.'

" 'Oh well said, Papa!' Anthony jumped up, clapping his hands, 'Oh, well done.'

" 'Be quiet, you cur,' snapped the Colonel. "Keep out of something which does not concern you. Do you not care about your welfare or that of your sister? Or your father? He has not a penny, man, he is a beggar!'

" 'Father won't sell to you, Jack,' Margaret said, showing that she too was in the same mind as the rest of her family. 'He said so. Oh what is it between you that you hate each other so! Would to God that I could make my father and my husband love each other, then maybe I should love both, for only one I love now and that one is he who gave me life. Cannot you find it in your heart, Jack, to make amends to my father, for whatever it is that has come between you?'

"The two men were staring at each other and such was the hatred and venom on the face of one, and the fear and contempt on the face of the other, that I knew Margaret's plea would be like the seed which falls on stony ground.

" 'I am willing to shake hands with your father and buy his house,' the Colonel said at last. 'I think my terms are fair.'

" 'They are not fair. You are humiliating Papa; you have always wanted to humiliate him. Why, Jack? Why?'

" 'Get upstairs woman,' the Colonel said roughly, 'and disturb me no more. You tire me with your puking and moaning. Be off with you.'

" 'You can't speak to my sister like that!' cried Anthony, jumping up. 'Withdraw those words!'

" 'Oh, oh, oh, listen to the champion,' said the Colonel, laughing cruelly. 'Don't you know, young cub, that a man's wife is his chattel? He owns her, and short of murder, can dispose of her how he likes. Your sister, I can tell you, is headstrong. She does not appreciate sufficiently the love and care of a good husband. What manner of woman have I married, I sometimes ask myself? She has little to commend her and now will not even obey. Upstairs, Margaret, do you hear?' And he moved towards her as though he would strike her.

281

Anthony leaped forward and seized his arm, only to be brutally beaten down by the Colonel who was a much stronger man.

" 'Off, cur! I'll set about thee all with a whip if I am provoked much more. Lay a hand on me and I'll break your neck. And as for this chit, this girl . . .' he seized my mistress by the arm and dragged her roughly to the door. 'Yes, she is a *girl*, no woman. She has no brains in her head or fire in her heart. Once I had savoured her attractions I had had my fill; I'll keep her for breeding and maybe put her in the stables where she belongs if I have aught more truculence from her . . .'

" 'How *dare* you . . .' Mr. Earnshaw was on his feet and quivering, his stick raised about his head.

"But the Colonel, like a man possessed by a demon, appeared not to hear and stalked up and down muttering to himself:

" 'When I think she is her mother's daughter I can scarce believe it. That angel for whom I would have given my soul to bear . . . *this*.' And he paused and his finger shook as he pointed it at his wife who stood by the half-open door. 'You are not worthy to be your mother's daughter. I loved your mother such as I've loved no woman, and I thought I'd found her again in *you*. I was prepared to worship you as I worshipped her, but what did I find? Emptiness. Silliness. A little girl in woman's garb. One who knew not her way in the world . . .'

" 'My mother . . .' she gasped. 'Papa . . . what is he saying?' I could see already that she knew, only dreading to hear the words.

" 'Aye, I went off with thy mother,' the Colonel cried, '*after* you were born. She came right willingly; so much for your father's attractions. And she wanted to follow me to the ends of the earth, so she said, but I had my duties in the Army and if I regretted it I've paid for it over the years by the memory of her, Aye, and Anthony's *my* son, can't you see it? You're a Heathcliff through and through, boy, even to your truculent nature and this fellow here, this Earnshaw, pretended he was your father but, to spite him, you have grown year by year more like me. Isn't it so, Agnes?'

"But I by now was shrinking in a corner and dared not open my mouth, though I would have liked to have given him a piece of my mind for the wrong he did his wife.

" 'You monster,' cried my mistress, rushing back in the room. 'You foul monstrous fiend . . . you married *me* after lying with my mother? 'Tis disgusting, 'tis obscene. Papa, *say* it is not true.'

"But Mr. Earnshaw sat on the edge of his chair, nodding his head, his hands loosely joined in front of him in an attitude of dejection.

" 'It is all true; alas, it is true. He has destroyed my family; the family that I so loved. He seduced your mother, and then you, and now he has taken all my land and there is nothing for me to do but die, dear Margaret, for I think he is in the grip of Satan and who am I to oppose such evil?'

" '*I'll* oppose it,' Anthony said, and he sprang for him and brought him down in a tackle that I thought would split his skull open on the floor. But no such luck. The Colonel roared like a bull and the door burst open and the servants came running and separated the two men and, once the Colonel was on his feet again, he seized hold of a stick which lay in the corner and was starting to thrash Anthony, but he was held back by a servant and Margaret cried:

" 'Get away, Papa and Anthony, get away, for he will kill you. Oh for my sake, I *beg* you, go.'

"And I added my voice to her pleas and, in fact physically ushered the master and Anthony out of the house where, quivering and dishevelled, they both stood by the gig.

" 'Agnes, take care of my daughter. He will kill her. He is mad. Oh God that we have come to this. Anthony . . .' and Mr. Hareton looked at Anthony who, however, avoided his eyes and I could see that of all of them he was the one most troubled and perplexed by the scene he had just witnessed and the awful words he had heard. As well he might be; for indeed it was a

283

terrible thing for a young man to hear that the father he worshipped was not his own and that his mother and his sister had loved him and lain with the same man, and had had children by him.

"Suddenly he turned away from the gig.

" 'I'll walk,' he said. Nothing else, and then he set off down the hill, first at a trot and then running as though he was pursued by a thousand fiends, but I knew that what pursued the poor young man was the awful memory of what he had just learned.

" 'Can you manage the gig back?' I asked Mr. Earnshaw. 'Or will I get a servant to drive you?'

" 'I think I can manage the reins, Agnes. What is to become of us now, good friend of our family?'

" 'Oh, Mr. Earnshaw, I am just a poor country woman. Sometimes, though, I doubt that God is good if he lets such evil things come to pass.'

" 'I have no money, Agnes. Heathcliff is right.'

" 'Then *let* him have the Grange. At least Margaret will have a home.'

" 'No, I'll not sell to him. I'd rather die. What, and let him own the whole of Gimmerton and spend the rest of his life crowing over me?'

" 'He'll do that anyway. You'd best go now and look to Anthony. A lad who finds that his father is not who he thought has sustained a severe shock. He'll need the comforting more than anyone.'

"And I patted the flank of the pony as Mr. Earnshaw set it jogging down the hill in the direction of his home. Inside I found that the chaos to which the room had been reduced had been put to rights and the Colonel, still breathing heavily, was drinking a glass of whisky.

" 'Well, a fine to-do we've had today,' I said. 'A right mess and no mistake. I hope you're proud of yourself, Colonel Heathcliff.'

" 'It wasn't my doing,' he said, tossing the contents of the glass down his throat and pouring another measure as large. 'I *would* be a good man, Agnes, but no one gives me the chance. Margaret hates me; her father detests me, now my son . . . An-

284

thony. All I wanted was for him to go for the Army, to help him . . .'

" 'You don't see yourself, Colonel Heathcliff,' I said, 'as others do. You are a mean, ruthless man and you have brought on yourself your own misfortune. You have no knowledge of how to treat people. You trample on your wife's feelings by calling her a chattel and then you expect her to love you and lie with you . . .'

" 'Oh, she'll lie with me all right,' the Colonel said grimly. ' 'Tis her duty and I'll enforce it . . .'

" *'Willingly*, I was going to add,' I said. 'Oh, I've no doubt you'll enforce it, for you have the strength. But is this what you want out of life, always to have to force people to do your bidding? And then to say that Margaret is not what her mother was. How *can* you say such a thing? You dallied with Catherine for but a few idle weeks. What makes you think that eventually she too would not have failed to please you, for she was a simple country girl at heart too and not nearly as strong minded or as capable as your wife whom you now abuse so unfairly. There's nothing to please you, say what you like. And what mischief you've caused by revealing all. How can you hope to mend that! You're a wicked man, and don't pretend you're any better than you are.'

" 'You get upstairs and see to your mistress,' the Colonel thundered, 'or I'll despatch *you* next. See to it.'

"Upstairs I found my mistress curiously calm, considering the trials she had endured. She was sitting comfortably on her bed, one babe held in each arm."

" 'They were crying, Agnes,' she said. 'I doubt not that the noise disturbed them. Oh Agnes, what is to become of them? Or me?'

" 'He's proud of them,' I said, jerking my head in the direction of the door, 'and I think in his funny way he loves you, despite what he says. I think he has found a lot more in you than he thought. He loved you at first because, of course, you resembled your mother and though he was unable to do it he loved her and was with her when she died. In many ways Mrs.

285

Heathcliff, and I know you may not agree with what I say, your husband is a pitiful man. He knows not how to obtain what he wants, and he destroys that which he loves most. I think it is his ancestry, for old Mr. Heathcliff was thought by many to be a wicked man.'

" 'And yet my grandmother loved him, and Papa says he loved him and, 'tis true, I worshipped Jack and Mama and thence loved him once.' She faltered and looked at me pitifully. 'Oh Agnes, I cannot bear to think that what he says is true, about Mama . . .'

" 'Aye it is,' I said reluctantly. 'It was a folly for them both, for your father was always a good man and much better than your husband, if you don't mind my saying it, ma'am. But he was a fine, handsome man— as he is now—young then and bold looking. There was a fire in his eyes that invited flirtation; but it got beyond that with your mother who was restless and, I'm sorry to say it, but 'tis true, tired of your father. Your mother was much younger than you at the same age; a child in many ways, discontented and always looking for the moon. Do not blame her, ma'am. Only love and pity her, for she died before her time.'

" 'Oh, I do,' Margaret said tearfully. 'I do pity her, to be loved by this man who would have cast her aside as quickly as he did me.'

" 'I have no doubt of it,' I said firmly, 'and I told him as much. They were only together a few short weeks before he left for the Army. 'Twas but a dalliance . . .' I added lamely.

" 'No, it was deeper than that,' my mistress said, her stoicism returning to her face, her tears dry. 'If you love a woman so much that you marry the daughter because she reminds you of that woman it was more than mere dalliance. Oh what fatal thing do these Heathcliff men have that draws us Earnshaw women to them, Agnes?'

" 'I know not,' I said, shaking my head. 'And there you see is young Anthony. You know you always loved him, preferred him to your brother Rainton: so you see he attracted you too, whereas what charm he had was always lost on me. He was a truculent, moody boy and

286

now see if he doesn't go and brood about what he heard today. He won't thank your father who brought him up and was so good to him, treating him as his own. And this was another source of discord between your father and Colonel Heathcliff because your father insisted that Anthony was his son when he knew 'twas not so; thus the Colonel nursed this grievance . . .'

" 'While father brooded over the fact that Mama had left him. No wonder they hated each other. Oh Agnes, see, Elizabeth is gurgling. Take her from me.' I was thankful that this disturbing talk was at an end.

"Such was our domestic tranquillity, loving and caring for the children, and so it was to continue for some days. Only occasionally did my mistress pause sadly to consider her own fate and that of her poor mother, but I did all I could to deflect her attention to something more pleasant. The Colonel was seen less at the house and stopped away for nights on end to go to London on business or visit his mother in Liverpool.

"Mrs. Ibbitson had kept very much out of her son's life since his return from abroad; it seemed to be her wish rather than his. She had not seen her daughter-in-law and seemed now to have no desire to see her grandchildren which I thought strange when I considered how fond she had been of them all, and especially Anthony, as children. I'd heard she suffered from bad health, the results of a slight stroke, and maybe it had weakened her brain. But I wondered too if she were not troubled by guilt because of what she had done to encourage her son to court so wantonly the daughter of the woman he had once loved. Maybe old age and ill health and the knowledge of the mortality of life made her afraid to answer to her maker for her evil schemes of yore.

"The Colonel's frequent absences gave us all a bit o peace and allowed Mr. Earnshaw to visit his daughter again, and one day he gave her the bad news that Anthony had disappeared from home.

" 'I never saw him again after he ran down the hill. I imagined he was in his room brooding and judged it best to let him be, but the next day when I sent for

287

him the servant said he had not returned home. Oh, what shall I do?'

" 'You best leave him,' I said. ' 'Tis all you can do. He is a gradely lad, able to look after himself. He'll get over it and sort himself out as best he may. He'll be making up his mind what to do. 'Tis all you can expect for the shock it has been to him.'

" 'And Margaret, my darling daughter, on whom I have brought so much misery, what will you do? I should have told you about Heathcliff and your mother; then you would never have gone away with him. It seems the wisest thing now, but then I did not think so. I did not want you to know.'

" 'Don't reproach yourself, Papa. I might have gone away with Jack even if I *had* known about Mama, I was so perverse and headstrong and foolish that it might have not mattered to me then. What shall I do, Papa? I shall stay with Jack; what else can I do? Neither you or I have any money; we have no other home if you are forced to sell the Grange; and what can a woman do when she is owned by her husband body and soul without any rights to call her own? I shall not be a loving wife to Jack, because I shall never forgive him, and I can no longer love him; but I shall be a *dutiful* wife for my children's sake. At least let us give them as good a life as we can, Father.'

"Mr. Earnshaw took her hand and pressed it to his lips, deeply moved.

" 'You are like the woman in the Bible, the pearl of great price, putting others before yourself. Would that you had the sort of husband you deserve; but you will be rewarded, Margaret. One day God will reward you. Now Margaret, if you don't want your husband to have the Grange I will shortly put it secretly on the market; he shall not know of it.'

" 'Of course, I don't want it, Papa! Your home? I could never live there in peace. Let him buy another, or build one. There are plenty of fine homes in the vicinity and plenty of land on which to build. But stay near us, Father, do not go far away—for I could not do without your loving counsel and wisdom.'

"And while Mr. Earnshaw wept, his daughter—dry-eyed as she nearly always was, such a stout-hearted creature was she—put her arms round him and comforted him."

Chapter 16

"Well, the days passed pleasantly enough except that my mistress complained about the harsh weather up on the moors, and about the inconvenience of her home. I would often see her gazing out of the window, watching the thick black clouds which hung so low you would have thought that, merely by reaching out your hand, you could touch them. And she would sigh and say:

" 'I know not up here whether 'tis night or day, Agnes. How I long for the plains again and the sight of green fields and hedgerows.'

"And I would shrug and say nothing for I knew that, if the Colonel had his way, my mistress would pretty soon be back in her old home. For Mr. Earnshaw's difficulties were common talk in the village, and it was known that now Anthony was gone—and still no word heard of him—my former master was without help of any sort in his business affairs and I heard too, through Dr. Clough who came up to see Mrs. Heathcliff and the twins, that Mr. Hareton had now a paralytic condition that would gave him only a few years more of life.

"But these things I kept from my mistress who was so engrossed in her babies and so determined to be strong that I would do naught to disturb her. By this I mean that her difficulties with the Colonel, her sorrow about her father and the sad state of his affairs, and the worry about her two brothers, she had somehow learned to put on one side so that they did not distract from the innermost calm of her being—her delight in her motherhood and her acceptance of her station. For we all have our stations in life, as you know, Mr. Lockwood, and those who rebel against them or nurse resentment are the least happy of God's creatures. For all the attention she paid him Colonel Heathcliff might not have existed, yet though he perceived it and was deeply angered by it, you could never fault her or say that she had been rude or wanting in her duties—except that there was one duty I know she did not fulfill. She kept her bedroom door locked at night, that I know, for I once tried to waken her when the babies were crying and she had overslept.

"And then, shortly before Christmas, the tragedy I had been dreading struck. I mind exactly the date because we were busy hanging up the holly and mistletoe and trying to make the place look as bright and cheerful as we could for the Holy Mysteries, not that I expected to have a merry or even normal Christmas with the situation as it was.

"We had had nothing but bitter weather with the wind driving strongly from the north so that all night it howled around the house, its buffeting seeming to shake it to its foundations. Many a day Colonel Heathcliff lamented the journey he had to make, and for that reason he would stop in the town and return when the weather had improved. We were warm and cosy in the house; there was no lack of fires or warming pans for the beds, and there was plenty of hot, nourishing food, but my mistress began to look pinched and chilled as though the starkness of her abode and the desolation she saw around her, unlivened by varieties of colour of scene, had penetrated to the fibres of her being.

"Anyway, this particular day late in the afternoon the Colonel rode home after having been absent for a few days and came straight to the nursery where my mistress was with the babies. I'd seen the Colonel coming from the window as I glanced out—for you could see the long, clear path down the moors to where it joins the road to Thrushcross Grange, and then it is lost in the fold of the hills; so the mistress was alerted as we listened to him shouting for the groom in the yard—the Colonel seldom talked normally to servants. He seemed to think they were all afflicted with a hearing impairment and had to be bawled at—and then we heard his heavy steps below and he ran up the stairs and came thrusting into the nursery, his face aglow as though alert with some good tidings.

" 'Well, how are my babes?' he boomed, rubbing his hands and leaning over his progeny possessively, like a miser over gold, but with the loving indulgence of a father towards his children which I had often remarked in Mr. Hareton's face. And then I saw the Colonel pause and look furtively at his wife, and his countenance again changed as he marked the serenity of her expression as she gazed not at him but her babes. And his face was such a mixture of emotions as I have seldom seen—missing was tenderness but most of the deadly sins were there, including pride, lust, and anger.

" 'Well Margaret, your father is a further step towards being a bankrupt, the course he has set himself. I have today acquired all his holdings in the Ribblesdale Mills, the largest spinners of worsted cloth in the north of England, and for a song, because he was forced to sell. He'll have to sell me the Grange as well now—it's his only way, and even then he'll owe all the money he gets for it to pay his debts, otherwise he'll end up in the debtors' prison.' He rubbed his hands with satisfaction, keenly marking the expression on his wife's face.

" 'That must make you feel very content,' she said at last, and how I admired the control and the dignity with which she spoke. 'It was a good day's work, Jack. I wonder my father sold aught to you, feeling about you the way he does.'

" 'Oh he knows not 'tis I!' roared the Colonel. 'I do everything through an intermediary, a broker versed in these matters. In fact I didn't know that Earnshaw still had holdings in Ribblesdale until this man alerted me to the fact. After the collapse of Butterworth there are a lot of good pickings to be had for those kept well informed, as I am. I shall have a fine empire to leave to my children.' And there was a hideous gloating on his face as he brooded on his rapacious misdeeds and feasted his eyes on her beauty and his fat young babies—all his property, all owned by him. I had to turn away such was my revulsion, and then my master broke another piece of news.

" 'I hear thy brother Rainton is come home, doubtless to cheer thy father or maybe to show us some example of business acumen we did not know he possessed, a quality that seems sadly lacking in your family.'

" 'Where did you hear this?'

" 'Oh I hear everything. I have ears and eyes perpetually focused on my behalf on the Grange, for I know that when that other Earnshaw is of a mind to sell, it will not be to me. Well, Margaret, I'm hungry. I expect you at my table presently, and we'll share a bottle of good wine to celebrate my good fortune, eh? *Our* good fortune, my dear, for soon you shall have your heart's desire and be mistress of Thrushcross Grange once more.' And he leaned over her and breathed in her face, his eyes alight with lechery, and I could see how she withdrew her head and her eyes closed in a momentary spasm of disgust.

"After he had left the room I could see her expression was thoughtful.

" 'Rainton is here—oh, can Rainton *do* anything, Agnes? I long to see him. He was always such a tower of strength, but father upset him by preferring Anthony. I think we both hurt Rainton in many ways but,

Agnes, I feel good that he is here. I think he may do something to help us.'

" 'Madam,' I said, looking at her piteously. 'What can a young man to who is scarcely two and twenty years old? He has no experience of the world or the ways of someone as skilled as your husband. Mr. Rainton was always more interested in the wonders of nature, in the fauna and flora that he observed about him than in any clever business deals.'

" 'I still feel that Rainton will do something, Agnes. I know not why, but 'tis in my bones. Oh, send word by George or Jennie or whichever of your children comes next that I must see him. I can't tell you why, but my heart is uplifted by hope.'

"However my mistress's happiness and optimism were short-lived, Mr. Lockwood, and I can scarce bring myself to tell a young man of your refinement and breeding what happened next, so I will pass over it as quickly as I can; but I have to tell it to you to show you the depths of degradation to which that ogre stooped, and to explain what subsequently happened.

"He dined well with his wife, that I know because in the kitchen we afterwards had what was left and it was enough for an army—roast capon, half a ham, a side of beef, tarts and quinsies and plenty of the finest French wine. Once again those who waited on them reported that no words were exchanged, but rather that my master kept up a restless monologue to which his wife would occasionally nod her head but no more, as though she had her mind on something far more pleasant and interesting than listening to one who was becoming increasingly drunk. After dinner my mistress got up as usual to go to her room but my master barred her way and tried to put his arms about her in a clumsy attempt to kiss her.

" 'Jack!' she cried. 'Pray let me be.'

" 'Margaret,' he murmured, trying for once to be cajoling and pleasant instead of tough and demanding. 'Cannot we try again? I am infatuated by you, Margaret, you know that. I will do all I can to please you.

I have *everything* to give you, and you shall never want for anything.'

" 'What I want cannot be measured by money nor yet by property,' my mistress replied coldly.

" 'But Margaret, I want to give you my *love,* too. I swear to reform, to be faithful. I will never look at another woman if you will be a wife to me again, Margaret.'

" 'You thought I was but a *girl* who was no longer capable of satisfying you, after you had had your fill. You said as much before my father; you had to seek other satisfaction. You said it yourself.'

" 'No, Margaret, no! I was wrong. You *are* a woman, a wonderful striking, beautiful woman and when I saw you with my children today, looking so lovely and serene, I wanted you passionately, Margaret, and I still do. I will be faithful, I swear . . .'

" 'You'd best keep out of the nursery then if such a sight inflames you so,' my mistress said contemptuously. 'No, Jack, you have done too much that is wrong to make me ever love you again; you have hurt me and my father. You think I want my mother's lover in *my* bed? Even if nothing else had happened between us, that would be enough to disgust me forever. As long as I have to, I will remain in your house. I have a duty and I will see that I do it; but make no mistake, Jack Heathcliff, between thou and me is fixed a great gulf and no bridge will pass over it nor is there earth enough to fill it in.'

" 'But Margaret, you're my *wife,*' my master shouted, aware that his pleadings had brought him nought but humiliation. 'You have duties to *me,* not just my children and my household.'

" 'I thought you got your pleasures elsewhere. Don't they suffice? There must be any number of women in Leeds and Bradford willing to serve the needs of Colonel Heathcliff who can certainly afford to pay for them . . .'

"And with that my mistress swept out of the room while, according to the servant who reported this scene, my master growled like a maddened bear and

296

filled his glass once more with claret and sat brooding by the fire.

"As usual I put my mistress to bed, perceiving her to be more tired and agitated than usual, and there were dark shadows under her eyes. I realised that, gradually, the strain of her life and the effort she had to make to appear normal was robbing her of much of her robustness and beauty. But all she said to me then besides the ordinary things about the children, was that she wanted to see her brother Rainton as soon as possible and that when the Colonel next left the house I had to send word to the Grange or go myself.

"That night, as it happened the babies were fretful and, as I did not wish to disturb my mistress, I stayed with them myself in the nursery which was next to their mother's room, trying to calm them with feeding bottles, so as not to disturb her sleep. At about midnight I heard the sound of a terrible crash from the sitting room, which was under the nursery, and then my master's heavy tread on the stairs. I listened fearfully as he lumbered towards my mistress's room and banged heavily on the door.

" 'Margaret! It is your lawful husband. Let me in.'

"There was no reply and my heart beat quicker and, oh, how I prayed he would leave her be and go away. But of course he did not and banged again.

" 'Margaret, open the door! 'Tis writ in the marriage bond that thou shalt comfort thy husband and obey him. OBEY, do you hear, Margaret? I'll beat down this door unless you open it.' And he began to thump on it so that the whole house reverberated. I wondered that the servants did not come but I suppose that, like me, they had heard and knew not what to do. In fact there was not one strong enough to stand up to the master, either physically or verbally, or of course any who had the right.

"Then I heard my mistress's voice saying calmly:

" 'Jack, you will wake up the house. Go to bed.'

" 'I want to go to bed,' the master thundered, banging the door repeatedly.

" 'I want thy bed. I care not who knows it. Open the door, Margaret!'

"Oh my heart beat so wild I thought it would burst. But what could I do? In the master's present mood he would surely strike me down if I tried to interfere.

" 'Jack, go away,' my mistress whispered again. 'You disgust me. I want nothing to do with you.'

" '*Disgust,* is it?' roared her drunken husband. 'Disgusted with your lawful spouse? Oh, how you threw yourself at me once, Margaret. I detected no disgust then. Aye and thy mother too—a right pair of wenches in heat if ever there were. Think back on those days of your ardour, Margaret, and let me in. You will not be disappointed.'

"Oh, what shocking words! I could hear his heavy breathing, but from my mistress there came no sound and then, to my horror, there was a terrible sound of splintering wood and I knew that the Colonel had put his huge frame to the door and taken it off the latch. My mistress gave a sharp scream, but he quickly overpowered her and the fearful sounds I heard I cannot describe to you, only I wish I could not recall them as vividly as I can. A man was violating his own wife against her will and it seemed to me that nothing said in the marriage contract or anywhere else could ever justify that.

"Well soon everything was quiet—for there was nothing tender or skilful in her husband's caresses—and I could hear my mistress sobbing very quietly, and shortly after this the Colonel left her room and stumbled down the corridor to his own. And I waited for a while to be sure that he would not return and then, very timidly, I went to my mistress's door and perceived that it hung loosely on its hinges, and I knocked quietly.

" 'Madam, it is I,' but she didn't answer, and I knocked again but there was no reply and after a time, thinking she was either asleep or preferred me not to see her thus, I crept away. But I stayed all night in the next room without sleeping in case she wanted me, and I also swore that if I heard the Colonel attempting to approach her again I should get one of the guns that hung in the gun room and blow out his brains.

"The next day, which I shall never forget for reasons which you will hear in a moment, was such a contrast to all the grim and gloomy days that had gone before. There had been a white frost overnight and there was snow on the hills and the earth gleamed and sparkled as though sprinkled with clusters of newly polished diamonds. The sun was a great orange ball low in the sky and the mistle-thrush and blackbirds were out in full song as though to express their joy at the beauty of the day. The sky directly overhead was a hazy blue growing pink towards the horizon, where the mist concealed the hills which we could usually see on a clear day.

"As though unaware of the desecration he had committed in the night, my master was down betimes, *singing,* can you believe it, and calling for his valet to get his guns for he was shooting grouse. As soon as I had seen to the babies I went into my mistress and found her awake and up, all ravages of the night before repaired except that I marked her lip was swollen and there was the suspicion of a bruise over one eye. She even smiled at me, remarking on the beauty of the day and my heart once again was filled with veneration at the spirit of such a woman and thought how her mother would have lain in bed for weeks after such an ordeal, lamenting loudly and calling for the doctor.

"Her only reference to the night before was to ask me to have the door mended and a bolt put on, and then she went into the nursery to greet her darlings. From downstairs came the smell of breakfast cooking, and the sounds of Colonel Heathcliff shouting for his horse and for his boots to be cleaned and goodness knows what, as though he thought it good to be alive and was untroubled by anything on his conscience. And this was probably the case, if he *truly* regarded that noble woman, his wife, as a chattel.

"But I marked, as my mistress began to feed the babies, that her chest was bruised and that she winced as they vigorously attacked her nipples. We soon per-

299

ceived that all was not well and at last my mistress said to me 'I think my milk has gone, Agnes. There is nought for them to suck. Pray prepare their feeding bottles.' The shock to her delicate system had caused my mistress's milk to addle.

"I knew that she did not wish to go downstairs as long as her husband was there, and I fetched her up some tea and toast, which was all she normally took in the morning, and then she sat at the window and as he galloped off with his valet James, a creature almost as evil-minded as his master, she watched then until they disappeared over the horizon towards Pennistone Crags.

" 'Madam, will you stay here?' I cried. 'Who knows what he will do next?'

"She blushed and turned her head away, but I had to express my concern for, such was his brutality, I wondered if her life was in danger.

" 'I don't think he will come again for a while, Agnes. It was the drink as much as anything else. Where can I go and what can I do? My father is a pauper, my brothers have no fortune. I have no relations, few friends. How can I take my children when I have no roof for their heads? No Agnes, I am better here, evil as Jack is; I must be patient. But, oh Agnes, send for Rainton. I *long* to see him.'

"But before I had the chance to brief a messenger we discerned a rider on the horizon coming up the hill, and I called to my mistress to come quickly:

" ' 'Tis your brother Madam, Master Rainton! Oh what a fine fellow he has become. See the girth of him.'

" 'Oh, let me see! Oh Agnes, he is a *man*. I have not seen Rainton since my marriage. Oh let us go and welcome him!' And she flew down the stairs and was out of the house and by the gate before her brother's horse had stopped. Then he leapt from the saddle and ran towards her and they embraced almost like lovers, and I thought that at last she would release her feelings and allow herself to weep; but no. She was laughing with joy and hugging him and looking up into his face and, oh, how my heart contracted, for to look at Master

Rainton was like going back over the years and seeing again the fine face of his father, that handsome strong man whose wedding I had attended and who was now a pitiful wreck dying of palsy.

"Rainton was almost as broad as he was long—that is not to say that he was fat because it was all strong muscle, and he was so bronzed and fit that I knew he had not acquired that complexion in this bleak land of ours. He walked with a spring in his step and exuded good health and clean living, and to see him was to feel the better for knowing that such a strong upright presence was at hand.

" 'Oh Rainton, Rainton, come in and tell me where you've been and why you didn't write and, oh, Rainton you look so fit and strong—what have you been doing? Agnes, pray get some tea for Rainton and then come and join us and hear what he has been up to.'

"After the shocking incident the night before, about which not one servant remained in ignorance I may say, the joy of my mistress on being reunited with her brother infected the whole house. For once, the Christmas decorations seemed in their rightful place and the pale wintry sunlight lit up the dark corners and shone on the tree decorated with tinsel in the sitting room. I wished that Colonel Heathcliff would never return to spoil the enchantment of the day.

"When Master Rainton had admired his niece and nephew and kissed his sister again at her good fortune in acquiring them, we returned to the sitting room and sat by a huge fire, my mistress gazing eagerly into her brother's face.

" 'Tell me Rainton, where have you been?'

" 'Why, Margaret, when father could no longer afford to keep me at Oxford I set about looking for employment. You know I was attracted to the Navy but had not the means to purchase myself a commission. But one of my masters at Oxford was a friend of Captain Philip Parker King who was about to set out with two ships *The Adventure* and *The Beagle* to survey South American waters, for ore and raw materials in plenty—the new nations of South America, following the collapse of Spanish and Portuguese domination during the Napoleonic Wars, were sorely in need of trade. Vast sums of money have been invested in operations in the South American continent, and hundreds of British merchant ships are carrying on a thriving trade with them.

" 'I managed to procure a passage on a ship, meaning to pursue my botanical studies, and I was able to assist the Navy with its survey because of my scientific knowledge. But Margaret, the opportunities in South America! You can become a rich man overnight. I have already staked claims to many mining concerns and without a penny of capital needed, though I lacked not for influential friends, thanks to the education father gave me at Rugby and Oxford. So I soon gave up the hydrographic surveys for business, and then the chance came to take a ship home and I felt the need to see father again, and you, and when I did my visit gave me both joy and pain. For I heard that father was ill and almost destroyed by your husband, and also something of how he has treated you, and our mother before you.'

" 'Oh Rainton!' My mistress embraced him again and kissed his cheek, seeing the expression of grief on his face. 'I would have spared you that.'

" 'One of my purposes in coming today—apart from seeing you—was to have words with the Colonel whose treachery to my own father I like not. He is a wicked, evil man, Margaret. Why don't you leave him?'

" 'And go where? And my children? Father is a pauper.'

"Rainton puckered his brow and began to pace the room.

" 'I came just in time. I am no rich man yet, but the pickings are there. Wait a year or two, Margaret, and I will have money to spare, for Father and for you. You can get a divorce; it is done. But, were it not for you, I'd get a whip to Heathcliff.'

"My mistress's eyes lit with hope at the brave words of her brother and, at the same time, the silk shawl that she had draped over her shoulders came unloose

302

and the terrible bruises on her chest which she had tried to conceal were revealed. Rainton saw them immediately and, going up to her, looked carefully into her face, noting her eyes and brow.

" 'What is this, Margaret?' he cried, his voice rising. 'What are these bruises I see, that cut on your mouth, the discolouration of the eye? Does he ill treat you, too? Say he does not, I beg you, or I will get a whip to him this very day.'

" 'Oh no, no. It was a fall.' Mrs. Heathcliff cried quickly, drawing the shawl over her bosom. But Master Rainton turned to me, his face like a thundercloud.

" 'Agnes, does Heathcliff beat my sister?'

" 'Oh sir . . .' I began, and then I buried my head in my hands and wept for I had had no sleep the night before and the shock of what had occurred was still with me. Alas, my action was more potent than words.

" 'What?' cried Master Rainton. 'He *dares* lay a hand on you, besides what he has done to our family. Where is he? I'll horsewhip him,' and Mr. Rainton strode from the room towards the outbuildings, and when he returned, he had a long carriage whip in his hands which he doubtless had procured from the barn.

" 'Where is he? I'll wait his return. Lay hands on my sister, does he? I'll have the hide off him.'

" 'Oh Rainton, I beg you. He is my husband. Please, Rainton, not here . . .'

" 'He's on the moors,' I said. 'A whipping will do him good. I'd like to see it. He rode over to the Crags; but be careful, sir. He has a gun and a servant with him.'

"But Mr. Rainton was so enflamed that I scarce recognised him. He had been angry enough before, but the violation of his sister had sent him over the edge and, without another word, he strode out of the room and in a trice we heard his horse galloping past the house.

" 'Oh, Agnes, fetch help!' My mistress cried. 'Jack will kill him. Quick, let us go after him with John. Oh Agnes, you should *never* have told him where Jack was.' And my mistress fled from the room, crying for John the groom, and a stout lad to saddle her horse.

"My heart was filled with such dread and foreboding that I sped after her, telling John that if he could not stop my mistress, I would ride behind him. Another servant I directed to go quickly to the Grange to fetch Mr. Earnshaw.

"But scarcely had I done this when my mistress was away—she had not the skill of her mother, but she could ride well even though it was years since she had been on a horse. I got behind John and urged him to follow our mistress, and not let her out of sight; but of course we knew not where we were going, and at one time we seemed to go round in circles looking for figures, dreading to hear the sound of a shot.

"And then in the distance I saw the gaunt outline of Penistone Craggs rising above the valley, and I perceived what I thought were figures, and I cried and pointed, urging my mistress to take care. The agony of talking in that harsh air made my lungs hurt and my breath grow cloudy with the cold.

"From Penistone you could see all over the valley, but already a thick mist was rising and the morning sun was hazy and overcast. Mr. Rainton had obviously been conversing with the Colonel, the two of them on horseback, the valet, James, some way off, and then Rainton jumped off his horse and on to the stone and the Colonel did too, giving the bridle to James, and as Mr. Rainton lifted his whip the Colonel reached for his gun, but Rainton struck first and the shot went wide. There was no doubt in my mind that Rainton would be killed, for how could he survive against a heavy musket loaded with shot? By now we were in sight and both the men stopped and Mr. Rainton cried for Mrs. Heathcliff to get away.

" 'Stop, I *beg* of you!' Margaret screamed, dismounting from her horse. 'He will kill you, Rainton; he will use his gun.' And then I saw the sneer on the Colonel's face and I knew that he realised he had the upper hand, and that he could take his time about despatching his attacker. Margaret, stumbling on the coarse heather continued running and crying, and I behind her aware all the time of the birds wheeling overhead, the gulls and the crows as though in anticipation of a gruesome feast. Rainton ignored his sister and again raised the whip and had it about the Colonel's legs, but the Colonel sidestepped and steadily aimed his gun. From where he stood the shot would blow off Mr. Rainton's head and send him plunging into the valley below, for he was perilously near the edge.

" 'Get back, Margaret,' the Colonel cried, a fiendish smile on his face. 'I shall despatch thy brother over the edge, and then I shall deal with thee and see if I can administer a few more bruises to add to the collection I hear you have!'

"And those were his last words, Mr. Lockwood, awful as it is to say that he went to his Maker with such a cruel jest on his lips. For at that point he backed to gain advantage over Mr. Rainton who was advancing with the whip and as he raised his gun to take careful aim he slipped, for I think I told you the ground was covered with ice and, struggling to gain his balance to no avail, before our astonished eyes he disappeared over the edge and all we heard was a resounding cry, like one of the damned descending into hell.

"Even after he had disappeared none of us realised fully what had happened, nor could we believe our eyes. We continued to stare into the space recently occupied by the Colonel.

"Margaret continued running as though nought could stop her, and then Rainton caught her, and John took another arm and they pulled her to a halt, for fear she too would go straight over the edge. Her face, which had already been distraught, looked as though she were on the edge of frenzy.

"Because of the slipperiness we did not dare look over the rocks in case we should follow him, but John and James quickly climbed down, followed by Rainton, while Margaret and I, huddled together for warmth and protection, stood at the top for I know not how long, wondering if by any chance he could still be alive.

"But chance there was none. He had fallen from the highest rock and his head was broken by the stones that jutted out beneath and, oh, much as I hated him, what a terrible end it was and what a mournful sight to see his body brought up and laid on the ground, his head lolling at an unnatural angle because his neck had been broken. His eyes were still open and from his forehead and mouth there issued twin streams of thick, black blood.

"I recall, at this moment, the sun disappeared completely and a chill wind sprang up, as often happens when the sun goes in and, oh, what a desolate scene it was as Margaret knelt by the body of the man she had once loved so passionately but whose misdeeds had driven her to hatred. What did she feel as she knelt there gazing on his face, into his dead open eyes which had once reflected all the emotions we mortals are prone to—fear and greed and hatred, passion and hope and, once perhaps, love? Love, certainly at first with Catherine and then Margaret, love as he'd looked on his children, love, maybe, for his mother and the kind man who had adopted him. But all the other less noble emotions had been reflected in those eyes all too often in the years since I had seen the deterioration of a once brave and noble man.

"I think Margaret felt that too, for she closed his eyes gently and then she kissed his cold lips.

" 'He was my husband, the father of my children,' she said as she got up and looked at us. 'And whatever he has done to me since, I did love him once. Oh, Rainton.'

"And her brother took her in his arms to comfort her, while those choking tearless sobs that I knew so well racked her slender frame, and what his own thoughts were I know not, for what was done was done and a dead and broken body could not be mended."

Chapter 17

"The death of Colonel Heathcliff was an accident of course—though I sometimes think intended by God—for there were witnesses to prove it, and no one cared sufficiently about him or liked him enough to try and implicate Mr. Rainton in the matter, although it was known that he had gone after the Colonel with a whip. It was also known that the Colonel would have shot him with his gun given half the chance. Indeed that was his evil intention at the moment he fell, and the magistrate paid full regard to this when he brought in his verdict of accidental death after the inquest.

"Yet because of the scandal all the villagers came out to gawp at the funeral and to see the remains of Colonel Jack Heathcliff placed, as was his wish, by the side of his father. Margaret, still shocked and stunned by the event that had made her a widow and her children orphans, left Wuthering Heights immediately to seek the safety and familiarity of Thrushcross Grange and the protection of her brother and father.

"But alas, before the winter had passed it became obvious that Mr. Hareton would not long survive his detested son-in-law. It had an irony to it—when you think how much Mr. Earnshaw had suffered at the Colonel's hands—that now he was not able for long to enjoy a peaceful life. He had a paralytic affliction, as I think I told you, Mr. Lockwood. His limbs shook, and he found it increasingly hard to move about. And, despite the loving care of Margaret, and his joy in having Rainton home at last, he pined for Anthony and longed to see him again before he died. Such was his grief and longing that Mr. Rainton did all he could to have his half-brother found, but there was no more word from him since that day he had disappeared running down the hill.

"I think that grief as well as the other sufferings which the poor man had had to endure accentuated his physical illness and on March 15, 1827, he died peacefully in the presence of his children and me, and Rainton closed his eyes and became the head of the family.

"And the sad thing was that a few days after his adopted father's death, Anthony was apprehended in London by agents sent to look for him by Master Rainton and brought home on the promise of money, for he had been found in miserable lodgings in Cheapside and heavily in debt.

"And a pathetic, sullen creature we saw as he walked from the carriage that brought him home into the house. He was thin and unshaven, his hair unkempt and his clothes threadbare.

"I know not what happened at the first interview with his brother and sister for I was not there, but Margaret told me something of it the following day as we busied ourselves with the twins in what had been her old nursery.

"Oh I cannot tell you the change in my mistress, despite the sadness of nursing her ailing father, and the shock of her husband's death. Now that she was away from Wuthering Heights, which she had hated, and once more in the comfort of her own home she had grown plump and wholesome and the haggard lines and careworn look had vanished from her face. When I say plump I do not mean that she was large, for she was so tall that she easily absorbed the extra weight; but oh, she was a fine-looking woman, comely and with a clear healthy complexion. And what with her flashing dark eyes and bright golden hair it seemed certain to me that any man who allowed her to be a widow for long would be a fool; but she used to tell me that, after her experiences with Colonel Heathcliff, she did not wish to rush into matrimony again.

"But the day after Anthony's return I marked that once more my mistress's expression was careworn, and she looked as though she had slept badly and she hardly waited for the babes to settle down for the morning rest before unburdening herself to me.

" 'Oh Agnes, we had a fearful time with Anthony. He is so full of hate and resentment. Rainton was so kind with him and gentle and said we loved him and he was our brother, and we had tried to find him to tell him that father was dying and then he said suddenly:

" 'And what about my *real* father? I hear Rainton killed him! Aye 'twas told me on the journey up how he died.'

" 'Oh Anthony, 'tis not so,' I said, aghast. 'It is true there was a quarrel, but he was about to kill Rainton with his gun; he had his eyes on the sights when he slipped on the frosty stone and fell backwards. I saw it myself and Agnes.'

" 'Aye, all covering up no doubt from the magistrate,' Anthony said brutally.

" 'No!' Rainton cried, pale now and hurt as well as angry. 'James, who was Colonel Heathcliff's valet and loved him, was there too; he saw it all.'

" 'Aye, paid no doubt to keep his mouth shut by you.'

"I could scarce bear to hear this from someone whom I had for so long loved as tenderly as a mother and sister combined.

" 'Anthony, you know your father was a harsh man. You know that, for you threatened to kill him yourself. What has changed you? He showed you no love, he has not provided one penny for you in his will. It is we who love you and always have, and our father too, Anthony, for I want you to think of Hareton Earnshaw as your father. Indeed I often think he preferred you to either of us. You loved him, didn't you, Anthony?'

" 'Aye, once,' Anthony said sullenly, and then he stood up and turned his back to us as though he wanted not to see our faces.

" 'But a lot has changed since then. It seems that my own father wanted me after our mother died, but Mr. Earnshaw would not have it that I was Heathcliff's son. He did want me and to provide for me; but it was denied him. All this I learned before I went to London because there are enough people in the village who know the truth, many of them who have been in service either at Wuthering Heights or Thrushcross Grange. Heathcliff *did* want to love me but he had not the chance . . .'

" 'But Anthony, he went away to the war. What would have happened to you then? He was away ten years. Besides, we were your brother and sister, and our father gave to you twice the love he gave to us.'

" 'To appease his conscience, doubtless,' Anthony went on in the same bitter voice. 'If he felt that way why am I not remembered in the will? For I believe everything is to Rainton, Margaret having been provided for by my father. Why did he cut me out?'

" 'Because there was nothing left to leave,' Rainton said gently.

" 'Our father was bankrupt; even the Grange was mortgaged and, apart from a few worthless stocks and shares, he possessed nought. Thank God I am able, with the help of friends, to raise a loan to keep the Grange, but I must shortly return to South America and develop the business interests I have begun there.'

" 'But I am wealthy, Anthony,' I said, 'and you shall share every penny I have and take an interest in your father's business if you have a mind to. He left his affairs very orderly indeed.'

" 'Aye,' Rainton said eagerly. 'You can look after your father's interests. How about that, Anthony?'

" 'I have no head for business,' Anthony replied in the same sulky way. 'My father made that quite clear

310

the day I saw him at the Heights. He was right. I tried, but I am not interested in it.'

" 'Then what is it you'd like to do, for we have the means?' Rainton said, going over to him and trying to put his hand around his shoulder, but Anthony backed angrily away.

" 'I think I'll spend some of the money lying around—how about a few wenches and the gambling tables in Leeds. Eh?' And he laughed so evilly, Agnes, that for a moment I saw the living image of his father, my late husband, and I shuddered. Then Rainton said sternly:

" 'Anthony, there *is* no money "lying around," as you put it. The bulk of your father's wealth has gone to the twins in trust. Margaret just has the interest on the capital and I will make sure it is not squandered by you on whores or the gambling tables.'

"Then I went up to him and put my hand on his arm, saying gently:

" 'Anthony, do not be bitter. You *have* a lot to be bitter about, but it is a sterile emotion and, thanks to the providence of God, we are now well provided for; but you are a young man, a fine man with all your life in front of you. Why waste it? Your father didn't. He served in the Army with distinction. There's an example for you. Would you like to go for the Army or the Navy? Rainton will purchase you a commission.'

" 'Happily,' Rainton said, looking eagerly towards Anthony who now turned round with a cunning expression on his face.

" 'Maybe I *will* have a commission in the Army. Be sure it's the best regiment, Rainton, that money can buy; there are few wars about at the moment so I'll have a life of ease, which is what I deserve, I reckon, after the hardships I've been put to. You'll be well rid of me too, won't you, my loving sister Margaret and devoted brother Rainton? But don't worry, I'll be back. I'll not forget the man who killed my father . . .'

" 'Anthony!' I cried, *really* vexed with him for the first time. 'That is the most unworthy and unfair thing you could say. If you knew the truth . . .'

311

"And I stopped, Agnes, for the sake of modesty, but he would not let that be.

" 'Yes, what *is* the truth, Margaret?'

"But I turned away, and Rainton said very quietly:

" 'Since you will have it, Anthony, and are not content without it, I must tell you that Colonel Heathcliff attacked his wife physically; he abused her. Need I say more?'

"You would have thought that would be enough to silence a man of decent feelings, but Anthony said with a snigger:

" 'But she was his wife! Wasn't she performing her lawful duties? Maybe she deserved a thrashing, for I found in London that women like a good beating from time to time and are all the more pliant for it.'

"And as I looked, horrified to hear these foul words from one who had been so gently reared, I thought Rainton would strike him, but instead he turned away and stood beside the fire, his head sunk deep in his chest.

" 'It grieves me to hear you talk like that, Anthony, and it shows me what sort of company you were keeping in London. Thank God we found you, for you are but a lad. Our father grieved for you, and the fact we could not find you hastened his death; but to speak like that of your sister! No woman, however lewd or loose, deserves violence; but your own sister!'

" 'Oh, they're all the same,' Anthony said casually, 'or so it seems to me; should be treated like a good dog or horse and thrashed when they don't obey.'

"Of course my instincts were to leave the room, Agnes, but I had almost reared Anthony myself so, if he thought this about me, what chance was there that he would treat a wife better?

" 'Anthony,' I said. 'If you think like this there must be something Agnes and I have done badly when we brought you up; for respect for women is part of a gentleman's training and I'm sure you never heard that kind of speech in this house. But you were shocked and hurt that day at Wuthering Heights at the revelation of your birth and for this I forgive you much. It also is obvious that you have got into bad, loose company in London and I hope that it will not mar you permanently. But I am always your loving sister, Anthony remember that, *whatever* happens. We had the same mother and we were brought up together and if an accident of birth has made you bitter there is nothing I can do. But let us all try to live in harmony and peace. Though you may reject us, we shall never reject you.'

" 'Will you give me the Heights for my home?' Anthony's next astonishing question was to Rainton. 'I have a taste for independence and I love the place. Say you will and I'll not bother you or shock you again with my coarse words.'

" 'But Anthony, this is your home, you are our younger brother.'

" 'No, I want independence. I'll go for the Army as soon as you have purchased a commission; but I want to know that, whenever I come back, my home is not here but the place my father loved and my grandfather before him, aye, and my mother and grandmother, too. My roots are *there*. And I'll change my name to Heathcliff to boot, so that I'll make a fresh start. I am best away. You and I never loved each other, Rainton, and now you've killed my father. I owe it to his memory to take his name and live in his place. Margaret, yes, I love her, but who knows that she says what she means? Give me the Heights and I'll be happy.'

" 'I have to think about it,' Rainton said unhappily. 'For 'tis not mine to give; it belongs to Colonel Heathcliff's estate; but Margaret and I will talk about it . . .'

" 'Of course, he can live there!' I cried, wanting to placate my wounded younger brother, for I did think this was but a momentary aberration that came out of a deep feeling of hurt and rejection. After all it is the duty of women to show love and tenderness when there is only harshness and fear. 'He can have it as his home, for I dislike the place; but whenever he wants another

313

he knows he always has a welcome place with us here.'

"And close to tears, I'm sorry to say, Agnes, for I loved Anthony and was deeply wounded by his brutality, I left the room.

" 'Well,' I said, 'blood will out. I'm sorry, ma'am, but they say it and it's true. You'll have nothing but trouble from Anthony, mark my words, whatever you do. Let's hope they ship him out to India in the Army and we hear and see no more of him for many a day.'

"And indeed, Mr. Lockwood, that is what happened, for a time at any rate. Anthony's commission was soon purchased in his father's old regiment, the Foot Guards, where his name was then a legend, and he did go out to India where there was a permanent Army, and for a time he did well; but we scarcely heard from him, for he seldom wrote. And then Mr. Rainton set sail for South America and for the next few years peace reigned once more at Thrushcross Grange while the babies grew strong and beautiful and my mistress lovelier as she became more mature. And eventually it happened, as I knew it would, that she caught the eye of a man who was a prize for any woman, even one as gifted and beautiful as my mistress. This was no less a person than John Broughton Tempest of Castle Crawford, whose family were one of the oldest and grandest in all Yorkshire, and now we come to the third and last part of my story."

"It was the year 1830 and the twins were nearly four. Mr. Rainton had been away for almost three years, but he had left the English business in the hands of a capable manager while he rapidly made a fortune in trade with South America. He wrote to us frequently, and how we loved his letters and his descriptions of the places he visited, which my mistress read to me with great excitement. But he always longed for his Yorkshire home and told us he was coming back for good, and that we should find a wife for him for he had a mind to settle down and raise a family! Mr. Rainton was twenty six in 1830 and, indeed it was time

314

to found his dynasty, and how I prayed it would thrive and be happy at last.

"Oh with what joy my mistress looked forward to his return, though the years he had been away had not been unhappy ones for her. For, as I have told you, she was a clever and thrifty woman, a good housewife and a loving mother, and although she did not lack male admirers, she gave her heart to none of them.

My mistress very occasionally went to London to see the shops and to keep up with friends she had made there in 1823 and it was at the house of Laetitia Talbot, the sister of her one-time suitor Charles, now married to a prosperous landowner and member of Parliament, that she met Mr. Tempest at a dinner party given in his honour. For he was lately returned from a business visit to the Far East and was on his way home to the North, and it was the purest coincidence that my mistress was staying with Mrs. Laetitia Chetwynd, as she now was in the spring of 1830 at that time, and this is her account of the dinner as she later told me.

"It was very grand, Agnes, and I was so pleased I had taken my green French silk for there were about twenty guests to dinner at Laetitia's house in Mount Street, Mayfair, and the table glittered with glass and silver and fine linen, and the guests, many of them distinguished, were splendidly attired. And although I knew I looked well in my silk and had had my hair coiffured, I felt once again that I had been too long immersed in the country for the talk was all of politics and the agitation for the Reform Bill and whether the government would fall and what would happen, because the King was very ill and expected to die.

"And all the time at dinner I was aware of the man sitting opposite me who was slight and fair and had a superior rather disdainful cast to his face, but at the same time a quizzical look in his eyes which, I must say, were often turned in my direction. I was not surprised at the concert afterwards that he contrived to sit next to me and his first words were:

315

" 'And what do you think of Reform, ma'am? Are you for or against?'

" 'Sir, I am not a politician,' I said, laughing to hide my embarrassment, 'but I do think the electoral system should be changed, and it should be fairer than it is. Near where I live large towns have no suffrage, while tiny villages in the South return ten members or more.'

"The man, whose eyes twinkled attractively, I noticed, and who was not as severe as he had at first appeared, nodded and said: 'And pray where do you live, ma'am, to have acquired so much knowledge?'

" 'Oh, 'tis a tiny village in Yorkshire. You will not have heard of it, sir. Gimmerton, by Keighley way.'

" 'Indeed I know of Gimmerton, ma'am, though I was never there. But I am a Yorkshire man myself, from Crawford, near Skipton, of which you may have heard, and I have business interests all over Yorkshire, Keighley, Bingley, and Bradford. But is not Gimmerton very isolated for such a beautiful woman? Is your husband in this company, ma'am?' And he looked about him enquiringly.

" 'I am a widow, sir,' I said, 'and if Gimmerton is isolated I am used to it, for I was born there.'

"And just then Laetitia came over and, clasping her hands together in mock surprise exclaimed:

" 'You two have sought each other out! For you *must* be acquainted. You are from the same part of the world.'

"But the fair man said:

" 'Pray introduce us, Mrs. Chetwynd, for although it appears we are neighbours we have never had the pleasure of meeting before.'

" 'Mrs. Jack Heathcliff, may I present Mr. John Tempest,' and as she pronounced our names we both looked at each other in surprised recognition for I, of course, had heard his name—who has not heard of the Tempests of Castle Crawford? and he cried out:

" 'I was briefly acquainted with your late husband, Mrs. Heathcliff! We did business together, and now your brother Rainton and I are on the boards of several companies. This is fortunate, Mrs. Heathcliff, only unfortunate that we did not meet before!'

"And standing up, he bowed low, Agnes, and kissed my hand and I felt an emotion stirring within me such as I had not known for years, and I needn't tell you what that was.

"Well, we talked for the rest of the evening. It seemed we could not find enough time to say all that we had to say and goodness knows what it was, certainly not business and the like. But he was such an enchanting speaker when he told me of his travels that he made me laugh and cry almost in equal proportion, and goodness, he even seemed interested in what *I* had to say and asked me about the Grange and my life in Gimmerton and the children. So that when it was time to go he asked me how long I was staying in London and if he might escort me to the Opera.

"Later it transpired that he had been due to leave the following day. But, just to be with me, Agnes, he stayed another week and we saw each other every day; and then he drove me all the way home in his carriage and we stopped overnight at Castle Crawford where I met his mother and sister Jessica and his father Sir Charles Crawford, who is a very old man.

"Oh the time we had in London! The balls and dances we went to. We were at the theatre or opera or a ball every night and danced the new *galop* which is all the fashion. I remembered, Agnes, how when I was young, the waltz was the latest dance and how daring we considered it then. Indeed this time was like a dream revisited and I was not a matron but a girl again.

"Well, Mr Lockwood, when my mistress came home that time driven up in style in a fine carriage with a coachman, and escorted up the stairs of the front porch by this elegant gentleman in a grey frock coat, pale grey trousers and tall grey hat, I knew better than any words could describe, merely from glancing at their faces, that something special had occurred during my mistress's visit to London. She ran towards me, her arms outstretched, and planted such a warm and affectionate kiss on my cheek that her happiness was something you could almost touch as well as feel.

"And then she turned and shyly brought forward this imposing gentleman and introduced me to him. I was so impressed by his aristocratic air and beautiful manners as he bowed and shook my hand, and then took my lady's arm and accompanied her into the house where her first action was to ask me to bring down her children who were taking tea in the nursery.

"Mr. Tempest was very tall, not well built as Mr. Rainton was, but lean and strong looking. He had fair hair that waved at the sides and a long, clever face, striking blue eyes and the most fastidious elegant hands I ever saw on a gentleman. And as I brought the little ones in and they ran to their mama and she covered them with her warm maternal embrace, I saw how he gazed at *her*, scarcely able to take his eyes away from her for one instant. But then he bent down and kindly greeted the children and, as tea was served, I thought what an admirable family scene we had here round the fire on a chill March day, just before Mrs. Heathcliff's twenty-fifth birthday. However I dared not let myself hope too much for, although in poise, grace, and beauty I held my mistress second to none, the Tempest family were of the old nobility as well as being enormously wealthy, and it seemed that for my Margaret to marry into such a distinguished family, after her treatment at the hands of the Colonel, would be a dream.

"However, that night as I did her hair and prepared her for bed I could sense her happiness; she was like a bairn again and not a woman weighed down by the responsibilities which, as a mother and the mistress of Thrushcross Grange, she had to carry. She hummed as I brushed her hair and her face dimpled in the mirror as I said:

" 'I am right glad to see you so happy, ma'am,' and it was then that she told me of the events I have just outlined to you, concluding: 'I have never been so

318

happy in my life, Agnes; well, not so happy for years for, it is true, that when I first met and married Jack I was very much in love; but it was a different *kind* of love, Agnes. I know not if you understand what I am trying to say. Then it was young, heedless, wild, ecstatic love. And this . . .' her voice trailed off and she looked at me gravely, 'but what am I saying? I have known him scarce a week!'

" 'I don't think Mr. Tempest is one to trifle with the affections of a mature woman, a widow,' I said. 'He would know that this was not an honourable thing to do.'

" 'I think you speak reason,' my mistress whispered. 'I could feel that every moment we were together his eyes were upon me and his heart engaged to mine. But dare I hope? What about the children? And the unsavoury reputation that my late husband left in the low districts of Leeds and Bradford? Would my past not be a burden to a family like the Tempests?'

" 'I'm sure that Mr. Tempest cares not what his family think or do not think,' I declared. 'He is too fine and upstanding a gentleman. If his heart is engaged then he is the master of his fate.'

"And indeed I was not wrong; for we had a beautiful spring that year and the Grange had been freshly papered and painted inside and out in preparation for Mr. Rainton's homecoming. And every weekend and some weekdays, too, Mr. Tempest rode up in his small, elegant carriage to take my mistress on outings with the children, or alone to visit friends and attend dinner parties.

"Occasionally he whisked her off to some grand party at Castle Crawford where it was his pride to show her off to his friends and family.

"And then it was the month of June with the grounds of the park a riot of colour and the leaves hanging thickly on the trees; the lawns had been cut, the gravel raked over and the horses rubbed until their coats shone, and Mr. Tempest arrived to take Mrs. Heathcliff to Liverpool to meet Mr. Rainton. Looking lovelier than ever I had seen her, she was waiting for him at the bow window in the sitting room. As soon as he saw her, in a yellow muslin dress sewn with small flowers, her thick golden hair dressed high on her head so that she seemed at the same time both maidenly and yet mature—an irresistible combination, Mr. Lockwood—he went over to her and before I could close the door behind me I heard him say:

" 'Margaret, I want to speak to you before your brother comes; look at me, Margaret, and tell me if you like what you see?'

"And I confess that for the first time in my life I deliberately *eavesdropped,* Mr. Lockwood, to my shame. I left the door open a crack so that I could see and, in justification, I can only say that my mistress's happiness was to me more important than my own. My mistress was looking up at him with the grave, composed face that was so enticing because on her lips there hovered a smile and you never saw such a flirtatious expression in your life.

" 'You know well I like what I see, John.'

" 'Then will you have me for your husband? Am I good enough for you? Oh Margaret, I hardly dare say the words, nor beat about the bush, for fear you will refuse . . .'

"And he stared at her, an expression of such comical pleading on his strong, handsome face, that my darling first looked amazed and then her face was transformed into absolute enchantment.

" 'I refuse *you?* John Tempest, since when have you become so modest? It is I who wonder if I am good enough for you. The Earnshaws are but ordinary country folk, not gentry, and as for my late husband—despite his prowess in the Army and the skill of his business enterprises, you could scarcely hold a candle to the honour of his name. Then I have two small children . . .'

" 'And I love them as my own already, my dearest Margaret. I want to make you and them happy for as long as I live; it is my only mission in life, my deepest desire. Oh Margaret, do not keep me in suspense . . .'

320

"And with that he drew her to him and as they locked in an embrace—such a handsome pair, both tall and fair, the yellow of her dress and the grey of his suit a pleasing combination—I thought I had never seen two people more suited, so that, well-satisfied with what the answer would be, I closed the door and went to order tea, my heart singing so much that I could say I was as happy as my mistress.

"And oh, that laughter and joy in the house that day and the day after! It rang with the sound of merriment from morning until night for Mr. Rainton was brought home and told of his sister's engagement and the children were told about their new papa, and there was such feasting and merrymaking as I had not seen for many a year or expected to ever see again. And then the whole family went off to Castle Crawford for the weekend and, a few days later, Mr. Tempest's sister and mother came to the Grange for dinner, and there were dances and visits to the theatre and endless activity as people came and went and dressmakers were summoned, for the wedding was not to be delayed.

"And I have forgotten in all this excitement to mention Mr. Rainton, who we had not seen for two years. He was grown even fitter and more handsome than ever, and more prosperous too, and he had become quite a dandy with exquisitely cut clothes and, as though to complete the picture of elegance, he had brought with him a black fellow as a servant who was called Peter and who could not speak a word of English. Gimmerton had never seen the like, I can tell you!

"It was several days before Master Rainton and I had the time to be alone together and then he called me into his study and thanked me for what I had done during his absence.

" 'You have always been a mother to us both, dear Agnes, and I know your joy will be as great as my own to see my sister happily wed to this excellent fellow and my niece and nephew with a father once again. Now you know they plan to live in the dower house in

321

the grounds of Castle Crawford. 'Tis no great size but 'twill suffice, and I want to know what plans you have. Would you like to stay on here with me, or go with my sister? You know whatever you decide your home is always here, and George and Jennie and Anne will always have a home with us and a father in me.'

" 'Oh Mr. Rainton,' I said, 'you are goodness itself . . . If my mistress commands me I will go with her, but I am not a young girl any more, sir, and I own I would like to end my days in the Grange where I have spent most of my life. Jennie is now fifteen, and, though young, is fully experienced as you know, sir, having worked in the house here since she was eight. She would be honoured to go with my lady as maid if Mrs. Heathcliff does not consider her too young.'

"I could see the pleasure on Mr. Earnshaw's face as he answered.

" 'I will ask her, Agnes, though she will be grieved to lose you, and the children, too; but she will be here often and of course we have known Jennie all her life.'

"And indeed so it transpired. Although saddened that I would not go with her, my mistress understood the reasons. For one thing, much as I loved Mrs. Heathcliff, I had a better position at the Grange than I would have at the dower house, and my own comfortable cottage. And Jennie was an admirable nursemaid for the children who knew her and loved her, and moreover, she was the third generation of the Dean family to be taken into a responsible position in the Earnshaw household—my great Aunt Ellen having been the first, as you know.

"The wedding was in September and the kind weather was with us again as Mr. Tempest led his bride down the aisle of Gimmerton church to face the throngs of well-wishers who gathered outside. All the village turned out to see the beautiful bride and the handsome groom, and Josiah and Elizabeth acting as page and bridesmaid to their mother. Oh, it was a sight to gladden the heart and I recalled the first time I had seen the four of them sitting around the tea table six months before. What then had been a faint hope had been turned into reality by the grace of God who surely, now, would bless this family and its descendants to the end of their days.

"But then of course, I had forgotten about Anthony Heathcliff and the legacy that his dreadful father had left behind."

Chapter 18

"My mistress had been married a year when Anthony Heathcliff was sent home in disgrace from the Army. It was sometime before I got to the root of what the dreadful business was, for it was hushed up even to one as close to the family as I was; but I know that he misconducted himself with the wife of one of the officers in his regiment and this had resulted in some sort of duel in which the offended husband was either gravely wounded or killed.

"The day I saw his spoiled, marred face gracing the doorstep once again, my heart turned to lead as though someone has cast a new and heavy burden upon me. Not that he didn't look well, Mr. Lockwood. He had fattened out and it suited him and, with his face bronzed by the Indian sun and his dark good looks and black flashing eyes, I was hard put to decide it wasn't a spectre, a reincarnation of his father as a young man returning from the past.

"For he looked just as his father had looked when he had stolen the heart of his mother, Miss Cathy, although he was a few years older than his father then had been.

"And indeed Mr. Rainton had more reason to be joyous and forgiving than ever for he was about to be married to Mr. Tempest's youngest sister, Jessica, whose affections he had succeeded in capturing in the face of much competition for, at the age of but one and twenty, as she was then, she was one of the prettiest girls for miles around and had a reputation not only as a beauty but as a tease and a flirt. She had all the young men sighing and swooning for love of her and threatening to blow out their brains if she scorned them.

"And indeed I think it was Mr. Rainton's *mature* charms that attracted this pert young miss, besides the fact that he was a fine-looking man and grown very wealthy to boot. For you will know, Mr. Lockwood, that the thirties saw the development of the railways which began here in the north with the Stockton to Darlington line in, I think, 1825 it was or thereabouts. And then in 1830 the Manchester to Liverpool line, which had been so bitterly opposed by those with other interests—I understood from Mr. Rainton who was my informant in all these matters—was opened by no less a person than the Duke of Wellington himself who was Prime Minister of the day.

"Mr. Rainton, who early on had seen the importance of the railways as opposed to the slow journeys by barge on the canal, had invested in them heavily and, as one of the principal share holders in the Liverpool to Manchester line, had for the opening taken all his staff to see the great occasion. That was the furthest I had ever moved from Gimmerton, Mr. Lockwood, or am likely to, and a wonderful day it was that I shall remember all my life, to see the hero of Waterloo, and Mr. Rainton walking in the retinue that surrounded that famous man.

"Anyway, I digress. To return to Jessica whom I had seen many times before I marked the interest my master had in her, for my dear mistress Margaret soon became *enceinte* after her marriage and I went fre-

326

quently back and forward between Thrushcross Grange and Castle Crawford as much to be sure that my daughter Jennie was carrying out her duties as anything else.

"I'll own that Miss Jessica was a beauty, but she had the superficial kind of good looks that, in my view, do not compare to those of Mrs. Tempest and which I personally have never found attractive. Her hair was very fair, almost white, and she had a pale skin with light blue eyes and arch, pretty lips on which I am sure she used paint. She had a very high childish voice and spoke quickly and breathlessly as though all the words contained in her mouth were bursting to find an outlet. And she always dressed in keeping with her doll-like appearance, with many bows and flounces and pretty floral muslins and cottons.

"Mr. Rainton had told me that he was smitten with her at first sight but that, with all the admirers he knew her to have, all younger than he and more stylish and dashing—for most of them were wealthy and didn't do a day's work—he didn't think he had a chance. And indeed I think his suit was not much favoured by his sister who, being of a very different character and disposition from her flighty sister-in-law, could not find much to commend her for someone as serious and worthy as her brother Rainton.

"But then we know, do we not, Mr. Lockwood, that worthiness is no special commendation in the eye of someone in love, and that one of the mysteries of life is why some people attract, and are attracted by, some and not others. And Margaret and her husband John were perfectly suited in body and temperament—for besides looking so well together they had many common interests, sharing a passion for music and books and of course opera and the theatre. And then Mrs. Tempest also loved parties and dancing, for there was this lighter womanly side to her, and I heard that no partners looked so well together as they did on the dance floor. Oh, they were such a perfectly matched pair and so deeply and seriously in love that it was the greatest joy to behold them or even to be near them.

327

She, of course, was the perfect wife and mistress of his household, although I confess that secretly I longed for the day when his frail old father would be taken to his rest and the young Mr. Tempest and his wife would inherit Castle Crawford, one of the grandest houses as well as one of the oldest in Yorkshire.

"And the twins adored their step-papa who gave them as much care and consideration as if they had been his own. I knew that he hoped for a large progeny for he was a vigorous healthy man and his wife in the prime of her womanhood and but two years younger than he.

"But, as I said, Mr. Rainton's wordly experience and manly charms no doubt attracted Jessica, for soon she put away all her other suitors and had eyes only for him, despite Mrs. Tempest's reservations. These I know she kept to herself and did not share with her husband, who had a proper regard for his sister. She spoke of her doubts only with me who had known her since birth and loved her as a daughter.

"I would say that Mr. Rainton was besotted by Jessica. I have never known a man so silly in love. He spoiled her from the day she consented to be his wife and showered her with presents large and small, never returning home without a gift or, if he was away on business, sending her some tokens of his esteem. And when she came to look over the Grange before their wedding I knew pretty soon who would be in charge there for she ordered half the furniture out of the house, and a lot of it good modern pieces by Mr. Chippendale and Mr. Hepplethwaite, and had sent instead the heavy oak early Georgian pieces that was the type of decoration she preferred.

"Anyway it was a few weeks before the wedding that Anthony darkened the house with his presence and was promptly set up in style and splendour by his brother, because he was so happy with the world that he wanted everyone else to share his happiness too, forgetting the former discord that had existed between them. Anthony seemed quite happy to have his accommodation in the Grange and showed no signs of

328

wanting to remove to Wuthering Heights which had re-mained isolated and unused since his departure in 1827. Nor did he show any inclination to do a good honest day's work but stopped in bed until afternoon, dressed himself up, and was away to the town some-times not returning until dawn.

"One day I said to my master:

" 'Sir, is Mr. Anthony to remain here after you are wed?'

" 'Indeed I have not asked him,' replied that good man cheerfully. 'I think he talks of going to London, or taking a house in the town.'

" 'I wonder you give him houseroom,' I said bitterly.

" 'Why Agnes,' said my master with some asperity. 'I find it strange that you should say that when he is our brother and we have promised to look after him.'

" 'But with his *reputation,* is it wise to keep him un-der the same roof as your young wife?' I said boldly. I felt I should speak frankly to those who, though they were my employers, I also regarded as my children. I must say that though this remark appeared only to an-ger my master and he dismissed me from the room, I think the wisdom of it implanted its seeds in his mind for, shortly after, Anthony was despatched with an al-lowance to London, but not before he had been up to the Heights and taken stock and said that he would use it as his country home, for he intended a life of idleness and ease.

"He was also beside his brother at his wedding and I must say he looked very fine in his dark frock coat and high starched cravat and I noticed even then how he ogled the bride, but I am glad to say that on that occa-sion, at least, she behaved with the greatest propriety and had eyes only for her handsome husband.

"And I will say they made a comely pair—he very big and strong with the dark Earnshaw looks and his fine head of chestnut curls, beside his dainty wife with her pale hair and complexion. They were a striking contrast; for he seemed all harsh masculinity and she everything that you would expect of frail femininity.

"They were married early in September 1831 and he

329

took her to South America on a tour that did not end until the following January, and during that time I left the Grange to be with my mistress who, in November, was delivered of a fine boy, the heir to the Tempest estates, who was christened John Dugdale Tempest but was always known as Dugdale to distinguish him from his father. And then sadly, for a death is always sad however much it is expected, Mr. Tempest's old father Sir Charles died soon after Mr. and Mrs. Earnshaw returned, and the new Sir John Tempest and my mistress, a titled lady at last as she had every right to be, moved into Castle Crawford and began one of the most glittering and extravagant episodes in its entire history.

"For I must tell you that Sir John and my master, Mr. Rainton, had enjoyed unparalleled prosperity in these years due to careful business enterprises and the management of their estates. They both had large shares in the railways and in woolen mills in Yorkshire and cotton ones in Lancashire. And, in addition, Mr. Earnshaw had extensive business interests in South America where he had taken his bride for, despite his joy, he had a skilful way of mixing business with pleasure.

"Castle Crawford, you might know it for it lies beyond Skipton in the beautiful dales country, and is well hidden by trees and parkland, is a huge mansion with, it seems to me, as many rooms as there are days in the year and of all periods because over the centuries it either had been added to or diminished by wars. In appearance it looks like a castle with crenellated turrets but parts of it are quite modern as Sir Charles had it expanded in the modern Palladian manner by a close associate of the late Mr. Nash. The effect, instead of being incongruous as you might expect, is very grand and Sir John has just had the whole front altered and extended so that it has a huge forecourt for the accommodation of all the carriages that are there so frequently, for he and Lady Tempest are given to frequent entertaining now that he has entered Parliament as one of the members for the newly created bor-

330

ough of Bradford. They say he is all set for a place in government anyway, he is that well thought of. However I am leaping ahead a few years and I have yet to bring you up to date with the tragedy that, despite my prayers to God, once more was to befall the luckless Earnshaw family.

"The new Mrs. Earnshaw had scarce been at the Grange for a few weeks when I realised what an unsuitable companion my master had selected to share his burden in life. For one thing, used to the splendour of Castle Crawford, she found the Grange—a sizeable house by any standards—too small and said it made her feel cramped! She also hated its wilderness and remoteness and the fact that the moors loomed behind the house like, she said, some threatening presence.

"She had little to do all day, for she was an inept housekeeper and found neither needlework or reading to her liking. What she did miss was the company of her mother and sisters and her many friends, for she said she had been forever moving about the country, staying at this grand house or that, or spending time in London to attend the fashionable dances and visit the theatre and opera.

"And then, of course, my master was away all day and often nights as he visited London or his many interests round the country and although on his return he lavished her with presents—I never saw so many gifts of expensive jewellery or lengths of silk or brocade and muslin for dresses—she was ungrateful. And whereas to be home by his wife's side was Mr. Rainton's dearest wish as a rest from his labours, she nagged him all the time to go to this place or that and gave him no peace at all.

"Then, fatally, I feel—for had he not left so soon things might have settled down—Mr. Rainton was suddenly called to South America to see some of his most important possessions which were threatened by war in the country, I forgot which. My mistress, who had but lately returned from South America and had found it primitive and the climate oppressive, had no wish to go again, even if Mr. Rainton had wanted to take her

331

which—only for her safety, because otherwise he loved nothing better than to have her with him—he did not. Thus it was that the newly married lady, restless and discontented to boot, was left to her own devices in the late spring of that year only a few short months after she had returned from her honeymoon.

"Lady Tempest, aware of her sister-in-law's discontent, invited her to stay, but Castle Crawford was being refurbished and buildings added so that she and Sir John were staying in the dower house. Mrs. Earnshaw said she neither liked the dower house nor small babies and refused the invitation, but she did make a trip to London and one to Bath and another to Hull. And then even she, restless and discontented creature that she was, had to come home some time and when she did it coincided with the fact that Anthony, pressed by debts and hounded by his creditors, took refuge once again in his native soil not knowing, of course, that his brother was away.

"I well remember the night Mrs. Earnshaw returned home from one of her many shopping trips to Bradford to find that her brother-in-law had installed himself comfortably in what used to be his old room. I even recall their meeting in the hall, for I was passing through with clean linen for Mr. Anthony's bed, and such events which are to have significance seem to imprint themselves on one's mind, so that one has no difficulty in recalling them later, have you not found that to be the case, Mr Lockwood?

"There was my mistress (for such, alas, I had to call her though I would always think of Lady Tempest as my real mistress) all bothered with her parcels and packets and her maid stumbling up the stairs behind her likewise burdened, and even the footman behind *them* stooping under the weight of what he carried, such was my mistress's prodigality with her husband's money, when Anthony emerged from the parlour and, looking in amazement at the sight before him, began laughing.

" 'Why 'pon my soul, sister-in-law," I think you have brought up the whole town. 'And he hurried forward to help her and you could see her face light up as she saw who it was and, letting go of her packages, undid her bonnet and shook out her hair as though he should immediately see her at her best, a gesture I considered premature and flirtatious into the bargain.

" 'Anthony!' she cried. 'What a delightful surprise! Are you come to visit *me*?'

" '*You*, ma'am? Why no, I was visiting my brother's house, but I understand he is abroad.'

" 'Aye and likely to remain so,' said my mistress petulantly. 'He neglects his little wife for his business affairs. I have scarce seen him since our wedding and am become *very* bored, brother-in-law,' and she gave him such a saucy smile that I swiftly gathered up my skirts and proceeded to the stairs for fear I should burst with indignation.

"I think then I realised that we had trouble in store at Thrushcross Grange and, of course, I was right.

"Anthony and Jessica were never out of each other's company, certainly during the day and, as for the night, I do not like to consider what went on for I was safely home in my cottage. But to all the world they behaved like a pair of young lovers and of course they were of an age because he was but four years older than she and so youthful and immature in comparison to his brother that you would have thought decades separated them rather than a few years. And then I saw, and wondered why I had not observed it before, that of course they were very well suited because they were both attached to what was trivial and unimportant; they were both excessively pleasure-loving and had no interest in the higher things that lift the human spirit above that of the animal. Their own immediate self-gratification was all that each sought and, to the extent that these needs coincided, they were ideal companions.

"Oh, how I longed for Mr. Rainton to come back, seeing the harm that was being done to his home, his happiness; but the weeks went by and all the news we had from him—passed on by his ungrateful wife who scarcely bothered to read the pages of passionate outpourings he sent her, to say nothing of the many gifts ordered from silversmiths and jewellers in London and Bradford—was that he had things under control and hoped to return home soon.

"Mr. Rainton had been gone four months or more when I decided to visit Lady Tempest and alert her to the situation at Thrushcross Grange, believing it to be my duty to do so. Oh with what joy my beloved Margaret, whom I had not seen since I had been invited for the Christmas festivities when Mr. and Mrs. Earnshaw were still away, greeted me and I her and oh, the happiness to see the twins thriving, both of them beauties. They were, I'm sorry to say, dark like their father, but they lacked the swarthiness and certainly the harshness of his disposition. Elizabeth was a striking girl and had such an air of happiness about her that I was reminded of her dear mother and when I said so my lady burst out:

" 'Oh thank you, Agnes! Thank God they have developed so well, and have such peace and contentment around them. For you must know that my darling John is everything you could wish for in a husband and father and treats them as his own and spends hours romping with them, giving them as much time as our darling baby Dugdale and, Agnes, I must tell you we are shortly expecting again! I am so happy for, in having babies and pleasing my husband, I find my full satisfaction as a woman and want for nothing more.'

" 'I am delighted to hear it, your ladyship,' I said, though I loved her as a daughter, and she me as a mother, there was never any familiarity between us of the kind that might make her think I was not aware of her station or the exalted position that God had now been pleased to call her in life. 'There is nothing more in the world I wish to see than your happiness and right well deserved it is; but ma'am, I would wish all were as well in your *brother's* house."

" 'All is not well, Agnes? But Rainton is away and not expected back until the winter. And I understand that Jessica flits all over the place and is scarce at home.'

334

" '*That* is the point, ma'am; she is at home—ever since your brother Anthony returned from London!'

" 'But what do you mean?' my lady said, the concern showing on her face as her suspicions began to mount. 'I thought Anthony would be at Wuthering Heights which we gave him for his own use. When he visited us here on his way up from the South he said that was his intention.'

" 'No ma'am, under the pretense of having Wuthering Heights redecorated, your brother stops at the Grange . . . under the same roof as his sister-in-law.'

" 'But Agnes, that is disgraceful!' my mistress said, jumping up in alarm. 'It is simply not done; he must not stop under the same roof as a married woman whose husband is away. It will create a scandal.'

" 'It *has* already, your ladyship,' I said, 'which is why I am here. I fear it is not only causing scandal; it *is* a scandal, for they are seldom apart. They are completely wrapped up in each other, ma'am, and I am sorely afraid for the outcome.'

"So great had been our absorption that my lady and I had not observed Sir John enter the room and, during the pause that followed my words, he said:

" 'If what you are saying is true, Agnes, and I am sure it is, knowing that you are not a woman to gossip maliciously or to create scandal, we must go over there immediately and either bring Jessie here or force that scoundrel back to London where he belongs, among the brothels and the gaming houses from what I hear.'

" 'Oh John!' Lady Tempest cried in distress, 'do not speak of him like that. He is my brother.'

" 'I know, my love,' her husband said, going up to her and tenderly kissing her cheek, 'but you know it is true. He was driven up by debts and you have paid them off for him, like you settled the matter in India. But something will have to be done about Anthony, my dear, and that right soon for he is no fit companion for my sister. Oh my God, I thought she was staying for the summer with Lord and Lady Dene at Scarborough as Lady Dene's daughter, Sandra, is a particular friend of hers. I'm sure she told us as much.'

" 'Then she deceived you, sir,' I said, 'probably deliberately; for she has spent these last months continually in the company of her brother-in-law; they are scarce out of each other's sight.'

" 'I will have the carriage prepared and we will return with you immediately,' Sir John said, and I admired the masterly way he took command of the situation and at the same time the tender glances he gave to his wife as though aware of her own suffering in the matter.

" 'But, my love,' he said to her, 'do not come with us; for I would hate you to be upset in your condition.'

" 'John, my darling, I am a strong woman! I assure you I shall not miscarry on account of Jessica and Anthony, however distressing the situation. And it is my duty to my brother Rainton to come with you. I must be there, John.'

" 'Very well,' he said, and left the room to give instructions.

" 'Now that the Reform Bill is passed, John is standing for Parliament,'' my mistress said, her eyes lighting with joy. 'He will have a lot to offer, for he is a good man and the conditions in his factories are models of humanity and limit a ten-hour working day for women and children and a half-day holiday on Saturdays. Ah, here is Jennie with my cloak. See, Jennie, the surprise I have for you.'

"And my daughter dropped me a shy bob and then remembering she was but a girl ran into my arms and kissed me while her mistress looked on benignly.

"But it was not a happy journey back to Thrushcross Grange and the weather was not with us either, for it was cold and wet and the storm clouds promised worse to come; but as we came to the edge of the moors Lady Tempest cried out, for the heather was in full bloom and what stretched before us seemed like an endless carpet of purple and green.

" 'Oh, John, look! You know I am beginning to miss the moors surrounded as we are at Castle Crawford by the soft hills and green fields of the dales country. It is funny, is it not, how you appreciate a thing only when you have it no more?'

" 'Why, my love, if that is how you feel and if Jessica will allow us we shall spend a few days at the Grange and I'll send for our baggage and my guns and see if I can catch me a few partridge. Would that suit you?'

" 'Oh yes, if she will allow it and after what we have to say to her she might not.'

" 'My sister is in many ways a silly girl,' Sir John said grimly, 'but I think even she can be shown where her duty lies and, if all Agnes says is true, and I am sure it is, I shall despatch a letter tonight calling Rainton home by the next boat.'

"And indeed when we reached the Grange it was late afternoon and of Mrs. Earnshaw and Anthony there was no sign. The visitors sat talking in the parlour while I had tea served, and then we heard the thud of horses' hooves and laughter and the sound of voices raised in excitement in the porch and, like young lovers, my mistress and her brother-in-law ran up the stairs and along the corridor bursting into the parlour, their hands entwined, before they saw who was there.

"I must say that even Mrs. Earnshaw, that brazen hussy, looked somewhat abashed at the upright figure of her stern-faced brother. My lady remained where she was, as though preferring to take a back seat in the distasteful proceedings that would ensue.

" 'Why John and Margaret! We didn't know you were coming. What a surprise, an, er, delightful surprise,' and she looked at Anthony who glowered on seeing the visitors and made no pretense that they were other than unwelcome.

" 'We are here on a serious matter, Jessie. I'll not mince words. I hear that Anthony is stopping under this very roof along with you and I'll not have it.'

" 'And how did you *hear,* dear brother?' said Mrs. Earnshaw, meaningfully gazing the while at me. 'No doubt Agnes Sutcliffe with her tittle tattle. Well, she is dismissed . . .'

" 'But ma'am . . .' I gasped.

" '*I'm* mistress here, Agnes, or did you forget it? Sometimes I think you believe you own the place, not my husband . . .'

" 'If Agnes is dismissed I will gladly take her to my home,' Lady Tempest said quietly, 'but she has done nought but what a good servant should do. She wishes to save you from scandal and the dishonour that goes with it; it is not fit that a married woman should be under the same house as an unmarried man to whom she is only related by marriage. However *innocent* the arrangement,' added my lady with a sly glance.

" 'I thought you were at the Heights for the partridge shooting, Anthony?' said Sir John trying, you could see, to be as pleasant as possible and giving them every chance.

" 'It is being redecorated. I can shoot just as well from the Grange. I didn't know it was a crime . . .'

" 'Oh Anthony, don't pretend!' Mrs. Earnshaw cried impatiently. 'After all, you said you loved me and cared not who knew it. Well, now they know it and shortly all the world will,' and that little minx paused for her words to take effect, while her eyes sparkled with defiance and a blush suffused her cheeks. 'I am to have Anthony's child,' she said. 'The doctor told me yesterday 'twas certain.'

"I must say the silence that reverberated in that room could surely have been heard on the top of the moors; no one spoke or so much as breathed for at least a full minute, and then Mrs. Earnshaw sat down and draped herself becomingly on the sofa while she stared boldly at her brother, as though daring him to castigate her.

" 'Can you know for *sure* it is Anthony?" Lady Tempest said, her calm, practical good-natured voice coming from the corner. 'Could it not be Rainton's child? Or is it that you don't *want* it to be Rainton's child?'

" 'I understand, ma'am, that a baby is in the womb for nine months,' said that strumpet. 'I am three gone, and Rainton departed five months ago. Besides I know it is Anthony's child; I *have* wanted it.'

" 'You have *wanted* it!' cried her brother. 'Jessica, are you mad? You have not only married into the honourable and worthy family of Earnshaw, but you are a *Tempest* and that alone should have been enough for you to remember you came from a long and distinguished line. Our women have always been the daughters, wives, and mothers of gentlemen and have not disported themselves like common whores!'

" 'She is not a whore!' Anthony said fiercely. " 'Tis true we love each other; I have never known love like it and I've looked for it often enough. I am not ashamed of what we have done and it serves my brother Rainton right if he goes gallivanting off, leaving such a woman on her own.'

" 'There was no gallivanting about it!' sputtered Sir John. 'He has half his fortune tied up in South America and, but for the situation there and her reluctance to go, would have taken Jessica. He had no choice; but it was the duty of a wife, scarce a bride, to remain virtuous in her husband's absence and not get with child by his brother.'

"And he spun round and marched to the window where he stood brooding out onto the grounds.

" 'It *is* a terrible situation,' Lady Tempest said, getting to her feet and then, gently, as though trying to take the heat out of the situation. 'What did you plan to do, Jessica? *Had* you any plans, for you must have suspected this even though 'tis just confirmed.'

" 'I want to marry her,' Anthony said. 'It will be the best thing.'

" 'I don't even know that you *can* marry your brother's wife,' Sir John said. 'Tis against the laws of consanguinity.'

" '*That's* the Bible,' Anthony said contemptuously, having as little respect for the good book as he had for other men's wives.

" 'I'm not sure it is not the law of the land,' Sir John replied, 'but that's not the only thing. Did you know, Jessie, that Anthony has no money? You who so love fine things, who went through my father's fortune like a knife through butter, and I dare say are doing the

339

same with Rainton's—which is doubtless another reason he had to hasten to South America—can you live just with love and without money, Jessie?'

"At this my mistress, for the first time that day, looked really disconcerted. The shocking things she had said, the appalling nature of her confession had upset her not at all; but the thought of penury . . . yes that was upsetting.

" 'Anthony has ample means. At least I think so. *Haven't* you, Anthony?'

" 'He has no fortune of his own,' Sir John said, 'not a penny. He is dependent on the good will of his brother and sister, and while they work hard and are industrious, husbanding what they earn or, in Margaret's case what has been left her, Anthony does nothing but live on the generous allowance they make him. Indeed he does not live on it, for he is always in debt and one of the reasons he came up here this summer was not to lead the life of a gentleman shooting grouse on the moors, but to escape from his creditors who threatened to throw him into gaol. Did he tell you *that*?'

"My mistress was struck dumb and Anthony's face grew blacker as he listened to the speech of his brother-in-law.

" 'Did he also tell you, Jessica, that it has happened often before, and that he was asked to leave the Army, an honourable regiment, for seducing the wife of his commanding officer and then trying to shoot her husband dead after he was caught in *flagrante delicto*? How much of his past has Anthony told you, or about the loving care of his brother and sister who have done all they could to help and protect him, wrongly in my opinion, for they should have given him a whipping and flung him out long ago.'

" 'Oh John, please,' cried his wife in distress, for I know that for all his faults she loved her brother and the recitation of his misdeeds was awful to hear, even to one such as I who had never cared for him.

"Indeed it had impressed itself on Jessica who

looked truly thoughtful at the end of her brother's speech."

" 'Jessica cares not for this malicious twaddle,' Anthony burst out angrily. 'She loves me for what I am, and she will wed me. She has told me so.'

" 'But *had* you told her the truth?' enquired Sir John, still speaking quietly and with admirable control. 'A woman, after all, has to live, and if my sister has a fault, and she does have a few, it is that she is inordinately fond of money and the pleasures it can bring. You have shown yourself singularly unable to earn a living, and I shall see that your sister does not continue to shower you with a fortune that properly belongs to my beloved stepchildren, Josiah and Elizabeth. I have the power for I am their legal guardian, and I doubt that Rainton, generous man that he is, will care to keep his ex-wife and her husband in a style as fitting as the one to which she has become accustomed.'

"At this Mrs. Earnshaw burst into tears, an action I had anticipated seeing her face grow more crestfallen as her brother's measured but blistering words continued.

" 'Oh, Anthony! You didn't *tell* me all this! You *didn't* tell me you had no money.'

" 'What is *money?*' cried Anthony fiercely, 'when we have a love such as ours? I care not for the stuff; but I cared for you and I thought you cared for me.'

" 'Oh I do, I do,' Mrs. Earnshaw went on between sobs, 'but we cannot live in *poverty*!'

" 'Poverty, what is poverty? I have a house which I don't think my sister will take away from me. Even *she* couldn't be as cruel as that if we are determined, and we will farm and have a few sheep . . .'

" 'Do you mean Wuthering Heights?' cried Mrs. Earnshaw, her tears drying as rapidly as does rain in a hot sun. 'You do not speak, surely, of *Wuthering Heights?*'

" 'Of course I mean Wuthering Heights. Where else did you think I meant?' he replied scornfully.

" 'But I cannot *live* at Wuthering Heights! Oh, the very place makes me tremble. It is so cold, and bleak and,' she shuddered, *'small* and they say it is haunted! Oh I could *never* live there.'

" 'But where did you think we were going to live?' By this time Anthony's face was becoming mottled and ugly with anger.

" 'Why, somewhere pleasant, in the south perhaps or abroad. I didn't know you had no fortune, Anthony. I have never *known* anyone who had no fortune . . . you should have told me you had no fortune, shouldn't he, John?'

"And she looked for all the world like a petulant child as she gazed first at her brother and then at her sister-in-law for assistance.

" 'What's to be done?' Lady Tempest said with her usual practical calm. 'Rainton will soon be home and he will know the child is not his. What are you going to do?'

"But Mrs. Earnshaw commenced weeping again and Anthony, angered and humiliated, did nought to try and comfort her. Then Sir John who had, I do not doubt, his own reasons for stoking the flames of discord between the two lovers went up to his sister and bade her stop crying and listen to him.

" 'Jessie, I tell you what we shall do. We will take you back with us. The Castle is almost ready for us to move into and then when your husband comes home he will decide what to do with you; but I forbid you to see Heathcliff again or to have ought to do with him until Rainton decides and, in the meantime, he will be given a small allowance as long as he stays away from London and lives quietly at Wuthering Heights. And with it he can purchase a few cows and some sheep and learn to be a farmer just in case the day *does* come when Rainton turns you out and Anthony has to support you and his child. For Rainton is a good man, but he has been sorely tried and God alone knows what he will decide or what the future holds in store for you.'

"And although I doubt that Sir John had the gift of prophecy, he as near foretold the future as anything I ever heard, Mr. Lockwood, and that's no exaggeration."

342

Chapter 19

"Rainton Earnshaw had already left for home when his brother-in-law's letter was sent, so he had no idea of the dreadful tidings that awaited him when he landed in Liverpool in October until Sir John greeted him on the dock and, I believe, acquainted him with the news on the way back to Castle Crawford. I had remained at Thrushcross Grange to look after the house as I thought that, as I grew older, I deserved a little leisure and comfort such as I had never enjoyed in my life. Let those who were younger sort out the excitements at Castle Crawford.

"I did, however, go over for Lady Tempest's confinement, as my place was always by her side on these occasions, and lucky I did for the doctor was late and her labour very swift and I helped to bring into the world a girl who was called Emma Jane Tempest and was as fair as her sister Elizabeth (now a comely eight year old) was dark, so that I was present on that solemn day when Sir John drove up the long drive to Castle Crawford with a very grim-faced Rainton Earnshaw at his side.

"Lady Tempest was still in bed following the birth and it was thus that she was able to tell me what had happened, for it was relayed to her by her husband John and the following story, that I shall tell you, is caused by me putting two and two together and using my wits besides."

"Mr. Rainton was delighted to see his brother-in-law at the dockside and had hoped to see his wife as well, and on enquiry, Sir John told him merely that she was indisposed but was being well taken care of at the Castle.

"Sir John, however, was wise enough to stop at a hostelry on the way back for refreshment and there in a private room he told Mr. Earnshaw what had passed. Apparently the poor man was stunned, and too shocked with grief to speak, but Sir John tried to make out that it was hardly her fault for she was but a young and foolish girl prey to a vile seducer and he had been gone too long.

" 'But does she love me, John? How can she love me?'

" 'There is a way of dealing with women,' Sir John replied, 'and it is to keep a warm bed for them and a full table and plenty of money in their purse. That makes for a happy and contented woman, aye, and a happy husband too. It is for you to decide, Rainton, for I cannot tell you what to do, and indeed I would not be certain what to do in your position; but you are a good man and if you can find it in your heart to forgive my sister it is something my family and I will not forget for the rest of our days.'

" 'And to have his child as mine?' cried my anguished master. 'No, never.'

"But Rainton was a God-fearing Christian man, and, no doubt, consulted with his conscience and, above all, by the time he had seen his wife again and he found he still loved if not as besottedly as before, he said he would forgive her. He agreed to raise his brother's child as his own, so long as his brother never came to his house again or troubled him in any way because,

344

although he could find it in himself to forgive the woman, he could never forgive the man. For deep down, you know, they had never liked each other. Hard though Rainton had tried, I think that Anthony was too provoking to someone as solid and sensible as he.

"And so Mrs. Earnshaw was reunited with her husband who instead of going home had the good sense to take her to London immediately where he rented a house so as to keep her away from Anthony and to be out of the district when the baby was born in February, a girl who was called Catherine Margaret after his mother and sister. And when I saw her later that year and realised she was really a Heathcliff and her name was Cathy I thought there was some very sinister influence abroad in the world that could bring about such curious combinations of inheritance. For Cathy was fair again, as fair as her grandmother and her aunt, and she could easily have passed for Mr. Rainton's child, or anyone else's. Of her father Anthony, I'm glad to report, there was not the slightest trace.

"But by the time Mrs. Earnshaw came home her baby was six months old and she was with child again, and this time by her lawful husband. Once more it was August and acres of purple heather stretched as far as the eye could see and the birds flew overhead uttering their many different calls, and the trees in the park waved in the wind as Mr. Rainton Earnshaw brought his errant wife back to Thrushcross Grange.

"But what a different woman she was from the one I'd last seen nearly a year before! I scarce recognised her, for her face was drawn and, apart from her belly, her body was terribly thin. Gone was all the life and vivacity which, although I confess I hadn't much liked—a bit too much of it there had been, if you ask me—seemed preferable to this pallid scarecrow I saw before me. And the attitude of Mr. Rainton had changed too. He no longer ran after his wife, indulging every whim and showering her with presents. Oh no; he shut himself in his study for the best part of the evening after dinner and, during the day, he left early

345

to see to his business affairs, and I can tell you that they were very good indeed. Mr. Rainton was a man of considerable wealth and prosperity, which showed in the number of servants he now employed and the property and stock he was daily adding to his already vast possessions. He now owned about twice as much land as his poor father had before he lost all his money and had to sell to Colonel Heathcliff. Indeed most of the land and villages round Gimmerton were owned by either Mr. Rainton or his sister Lady Tempest. They had any number of tenant farmers because, once the fields started to be enclosed, the poor could no longer afford to graze their sheep and moved to the towns and the factories; and there were so many souls dependent on Mr. Earnshaw and his sister for their very existence that one could only thank God they were such good people and so kind to those who worked for them or were dependent on them.

"And I think it was this kindness and good nature and his concern for the poor, as well as the tragedy he had suffered in his personal life, that caused the greatest change in Mr. Earnshaw after he came home to Thrushcross Grange. He had become greatly influenced in London by the supporters of evangelical religion, so that we now had Bible readings every day and prayers every morning and evening at which all the staff assembled. I think it was this intensely religious attitude that marked Mr. Earnshaw more than anything else— I can't say for the better, because he became so much graver and solemn as religious people tend to, don't you think so, Mr. Lockwood? It is as though in trying so hard to please the Lord they lose the ability either to give pleasure to themselves or others.

"Well, we became a *very* sober household indeed and righteous too, and Mrs. Earnshaw was never again seen in a dress with a low neckline, but was always well covered from throat to the tips of her feet and her dresses were made from sombre hard-wearing materials such as were woven in Mr. Earnshaw's mills. Never was a brocade or satin to be seen except for the very

346

occasional ball or dinner the Earnshaws went to, and then the colours of Mrs. Earnshaw's gowns were subdued matronly greys and browns and not the pretty pinks and blues that she had loved when I first knew her as a bride not two years since.

"It was an awareness of her increasing sadness and melancholy that drew me to Mrs. Earnshaw and made me revise my former harsh opinion of her. I perceived she was a good mother to the baby Catherine and, as the date for her second confinement drew near, I was able to spend more time with her as we sat sewing the little garments in preparation for the new baby. It was the end of the year, a downcast December day, when she first bared her heart to me and she was gazing out of the window at the rain beating down on the hills and the sodden branches of the trees in the park which looked bedraggled with a few wintry leaves clinging to their branches. The sky was so overcast we had to light the candles before morning was out, and the wind which had howled all night continued unabated during the day.

"'Oh,' Mrs. Earnshaw sighed, 'this baby is very heavy, Agnes. I am sure it will be a large boy. Mr. Earnshaw dearly hopes for a son to carry on his inheritance,' and she moved uncomfortably in her seat and, as I had already noted her size, I wondered if twins were once again expected in the Earnshaw family.

"'I'm sure you will have many fine children yet, ma'am,' I said, 'for you are but a young woman and Mr. Earnshaw a fine, vigorous man.'

"But Mrs. Earnshaw continued sighing and seemed not at all delighted by the prospect of the large family Mr. Earnshaw intended for her.

"'Oh Agnes, I wish one could live life again, go back, undo the past. Do you know what I mean?'

"Of course I *thought* I knew what she meant, but judged it more prudent to wait for her to say it.

"'What a silly young girl I was, Agnes, to behave as I did; you know to what I refer. For although my husband had been nothing but good and considerate and treats the baby as his own, I don't think he has really found it in himself to forgive me for what I did. Much as he has tried, I am no longer important in his life as a wife and companion. I think if it had not been for my sin, for a sin it *was,* Agnes, he would not have been so eager to hear Mr. Gifford, the evangelical preacher in London, who taught us how unregenerate were our ways, how sinful we were, and how our only hope was in God. Once my husband had heard Mr. Gifford preach he invited him often to our house and it was from that time that I noticed a change in him. I remember him saying to me:'

" 'I have been sorely troubled by what happened, Jessica, but now I think I see a way to get God's forgiveness for you; for what you did was a terrible sin and it will take a lifetime to repay it. But I will help you and, if we lead a sober, upright life and see to the poor and needy, surely God will take you into his kingdom at the end.'

" 'I think he only took me back because he felt he *had* to, and because of the pressure of his sister and brother-in-law to save the family name; but forgive me, no. I think he does not even *like* me, and one night he told me that every time he looked on me he saw Jezebel and, but for his promise, would have cast me out of the house. And he had to have frequent recourse to prayer and the Bible to stay his wrath. Thus it is that we lead such a mean and miserable life with no parties or fun except if they're given at the Castle. Then he deems it his duty to go. I never saw a man so changed.'

"And she sighed and went on hemming the napkins for the new baby.

" 'Indeed, Mr. Earnshaw has changed, ma'am, I'll not deny it; but he has so many more responsibilities and so much more wealth. It is a pity he has took to religion so hard, but I think he feels, if you will pardon me saying it, ma'am, that the women in his family have shown a wayward streak and maybe, by frequent prayers and Bible readings, he hopes that such occurrences will be prevented in the future.'

" 'You mean his mother of course,' Mrs. Earnshaw said, looking at me keenly. 'He told me about that be-

348

fore we were married, and how his brother Anthony was not his father's son. Yes, poor Rainton, I suppose I must try and understand him; but at times I find it hard, such is the drabness of my life, for I so loved parties and balls and shops, and visits to the dressmaker and milliner, and, Agnes, I am *still* young, am I not?'

"And for a moment the poor girl's eyes lit up at the memory of far-off happier times and the emotion in my breast was one of pity. I thought that the course of her life had now been decided for her, and that Mr. Earnshaw had told her only of his mother and *not* of his grandmother, or his sister's elopement; maybe if he had she would not have married him!

"Mrs. Earnshaw's next child was born in February after a long and agonising labour, which Mr. Earnshaw saw as the wrath of God punishing his wife for her misdemeanour and, instead of sending for the best physician as he ought to have done to relieve her pain, he spent the time on his knees seeking the intervention of the Almighty. Well, maybe the Almighty intervened or maybe he didn't and it was simply nature taking its course; but in due course the poor woman's travail came to an end and she was delivered of a puny girl who was given the biblical name of Ruth and I never expected her to live, for the baby looked as exhausted as the mother after the ordeal, and an alarming time elapsed before she cried.

"You could see that Mr. Earnshaw was disappointed the child was a girl for, after briefly inspecting her, he shut himself in his study for the rest of the day and never went near the child or his wife. Nor did he think to summon a clergyman to baptise the sickly creature, which you would have thought would have been the first thing on his mind, him being so close to God. Indeed he paid but perfunctory visits to his wife who lay in bed for several weeks while we tried to restore her strength with broth and roast chicken mashed with potatoes and reduced to a thin gruel-like substance so that it might be more readily digested. Although he was low church and not a dissenter, Mr. Earnshaw was convinced that the cause of many evils lay in the abuse of alcohol, so this nourishing beverage in its many forms was forbidden in the house and my poor mistress was denied even a glass of brandy or claret in whose restorative properties I was a great believer.

"The only bright thing that happened following my mistress's confinement was the visit of Sir John and Lady Tempest to see Mrs. Earnshaw and the baby Ruth and, as they had been abroad, that took place some six weeks after the event when the earth was beginning to dry after the winter's rains and the first crocus, celandine, and snowdrops were appearing in the park and small undeveloped buds on the trees.

"And if Mr. Rainton had grown gloomy and religious, the very opposite seemed to be the case with my beloved Margaret and her handsome husband, who bowled up in a fine new carriage with a liveried postillion. As my lady alighted, I could only gasp at the magnificence of her dress, a richly embroidered silk, no doubt from the Indies, and a bonnet with a plume that concealed half her face, and she wore a purple velvet cap she gave to me as she kissed me in the hall. And, oh the wonderful *smell* of her and the opulence of her person, for she had grown plumper but even more comely, if that were possible, and I saw that as well as perfume she used rouge and powder and I'm sure my master who had received her on the steps would not approve of that!

"But, oh, the contrast between poor Mrs. Earnshaw in her brown high-necked stuff dress and with her plain hairstyle, her thin emaciated figure and lustreless eyes, and Lady Tempest who had about her a new aura of distinction. You could see how proud her husband was of her, for he was forever glancing at her and making sure that she was comfortable or that she had everything she required.

"And I think that the first inkling the Tempests had of the change in the household was the very plain meal that was served of boiled beef and vegetables, and water instead of wine, which was exactly what we had in the kitchen, although now I took my meals alone in a small parlour Mr. Earnshaw had given me for myself as the housekeeper in charge of such a large staff.

"But my chief joy that day was to see Master Josiah and Miss Elizabeth who were now eleven, and as bright and as pretty a pair of starlings as ever you could wish to see. Dark haired and dark eyed but with their mother's very white skin, thank God, and the sunniest and most playful of dispositions. They even brought a smile to the wan face of that lady, the mistress of the house who looked more likely as though she were employed as scullery maid. They scampered in and out of the house making muddy marks all over the hall until called to order by their stepfather and you could see with what joy and affection he regarded them.

"It was a happy time. All day long the house reverberated to the sound of laughter, and even Mr. Rainton looked happier and less preoccupied with thoughts of doom and judgement and to see her brother was, for Mrs. Earnshaw, the best tonic she could wish, for the colour slowly came back to her sunken cheeks.

"But if the Tempests brought joy to us; joy was far from what they got from their visit for, later in the afternoon, when I had gone to my cottage for the two hours I habitually had alone to myself during the day, there was a knock at the door and my lady stood there smiling down at me. And how my heart flooded with joy and the tears came into my eyes as she stepped inside and took me in her arms and patted my heaving shoulders as though I were the child and she the mother, because 'seeing her there had reminded me of the day, so many years ago, when she had left Colonel Heathcliff and came back to seek refuge with her father. And oh, what a change there was between that day and this.

" 'Agnes dear, what is it?' she said with concern in her voice. 'I thought you were so happy to see us?'

" 'Oh madam, Lady Tempest, I am so happy to see you and grateful to God that you are looking so well, so fulfilled, with that good and righteous man by your side. My tears are of thankfulness.'

" 'Dear Agnes,' said, her ladyship leading me to my chair, 'I could not have wished for a better man, kinder, more noble or affectionate, clever, and compassionate too; for now that he is in Parliament he is taken up with all sorts of causes for the betterment of the new industrial class, and he was active in the Bill that abolished slavery in the British Empire last year. We are to have a house in London, Agnes! Oh I shall like that so much. I have already seen one in Grosvenor Square which is near the shops and Regent Street which I love, and the Park, and not too distant from the Houses of Parliament where Sir John will spend so much of his time. And I shall entertain *all* the famous politicians and their wives and do everything I can to help my husband with his career and, oh, I shall enjoy myself vastly too! But Agnes, dear, I have come to talk matters of graver import. Both Sir John and I are much distressed about the appearance and generally low condition of Mrs. Earnshaw. Can it be *only* attributed to childbirth? She looks as though she is in the last stages of a mortal illness which God forbid, yet when we suggested that she should come for a few days to Castle Crawford, Rainton put up such a string of reasons as to why she should not go that you would have thought we were suggesting a plan to abduct her!'

" 'And while we were discussing this I noted she said nothing, but kept her eyes cast down and her face expressionless. I never saw such a change in a person in my life. And my brother; is he so *very* virtuous now? No wine at dinner, the plainest food, and Sir John was much put out at not being offered a glass of brandy and a cigar afterwards, which he greatly enjoys; but Rainton says he will not allow the stuff in the house! I tell you we shall not stop here long at this rate or visit again soon. Sir John is rightly concerned with his food and comforts. He is chafing already to be at home! What can you tell me, Agnes dear, mother of us all?'

" 'Mr. Rainton has taken strongly to religion, my lady,' I said, not mincing my words. 'There was some evangelical preacher who influenced him in London

352

and made him see the error of his ways, but more particularly those of his wife, I believe. It appears she is to spend the rest of her days in atonement. We have prayer meetings twice a day, every day, ma'am, which all the staff have to attend, even the boys in the stables and the gardeners from the ends of the park. Mr. Rainton reads from the Bible and says prayers and if the fancy takes him delivers a little homily. It is all very uplifting, but tedious if you will pardon me saying so, ma'am, and it has made this house a drab place and the master and mistress too solemn for words. Mr. Rainton believes in thrift and hard work, he is forever telling us, ma'am. And he carries out these precepts in his own life, for he is hard at work all day and half the night, neglecting his wife I might say, but that apparently does not signify, and although our food is plentiful and nourishing it is simple and ordinary.'

" 'What a dreadful thing to happen!' Lady Tempest exclaimed, sitting down by my side in the familiar manner she had as a girl. 'Poor Jessie is to pay sodden for her weakness. I know not what my husband will say. To my sorrow, he forbids me to see my brother Anthony whom I would dearly love to have sight of, despite what he did. Do you know aught of him, Agnes?'

" 'I hear he is become a hermit,' I said, recounting the village gossip. 'They say he looks like John the Baptist in the wilderness and is ill clad in all weathers. He has no servants to look after him, and grows his own food, and kills his own cattle for he has a herd of sheep and cows. They say he has a wild look about him and will greet no one civilly on the rare occasions he comes to the village to buy provisions or to have a horse shod.'

"Now tears came into her ladyship's beautiful dark eyes and I thought how, despite her grandeur, she was as simple and unaffected and concerned for humanity as she had always been.

" 'Oh Agnes, what a contrast between my own happy luxurious life and that of poor Anthony! Sir John sees that his allowance is regularly paid through

353

the lawyer but, apart from that, we have lost all contact. Both he and Jessie are paying for their sin.'

" 'And it *was* a sin, ma'am, make no mistake about that,' I said. 'For although I don't hold with Mr. Rainton's excessive piety I do think it was awful for a man to bed his brother's new wife, and wicked for her to be bedded, for she was old enough to know what she was about.'

" 'Jessie was very spoiled by her father who adored her, for she came to him late in life. She grew up used to having her own way. Even now she is like a petulant child who has had her toys and playthings taken away; and the baby is so frail! Will she survive? Thank God it is the spring, or else I think the winter would have killed her. And she is so plain and ugly. I see neither Earnshaw or Tempest about her.'

" 'At least she is no Heathcliff either,' I said grimly, 'and thank God for that.' Then, when I saw my lady blush, I took her hand and begged pardon for my foolish words.

" 'Oh, I deserve to be ribbed, Agnes. I was a foolish girl too, headstrong and wayward; but God was good to me and spared me the fate of poor Jessie. Well, Agnes,' and here she got up, 'I think there is nothing more we can do in this sad house; for Rainton will have no interfering and John is heavily engaged with him in business affairs and would not cross him and, besides, he respects and likes him. I daresay he will have a word about Jessie by and by and see if he can improve her lot; but we shall be more in London and only at Castle Crawford during the parliamentary recess.'

" 'Do not worry yourself, ma'am,' I said. 'I have grown to like my new mistress, though of course no one could ever replace *you*. I will do what I can for her, you can rely on me.'

"And with kisses, and renewed tears on my part, we said goodbye and I watched my lady walk back thoughtfully to the big house and shortly after that I heard the sound of the carriage wheels and knew that they were gone, and my heart felt emptier for it."

354

"But despite my promise to Lady Tempest, there was little I could do to cheer Mrs. Earnshaw. Three months after the birth of Ruth she was expecting another, but of course she was too frail to keep it and miscarried soon after she conceived; and the fact depressed her and she was forever feeling ill and in tears and swooning about the house.

"But even her weak condition caused her husband no pity and she was quickly with child again and, indeed, she spent the next nine months confined to her bed, for the doctor said that she never ought to have been got with child so soon but, since she had, they only chance of keeping it was to lie down.

"To me Mr. Rainton was still a kindly man, a good employer, and as to his God-fearing qualities he left us in no doubt; for the prayers got longer and his homilies more solemn and all the time his wife lay upstairs nearer death than life, just for the fact that he wanted an heir. And that was *all* he wanted from her, for otherwise he scarce went near her or to her bed that I knew and, poor soul, she told me most things for she had no friends but me; none came to visit her and she was not allowed out.

"But, thank God, in due course the doctor's care bore fruit and in April the following year Mrs. Earnshaw was delivered of a full-term healthy son and great was my master's joy as he was given the name Matthew, after the Evangelist, no doubt. The birth almost killed my mistress because the boy was so large, a real Earnshaw if ever I saw one. For weeks the doctor despaired of her life; but now that she had done her duty and provided an heir, Mr. Rainton obviously felt that her life could be dispensed with if necessary and he no longer petitioned the Almighty on her behalf, or, if he did, it was in private. For her name was never mentioned at daily prayers, other than in the dutiful reference to the King and Queen and the master and mistress and all those over us.

"But I think Mrs. Earnshaw was determined to live, for what reason I know not because, for what I hear, her life now is no better than what it was then. And

355

now we are coming to the end of my story, Mr. Lockwood, and weary of it you must be; but you have been
very patient and, no doubt, even enjoying yourself as I
see you are, sitting there scribbling notes on your
block. If there ever is a book of this you must let me
see it, sir. Oh yes, it is almost evening and your servant
will be seeking you out again—how he *does* take care
of you. At any rate, after tonight, you may do as you
will for I am about to tell you how the story ended
and, as you may guess, it was tragic, at least for Mr.
Earnshaw, but in many ways for all concerned. For
once again the Earnshaw family seemed dogged by
misfortune and all were affected in some way or another; the children, Matthew and Ruth, and Sir John
and Lady Tempest, who suffered the sort of shame that
such a noble family can well do without, especially
with Sir John being such an important man and some
say about to be selected for advancement.

"Well, as I said, Mrs. Earnshaw was determined to
get better and she did and, with it, I noticed a harden-
ing of her attitude towards her husband whom formerly
she had tried to please as though hoping to woo his affections again. Well now she no longer cared aught for
his affection, indeed she could well do without it for
the doctor told her that another baby might well kill
her, and he told her husband too. So he kept away
from her bed and, but for dinner times, they had
hardly any contact. She was a good mother, as I have
said, and gave such love and nourishment to the ailing
little Ruth that she picked up and put on weight
though even at a year she looked puny by the side of
her newly-born brother. Honestly it was hard to believe
they had issued from the same womb, for the boy was
strong and comely and the girl scraggy and downright
ugly and until she was twelve months I wondered if she
would ever have a hair on her head for she was as bald
as a coot and then, when it did appear, it was thin and
mouse coloured, while Matthew had emerged from the
womb with a mop of brown curls, just like his father,
of whom he was the spitting image.

"However she loved both equally and little Cathy

356

too, though I will not hide from you the fact that Mr. Rainton showed no interest in his brother's child at all, which I suppose is hardly surprising. I know he thought he enjoyed a close communion with God, but he would have been a saint indeed if he'd loved Cathy as his own knowing that she was a child of sin. But she was a lovely little thing, fair and pretty and winsome, as though always trying to please her stern father, and that bright she was! She was talking before she was two years and I have scarcely ever known *that* I can tell you.

"Anyway during that summer following Matthew's birth Mr. Rainton was away a great deal. I think he did not dare to go to South America again or perhaps he did not need to, for he certainly did not confide in me, but he went abroad and several times to London and Scotland on business. I can't exactly tell you when it was that I began to notice an unaccustomed sparkle in Mrs. Earnshaw's face and that she now walked with a lilt, instead of dragging one foot after the other as though she was on her way to the grave; but her old comeliness returned and I would often hear her singing as she sewed or went about her household tasks. When Mr. Rainton was at home there was none of this sprightliness at all, as though by careful calculation she kept herself deliberately drab for him (no doubt reluctant to put the idea into his head that her bed might once more be an attractive place); but when he was away . . . it was a different tale altogether.

"And then I perceived that my mistress walked a lot in the park and one day, growing curious, I watched by the window and saw her take the back door on to the moor and then I knew, without any doubt, what had put the spring in her step and the light back into her eyes, for I saw her out of sight, and the direction she had taken was towards Wuthering Heights.

"But I said nothing, for I bided my time and then one day after I saw her go, I put on my shawl and followed her, keeping well behind. But oh, I was no longer the woman I had been and that toil up the moor made me pant and heave so that I was almost col-

357

lapsed when I at last arrived at the Heights and stood breathlessly at the gate.

"And then the most dreadful apparition appeared. I thought at first it was a bear or some unknown mountain creature until I perceived it was Mr. Anthony grown a beard and looking even more like the prophet John than I'd heard.

" 'Snooping again, Agnes Sutcliffe!' he shouted at me. 'Following thy mistress! Well she's in yonder; go and see and then go back and tell thy master if that is why he sent thee.'

" 'Now Mr. Anthony,' I said, having regained my breath and my self-respect right quickly. 'That is no way to talk. You know quite well I am not my master's spy; but I have a mind to warn my mistress, and you, of the consequences of your meeting.'

"And just then Mrs. Earnshaw came to the door and stood looking at me.

" 'We know them, Agnes, and it is what we want. To be cut off, and to be by ourselves with our child and our love. For I have never stopped loving Anthony and he me, after his fashion, and we want to be together.'

"And then she came up to him and put her arm through his and over his face there stole the nearest expression to tenderness I had ever seen on him; but it didn't last long, for he was a surly creature and how she could bear to be near him I knew not. For, apart from being unkempt and hirsute, there was an odour about him as though he spent all his time in the barn with his cattle, and my mistress, brought up in a fine home, a castle, was so clean and fastidious and took a bath once a week by the fire in her bedroom. But he had something for her that others, including her husband, never had and what it was continues to be a mystery to me.

"But that day she did look content, and fulfilled, too, standing there with her arm tucked in his, her head raised proudly and the wind blowing through her hair and her face pretty again, alight with the kind of joy that it seemed only he could give her and I didn't

358

understand it then and I don't understand it now; but 'twas a fact. Those two poor lost outcast souls had found a home together and, as I looked at the bleak, gaunt house that had stood on the moors, firm as a rock, for centuries, I realised that it was as fitting a home for them as they were ever likely to get."

Mrs. Sutcliffe got to her feet stiffly and poked the fire and I put down my papers and, for a long time, neither of us spoke—indeed sometimes I felt I had almost lost my voice during the course of her narrative.

"And Rainton, of course, turned her out?"

"Well, he didn't turn her out because whether it had been her intention or whether my visit had provoked it, I know not, but she never went back home after that day and they never saw each other again. I had the task of delivering the note she'd sent him and the queerest reception it got. He read it, put it aside, thought a while and then said:

"'Pack Cathy's things and send her up to her mother in the gig, Agnes. She's not coming back and I'm not looking after *his* daughter. And tell her that the lawyer will see to the rest. She always was a wicked woman and she'll get a wicked woman's reward when the time comes; fire and brimstone, Agnes, fire and brimstone!'

"And that was all the emotion that extraordinary man showed. But that was only to me, of course. I know he went over to see his sister, and she told me later he did not appear fussed, saying it was the will of the Lord; but that he would not stop in the same part of the country with her. He proposed to leave a manager, as he had done before, and ask his brother-in-law to oversee his affairs and take his two babies to South America to get them as far away from their mother as he could, and that was Mr. Rainton's way of dealing with the situation and swiftly it was done.

"The Grange was to be shut up completely and I was forced to leave my comfortable cottage where I had been happy for so long and to say goodbye to my babies and it was a sad time for me, I can tell you.

And as for their mother, how she could abandon them I knew not, seeing the love with which she had nursed them. My guess was that knowing Rainton would not let them go, she accepted it. In her way she was as strange as he.

"But Mr. Rainton, although I could no longer love him because he had become so hard and remote, behaved to me and all the servants as well as he ever did and purchased for me outright this nice cottage as my home. He gave me a stipend and found as many of the others as he could good jobs, although some of them were in his factories and even these days, with all the laws they have passed to try and improve conditions, they're bad places to be and people work long hours, and the noise is deafening and sometimes there are accidents and many folk are crippled or even killed and no one looks after them then.

"And that is the end of my story, Mr. Lockwood. I never saw Mrs. Earnshaw again to this day for she never goes abroad and I have not been asked to the Heights. But I often think of her and Cathy there and that bear Anthony, the madman as they call him, and wonder what will become of them all."

"And Sir John and Lady Tempest?"

"Oh, they are become very celebrated. My Lady had another child two years ago, a boy called Henry, but this time I did not attend her confinement because I had the influenza and was very poorly that winter; But she always keeps in touch and writes and I spend a few days with them at Castle Crawford once a year, usually in the summer, and thankful I am that at least one part of the Earnshaw family story had a happy ending. Josiah is at Eton College and Elizabeth goes to a very grand school for young ladies, and a beauty she is. And I'm sure she'll do well and marry well for she has had a good start in life, thanks to her mother, and has every reason to succeed."

My thanks to Mrs Sutcliffe were profuse and prolonged. I really felt I had made a friend and scarcely knew how I would spend my days or what I should do with my time now that this absorbing tale had been completed.

But as I approached my house my mind was immediately taken up with a new event, for outside the front door stood the stylish phaeton my brother Dalby chose to drive, fancying himself as a young buck as he roared along the new roads with a pair in hand. And there he was, standing at the door, stylish and handsome, a long cigar in his mouth, and he hailed me heartily and strode down the drive exuding the air he always had of a prosperous and successful man.

"Tom, you old rascal! I hear you haunt the house of a *woman* every day, and she tells you stories. Now come, my good fellow, *that* is a story I am like to laugh at; not but that it is out of character for you to chase the ladies."

"Oh come, Dalby," I protested, "the thought is unworthy of you. She is an *old* woman and she *has* been telling me a story; a long and fascinating one."

"Then tell it me."

"If I did, brother Dalby," I said taking his arm in a gesture of affection, "it would take a week or more, for that is what it took her to tell it to me; but one day I shall write it down and you can read it all for yourself."

But that was not quite the end of it, for that night as Dalby and I sat after dinner with our port and cigars recalling memories of Italy and talking of current events, he provided me with a curious and unexpected epilogue to all that I heard.

"Aye, and the railways will be all over England soon,' he said *à propos* of something we were saying. "You will be able to go from Leeds to London and my phaeton will be out of date! It is a great century of progress, Tom, an exciting time to live. Why I have been stopping not an hour's journey away with a fellow Member, Sir John Tempest and he . . ."

"Sir John Tempest!" I cried excitedly. *"You* were at Crawford?"

"You know the place?" enquired my brother in some surprise.

361

"Only by reputation," I said, and I was about to tell him my story, or begin it at any rate, but decided the night was too far advanced and it was too long and complex.

"Oh, 'tis a handsome dwelling and the family an interesting one. Sir John was with the Whigs over Reform but he has joined us, and Peel for certain has him in mind for promotion as soon as we get rid of Melbourne and Sir Robert is asked again to form a government."

"And you think he will be?"

"Of course, the Whigs have had their day; the Reform took the stuffing out of them."

"I hear Sir John has a lovely wife," I said, carefully tipping the ash from my cigar into a tray so that my brother did not observe the eager expression on my face.

"Oh you've heard that *too,* have you, you rogue! Indeed Margaret Tempest is the toast of London, one of its greatest hostesses since Lady Holland relinquished the title. She is clever, she is witty, and her beauty," my brother kissed his finger tips in that Italian manner that is no doubt natural to him from his years in the country of our birth, "she is divine."

"Though of course she is *mature,* no girl you understand, having had two husbands and given birth to five children. But rumour has it, and it is said most discreetly but I have a way of hearing these things, that she is or was until his recent marriage the mistress of the Foreign Secretary, Lord Palmerston."

"But he is an old man," I exclaimed in amazement. "He must be over fifty!"

"I hope, Tom Lockwood," my brother said reprovingly, "you will think differently when *you* are that age, to call yourself 'old.' Lord Palmerston is a fine-looking man and a great one for the ladies and 'tis said he was much taken by Lady Tempest when she first came to town. He has prestige and vast power and influence, all the things Lady Tempest prized for she was new to London, and in no time at all Palmerston had introduced her to everyone, and everyone to her. 'Tis true last year he married his old flame, Lady Cowper; but

362

he'd known her thirty years so there's not much heat left there and he, with Lady Palmerston or without, is always at the Tempest's house in Grosvenor Square and they say my Lady is (or was) not unfamiliar with the back entrance to his own house opposite Green Park!"

"Margaret Tempest, Lord Palmerston's mistress!" I mused, thinking of her past, and how well it fitted in with what I knew of her, that wild romantic streak she'd shown as a girl come out once again to achieve practical gain: to help her husband's ambition.

"You sound as though you know her," my brother said, intrigued.

"I only know *of* her," I said. "She hailed from these parts."

"Indeed?"

"Yes she was an Earnshaw. They are from Gimmerton."

"Well, I know not the Earnshaws, though 'tis interesting news. Oh there is no *real* scandal attached to Lady Tempest. At least Queen Victoria knows it not for she is much taken with her Ladyship, and you know how particular Her Majesty is. But I have heard what I have told you on very good authority. Not that her husband is without his *amours,* he is rather less discreet. But you know, my dear Tom, society in London does these things with delicacy, and a couple can be loving and tender and still play about a bit. I know of dozens other than the Tempests. They say it is good for a marriage!" But here my brother's eyes grew bright and he poured himself more port. "The Tempests have such a daughter! Ravishing! She is at school and I only saw her when I visited them last week; but such a dazzler, I tell you I am hard put to rid my mind of her . . ."

"But she is a child. Really, Dalby!"

"A child? Oh you know about her, *too?* It must be these stories you have been hearing, Tom. Methinks I see a link. Elizabeth Heathcliff—for she is Sir John's step-daughter; no doubt you know of that as well . . ."

"Indeed." I concurred. "She could only inherit her

363

father's estate if she and her brother kept his name."

"Ah, then you have solved a puzzle for me. Well she is not a child, my boy! Tender in years, maybe not more than fifteen or so; but she is as well developed as a woman and as flirtatious as her mother and, I can tell you, half the men in London will be after her when she is launched and I among them."

"You!" I laughed.

"Why not? I can give her ten years, true; but I believe I am not without attraction and that I too will one day be in the government, along with her step-papa, and that should give me a head start. For the Tempests like successful men."

We said no more on the subject but, as I went up to bed, I reflected on the curious coincidence of my brother being so well acquainted with the Tempests; and I thought how droll it would be if fortune were to link my family with theirs, for, in fact, we had been linked, though in a most tenuous way, for the best part of this century.

But this I soon put out of my mind for a week later I left Gimmerton, rather abruptly it is true; but I fancied I was in for a fresh chill and my poor Nostro, who ached all over and longed to leave anyway, said it would be the death of him if he stayed in such an inhospitable clime and we should both end up in the yard of Gimmerton kirk. I had anyway obtained what I had come for and now, in the Italian sun, I would relive Mrs. Sutcliffe's story and commit it to paper.

But perversely I renewed my tenancy of the manor and asked for an option to purchase should the owner be willing for, much to Nostro's disgust, I felt an attachment to the place, and a bond that he could neither understand or approve.

The night before I left I took Patch along the moorland path until, in the far distance, I could see Wuthering Heights. It looked so peaceful in the fold of the hills with the smoke coming from the chimney and the sheep grazing around it, doubtless the same that Patch had chased and which had enabled me briefly to meet the inhabitants of that strange, unhappy house. But I cared not to let Patch loose again and kept him on a tight leash for I did not think I should receive a welcome from that fearful man, brooding on the imagined wrongs done to him by the Earnshaws—just as his grandfather, Heathcliff, had so many years before. And what awful revenge would Anthony try and extract, other than taking Rainton's wife, for no Heathcliff appeared to think that it was sufficient until they had taken all?

However, I doubted that Anthony, even if he had the will, would ever have the means to displace the family his step-father and brother had done so much to make prosperous. But I thought of the poor sad-looking woman I had seen, Jessica, and her pretty, lonely little girl who wanted a puppy as a companion having none other. What would become of them?

Then my mind turned to the other branch of the family, the Tempests, rich and successful and the new generation of Heathcliffs, a boy and a girl—one a beauty like her mother, grandmother and great-grandmother; the other growing to maturity, an heir to rich estates. And somewhere on the other side of the world, still infants, were a new generation of Earnshaws, also a boy and a girl, whose unknown mother still stayed in their native valley upon which I was looking.

And as I stood there on that clear spring evening, the many colours of that rich moorland glowing in the golden evening sun, with a soft breeze blowing from the Heights and curlews and gulls whirling in the sky above me, I knew that, much as I loved Italy, I would come back. For my father had struck roots here for me. He had given me a meaning and a purpose beyond mere idleness and pleasure: to be a writer and a man of letters as he had tried to be.

In a decade or two there would be another story for me to hear and, as I turned back towards the Manor House, my dog at my heels, I knew for sure that I, Tom Lockwood, was part of this wild mysterious moorland countryside with its deep feuds and bitter legends, its ghosts and its savage charm—and it was part of me.

A SELECTED LIST OF CORGI ROMANCE
FOR YOUR READING PLEASURE

All these books are available at your bookshop or newsagent, or can be ordered direct from the publisher. Just tick the titles you want and fill in the form below.

CORGI BOOKS, Cash Sales Department, P.O. Box 11, Falmouth, Cornwall.
Please send cheque or postal order, no currency.

U.K. send 19p for first book plus 9p per copy for each additional book ordered to a maximum charge of 73p to cover the cost of postage and packing.

B.F.P.O. and Eire allow 19p for first book plus 9p per copy for the next 6 books, thereafter 3p per book.

Overseas Customers. Please allow 20p for the first book and 10p per copy for each additional book.

NAME (block letters) ....

ADDRESS ....

JAN 78) ....

While every effort is made to keep prices low, it is sometimes necessary to increase prices at short notice. Corgi Books reserve the right to show new retail prices on covers which may differ from those previously advertised in the text or elsewhere.